THE SAGA OF
SALLY LUNNS

ALWYN DOW

Tales of murder and intrigue featuring Sue Parker Somerset Sleuth

Order this book online at www.trafford.com
or email orders@trafford.com

Most Trafford titles are also available at major online book retailers.

Printed in the United States of America.

ISBN: 978-1-4669-6663-5 (sc)
ISBN: 978-1-4669-6664-2 (e)

Library of Congress Control Number: 2012920541

Trafford rev. 11/07/2012

 www.trafford.com

North America & international
toll-free: 1 888 232 4444 (USA & Canada)
phone: 250 383 6864 ✦ fax: 812 355 4082

INTRODUCTION

Sue Parker is a young policewoman in Bath who finds herself propelled into cases of mystery and International intrigue as she tries to balance her career and her love life, usually to the detriment of the latter. A missing man, a series of bizarre accidents, the death of a very old lady and a body on the beach are cases that she has to deal with in the stories above. Were it not for these stories perhaps no one would have heard of Sue Parker. In many ways she was just an ordinary detective, but it was her sharp perception and dogged perseverance that made her a force to be reckoned with as a P.C or Sergeant in Bath, or as an Inspector in Frome. If she had a blind spot it was in her 'work/life balance.' Too often she was preoccupied with her work, and her social and love life suffered. She regretted it, but believed that love would last forever 'next time.'

In these episodes she is challenged by a bewildering array of criminal activity but she always trusts her instincts, and they never let her down 'Anyone may have a reason to kill and it's not always obvious.' she would say, 'and many might have opportunity and that needs scrutiny as well, but in trying to solve a crime, I've found that the answers usually lie in the way that individuals and groups distinguish between right and wrong. That's the key to understanding motive and method. It's conscience or lack of conscience that will give someone away in the end'

PART 1.
BATH BUNS AT
SALLY LUNNS

Summary

This is a love story set in Bath. It is also a tale of mystery, murder and intrigue spanning decades and continents. Above all it confronts and exposes the way that moral dilemmas are dealt with in a variety of different situations. The story begins in Bath. Peter Howard has not returned home after calling his wife from Sally Lunns that evening. Inspector Lockhart and Constable Parker set out to investigate.

A missing man (Where is Peter Howard?)

Sally Lunns (he was last seen in a small tearoom in Bath)

Sue Parker (a young PC has more on her mind than crime)

The Howards (we find out more about the missing man)

The Lamberts and the Grearsons saw him last.

Lambert gives them his life story.

Inspector Lockhart. (A family man.)

Alice spots Diana and Denis.

Cap'n Jack (Alice Appleton remembers old and new loves)

Sue visits Sally Lunns (Sue gets a lead, of sorts)

The Affair Part Two. Hotel Miramar. Love, lies and logistics.

Sue thinks about love (a day at the seaside and an illicit love affair)

Denis Grearson (Denis examines his own conscience)

Denis and the Geisha 1965 (Denis does the decent thing)

Colonel Lambert (cv comes out clean)

Herr Gieseling and Charlie Chan.

Another missing person (Charlie Chan, Losie Lee and Frau Gieseling)

The Kitchen Table Munich 1936 (and that's how it was you see)

More Howard clues at Sally Lunns (good police work)

Denis Grearson in the spotlight (What affair? Oh, that affair.)

Lorna Howard confides in Sue (Peter got on with everyone . . .)

The Ellsberg Affair 1965 (Hot water in the Cold War)

Lorna's African tale (Tennis in Dar-es-Salaam)

UDI in Rhodesia (Peter gets more than he bargained for)

The Hell Run 1968 (The Mariakos story as told to Lorna)

Simon of White Rose farm. (a statement by Doog Moss)

The Kariba courtroom (a finding of eternal damnation)

Lorna's regret her story we came to Bath to put it all behind us.

(The answer's in Somerset not up the Limpopo)

Teamwork? (Harmony at Police HQ? That's a joke.)

Sue checks out the Hotel Miramar (What is a dirty weekend?)

Sue and Kath (The girls get a fright and Sue finds the files.)

The burglary (It's the only way, but I'm scared)

The denouement. (Two jigsaws become one)

BATH BUNS AT SALLY LUNNS

Introduction

A man had gone missing, or so his wife said. However, it soon became clear to the investigating officers that all was not as it seemed, especially when he failed to turn up in a matter of days. Questions needed to be answered, and fast. Firstly, who was this Peter Howard who had disappeared without a trace? What was his background and who were his friends and acquaintances, this man who appeared to be such a respected member of his local community? Secondly, what reasons could lie behind his disappearance? These might be simple enough of course, but as they dug further into the details of the case, the police began to unravel a far more complicated scenario in which secrets that had remained hidden for so long behind comfortable lace curtains in Bath, now began to surface. Peter had last been seen at the Sally Lunn's tea shop in Bath, and it was here that Constable Sue Parker became involved in a case that seemed at one time to have no motive or suspects, and then too many of both.

Sally Lunns

If you know Bath you have probably been to Sally Lunns. Right in the heart of the City and home to the famous 'Sally Lunn Bath Bun' it is easily reached from Pulteney Bridge, past the Weir, around the Abbey, down North Parade and it's on your right just before Tilley's which is another small restaurant worth a visit. It is part of the fabric of the city, along with the Jane Austen Museum, the Abbey and the Baths. It claims to be Bath's oldest house, circa 1482, emphasis being on 'house', because, built 10 years before Columbus, it cannot really compete in longevity with the original Roman Baths around the corner. As you step down, and down again, there are remains of the early footings, and an original kitchen with a faggot oven, Georgian range and old baking utensils. Adjacent is a rather remarkable stalagmite and stalactite cellar and, next to all this, a friendly face sells buns, cakes and sweets to a suitably impressed public. On the first and second floors there are neat tables and cosy corners for the visitors. If walls had ears this place would have many tales to tell, perhaps none more interesting than that which you will hear in this story.

Sally Lunns is a must-see venue. It is so small that one is touching knees with the person on the next table, especially when a guide brings a group of visitors to marvel at it's charms and taste the legendary Bun. Visitors come and go, ticking the 'Sally Lunn' box on their itinerary with great satisfaction. Exceptions to this rule are the few regulars who pop in for a take-away coffee or Bun and those few who come in to read the paper or plan their day, such as Tom and Iris Cavendish who own the flower stall just down the street. Less typical, but habitual visitors, are three men in their seventy's. Firstly there is Daniel Ziegler (Ziggy), first violin with the CBSO (retd) and originally from Poland. He is the slightest of the three and, although he doesn't talk about it much, he is a survivor from the Nazi death camps. He has his identity numbers still on the inside of his left forearm, and these are the ones he always remembers, not his army or national insurance numbers, just these. They are embedded in his arm, his memory and his soul. '434434437438.' He would never forget nor forgive. His friends had tried to persuade him that it was a long time ago, and that justice had been served at Nuremberg and elsewhere but his reply is always the same. 'We couldn't do anything in the camps but if only I had a chance now. If only; just one chance.' So the three friends tended to avoid the subject especially as Ziggy was such a delight in every other respect and they were never been short of other talking points. Then there's Pete Ferguson or 'Cabbage' to his friends because of his devotion to his allotment, and lastly Leslie Jackson, or 'Jacko'. He has had his sobriquet for many years having been 'Jacko the Clown' in Billy Smart's Circus. These three are indeed seemingly without guile or artifice, but this can hardly be said of other visitors who may be whispering their undying love, or planning their next betrayal in quiet corners at this very moment. Sally Lunn's is that kind of place.

Others may tell tales, but places like Sally Lunns are silent witnesses to people's everyday lives. They do not record a situation, nor do they judge the outcome, so visitors to its' darkened rooms can always feel comfortable that 'their' liaisons and betrayals (so many over the years) will remain secret. There is in fact but one thing that might reveal their secrets and that is the secret itself, because love and treachery are close neighbours, fickle as well as faithful, and the wild card of fortune or misfortune can so easily change romance into revenge. This is such a story, a story in which the unexpected seems to be the rule and where imperatives to action are so strong that normal considerations of right and wrong are ignored. Indeed it is a tale much like any other, where conscience is shelved for convenience.

*   *   *   *

Peter Howard was missing. He had telephoned his wife Lorna from Sally Lunns at about 6pm, but he had not yet come home. Now it was eight and she was wondering what to do. Firstly she went down the garden to his work shed and then to their narrow boat, which was always moored at the bottom of the garden, calling out as she went along, 'Peter, are you there? Where are you?' she sang out in a musical voice. 'It's Laura here' This was a pet name between them because they couldn't find a boat called Lorna, and Peter had said that she would have to change her name to stop any jealousy. It was his 'other girlfriend' and sometimes she wondered who came first but if Peter was happy then so was she. 'Come out, come out wherever you are' she continued in a sing-song tone now, as in the Third Man, when Holly Martens located the shadowy cat, then the feet, and then the face of the inscrutable Orson Welles in the lamp-light. There was no response, so she strolled around to the neighbours to see if he was there, but no one had seen him that day.

It was getting late, about 9pm when she started making phone calls. Just a few friends, and of course the Lamberts and Grearsons who were supposed to have gone to the Abbey for an ecumenical meeting with him. Mike Lambert confirmed that he had been with them but they had gone off shopping and didn't see him after the meeting; 'Did we Diana?' he called out, 'No, she says we didn't see him again; why? Has he been a naughty boy and stayed out late?' This was said in a joking tone, but Lorna was rather worried by this time, and all her other calls, including the local hospital and the AA, had been fruitless. The Grearsons were out so it was past midnight when she decided to call the police; not 999, that would seem to be too dramatic, but that nice Inspector Lockhart that Peter knew from the Round Table and the Bowls Club. She picked up the phone nervously and dialled his private number, aware that it was really too late to make personal calls at midnight. It rang for a while then she heard his voice. She was relieved. 'Hello Steve, is that you?' she spoke softly, as if slightly out of breath, as if she couldn't believe he was there or even that she was here and making the call. 'Yes, Steve Lockhart here, who's that?' He felt like saying 'at this time of night' in his brisk northern manner, but refrained as he sensed some urgency in the tone of his caller. 'It's Laura, I mean Lorna, you know; Lorna Howard' 'Of course Lorna, what's up?' he replied, 'It's Peter, I can't find him, I can't find him' she felt her voice faltering and he noticed an increased desperation in her tone. 'I suppose you've tried everywhere?' 'Yes, of course, of course I have, what shall I do, what should I do?' She was repeating everything and he tried to calm her down. 'OK Lorna, just take it easy. I'm sure it will be all right. I suggest you try to get a few hours sleep and I'll phone you first thing from the station. He may have turned up by morning.'

She sounded relieved, 'Oh, thank you, thank you, I'm so sorry, I'm so sorry to trouble you.' Lockhart sighed and went back to bed and Lorna curled up on the settee, listening to every sound, and watching the sky turn from a dark drizzly night, to a bright sunshine morning. She must have fallen into a deep sleep and awoke with a start when the phone rang. She grabbed at it, knocking it to the floor and disconnecting the caller. 'Bugger! Sod it! Come on, call back . . . call back damn you' she cried out, and fortunately the phone duly responded to her frantic calls before it would have been hurled across the room. It rang again. She picked it up, this time in a movement of exaggerated calm, 'Is that you Peter? Thank God,' she gushed out the words in a torrent but then stopped sharply 'Oh it's you Steve, have you any news?

No he's not here.' She started to cry so Lockhart stepped in, 'Now, Now Lorna, I'm coming round right now and I'll bring Constable Sue Parker with me. Put the kettle on and we'll have some tea. We'll be with you in about ten minutes'

Constable Sue Parker

Sue Parker was in her first year as a Police Officer. She was very conscientious when on duty, but she also liked to have a good time and she frequently went to Sally Lunns, herself, to meet friends. She usually met up with Adrian on a Thursday but since she had met Denton she'd almost forgotten about him. He was such a kid and Denton was, well, after all he was an Australian, and he was kind of experienced, in ways that girls like, ways that Adrian would have never thought of. Poor Adrian, he was very upset when she started going out with 'Big D' and she couldn't help feeling a little sorry for him, almost guilty that he had felt let down. But his feelings were not her responsibility, were they, she thought? The trouble was that she had told him things and they had done things together, because she wanted to, at the time; but when she didn't want to anymore she felt she should be able to stop. Funny she thought how a touch and an aroma so appealing could become almost repulsive. It's not like they were married, that would have been different, she thought, or, on second thoughts, would it? If a person doesn't 'want to' any more, but there are ties, what should they do, she thought? Well we didn't have ties so he shouldn't have got upset should he? She half persuaded herself, that things had not been good anyway, but she really knew that it was Denton who had changed everything, and that someone, or something, can come along and turn anyone's world upside down. She knew this by instinct, but even so she was still not prepared for the way in which the Howard case itself would hinge on that same randomness.

It was a coincidence but Sue had actually been at Sally Lunns herself on the day in question with her friend Amy, but the two girls had other things on their minds at the time, and it was 'boys' again. Denton had said that he had to go back to Australia so she had placed herself 'on the market' once more, and Amy was a good 'hunting' pal.

They had been at University together and shared most things including their taste in the opposite sex. This had resulted in some fun times, and also some squabbles between them from time to time, but despite this, they had remained firm friends. Amy had gone on to Teacher Training and was now at Ralph Allen School in the City, whereas Sue had joined the Police Force. The restaurant was busy, so they sat at a table and chatted about old times and their jobs for a while, until Amy changed the subject. 'That one over there' she said. This was their customary hunting ploy, sometimes it was only a nod in the direction of some hapless male and it was often followed by hilarious laughter from the girls. 'What him?' responded Sue with a grimace, 'Not bloody likely!' and, true to form, they burst out laughing. 'Well what about him then?' she persisted, nodding in the direction of a young man seated a few tables away. This time Sue was a bit more positive, 'Mmm not bad, not bad at all,' she said and they both laughed again. Just then the waitress appeared to take their order and Amy spoke first, 'I'll have some of that over there' she said, pointing to the young man at the table. 'Yes madam' the waitress replied, 'that's a Sally Lunn Special Bun with extra Stilton.' She paused with her pencil held over her ordering pad. 'Not quite what I meant,' laughed Amy, 'but I'll have some anyway.' 'Me too,' said Sue,' I rather fancy it myself!' The girls hooted with laughter but the joke seemed to elude the waitress who went off with a rather disapproving look.

By now the young man had noticed them because, after he had paid his bill at his table, he strolled over to theirs. 'I like a good joke' he said with a smile, 'and you certainly know how to enjoy yourselves don't you. By the way, my name's Adam. How would you both like to come to the Old Farm House next week? It's The Pete Allen Jazz Band. Tuesday I think.' They both stared at him disdainfully (they had practised this many times) and, once more, Amy spoke first. 'Actually we don't like Jazz but we'll have to see.' she said, and then they began to chat as if he wasn't there. He seemed a little put out and, mumbling 'Goodbye then' he left. The girls did not look up until he'd gone and then Amy burst into laughter again. She looked up at Sue but stopped when she noticed that Sue was not joining in 'What's up Sue?' she asked, 'Cat got your tongue?' Sue smiled,' Tom cat I think, shall we go?' she replied with a smile. And that's how it started. Adam was to be her next target but he'd never know it. She knew that she was a 'Will o the Wisp' or a Butterfly or better still, a Moth attracted to a flame, but actually there was something of the Spider about her as she began to spin her web once more, this time with the luckless Adam in mind for lunch.

The Howards

Peter and Lorna Howard had only lived in Bath for about four years and were still considered newcomers by some. In a way they stood out because they did nearly everything together, this in a place where 'own interests' seemed to prevail. No separate bridge clubs for them; if she went, he went and vice versa. They just loved to be together, in fact they just loved each other, and it had been like this since they met at the London Hospital Six a Side tournament many years ago. She was a nurse on a night out; he had scored the winning goal and was ready to celebrate. He was tall and slim and she was quite tiny, with dark features and a big smile. She danced all night and, as she danced, he could not take his eyes off her. True he had been drinking a bit, but he was mesmerised, and forgot all about his current girl friend Alice. People had remarked that Alice and Peter were the perfect couple because they shared an abiding interest in boats, as well as all the usual things that young people did.

They were on the water at each and every opportunity and she called him 'Cap'n Jack' affectionately. But, at that moment, at that very moment, Peter's world changed forever. This was serendipity indeed, with consequences that he could hardly imagine at the time. Suitor after suitor had whisked Lorna around the floor until finally an opportunity arose when she was alone for a moment. He moved in, feeling rather tongue tied for a moment. 'May I have this dance?' he asked very formally. She threw her head back and laughed, 'I was wondering when you'd ask me' she replied, 'You'll have to be quicker than that to get the girls!' He felt reassured and suddenly became quite bold 'Well I've got you now and I'm not letting go' he said as he held her very gently and then very tightly. They were married within twelve months, much to everyone's surprise, and to Alice's fury who continued to harbour a seething resentment for years. From then on Peter and Lorna became inseparable and Bath was their retirement dream.

*   *   *   *

Lorna saw the silver Audi pull into the drive. She recognized it as Steve's car because he sometimes picked Peter up for golf or bowls or a day out at Bath Rugby. They were both rugby fans and they usually took Lockhart's boys, Samuel and Stephen along. There was a second person, a woman, with him. Neither was in uniform. She opened the door before they had a chance to knock or ring the bell. 'Come on in, forgive the mess' she said as she led them into the lounge, which overlooked the garden at the back of the house. 'Please sit down.' she said, then paused, 'Is there any news; about Peter I mean?' she asked nervously. 'I'm afraid not' Lockhart said 'By the way this is Constable Parker from the station.' Lorna turned with a smile. 'Oh hello, pleased to meet you, can I get you some tea or coffee?' Sue looked at Lockhart, but he frowned, so she answered 'No thanks Mrs Howard, we are just here to ask you a few questions, the quicker the better and we can get on with finding him.' she looked over again at her boss. 'Right' said Lockhart 'let's get started. Tell me about yesterday' Lorna hesitated 'what do you mean exactly, everything?' 'Yes,' he replied 'every little thing you can think of, no matter how small. Start at the beginning and take your time.'

'Well' she said 'I'll have to think. Let's see now. I got up to clean my teeth, probably about seven then I went down to make a cup of tea. He was getting ready to go to the Abbey for a meeting of 'Bath Churches Together.' He went into the shower, took rather longer than usual as I remember and then joined me in the kitchen but the toast had gone cold and he complained so I just said, 'You must be meeting someone special today, you've been ten minutes in the shower and you've got that 'Old Spice' after shave on, but he just laughed' she paused, then continued, 'but isn't all this rather trivial when, after all we should be looking for him shouldn't we?' Lockhart sniffed 'Not at all. We don't want to miss anything do we eh constable?' 'No sir' she replied dutifully 'but may I ask a question?' Lockhart frowned as he had done earlier, and was wont to do when he disapproved of something, even though he didn't always know why. Actually he tended to like centre stage. 'Certainly Constable, carry on, don't mind me' he laughed, but it was more of a snigger. Sue knew his brusque Yorkshire style well but she continued 'Well, Mrs Howard, did he have any other plans for the day as far as you know?' 'No, he was only going to that church thing at the Abbey,' she replied, 'nothing else that I was aware of, but he didn't always tell me everything unless it was really important you know.' She had suddenly become even more anxious and looked at Lockhart for some kind of relief from this line of questioning. He duly obliged and said, 'Well, that'll be all for now then Lorna but tell me, did anyone else from the church go with him to the Abbey?' Lorna was relieved at this easy question and replied straightaway, 'I know that Mike and Diana Lambert and Denis and Lucy, the Grearsons, were going. Would you like their numbers?' 'Yes thank you,' he replied, 'just give them to the constable and don't worry. Oh, and do you have a recent photo? Thanks, we'll be in touch.' With that he motioned to Sue and they both left the house and got into Lockhart's car.

'She seemed a bit unnerved, don't you think?' said Sue. Lockhart scowled, 'So might you if your husband was missing, that is if you ever get one.' Sue ignored this barb because she knew that she was right.

The Lamberts

Lockhart had arranged to see the Lamberts the next day at 11 am. He took Sue and another young constable 'Charlie' Charlesworth with him to make notes and when they arrived Mrs Lambert showed them into a very grand sitting room. The walls were covered in paintings of army life in India and Kenya and there were also a number of the popular series of prints of wildlife by David Shepherd including Zebras and Lions with a backdrop of Mt Kilimanjaro or Lake Naivasha. There was a corner dedicated to the East African Safari where it seemed that he had been an important organizer. Also on the walls were Zulu Shields and Assegais and these were complemented by many carvings of Elephants and Conche shells on every windowsill and on every shelf in cabinets.

Yet strangely on one wall there were a number of David Hockney prints, rather out of character with the rest. Lockhart did not seem to notice this but Sue did. She had already observed that Mrs Lockhart was a good deal younger than her husband. Was this wall a statement of her independence, in a house where everything else seemed to be to the Colonel's taste Sue would have loved to see their bedroom, or might it be bedrooms, she wondered. 'He won't be a moment' began Mrs Lambert, 'He's out with the dogs, I'll go and make some coffee' 'Thank you, and thank you for seeing us at such short notice' replied Lockhart as he looked around the room. 'Not short of a bob or two' he whispered to Susan 'Last of the British Raj I should think, and I wonder if that Shepherd print is one of the original; limited editions and all that?' He liked to show his cultural knowledge, (no simple Sheffield cop he), but Susan knew him all too well by now. She had him down as a bully with a chip on his shoulder and one who must be humoured lest sparks fly.

Just then Colonel Mike Lambert entered the room or, one might say, marched into the room, with a big dog at his heels. 'Sit, sit!' he commanded. Sue looked at Lockhart with a smile, as if the command applied to them as well, but he was not amused. 'Good morning Mr Lambert' he began, 'Colonel, man, Colonel, call me Colonel if you please.' interjected Lambert. 'Yes of course, sorry sir. As you know we've come to see if you can help us about the whereabouts of Peter Howard who hasn't been seen since Thursday, and you and Mrs Lambert were with him on that day. We are wondering if there is anything you can tell us about the day itself. Any small detail might help.' Lambert sat down and the big dog sat at his feet. 'Hound of the Baskervilles' thought Susan, but looked at her boss dutifully as Mrs Lambert returned with a tray of coffee, which she poured into four cups. 'Help your self to milk and sugar please do, and then tell us what you want to know.' she said. Lockhart was a patient man, he was prepared to wait for as long as it took to get results and he knew that the best information was obtained if small talk could be allowed to melt the ice. 'Well, it's such a lovely day,' he began 'I wonder if Mrs Lambert would mind showing Constable Parker round the garden, she has been admiring your roses' Susan was used to these gambits and so she smiled encouragingly. 'Will you? May I?' she said rather gushingly and thought she might have overdone it, but no, Mrs Lambert was keen to show off her garden and so she beckoned to Sue. 'Yes, follow me Constable, let's leave the men to talk shop.' she said.

In the sitting room Lockhart came straight to the point. 'This is Constable Charlesworth,' he said,' I hope you don't mind, he'll just be making notes for the record if that's all right. Now tell me Mr, I'm sorry, I mean Colonel Lambert, how well did you know the Howards?' Lambert thought for a while and then replied, 'Well, not especially well I suppose, they were quite new you know, They'd only been here about five or six years. We saw them at Church, down in the Canal Basin and at the Golf Club you know, not a bad handicap as I recall, Peter I mean, but Lorna played as well you know.' Lockhart looked thoughtful, 'You were on Christian name terms then, I mean, not just formal acquaintances?' Now it was Lambert's turn to pause, 'Well we weren't exactly bosom buddies if that's what you mean, but friends, yes, friends I suppose.' Lockhart stopped and made some notes. Actually he was not making notes but drawing a picture of a rather silly dog. This strategy had served him well over the years. It gave him time to think and, to a degree, it unnerved his 'target'. After a few minutes he got up, leaved through his notebook and walked behind the Colonel so that he would have to turn his head to reply. 'Right then that's clear enough' he muttered almost under his breath so the Colonel had to ask him to speak up. 'Sorry sir, clear enough, I said, but tell me about the day, what happened on Thursday?' Lambert craned his neck to see where Lockhart was. 'What do you mean, happened? Nothing happened as far as we are aware.' Lockhart smiled from behind the settee, 'You mean, as far as I am aware don't you, not we, I mean?' The Colonel spluttered as his face turned crimson red, 'What are you getting at?' he said, 'the 'memsahib' saw what I saw, we were together all the time, all day. We went to the meeting and then we went shopping together, then we came home together that's all there is to it.' Lockhart realised it was time to back off, 'Yes of course, thank you I do understand, just routine questions, purely routine.' he said.

At this point Charlie spoke up. 'I hope you don't mind sir,' he said 'as a matter of interest perhaps you could tell us a bit about your time in India and Kenya. I had some relatives out there once, in the Civil Service and I'd love to go one day. I would really appreciate it.' Lockhart was a good police officer and, although he did not approve of Charlie asking questions, he thought that a new 'Personal' angle might be a good idea to put Lambert at ease. 'Yes, good thinking constable, nothing to do with the case of course. Just tell us about the Army, we haven't got time for the rest. Do you mind Sir? Just to humour the lad you know.'

This was a bit of a tactic, and it worked perfectly. 'Of course old man,' responded Lambert, 'let's start with the photos shall we? Now that's me with the regiment up at Simla, just north of Delhi you know. Posted in Delhi but Simla was a great place for cooling off and most Europeans went there for a break. This next one's me with the King's African Riles in Gil Gil near Nairobi trying to clear up that messy Mau Mau business. I won't show you my official photos of the corpses we found in village after village where the Mau Mau had taken revenge on so called 'collaborators' with the British. No, let's move on to my Safari collection, there's Joginder in the Volvo (the winner in 1965) and Marshall in the Peugeot, killed soon after, ran into a truck without lights at night poor bugger. Sit down and I'll get some albums.' he said and left the room.

Lockhart was annoyed. 'See what you've done Constable. He's off down memory lane on total irrelevancies. You've got a lot to learn about police work my lad.' However he didn't want to refuse because he was still evaluating Lambert as a suspect, so he just growled and sat down. 'We'll have a word back at the station.' he muttered under his breath but it was too late as Lambert soon returned with an armful of books and sat down.

'Now I want you to browse through these while I tell you what it was like to be an organiser and marshal at the Rally. It began in 1953 you know, and was known at first as the East African Coronation Rally, in honour of the Queen's coronation. It takes place over miles of dusty murram roads through Kenya, Uganda and Tanzania. A VW Beetle and a Standard Vanguard shared the first honours, then a hat trick for the Mercs. Here, take this one for starters, that's just how it was, just like that.' The picture was of an upside down car in a ditch and Charlie laughed. 'Can't quite see what's happening there.' he said, with a smile. 'Well, just hold on and I'll tell you.' said Lambert. 'It was June,' he began but Lockhart soon interrupted, 'We really haven't got time Sir.' he objected, but Lambert was in a world of his own as he told his story with memories flooding back and there was to be no stopping him now. 'It was June,' he began again, 'It was hot and dusty, there had been no rain for months . . . .

The East African Safari 1965 (Lambert's story)

It was June. It was hot and dusty, there had been no rain for months and I was in charge of the organisation around Lake Nakuru, where all the Flamingos are. Bet we gave them a fright. I was used to heat especially the sort of damp heat in Delhi where it was stifling but here it was a dry heat that made you itch all over with no respite. Now here's a mystery for you if you want one. That photograph was taken at my checkpoint and it never should have happened, not there anyway. Ralph Steadman, the driver was from Pretoria, a sort of government official. His co-driver was a local farmer Jan Smoot from Eldoret, some 50 miles north of Nakuru and the car, as you can see, is a Toyota. Smoot was an interesting character, a descendant of those Afrikaaners who took part in the 'Great Trek' from the south in 1840, or maybe later after the Boer war in 1900. Either way he was one of many in East Africa and beyond, who resented British hegemony in the region. That year they were big rivals with the Mercedes, Datsun and Mitsubishi teams as well as Ford and Volvo etc. Steadman was killed but Smoot survived, saying that they had had no brakes since the last checkpoint. Steadman had refused to stop because, he said, they would lose too much time. He had kept it on the road, and to time, right up until the last bend as he approached my checkpoint, and then, crash! Killed outright.' There wasn't much roadside medical care in those days either, and poor old Smoot had to wait hours for an ambulance, and meanwhile of course the Rally went on.

We left Steadman's body by his car covered in a blanket, but it wasn't long before those fiendish Hyenas came sniffing round so we moved him into our tent but it didn't stop the smell, and it still didn't stop them so I took one of them out and the rest fed on that. The day was hot, very hot and there was dust everywhere. As I said, we were on a bend, which is usually a good idea for a checkpoint, because the cars are slowing as they reach you. The downside is that you can't see them until they're nearly on you, not like here in the UK where marshals are blowing whistles and hooting horns to warn of an approaching car. We did actually have a marshal on the bend, if you can call him that. He always seemed half asleep with the effects of the local 'pombi' beer. Just imagine the scene. We hear the noise of an engine and then suddenly a car thunders into the checkpoint at high speed in a cloud of dust as if it won't stop.

'Pesi, pesi, quick, quick what's the make and number?' It's covered in dust and we can't see. 'Yes, looks like number 99 Mercedes, (Lang and Richter) yes, time 3.09pm noted. Off you go!' And he's away, but another one's here already. 'Pesi, pesi, quick, quick. Number 72 Volvo, (Carlsonn and Thomas,) sounds rough, bashed up nearside front, Time 3.11. Gone!' And so it went on for hours, sometimes nothing to do and then a flurry of activity, and it was during one of those lulls that I went to inspect the doomed Toyota in order to make my report. There it was on its' side, crumpled and forlorn and a little sad. A beautiful machine reduced to scrap in seconds. Hardeep Singh was my engineer and it was he who noticed the first problem and called me over to where he was inspecting the brakes. 'Not wear and tear sir, cut right through I'd say, with a hacksaw or something. Look you can still see the teeth marks.' Hardeep was not an excitable man and he made his comments in a sort of professional monotone, but I was very, very interested in this development. We had been told to look out for instances of cheating or malpractice but this went way beyond that. It looked like sabotage and, for me, it was the Mercedes team whom I suspected, partly from my own observations, but also because it was well known that they were very keen to reinstate their position as market leaders in East Africa, and a Safari win would do a lot to help their cause.

Well that was the first surprise but nothing prepared me for the next, and I kept this one to myself until I could report it in person to my own Rally directors. It was a very hot potato indeed and I didn't want Hardeep or anyone else to get wind of it for now. I found it in a waterproof package tucked under the driver's seat. I might not have done but his seat had been thrown forward revealing a small brown box and an envelope inside the package. At first I thought it must be his personal belongings put there for safety but when I opened the box I was dumbfounded. It was diamonds! Hundreds of them shining and twinkling in the fading light. I opened the envelope and read a very formal but mysterious letter with an official stamp at the top. I did not recognise the logo but I noted the address. It was 179 Kruger Street, Pretoria and it was addressed simply to RS (which I took to be Steadman.) It was marked Urgent and Top Secret and this is what it said.

From the Office of the Interior
179 Kruger Street
Pretoria.

Urgent and Top Secret to RS

Collect Girl's Best Friend from contact KEY at Kigoma Hotel on Lake Tanganyika and carry with you to end of Rally at Nairobi. Deliver in plain parcel to Mrs Green, 39 Delamere Close. Do not open. Sgd JB.

Well, what was I to make of this? It seemed like smuggling, but why the official South African Government heading? In my innocence I suppose, I couldn't understand why South Africa needed to smuggle diamonds. Didn't they have plenty of their own? I think that's why I decided to keep it quiet, until I could get some advice that is. Eventually an ambulance arrived to take Smoot to hospital and to remove Steadman's body, and soon after a Toyota team delegation came to inspect and move the car. I told them that they could not do so until the Police had investigated the crash scene, which, to be frank, I knew might not be for some time. There were two Japanese engineers but the car was a private entry from Bulawayo in Rhodesia with 'factory backing' from Toyota. There were two other men in the car and I recognized Afrikaaner accents in their voices. 'I'll take responsibility for moving the car.' said one, 'I'm Louis Botha from the Pretorious Toyota dealership in Bulawayo. It's our car and I'm taking it away now.' He signalled to a tow truck that had come with them to move into position. 'I'm sorry,' I said, 'that would be illegal and we must wait for the Kenyan Police. They might be here soon.' I knew this to be unlikely but I didn't know what else to do, short of mounting an armed guard. 'I'll give you a receipt,' he said with a laugh, and motioned to his drivers to couple up to the stricken vehicle. Soon they were gone, taking any evidence of the tampered brakes with them and all I had was a receipt. Well, not quite all. Did I tell you that I still had the diamonds?'

'Yes sir, you did, at least I think you did,' said Charlie consulting his notes, 'It says here that you found them but not what you did with them.'

Lambert was amused, 'Yes I kept them and led a life of luxury from then on,' he paused and looked seriously at Charlie but gave Lockhart a big wink. 'Do you think I did the right thing then Constable?' Charlie was used to being teased so all he said was, 'Well sir why don't you tell us exactly what you did do then?' Lockhart interjected at this point, 'Come on Colonel put him out of his misery, just what did you do?' 'Well,' said Lockhart, 'being a good soldier and all that, I presented a full report to the Safari Directors and I was given a commendation for 'responsible service.' I was told to leave the whole matter in their hands and not to 'make waves old boy.' I did persist for a while, telephoning to see what had become of the diamonds and, of course the investigation into the brakes. They didn't actually say 'what diamonds, what brakes?' but their inaction meant the same thing to me. To cut a long story short I never did find out, and soon after I came back to the UK, met Diana and, as you can see, lived happily ever after.'

Lockhart didn't say much except to thank the colonel and ask him to see if the 'ladies' had finished. Then he turned to Charlie, 'Don't worry about all that irrelevant stuff,' he said, 'just keep your report as brief as you can and concentrate on Peter Howard. Remember, he's the missing man, not 'call me Colonel' Lambert and his diamonds. And next time keep you mouth shut until you know what you are doing.'

Actually Sue and Mrs Diana Lambert had been getting on very well. Mrs Lambert talked endlessly about the garden and the roses while Sue listened patiently. She was weighing up Mrs Lambert. The colonel was in his late sixties but this woman was only about forty and rather sophisticated she noted with some interest, and the Colonel did seem to be a rather stuffy character. Certainly their tastes seemed diametrically opposed, but what might this mean? Sue was good at observation but she was also a good police officer, biding her time to ask her questions. When Mrs L suggested that they sat down under the apple tree Susan quite properly admired the crop asking whether they had taken apples on a picnic on that Thursday or, she added, had there been a formal lunch? 'Why don't you take a few Constable' said Mrs Lambert, 'Well, there was coffee when we got there at about eleven o'clock. We had a talk until about one and then broke into informal groups at small tables where sandwiches and a soft drink were served. We finished at about two thirty and then the Colonel and I went shopping. She always called him 'The Colonel' to others, and especially if he was present. 'Does he like shopping?' Sue asked, seemingly in a rather absent-minded way, but it was actually her key question to determine if they had spent all of the afternoon together. 'Not really, I suppose' Mrs L responded, 'I suppose he couldn't get out of it this time' she laughed rather nervously. 'And did you do a 'Ladies shop' if you know what I mean?' asked Sue. 'Yes I did actually, because I don't get into town so often these days. I went into Marks and around the Paragon and then I popped into Sally Lunn's for a coffee before getting home about five. He, I mean the Colonel, likes me to stay at home you know. When I do get a chance he usually goes off somewhere and we meet up later.' 'And is that what happened on Thursday then?' Sue asked. She was closing in and her quarry was responding well . . 'Yes, we said we'd meet back at the house about sixish but he didn't turn up until after seven.' Here Mrs Lambert paused, 'Is that all now? I rather think we should be going in, he won't like me talking to you for very long.' She seemed to be getting rather anxious, so Sue touched her hand reassuringly. 'That's fine, you've been most helpful' she said with a smile, 'Let's go in then.' After calling them in Colonel Lambert had gone off with the dog again so she and Lockhart bid farewell to Mrs Lambert, and made their way out to the car.

'Well Sue, how did you get on?' Lockhart was looking quite pleased with himself. He smiled encouragingly. 'Well sir' she replied, avoiding the familiar which he deployed as often as the scathing, or merely irritable,

'Well sir, it seems they were not together all day Thursday. After some shopping they split up and he didn't get home until seven. They both had a few hours on their own.' 'Oh did they indeed?' he responded grimly.

'Good. Well done. Now I want you and Charlie to put your notes in a File marked <u>Lamberts</u>, keep them brief, none of that Rally rubbish, all red herrings in my opinion, put the rest in order, we may need them later.'

Back at the station Sue and Charlie assembled their notes. 'I may as well chuck my lot out.' said Charlie. 'Not on your life,' said Sue, 'Evidence is evidence. We just don't know where it might lead and I've got a hunch that there may well be something we might need later. Keep it all.'

Inspector Lockhart

Steve Lockhart was somewhat of a contradiction in many ways. On the one hand he was a rather tough and somewhat ruthless police officer, but on the other, according to his friends, he was an exemplary father of his two boys Samuel and Stephen on whom he absolutely doted, and a considerate and loving husband. He seemed to lead his life in compartments and adapted his personality to each. At work he was efficiency itself and he was strongly tipped for promotion, but he was not the same man at home. He celebrated every birthday and special day with his family and nothing was too good for them. There had been Balloon rides, ten-pin bowling and many trips out, including the 'SS Great Britain' and the 'Matthew' in Bristol docks. He told them about Cabot and Brunel and he took them to the Roman Baths as well as to the Jane Austen Museum. He sought out non-conformist Churches of all kinds, Methodist, Congregational, Dutch Reformed, Lutheran and others. This might seem rather strange, because they did not attend Church as a family but he always said that it was part of the boy's 'education.' Sometimes however they left him there alone as he seemed deep in prayer, but when asked he usually replied, 'Oh, just thinking about things you know.' When the boys played sport 'Mum and Dad' were always there. Lockhart's 'domestic' character was tuned in to his family life and it would seem that nothing could disturb it, but if, we are to gain more of an insight into the Inspector, we might reflect on an occasion when his guard slipped and his 'work' character intruded on a day out with the family.

On the day in question he had taken his family to Longleat (The BBC's Animal Park), which was only about twelve miles from Bath. Typically he had chosen a 'Longleat Rally' day featuring the Bristol Austin Seven Club thus giving the boys a double memorable experience. The day began well. The Audi Estate was, as usual, packed to the gunnels with every kind of 'little boy' survival kit, from 'wellie-boots' to wet wipes, a football, cricket gear, plenty of food and a picnic table and chairs.

They had decided not to look over the House itself this time, judging that it might be rather boring for the boys, so the first thing was the picnic, and what a feast it was. There were all the 'usuals' of course, but also a big cake in the shape of a 'Longleat Lion' and the boys were suitably impressed. When they had finished they joined strolled down to the Rally and poked their noses into Austin Seven bonnets of all types, shapes and sizes. There were Tourers, Saloons, Cabriolets and Sports models of every vintage, and Lockhart didn't want to leave but he knew they must because the evening was already booked. This was another treat for the family, an outdoor concert at Dyrham Park, some twenty miles from Longleat, where they had tickets for a fabulous Elton John concert starting at seven. Climbing into the car once more they set off to circumnavigate the Estate with all the other visitors. 'Over there! Look Mum! Those baby Giraffes . . . Look Dad, Zebra! Look, Look Rhinosristrices!' Mum and Dad laughed but didn't correct the mispronunciation. There had been quite a few of these over the years and they remembered them fondly. 'Beep-Beep!' was one that stuck in their minds when the boys had first spotted a Sheep.

They continued through the Wolves enclosure and past the Lions. 'Why are Lions always asleep Mummy?' came the question, so easily put, but so difficult to answer. 'I suppose they're tired dear.' she said. Lockhart smiled and said 'Yes, that's it, tired.' and they all laughed and were still laughing when all the cars in front suddenly stopped, seemingly for no reason. A few moments went by, then a few more and then more. Lockhart looked at his watch. 'Come on, get a move on.' he said but they did not move. 'What the heck's going on?' he continued, now sounding rather concerned, 'We're going to be late if we're not careful.' Mrs Lockhart and the children started to play a game of 'I Spy' but after a few more minutes he said, 'I'm going up there to see what's going on.' 'No dear, you can't' she said, 'it says, 'you must not leave your car under any circumstances' so we'll just have to wait, won't we?' 'Not on your life' he replied and, taking his walking stick, he got out of the car and strode down the road until he was out of sight. She decided to continue the game with the boys. 'Anything to distract them, and me as well.' she thought. She was rather worried, and more so when he didn't come back for a while, but soon the boys spotted him. 'Daddy, Daddy, here he is! Daddy, Daddy! Look Daddy they're moving, the cars are going!' Lockhart climbed in to the car and started the engine. 'Let's go then.' he said, 'we can't hang about here. We've got a concert to go to.' They set off and, after a while, when the boys were pre-occupied, she said, 'What was that all about back there?'

'Oh, nothing much,' he replied, 'some Baboons thought they ruled the roost around here, and no one would take them on.' 'So what did you do dear?' she asked. 'Well, I looked them in the eye and told them who was boss.' he said with a rather grim smile. 'Thank goodness you did.' she answered, 'Well done dear. Now we'll be on time after all.' She patted his arm as a sort of approval but, as she did so, she noticed that the sleeve was speckled with blood. She drew back, momentarily fearful to ask questions, and she just whispered so that the boys would not hear,'Don't forget to change shirts when we get there. That one's got rather grubby.' He smiled and said, 'Right.' Fortunately the concert was a great success all round, but as she sat there listening to Elton John's songs, she was thinking about her husband. Did she really know him? Had she ever known him? Was he just a man like all men, and did all men have that capacity to turn from peace to aggression in moments?' she wondered.

'No wonder he's got such a difficult job,' she thought, 'where anyone, absolutely anyone, can wound or kill given enough motivation. And this could include women as well.' she conceded, rather reluctantly 'and when would it be right?' she wondered. She looked across at her husband in his clean blue shirt and held his hand. She loved Steve and trusted him implicitly. She knew that he had been 'protecting' his family back there, and she supposed that would have been a good enough reason for anyone.

The Affair (Part One @ Sally Lunns)

On the day that Peter Howard went missing Diana Lambert was also at Sally Lunns. She was feeling anxious and very nervous as she sat at a very small table deep inside the restaurant. She wished she could go deeper inside, but then Denis might not see her. She looked aimlessly at the Guardian crossword on the table but could not concentrate. Grearson always did this to her. Why did she let him? Why? Why? He had told her to be there at three thirty, which allowed an hour after the meeting finished. Well, it was now four thirty, and she was starting to wonder, when suddenly there was a tap on her shoulder. 'Hello darling' a voice said. Her knees went weak. It sounded just like her husband's voice for a moment, but no, it was Denis. 'Thank God, Thank God it's you, I was getting really worried' she spoke in a soft whisper, as if Sally Lunn herself was listening. He sat down and held her hand gently. A shock ran through her whole body and she flushed a deep pink around her neck. 'Well I'm here now' he said, in a voice vaguely reminiscent of the Colonel's when they had first met. Perhaps that's one of the things that made him so attractive, that and the other things that were so unlike her husband after so many years together. Just then the waitress appeared and asked what they would like. 'I'm starving' Denis said, 'I'll have coffee and a Sally Lunn Bun please. What'll you have darling?' 'Nothing thanks, I've had a coffee while I was waiting' her voice tailed off because she did not want to upset him, 'Well, maybe just an Elderflower water please, with ice.'

She was feeling a bit too warm for comfort for one reason or another. He reached over, slightly under the table and touched her hand again. She smiled. His hand stroked hers and then very briefly, her knee. It was all too much. She sat back rather hurriedly. 'Not here. Not now . . . please.' He smiled at her, very assured, 'What do you mean by please?' he continued. 'Not now, I said not now' she repeated, but, after she said it, she immediately wished she had said yes please instead. He pressed her hand gently, 'Don't worry, I saw Mike about an hour ago, he seemed busy and won't be bothering us I fancy'. 'Where, where did you see him, and why didn't you tell me?' she asked anxiously, 'Didn't see the point.' he replied, 'He was just going into the Jane Austen Museum, looked as if he was meeting someone. He didn't see me and anyway he's out of the way now.' Once more he patted her hand. 'Well, it wouldn't be a woman,' she said. 'Mike's not like that, well, he couldn't be could he, not at all like that, but what do you mean by 'out of the way'?' she sounded nervous so he took his hand away and smiled. 'Well, he's not likely to come up here now is he. That's all I meant' 'No I'm sure he won't, do you think it's going to be all right then?' she asked. 'It certainly is,' he replied, 'all booked again. Who would believe that you'll be teaching me needlepoint at your Nadfas 'away weekend' this time?' Once more he was smiling and she felt safe, longing to be in his arms where she had felt so much alive, as if every time was a first time. It was only two weeks ago and she could not bear to wait another moment let alone two weeks more. She was alive, she was glowing; Mike would never, could never understand and he would not have noticed anyway.

But Miss Alice Appleton noticed. Miss Appleton came in every day for afternoon tea, usually with a piece of Fruit Cake. 'Buns are for the Tourists' she would say disparagingly. She noticed everything. It may have been because she had been a Chief Librarian that she noted down what she saw and mentally 'categorised' the scene. Mum and Dad with two children, well that was probably 'Sociology' or 'Money.' A young couple canoodling, Mmmm, probably 'Love and Romance.' An elderly couple, yes, 'House and Garden' most likely. As usual she was watching everyone, including Diana and Denis. She was seated too far away to hear their conversation but their body language did not escape her. The woman, she noted, was nervous, and the man was a little too pushy to be really thoughtful. So, she puzzled what category? Romance? No. No happy ending here, I think. What about Friends and Family then? No, not likely. Well, how about Crime, yes, or even Murder, yes, even better. The way they acted made them prime suspects in a tale of star-crossed lovers and murder she decided. Yes, 'crime' for sure.

She started to dream a little, thinking back to when she was young and in love with her 'Cap'n Jack.' What had gone wrong? She had not seen it coming, her life ruined in a flash. Over the years she had had many lovers, Paul, Tommy, Bill, Michael, she had forgotten all their names. To her they were all 'Cap'n Jack' her one true love, Peter Howard, who left her to marry Lorna. She slept for a moment, conjuring up old memories that she would rather forget. But she would never forgive. She had never married and some unkind folk called her Miss Haversham. But she wasn't like

Miss Haversham. On the contrary, she took her revenge for the disappointments of yesteryear by ensnaring and rejecting lover after lover, If only she could think of a way to sink 'Cap'n Jack' and his mate.

Cap'n Jack

Alice relived her memories frequently. Sometimes it was for no reason, but usually because someone triggered them off, as Paul, one of her ill-fated lovers had done, on an especially rainy afternoon when they had nothing better to do some years ago.

*　　*　　*　　*

'It was the boat you see' she said . . .
Yes
The boat was everything
Yes it meant everything
Well the boat was special
As being special is, you know, like it is sometimes

Yes, yes you do, I told you

It's you, your legs, Aaah that's better, the boat was so special, I told you

It was us, I mean him and us, and ours but his really, his and him.

Because the boat was everything
I mean everything, all, total, sum, best, complete. us, him and the boat.

Well, we kept it, I mean he moored it in the Harbour

'Was it?' Paul replied.

Go on
So?
To you?
In what way?

I'm not sure that I do
Tell me again and budge over please

Well then, how was it so special?

So why do you feel differently now?
Pass the soap. Thanks, go on

Tell me more about the boat

So was it big then, was it a
yacht?

Oh no, nothing grand   *How many berths then?*

What do you mean?   *Berths, you know, beds*

I don't know about that but it
was very comfy for two

It's comfy here isn't it? Would
you like some warm?

Yes please, good idea, we didn't
have a bath on the boat

Did you go out in the boat?

Out?   *Yes, to sea*

To sea?   *Well, out of the harbour then*

Maybe up the river, I think so,   *You don't sound very sure*
yes

'It all seems blurred and fuzzy sometimes, but it's all there, still there, still there. I remember the waves splashing against the side of the boat in the harbour' she said and closed her eyes dreamily.

The scene was as clear as it was back then, and she remembered everything as if in a trance. A scene opened up as if in a cinema, and she saw herself and Peter Howard as clearly as if it were yesterday.

Waves lapped against the side of the boat rocking it gently to and fro.

Alice, Alice darling, wakey-wakey, it's morning!

Alice awoke with a start and rubbed her eyes as Peter leaned across her to open the cabin window. She touched him gently as he lay over her.

'Make love to me Cap'n Jack' she said.

Not now, not now precious, we haven't got time, we've got to get under sail Matey, catch the tide me hearties! Anchors away! Don't forget we're meeting the Langtons for lunch at the 'Old Lock.'

Can't we just stay here? Look, are you looking? Yes you are I can tell.

Maybe I am but it's no use. Come on, shake a leg.

That's exactly what I am doing you spoilsport. OK, I'll get up if I have to.

(She said this with a mischievous grin as she moved slowly to the sink.)

She stood nude before a small washbasin and he smiled as she leant forward to wash her face, her curves even more evident than before. He moved hurriedly to the deck before he had a chance to change his mind. She finished freshening up and then stepped into her jeans and loose top before stating on breakfast. It was soon ready, bacon, hash-browns and eggs sunny-side up just as Peter loved them, and she loved him.

'Cap'n Jack' was her special, very special love name for him. He called her 'Matey' and it worked, oh how it worked.

'Vittalls, Cap'n Jack, come and get it!'

'Aye, Aye matey! Ah, good enough to eat, just like you Matey. Mmm lovely, lovely. Hoist the mainsail we're setting sail!!'

*   *   *   *

And so the day progressed and eventually the pub hove into sight. 'The Old Lock' was well known to river and canal users alike as it was situated on a small island between the two. It would be most unusual if a person did not meet up with a past acquaintance and so it was this time as Peter and Alice walked in. Choruses of 'Hi there!' and 'Where have you been?' greeted them and they waved. The joint landlords were Jeremy and Jeffery, the former a cordon bleu chef, and the latter an award winning interior designer, and their joint expertise showed. 'Look Jay, look who's here' called Jeffery to the kitchen, 'Come and say hello to Peter and Alice!' It was always like this so it took a little while for them to work their way through to the table where the Langtons were already seated. 'At last, at last, here they are, said Joan Langton with a big smile.

'Sit, do sit, Bernie will get the drinks in won't you dear? Usuals?' They nodded and Bernie went off to the bar. Joan continued, 'Well now we're all here we can get started. I fancy the Game Pie myself. By the way you haven't met Lorna Symington have you? Lorna, these are our best friends Peter and Alice. He'll surprise us all and name the day; one day!' Alice smiled politely and said,' Hello Lorna, very pleased to meet you, this is Peter.' Lorna shook the outstretched hand and said, 'Nice to meet you Alice and how are you Cap'n Jack?' Alice froze. She waited to see if Peter would reply, 'Aye Aye Matey' but he just said, 'Nice to meet you Lorna' and then Bernie returned with the drinks. Nothing more was said.

Soon Alice was forced out of her reverie by a voice that seemed to come from far away, as if in the clouds somewhere. She resisted at first but there it was again, and she finally awoke with a start

*   *   *   *

Alice, Alice! Wakey wakey, it's Paul here, we need some more hot.

Yes, yes of course, I must have been dreaming

Turn around, I'll scrub you back with the loofer. That'll wake you up

Yes, that's nice, very nice

Wasn't the boat nicer?

Don't be silly. By the way, have we done it?

You mean you don't remember?

I'm not sure
Well I'm blowed!
Sorry, nothing personal
Not personal? Anyway, the answers no
Good
Why good?
Because
You mean you didn't want to?
No. I mean yes
OK by me then. Just tell me what happened when you split up
Don't say that!
Well, is, 'went separate ways 'better then?
No, No! Stop it, Stop it!
I'm sorry Matey, let's dry off by the fire shall we?
Yes let's, and then make love to me Cap'n Jack

*   *   *   *

A few moments passed before Alice came out of her trance and she was back in Sally Lunns. Yes, so many 'ships had passed in the night' and so many Cap'n Jacks had come and gone. If only. If only she could think of another way to get her own back on Peter Howard. Did she have murder in mind or was that only in the books that she read in the library?'

Sue visits Sally Lunns

Lockhart had decided to ask questions about the missing Peter Howard in Bath and had divided the immediate vicinity of the Abbey between his officers. He would do The Paragon himself, and ask Sue to do North Parade, which actually included two of his favourite restaurants. First she asked questions in Tilley's; no luck there, so she went on to Sally Lunns. It is only next-door, and, as she approached she experienced that delightful aroma of coffee beans roasting, a temptation closely akin to the smell of Fish and Chips, but much more agreeable she thought. She could see that it was very busy; but nothing could have prepared her for what she found inside the tiny restaurant. The place was full of French and German pensioners, Japanese tourists, Chinese students and others at every table, on all three floors, and in every corridor. As she eased his way in she heard voices in German, Mandarin, Cantonese and a multitude of other dialects, not to mention the fevered calls to the kitchen by flustered staff, all of who were young girls, and most of who seemed to be from Eastern or Central Europe.

She cornered a young waitress holding a tray of Sally Lunn Buns. 'May I see the manager please?' she asked politely. 'Manager busy, not possible, come later' was the predictable reply but when Sue showed her warrant card she ran away and Mr Lorenzo soon appeared. 'Oh hello Constable, we're very busy today as you can see. Let's go through to the office. Will you have a coffee?' They had got to know each other quite well over the years and had remained amicable despite that unpleasant business over some rather dodgy 'illegal' workers. 'Thanks Jorge, but spare me the Bun!' she said with a smile. Lorenzo laughed, 'Well how can I help?' he asked. Sue came straight to the point. 'Well, we're asking questions all around the Abbey to see if we can locate a man who went missing yesterday. This is his photo and his name's Peter Howard. We know that he went to the Abbey in the morning for a meeting but he didn't come home that night' There was a pause and then Lorenzo said 'Yes of course, of course. I know him. That's Mr Howard, we know him quite well, he often comes in with his wife, but yesterday? I don't know. I'll ask Tatiana, she was on duty.' He stepped out into the corridor and called out in a loud voice. 'Tatiana! Tatiana! Come up here please. Come up for a moment will you?'

There was a moment's silence, broken immediately by the crash of falling crockery, after which Chinese and other voices seemed to rise to a crescendo, and then Tatiana appeared looking flushed. Lorenzo was tactful and didn't mention the incident but asked her if she remembered Mr Howard being there yesterday. She seemed scared at first, then said 'I theenk so. Just as we closing. About six, go to meeting, he say.' Sue was pleased at this outcome, it was a lead of sorts and she was grateful. 'That's very helpful' she said, 'Thank you, that could be very important indeed. You've been most helpful. Thanks again.' As she left she was wondering who Howard may have been meeting and why, and would he have wanted his wife to know, because she hadn't mentioned it.

The Affair

It was Saturday 20 March, and two weeks before Peter Howard went missing that Diana and Denis had arranged to go to The Hotel Miramar. It was their first weekend away. Diana had decided that she must go, she must. No two ways about it she had to go. So many loveless years with Mike, or was it that many? It seemed like a lifetime, and anyway he was always tied up in his own affairs while she was expected to stay at home. What happened to 'our' life she had thought? Well that's all water under the bridge now that I love Denis. Yes I do she thought; maybe only a few crumpled moments grabbed when Mike was away, and never at the Grearson house, but what sublime bliss. He had said it was 'too close to home at home' and laughed, but she thought that he also sounded a bit worried about the whole thing.

And now this was it, another weekend to lie about. Of course there had to be some planning, and this had created difficulties, not only with excuses and alibis, but also practical things such as 'names'. One of them had to leave credit card details at the hotel in order to book the room and she had positively refused, saying that Mike always checked their accounts, so they booked as Mr and Mrs Grearson at The Hotel Miramar in Bournemouth. And she had insisted that he made the phone call, otherwise it wouldn't seem right she had said, so he did. The Hotel had 'designated parking only', and only one car per room, so he had given them his car details as well. And obviously they would have to meet up somewhere and leave the car in a safe place where it would not be noticed, but where It should not be too close to Bath in case it was seen by someone they knew, nor would it be sensible to take it all the way to Bournemouth so they agreed on Frome, at the Leisure Centre attached to the College; no parking charges and probably unnoticed; not exactly on their way but not too far out either.

They agreed and now they were there, tucked in, and she was smiling again, and again. She felt wanted, wanton and womanly, but he was beset with a mixture of guilt and desire. This was lovely but he knew that it was wrong. Above all, it must be kept secret, at all costs, at any cost, and no one ever must know, ever.

Sue thinks about love

After their visit and interviews with the Colonel and Mrs Lambert, Sue thought she might be on to something. Mrs L was a very attractive young woman and he was, well, he was a bit of an old duffer, she thought. 'I wonder if they do?' she thought to herself, 'maybe she has a lover, maybe, but a lover's got to be special, I mean tingly and all that; like Adam and me. Yes like that, when you just can't stop. Or can you? I mean if it's not right? What if someone else is involved? Should you stop, or more to the point, should you start if you're not free?' Sue wasn't thinking about the morals of the situation, but of the practical implications in Police work where betrayal could so easily lead to murder. She thought back to how Adam and she had got started at the Farmhouse. Amy had only been in the running for a very short time because it was Sue that Adam had phoned the next day.' Amy'll kill me' she thought with a laugh but agreed to go to Weston-Super-Mare for the day. He had made it sound like a real adventure with extravagant promises of sunny skies and maybe sightings of dolphins, but of course it rained, and it was donkeys not dolphins that amused them that day.

They had paddled for a while and then as the sun went down over the pier he drew her close and kissed her on the cheek. She said nothing as he stepped back, but, placing her fingertips on her lips, she said, 'Here please'. Once more he drew her to him gently but this time with an urgency that made her gasp. They kissed with a passion that startled yet thrilled her, oblivious to the fun fare in which they were standing. 'Cor! Look at them Mum!' said a little boy, tugging his mother's sleeve. 'Yes dear,' she said, 'I think they need to cool off with some ice cream don't you? Come on let's go and get some!' . . . But Adam and Sue were still locked in an embrace, and ice cream was the last thing on their minds.

When Sue got home she lay on her bed thinking. Was she right about Diana Lambert? Had she sensed the 'Heart of the Matter,' just in her very brief visit to the Lambert house? Diana was undoubtedly a young attractive woman, with (to put it kindly) a bit of an old duffer for a husband but so what? Did she have a lover and what's more to the point, how might they fit into the case? Well, she thought, my money's on Denis Grearson. The Lamberts and the Grearsons were the last to see Peter Howard so let's start there she thought. What kind of man was he, and what kind of woman was she? She knew that they were involved with 'Bath Churches Together' a moral crusade perhaps, or more likely a convenient cover-up especially when Cupid came calling, she wondered. Finally she gave up, lay back on her bed exhausted and was soon asleep.

Denis Grearson—A double life

It was 9am when the phone rang in the Grearson house. 'Whoever can that be at this hour,' thought Lucy as she called out to her husband. 'See who it is Denis will you, there's a dear, I'm still drying my hair.' Lucy Grearson was always in a hurry on Sunday morning as they got ready to go to Mass. 'Gotcha,' her husband replied 'Hello, this is 474878 who's that please?' 'Steve here, Steve Lockhart, can you spare a mo' Denis?' Grearson grumbled under his breath but was, as usual, politeness itself.

He hadn't served in customer relations for nothing. 'Oh Hi Steve, yes but make it quick as we're just off to Church. If it's about Peter I hope you're phoning to say that he's returned to the fold, turned up I mean.' 'I'm afraid not. Not a sign so far. I was hoping to come up to see you sometime tomorrow, would eleven o'clock be OK? Just to go through a few things?' Grearson thought he sounded very 'Policeman Plod' but he knew better, knew that Lockhart was a potential high flyer with a faultless record tipped for stardom. He knew all this because Grearson himself had served on the Policing committee for Bath & North East Somerset. 'Hang on a minute' he said and, putting down the phone, he moved to the Stairway. 'Lucy, Lucy dear, it's Steve Lockhart; wants to come and see us tomorrow morning about Peter, he's still missing. Would that be OK for you? OK, thanks 'He passed this message on to Lockhart and went out to start the car. They were running late, 'As usual' he thought,

'Lucy was wonderful of course, but couldn't she be a bit more, well a bit more, a bit more like me perhaps, organized, get up and go, or more like Diana with her deep eyes and her . . . but no that wouldn't do at all would it?' He chuckled at the thought. Lucy was built for comfort not speed, and maybe she was not as she used to be, but she was a perfect hostess for a Garden Party or any social gathering for that matter. It crossed his mind that things might have been so different for them.

He remembered times when he was not tempted by other women, times when his thoughts were always with Lucy, and how he loved her. And he still loved her, although now his thoughts were more about Diana Lambert. 'So where had it all gone wrong' he thought and, 'would we still be happy if I hadn't met Diana.' Had he been given a test and failed miserably? Had Diana been that test, given to everyone, when it is up to them to decide, for good or for ill, the moment when conscience may be ignored, sometimes for duty, sometimes for revenge and often for love, no, let's call it lust because love and conscience are partners. Just then Lucy ran into the lounge, 'Hurry up dear or we'll be late for Mass,' she said, stopping to pick up her prayer book. 'You go on dear,' he replied, 'I've got too much to do today, to get ready for the garden party, mow the lawn and all that.' 'All right dear, I'll say one for you then, Bye darling.'

Denis breathed a sigh of relief. Why was he so troubled today he wondered. 'Stiff Scotch, that'll do it' he decided, saying which, he poured himself a double measure and sank down on to the sofa.

He was soon asleep and then awake again, drifting and remembering London and Tokyo in the 1960's when he was in Public Relations with Gifford PLC. Is that when he lost his moral compass, or did he find it there only to lose it here? As he dozed he remembered Tokyo in 1965.

*   *   *   *

Denis and the Geisha 1965

Giffords had been commissioned to work with Chrysler International, based at Bowater House in Kensington to bring about a 'fruitful liaison with MMC (The Mitsubishi Motor Corporation)' Initially this was to be on the world markets, but not in each domestic market. The first meetings were held in London in the Autumn of 1964. As Marketing Director it was Grearson's job to see that the MMC team of six were comfortable at the Park Hotel as well as to see to their timetables and flights etc. Almost as important seemed to be the requirements of their wives who had 'much shopping' to do. There were only three wives present, but that was complicated enough. Having seen to all this it was then Grearson's brief to attend, but not to take part in, the face to face meetings of the respective directors, and lastly to organize their 'entertainment' at night.

It might seem like a grandiose scheme but the two companies had divided the world into 'spheres of influence' in which one or other of the parties would take a leading role and this was the nature of those first meetings.

All models were to be included but especially important were the 'Chrysler Cricket' (The British Avenger) and the Mitsubishi Lancer, which were head to head competitors. In other words a world-wide cartel was being considered at that stage. Denis was encouraged to bring Lucy to London for the week. Most of Chrysler's management in the UK were still American at this point. They knew that the Japanese put family honour and prestige high on their agenda and Lucy was certainly worth showing off, not just for her beauty but also for her sensitivity to the situation in which they found themselves. The Chrysler team were led by Moises (Mo) Romane and Clemar (Clem) Danchon, and the Japanese team by Messrs Tanaka and Susuka and everyone seemed to get on fine. As well as other entertainments Denis had arranged a very traditional English evening out at Simpsons in the Strand (Best Aberdeen Angus) with a walk along the Embankment afterwards. Then it was back to the Hotel, although Denis knew that others might be seeing the night-spots and maybe more. Back in their room he had felt such an outpouring of love that Lucy was quite taken aback. Later she said, 'If that was the Saki we'd better get some in!' and they both laughed and laughed until they nearly cried with joy. The week passed all too soon but a further meeting was arranged in Tokyo for the following Spring, during which time, each side would prepare more comprehensive territorial pricing briefs. Giffords were kept on as PR consultants but there wasn't much to do on the account until January '65.

The January soon arrived and Denis packed his bag. He would be staying at the Tokyo Hilton but Lucy's mother was ill so she could not come.

'You will be a good boy,' she said as she kissed him goodbye, 'And don't overdo the Saki will you?' They hugged and laughed again, remembering that wonderful night once more. 'You know that I love you more and more each day,' he replied 'but I think I'll stick to Scotch just in case! Just joking!' The taxi was at the door and he was gone with a waved kiss.

The flight was excellent with only one short stop at Anchorage in Alaska. There was no snow but there were miles and miles of Evergreen trees and blue skies. Surprisingly there were 'Canadian Mounties' in their redcoats at the Airport, or was he suffering from flight fatigue, he wondered. The Hilton was, well, the Hilton the same as any Hilton he had seen in many cities, but the service was better. Inside the Hotel it was an oasis of calm. Outside it was organized chaos. Large sedan cars vied with tricycle runabouts and delivery vehicles for every space on the road. On the pavements anxious businessmen pushed their way past little old ladies dressed in the traditional manner. Denis was pleased to find his room to settle down for the night, but sleep would not come because there had been too much dozing on the plane. Must get an early night tomorrow. Some hope! His hosts treated him and his colleagues like royalty and every night was a new experience of entertainment. There was also a trip to Kyoto and a ride on the bullet train up to Mount Fujiyama. The previous week the train had broken down and, being fully electrified, the windows would not open and it was a blazing hot day. The windows had to be smashed and many people were injured. Denis kept his fingers crossed and it was indeed a wonderful experience.

Kyoto was different from anywhere he had been before, being one of the spiritual hubs of old Japan. Shinto, Buddhist and Confucian temples dominated the town but he did find a small Catholic Church tucked away in a quiet corner of the City. He sat and prayed his usual prayer, 'Please God let everything be all right. Amen.' He stayed on for a bit, wondering why 'Christians' had always tried to convert the world to their beliefs, especially the Catholics, he had to admit. He knew the answer of course. Jesus died for all mankind not just for Christians. For himself he appreciated all religions and none, and he tried to live a good life according to his own faith. He stood up, said 'Bless me Father' to no one in particular, but to the 'Stations of the Cross' on the walls.

The following days were taken up with intensive meetings in ubiquitous Hotel conference rooms. The issues were much the same each day and for each territory. If Mitsubishi were already in the market they would decide model pricing and vice versa. Denis was given detailed analysis from the MMC side to back up their costs, together with other competitive prices in the market, say from Toyota. The Chrysler file was sketchy by comparison, with very little hard evidence to underpin a comprehensive marketing strategy but he was assured that there was ample material back in London should it be required. On that matter he was reminded that he was an observer not a negotiator and how did anyone really know how accurate the MMC figures were anyway? So. In a way he was a witness to a game of cat and mouse played out on the large conference table. Sometimes the atmosphere was very tense and sometimes there were long periods of silence. This usually occurred when Chrysler posed a difficult question. Instead of a considered reply within a few moments, it seemed that the whole MMC team would go to sleep. Eyes closed and maybe, just maybe, an imperceptible movement, then still and silent again. It seemed like hours, but even so, it could be up to ten minutes before an answer was given. There were no fundamental disagreements on the face of it, but nothing was signed either.

*　　*　　*　　*

Back at the hotel Denis was worried. His colleagues had left the meeting as soon as it was over because they had a reception at the American Embassy and he was left to clear up the files. It was then that Tanaka came across the room to speak to him. 'So, how you enjoy Tokyo Grearson San, you like very much? Tonight we have big treat. Go to Hanamachi to visit Geisha. You like?' Grearson nodded and bowed, 'Thank you very much Tanaka San but I will probably have work to do. My humble apologies.' Tanaka seemed a bit upset. 'I'll tell Romane San to let you off,' he said and laughed. It was then that Denis noticed that some men were not only clearing up, but were making notes from the confidential Chrysler papers, one he thought he recognised from the MMC team. He was about to say something but when he looked again they had gone. 'Were those men from MMC?' he asked Tanaka, 'No, not ours,' came the reply, 'Only four here from MMC, one, two, three and me' he said as he pointed to the others in the room. Denis was concerned but after all, what could he say or do, he was an observer wasn't he, albeit employed by Chrysler? He had no witnesses to what he had seen and anyway it had been denied, and if he spoke up his own reliability might be called into question. He hesitated as he took his leave from Tanaka, it was now or never, he must make his case now and call Danchon or ignore the whole situation. 'So this is it' he thought, 'the slippery slope starts here. This is my moral crossroads, the time when I know I'm doing the wrong thing but I'm going to do it anyway because I'm scared to do otherwise. Let's face it I'm a moral coward. A row at this stage could bring the talks to a halt and I'd be blamed.' He could think of many reasons to keep quiet but they weren't good ones, and if it was the right thing to do to stay silent, why was he feeling so guilty, and why do us Catholics always feel so guilty about everything, he mused. Finally he decided to say nothing, and wait for 'fate' to take its' course. 'Maybe I'll get another chance to even my account 'up there' before I die.' he decided. 'Another place, maybe another time and I'll do it right next time dear God I promise. I'm sure <u>you</u> understand.' he added hopefully, with a glance up to the heavens.

Just then the telephone rang in his room. It was Clem Danchon, the Chrysler Marketing director, 'Hi Denis,' he said, 'All right if I come round for a minute? Mo wants me to talk to you about tonight.' Grearson's heart sank, he knew that he wouldn't be able to get out of it and, to be frank, he didn't know if he could trust himself, especially after what he'd heard about the legendary Geisha girls. He gave in graciously and said, 'Sure Clem, come round now, it's number 787, I'll crack open a bottle.' Danchon arrived soon after and they chatted about this and that for a while until Clem broached the subject of the evening ahead. 'Look Denis,' he said, 'I don't like to press the point but something tells me you're not too keen on going out tonight. Am I right?' It was no use denying it so all he said was, 'No, I'm not too keen, but I'll make the numbers up if you like.' Danchon smiled and said, 'I'm glad to hear you say that because Mo was getting a bit worried. Always thinking about sales, that man, and our image of course as we all do. So tell me, really, what's on your mind, pressure of work, homesick, jet lag hangover, which is it?' Denis laughed, 'Well, none of those actually, although homesick is nearer the mark. To be honest I'm a bit worried about spending an evening in a strip club with prostitutes. Tanaka said we were going to the 'Hanamachi' to see the Geisha' Now it was Clem's turn to laugh out loud, 'You're going to have no trouble on that score.' he replied still chuckling 'Because that is exactly what you won't be doing. Let me tell you a little bit about Geisha. You sound just like an innocent abroad.' Denis knew that this was true except, of course, he didn't like to admit it. 'I've been around,' he said rather lamely and Clem smiled again.

Clem Danchon was an interesting man. Swiss born, naturalised American he had been at the forefront of Chrysler's expansion into world markets, sometimes against the instincts of a rather parochial Detroit Board. He had led delegations to Iran where the 'Paykaan' (Hillman Hunter) was one of the best selling automobiles, especially for taxis. It was shipped from the UK in CKD (completely knocked down, or disassembled) packs, and assembled in Teheran. Iran seemed reasonably settled at this time under the firm grip of the Shah (Pahlavi), so wider ventures were being considered, as here in Japan. Danchon had certainly 'been around,' from the Casbahs of Casablanca to the 'salons' of Singapore and beyond.

'First of all Denis,' he said, 'Geisha are not prostitutes, nor strippers. Firstly they are not 'The' Geisha, they are, just simply, Geisha. The 'Hanamachi' is not a red light district either. The Hanamachi areas are sometimes called 'kagai' as well, and were originally established near traditional tea houses (the ochya). Remember the film,'Tea House of the August Moon'? Well many of them are still the same today. On the other hand, there are those that are larger Japanese style wooden houses with banqueting and hotel accommodation. Here there are usually smaller 'ochaya' rooms where geisha may entertain special customers.' 'That's what I'm worried about!' laughed Denis, 'Don't tempt me please!'

'Well, as I said before,' replied Clem, 'you've nothing to worry about. It's usually very formal. Just Tea and Saki later, lots of Saki!' Denis continued to look worried, 'Go on.' he said.' That's about it really although it might be useful to be aware that there are two kinds of geisha at least.' replied Clem, 'and usually a hierarchy of senior Geisha to keep an eye on things especially on the 'maiko' who are the youngest, and sometimes very, very young, if you get my meaning. The older Geisha are known as 'Jikata' and they generally sing and play musical instruments. If you get into conversation with a 'maiko' just make sure you've got an approving glance from a senior 'Jikata' That is usually sufficient for you to continue. Any questions?' Denis could think of many but he just said, 'No, that's a great help Clem. I'll try to observe the local protocol just as you suggest. See you later then.'

The evening soon arrived and they were whisked to the 'Hanamachi' area in no time at all. Their car was a luxury limousine of the kind that Denis had not seen before, not unlike a Lincoln Continental with leather seats and electric windows quite unusual in the UK. It had not been on the Chrysler 'shopping list' probably for that reason but Denis was very impressed. They were ushered into what seemed like a large dance hall with seats around the edge, some 'sit up and beg' and some comfy recliners. There was an excellent band that Denis thought to be Goanese or Filipino playing European style 'Tea for two.' Apparently the Japanese entertainment would come later. Gradually he began to feel more relaxed. Perhaps it was the Saki but anyway he was soon talking to a young Geisha, maybe about eighteen or so. Actually he felt safer doing this because he knew that the 'maiko' were out of bounds to predatory men. Her name was Lily and she was not only lovely but, as it transpired later, she was a very graceful dancer in the Japanese 'mai' way. The evening passed in a flash and soon it was soon two o'clock in the morning. Then, as everybody gathered to say goodbye, Tanaka called Denis to one side and proffered the following invitation.

'You are most favoured Englishman.' he said, 'Madame Nakano has said that you may take Lily back to the Hotel. She will come with her but wait in the lobby as long as necessary.' This was exactly what Denis had tried to avoid. He yearned to say yes, but something told him to say no. He also knew that Clem and Mo expected him to agree. Part of corporate entertainment they would say, to refuse would mean 'loss of face' (so important in Japan) all round, not just for Denis but for them as well. What could he say or do? Was this his moment to redeem himself but at what cost and to whom? Clem could see that he was hesitating, 'Come on old boy, the lady's waiting.' he said. 'Right,' Denis replied, 'tell her I am very honoured indeed and am pleased to accept.'

Now Denis knew that it was up to him to play his cards right, any slip and he (and Giffords) would be history! The limousine took him with Madame Nakano and Lily back to the Hilton. They left 'Madame' in the lobby and went up to Room 787 and closed the door.' I'll make some tea.' he said.' 'No Grearson San, 'that my job'. You get comfortable 'she replied, with such a sweet smile that Denis wanted to hug her.

He sat on the bed and probably looked quite forlorn. She made tea and sat at his feet. She took his shoes off and said. 'I know you not want me Grearaon San, but I will say nothing to Madame or to Danchon San if you promise to do same. I stay here for two hours, no sex, then gone. I understand you married but don't worry. It will be our secret.' Once more Denis could have hugged her but he just said,' Thank you Lily, thank you very much. I'll leave you a present.' He took out his wallet but she stopped him, 'It all on House.' she replied with a smile. He flopped on the bed and was soon asleep. When he awoke it was seven am and she was gone. There was only a small card with an emblem on it. No other name and no address, just a simple lily.

At breakfast nothing was said, no innuendos no knowing winks, just business as usual. He had got away with it. He had 'done the right thing' he had 'balanced the books' or had Lily done it for him?

*   *   *   *

Now he lived in Bath and had a lover but it was a very precarious arrangement. Actually he did not feel secure at all. In fact he thought that they might have been spotted together last time at Sally Lunns. Despite everything and his love for Lorna, he knew that he must protect Lucy and their marriage (until death do us part) whatever it took. If someone told Lucy or attempted to blackmail him what lengths would he go to, he thought. Indeed, would he be capable of the mortal sin of murder?

Lucy Grearson

The Grearsons were conscientious Catholics. Every Saturday they went to confession and every Sunday they went to Mass. Rather unusually Denis had not gone to confession this Saturday, saying he was too busy and there was a lot to do in the garden for Father Basil's party. Indeed there had been much to do because this Sunday was Father Basil's Birthday and the Garden party in his honour was to be at their home. Still, thought Lucy Grearson, it was most unusual, and anyway, who was it that had spent weeks in preparation with a small Church committee? Well, it certainly wasn't him was it? What with the local Bowls club and those business weekends away she hadn't seen so much of him recently. Still it was nice of him to do the heavy work in the garden, she thought graciously and he could be very thoughtful when he felt like it. He had certainly helped in re-jigging their Verandah that had not wintered well, but which was now looking at it's best. Quite took her back to holidays on the Costa Brava where they had spent so many happy moments, sitting out with friends and 'Sundowners'; and how they all laughed when Anne Butterfield had said that they should be called 'Sindowners'! The joke was aimed at Lucy but she didn't mind. Her faith had withstood far worse in the way of 'jokes.' It's funny, Lucy thought, how Catholics always seem to be on the fringes of whatever society they live in. Of course this would not pertain to Spain and probably much of South America but she only had experience of The States and, of course, the UK. They had lived in Manchester, Warwick and London and it seemed like that everywhere.

Actually she could not think of any of 'their' friends who were Catholic. Going to Mass on Sunday was like entering a different world. Where did they all come from, these Catholics? She never saw them socially elsewhere. Parallel worlds she surmised but why is it still the case? Suspicion from History dies hard it is true she thought, but surely prejudice is another dimension, one of uncorroborated suspicion, surely. She was not a Tory but she wondered why Bernadette Brearley, who had been a Conservative 'A' list candidates, had (allegedly) been asked but refused to use her second name Margaret in the recent local elections. 'Bernadette is just too, too Catholic my dear, and Margaret, well Margaret reminds us of our very own Margaret Thatcher of course,' the chair of the selection committee had said but to no avail.

Lucy was getting upset. She was not an intellectual but her Faith was very dear to her and she wished, oh how she wished that some amongst her friends might share it. Of course she was so blessed to have Denis, true and steadfast in their faith together. Yes, she decided, she was indeed very fortunate. Wasn't it a pity about Adrian though! They'd tried everything, but he barely paid lip service to the Church. He was such a good boy and hoped to go to University next year, but she was very worried about him, and especially about his choice of friends, who often led him astray, she thought. It was their fault, even that nice Susan. He could be such a good boy; but so easily led.

Luckily the day was fine and the Party was a great success. Father Basil got a bit tipsy and did a jig to a small Ceilidh band. The proceedings closed with some exuberant dancing from the large Polish contingent that now made up more than a third of the congregation; and then it was over.

The Grearsons slumped into their armchairs. Lucy spoke first, 'That went well didn't it dear?' she ventured. 'Wonderful darling, you really are the best,' her husband responded warmly, giving her a kiss on the cheek. 'That's nice dear, can I have another one?' she asked with a smile holding his hand in hers. He moved his hand from her grasp to pat her arm gently, 'Drinks my love, that's what we need don't we?' Lucy smiled again, but this time it was more a smile of frustration than pleasure.

'I thought that Father enjoyed himself tonight, don't you?' she said as an opening gambit that she knew would take them down one of those long discussions that they used to have when they were really close. Whatever has happened to us, she thought to herself waiting for Denis' reply, we used to understand each other so well. And so the dialogue began, old ground in new clothes maybe but she felt as if something had gone missing in their lives so she was pleased to get his attention like this hoping (and praying) that she would sense a spark again.

He- I'm not so sure, he seemed rather quiet I thought.
She- What do you mean?
He- Well there's always scandal about paedophile priests and all that. Maybe he's one himself!
She- Please don't say that, don't even think it!! He's such a sweetie.
He- Well you never know do you?
She- Don't you?

He- Well, how can you tell?

She- I think you'd know if someone close to you was gay or having an affair or something like that wouldn't you?

He- Would you really?

She- I'm sure of it. Remember Gillian Clarke? The minute she started an affair with George at The Bell everyone knew about it didn't they?

He- Bet his wife was the last to know.

She- I don't agree; not at all. A wife always knows.

He- Yes, I suppose you're right.

She- Don't you think it's hard though, say your marriage has fizzled out one way or another. How can people cope without the blessings of Mother Church that we have, to help them through difficult times?

He- They seem to, it's only us who are on a constant guilt trip isn't it?

She- What do you mean? Everyone knows right from wrong, don't they?

He- Maybe, but what is it that restrains people from acting on, let's say, selfish or convenient principles? We believe that Christ died for our sins on the Cross. So we have a guideline and, although others may say they do, they don't make a connection with his moral teaching. But we know that every time we transgress it's another wound in Jesus' side and that's why we feel guilty. As bad as life may seem for us, it pales into insignificance when measured against His sacrifice. He set a Gold Standard and we must follow or fail. Isn't that why we go to Confession because we're always failing? Everyone fails of course, but most don't know they do or they don't care. Many people do act morally of course, but this may be, for them, based on another kind of moral teaching, or just a sense of right and wrong from inside, a conscience perhaps. That seems to be something that everyone has, but it's not always listened to. Following orders, soldiers usually say.

She- So, why is it us that carries the extra burden of Christ's suffering?

He- I don't know. I suppose it's a matter of faith in the end.

She- Would you?

He- Would I what?

She- You know, have an affair?

He- Me? No. Never. One woman's enough for me, and you know that I have always loved only you don't you?

She- But what should a person do if they're tempted and fall and can't find a way out? What should they do?

He- I don't know darling. End it all I suppose, suicide, mortal sin or not.

She- We are so lucky aren't we? I'll make us some chocolate to take up.

The next morning Lockhart and Perkins arrived as arranged but their questions did not seem to shed much light on the matter. Denis Grearson had gone to the Abbey for the meeting as he said and he had gone home when it was over. She had stayed at home to prepare for the weekend and then they spent the afternoon in the garden. Much later Denis had gone to see Father Basil to go through the arrangements for his Birthday Party. He had come home about nine thirty. They were very sorry but there was nothing more they could do to help. 'Drawn a blank there I think' said Lockhart, 'perhaps we'll have better luck with the report on Lambert.'

Colonel Lambert

Lockhart was in the Office when a confidential report came in on Colonel Lambert. It gave details of his Army and Civilian careers and an update on his more recent activities. 'Hey! Constable Parker! Come and have a look at this' he called out. It was an order but Sue was curious. 'Right Sir, anything interesting?' she asked politely. 'See for yourself, nothing much I think, army service, jumped up Lieutenant if I'm not mistaken.'

Sue looked at the file. Lockhart may be right she thought, Lambert had been a Lieutenant in the Grenadier Guards served in India but somehow had got promoted to Colonel in the Kings African Rifles in Kenya during the Mau Mau Emergency in 1951. When that was over he had farmed for a while near Lake Naivasha then come home to chair the British Waterways Board from 1968 to 1973. He was appointed President of the Kennet and Avon canal Trust in 1987. 'Well sir, he seems pretty kosher to me 'she said 'although I suppose he could have had a row with Howard over his boat, Howard's I mean . . .' Lockhart frowned 'Maybe, could have, that's not good police work is it Constable? Evidence and connections, that's what we need, not guesswork. Just put it on file will you, we still have a missing person and conjecture won't help will it?'

'No sir but do you think it would be a good idea to see Lorna Howard again to see if there's some background that we don't know about?'

'I agree Sue' Lockhart said, this time a little more friendly and she wondered why. 'Why don't you go? I'm going to be busy tomorrow.' Now Sue knew why he was being nice, 'busy' usually meant Golf or Bowls. Still she preferred it that way, and she thought she might do better with Lorna on her own anyway. 'All right Sir, I'll do my best' she answered, tongue firmly in cheek 'just leave it to me.'

Murder

Sue had lunch and went back to the Station to do some paperwork before she called to make the appointment. She'd been at her desk for about half an hour when Lockhart came out of his office looking grim. 'They've found him' he said 'at the sports centre, with a knife through the heart.' Sue shivered. She was speechless for a moment. 'Oh No!' she said, and that was all she could say, what a turn up, poor Mrs Howard she thought.

Apparently the Bath Beavers gymnastics team had gone to use a vaulting horse in the gym but couldn't move it, and when they took the lid off they saw that there was a body lying crumpled up inside. Naturally there was a lot of fuss and the Paramedics and the Police had been called at once.

A driving licence on the body was in the name of Peter Howard.

'We'd better get down there Constable' said Lockhart, 'we don't want anybody messing with the evidence do we?' 'No sir, I mean yes sir' said Sue rather reluctantly. She had never got used to dead bodies.

When they arrived at the scene the Coroner was still there. 'What do you make of it Tom?' asked Lockhart in the most familiar friendly tone that he used when he wanted something. 'Strange case this one Lockhart' came the reply. Professor Tom Greene was not drawn into Lockhart's familiarities, 'Knife straight through the heart from the front. He knew his killer, knew his killer yes, but, and this is very strange, the victim's face has also been cut, in a number of slices on both sides. Oh yes, and what's more, he was dead when the cuts were made, and they probably weren't made until a little later. No blood you see, no blood, no heart beat no blood do you see?' 'I think we do Professor' said Lockhart, 'thank you very much, that's very helpful. Come on, let's go Constable, we've got a lot of work to do haven't we?' 'Yes sir' said Sue 'but where shall we start, it all seems so strange, macabre even don't you think sir?' Lockhart was back on professional ground again quickly, 'We're not paid to think Constable; evidence, evidence that's what we need. We'll have to question everyone again. I'll start with Sally Lunns, where he was last seen, try to pick up some clues, you go on to the Grearson's, too good to be true that pair in my opinion, but first we'll have to break the news to Mrs Howard and I'll need you in case she gets hysterical.' Sue agreed, noting that Lockhart showed little sign of being sympathetic as usual.

It was 10am the next day and Lockhart was looking grumpy. There had been a meeting in Superintendent Powell's office about the dramatic turn of events, and the Super had decided to set up two teams, one under Lockhart to follow up the immediate connections and another one under Inspector Jean Curtis to look into his work colleagues, wider family and friends. 'Let the dog see the rabbit, I always say. No point when you can't see the wood for the trees is there? A stitch in time saves nine I always say. Good, good. Just let me know if there are crossovers but I'm sure you'll manage. I know that you'll get on fine.' And with that he dismissed his two top officers with a wave of his hand. They both mumbled, 'Thank you sir' and left. Lockhart turned left in the corridor and Curtis turned right. She smiled at him and said, 'See ya Steve, and good luck' 'Police work isn't good luck' he replied 'and you won't see me if I see you first. Just keep out of my way' He didn't like to share. He had little respect for Curtis, but this sentiment was based on his prejudice against any high-flying woman police officer rather than anything else.

Lockhart had observed the rise of 'Feminism in the Force' with alarm just as he had misgivings about 'positive discrimination' of any sort. He was a middle aged, somewhat conservative police officer, and was much more comfortable with a world where women made the tea. Now it seemed that it might not be long before he reported to a woman, or even a black superintendent who couldn't cut the mustard, and maybe both! Time to retire then, he thought. Actually he quite liked working with Sue Parker because she seemed to be the traditional sort. He summed her up thus, 'Comprehensive school, Police College, respectful, co-operative and efficient within her own limitations.' Small and attractive, she didn't seem like a police officer at all, and that suited him fine. Jean Curtis was a different case entirely, 'Jumped up les. I wouldn't be surprised' he thought. Tall dark and slim, University First Class Degree, fast tracked to promotion and 'not up to it' was his opinion. He was wrong on nearly all counts about both.

Another missing person

The next day Jean was called into the Superintendents office again. 'Oh, come in Jean, do sit down.' he said. 'Uh-Oh something's up' she thought but just said, 'Thank you Sir.' and sat down. 'Funny business, police work,' he said, 'just like the buses, nothing for ages and the two along at once.' He smiled and waited for her response. 'Do I take it Sir that we have another Missing Persons case?' she asked. 'Bang on Jean.' he replied, 'a tourist has gone missing from a Shearings Continental Coach Trip. They had a day out doing the sights and then he went out for a walk before dinner. Didn't return to the 'Dukes Hotel' that evening and he's still unaccounted for. We've already sent out some dog teams and beat officers to make enquiries but nothing's come to light. You know the hotel I suppose, it's in Great Pulteney Street just a few minutes 'level' walk from the City centre. That's why it attracts Saga visitors or pensioners groups like the one he was with. I want you to give young PC Charlesworth the job. Probably open and shut, I wouldn't be surprised, but tell him to take PC Parker with him, umm yes' He looked at the file on his desk, 'Yes, take PC Sue Parker with him. Tell him he's in charge reporting directly to you. Keep me posted. Any questions?'

'No sir, I'll see to it right away. Thank you sir.' she said and left the room. 'And thanks for nothing' she thought to herself, 'doesn't he know I've got other work to do. This is the second job he's piled on in as many days. Still, maybe it will be as he said, 'open and shut." As it happened both PC's were in the wardroom when she came out of the Super's office. She beckoned to them both to come into hers and began. 'Well Charlie this is your big chance. The Super wants you to handle it and Sue, he wants you to help.' Charlie looked pleased, 'Oh thank you Ma'am.' he said, 'What's up?' Jean felt like saying 'open and shut' but she thought that this would give the wrong impression to the two young officers. 'Well you know about the murder case' she began, but before she could go on, Charlie butted in 'Yes, we certainly do don't we Sue. We were talking about it just now. Do you want some help?' Jean couldn't help smiling at the confidence of youth but she was tactful. 'Not just yet Charlie, it's actually a missing person's case. A tourist hasn't returned to his Hotel and the Super asked especially for you two to clear it up. It could be important for the City. He's an overseas visitor and we could do without the publicity. Do you think you can handle it?' Charlie looked at Sue trying to hide his disappointment 'Shall we have a go?' he said. It was her turn to smile,' Well Charlie I actually think it's an order. Put nicely of course. It seems to me that, when you're in uniform you follow orders don't you, otherwise there'd be chaos and we wouldn't want that would we?' Jean smiled and said 'All agreed then. Get down there as soon as you can and good luck.' The two young constables left her office and walked into the wardroom. There was an expectant hush from the other officers there. Had the two youngsters been fired or what? Charlie soon settled it. Turning to the room and rolling his eyes he looked to the sky with an inscrutable grin, 'Inspector Charlie Chan is on the case,' he said, 'with his lovely assistant Rosie Lee, soon all will be solved!' There was immediate clapping from his colleagues and shouting such as, 'Good on ya Chan!' and 'Good luck Charlie!' and 'Go for it Rosie!' Charlie and Sue waved graciously and left the room. They had a case to look into and now it seemed an exciting prospect.

Sebastian 'Charlie' Charlesworth was just 'Charlie' to everyone. This was quite understandable because most of his friends were not acquainted with the TV series of 'Brideshead Revisited,' which his parents had loved so much that it was probably the backdrop to his conception. He did well at school but chose a 'gap year' instead of going to University. Not to the wilds of Borneo or the Amazon rain forests, no, Charlie would 'find himself' in a crowded squat in Whitechapel that was already home to some of his friends, their mates and their girl friends and their boy friends and their mates and so on. Mum and Dad visited once but 'never again' was their verdict. Sally was his girl friend, at least he thought she was, but she was by no means exclusive as far as men were concerned. She used to say that monogamy was for 'mono-morons' and she just wanted to have fun. Charlie felt that this was OK as long as no one got hurt, in other words, as long as love didn't enter into it. Unfortunately it did for him, he just couldn't help it and Sally's comments that the 'other guys' meant nothing at all, was not very reassuring. He'd come to that place where he had to decide for himself, and that was a rather uncomfortable feeling. It was that moment when only he could decide what was best.

Fortunately the only other person involved in his decision to leave was Sally and she just said, 'Be happy Charlie,' kissed him on the cheek and ran to her room. She had said that she loved him and now she was gone. 'What had she meant?' thought Charlie, 'Yes that was it, she had meant it, but for her love was transient, a moment or moments of happiness shared.' Charlie was growing up. He had begun to accept that her way was not his way, so it never would have worked in the long term. That wasn't what he meant by love because he knew that it was the absence of trust that was most often the cause of unhappiness in relationships. 'So let's have Love without Loyalty' he thought 'that was Sally's motto, but then would it be Love at all?' he wondered. Fortunately he had been able to put these thoughts behind him for the time being because he had successfully enrolled in the Police Academy, passed his exams and now he was PC Charlesworth No. 667668, attached to Bath Police Station. And what's more he had a case to solve.

The next day Charlie and Sue made arrangements to meet up in a quiet room to read the 'Missing Persons' file. This is what it said.

<u>Missing person.</u> Walter Gieseling. Age 85 tourist Shearings. (Heart of England tour) visiting Stratford on Avon and The Cotswolds, Bath, Yeovilton and Bristol. Dukes Hotel. Frau Gieseling interview (PC Drew)

'Herr G was enjoying his trip esp. Bath; He had said that Frau G should wear a toga at the Roman Baths and how nice she'd look in the smart uniforms of the waitresses at Sally Lunns. He'd said it seemed like old times, when they were young together. She wanted a short rest before dinner so he went for a walk about 6.30 and didn't return. <u>End report.</u>'

When they had finished reading it, they made an appointment to see her the next day and arrived punctually at 9am. The manager had not turned up yet but he had set a room aside for their interview. They sat down and waited, Charlie helping himself to some of the biscuits that had been provide with coffee. Sue frowned and said, 'Can't you wait?' That's not very good manners is it?' Charlie felt awkward and put one back. 'There is that OK?' he said with a grin. 'Well I hope you didn't lick it' she said and they both smiled. He was sure that things were going to be fine. A few moments later Frau Gieseling arrived, a small frail looking lady, but she was not alone. 'They told me I could have a friend with me' she said, 'I don't always remember things clearly. Will that be all right? This is Frau Riedler.' The other woman was probably in her late fifties, dressed in a simple black dress with pearls around the neck. Her dark hair was tied back in a bun, which made her look rather like a schoolmistress or a warden in a prison. Sue spoke first, 'Yes of course. Guten Morgen. I'm afraid our

German is not very good so may we all speak in English?' 'Of course,' replied Frau Riedler, 'just go ahead and we'll try to help.'

Charlie began with the police report that they already had and, to be truthful, the ladies could not add much to the existing file. Frau Gieseling did say that her husband did not like to be away from home for long but she had persuaded him to come on a 'Holiday of a Lifetime.' Sue was curious. 'So where did you normally go on holiday then. Was this to be an unusual kind of adventure?' she asked. 'Well we had a wonderful time in Austria last year and before that we went on a cruise to Scandanavia, that was lovely.' replied Frau Gieseling, 'No it wasn't so much that it was unusual but that Albert always said he had no wish to go to England or America for that matter. It's been such a pity, Suzi our daughter lives in Los Angeles and I've never seen little Eric. Still, that's the way it was. I couldn't persuade him until now.' Charlie was beginning to show an interest in this apparent contradiction and asked. 'Frau Gieseling, can you think of any reason, any reason at all why he might have gone missing? Did he know anyone here? Had he said anything on the journey and had ever told you why he didn't want to go to the UK or the States?'

Frau Gieseling looked at her friend and was about to speak but Frau Riedler spoke first. 'I think that's enough for today.' she said 'I can see that she's getting very tired. Come back tomorrow please but perhaps Albert will have returned by then. Auf Wiedesehen.' With that she took Frau Gieseling by the arm and physically lifted her from her chair. 'Come Liebschen' she said, and guided her out of the room. Charlie looked at Sue, and Sue looked back. 'I wonder what that's all about.' he said,' do you think that they are, well sort of very-very close friends?' 'Not in the way you're thinking.' responded Sue, 'she seems more like a kind of guardian to me. Watch dog even. Very strange.'

The next day the Shearings coach was planned to go to an Air Show at Yeovilton and this gave Charlie a good idea. 'Let's tell Frau Gieseling that we won't be coming over tomorrow.' he said to Sue, 'She wouldn't be going on the trip anyway because of her husband but there's a good chance that Frau Rieding will.' Sue was impressed, 'Ah So Inspector Chan, Losie Lee velly implessed. Softly softly catchee Gieseling! 'This amused them both, but the serious point was that Frau Riedler might, repeat, might, be out of the way allowing them a free hand with Frau Gieselings secrets, if she had any. And so it turned out. They didn't go to the Hotel until about 11 am and just 'happened' to see Frau Gieseling having coffee on the patio. 'Oh hello,' said Sue, 'we're actually on another case but can we join you for a moment?' Frau Gieseling looked a little uncertain but then said,' Of course mein liebschen, has there been any progress?' Again Charlie was on the ball, if you can call it that. He didn't want to alarm her nor deceive her so he chose his words carefully, 'Well I don't want to say too much but we are following up some rather useful leads at the moment so we won't trouble you today.' He nodded over to Sue and she picked up his cue. 'It's such a lovely day isn't it?' she said, 'and such a shame that Albert left it so long to come to England don't you think?' Frau Gieseling looked at them both and smiled. 'You are so young, just as we were. You are so proud of your pretty uniforms, just like we used to be. I had a white blouse, full blue skirt, socks and heavy, rather unfeminine marching shoes in the 'Jungmaedel' and Albert was so smart in his neat uniform. I don't think you could ever understand what it was like. How wonderful it all was.'

Sue was a History Graduate and she had begun to put two and two together already. She remembered how Herr Gieseling had admired the waitresses at Sally Lunns in their uniforms. She reached over and held the old lady's hand. 'Tell us,' she said, 'tell us what it was like, and why it was so wonderful.' Charlie kept quiet. Frau Gieseling actually looked rather relieved. 'Yes I will, I must. I'm tired of all this secrecy after so long. You must try to go back in time, I mean really go back in your mind, back to 1936, well before you were born I know but try, do try, try to imagine it as it was then, in Munich at Christmas. It was snowing. sleigh bells were ringing, and we had a large kitchen table'

The Kitchen Table. Munich 1936

Papa, have you laid the table? Have you put out extra places for George and Helena? And a place for Mitzi, don't forget Albert's new 'Liebling.

Mama Gieseling was always like this at Christmas, and on Birthdays and any other special Saints days, or Public Holidays. She fussed a lot but everyone loved her. The table was always full of treats and simple food. It could seat about ten and was invariably full with an ever-changing caste of drinkers and diners. The room smelt of chestnuts and chocolate, and of mulled wine with cinnamon. There was always family, then there were friends and neighbours and just acquaintances who dropped by. Papa always said they couldn't start because he was waiting for 'The Good Samaritan'. Needless to say, they dug in regardless. That year I was formally introduced to the family. When we had finished dining Albert rose to his feet and chinked a glass with his fork. 'Mama, Papa, dear family and dear friends.' he said, very bravely I thought, he was only seventeen, 'Mama and Papa and everyone, may I introduce Fraulein Mitzi Dorfmann, the girl I plan to marry!' There was a hush and then a surge of quiet clapping then louder and louder and everyone was shouting, 'Wonderful news, Wunderbar, wunderbar!' and then everyone sang, 'For he's a jolly good fellow' and shook him by the hand and smothered me with kisses. It was a lovely moment. I joked later that he should have asked me first, but he said he didn't dare because I might have refused.

But Albert hadn't finished. He rose to his feet and once more chinked the glass with his fork. 'Ladies and Gentlemen,' he said proudly, 'I have one more important announcement to make.'

The assembled company was still once more, waiting. 'Mama and Papa and dear friends,' he said, 'Today is the proudest day of my life. Today I have been accepted into The Hitler Youth!' There was a gasp from the crowd and then, once more cheers all round, 'Well done Charlie, you'll make us all proud,' shouted Uncle Franz. Then my father got his feet. 'Dear friends and family, may I call you family?' There was a whispered assent and he continued, 'Dear family and friends I am so proud today. Albert is a very lucky boy. Just remember young man that Mitzi is only fifteen so you must be patient. But Mitzi is ahead of you in her love of the 'Fatherland.' She is already in the BDM (Bund Deutscher Maedel). She moved up from the junior group 'The Jungmaedel' last year when she was fourteen. What a team you will make and one day we'll have more 'Kinder' to spoil!' Frau Gieseling paused, 'Yes, it was all like a fairy story and we were so in love.' she said and then went on with her story.

The next Christmas, we were seated all around the table again. There had been some rather dramatic changes to Albert's career and to my home life. He had graduated at eighteen to join the Labour service and then the Army. The SA organized many fun weekends for the young people, mostly to do with Sports. There were boy's camps and girl's camps but they were often just a few fields apart so we used to meet up at night, as many did. And then it happened, I became pregnant just as Albert was selected to join 'The Ordensburgen' the so-called 'Castles of Learning,' taking only the best of the young Nazis for further education. They studied racial sciences, sport, politics, military tactics and lastly our desperate need for 'living space' in the east, known as 'Lebensraum.'

Albert was looking splendid in his uniform as were many around the table. Suzi, our daughter, was being spoilt by everyone as usual, and the wine was flowing 'Let's sing' said Papa. 'Yes, let's all sing,' said Albert, as he climbed rather uncertainly onto a chair, 'Let's all sing 'The Horst Wessell song. Everybody . . .' But then and there the atmosphere changed. There was a moment's quiet. You might say 'The Calm before the Storm' but there was no storm, just a feeling of apprehension that hadn't been there before. Not everyone was looking forward to the imminent war, and there was some discomfort over the treatment of some Jews who had been our friends . . . 'No!' shouted Papa, 'That's for another time and another place. Let's all sing 'Stille Nacht' together.' I looked at Albert as he stepped down but he wasn't smiling this time and he didn't sing either.

The next Christmas and the next we had the table all laid out again. There was less food and wine but enough for us. There were fewer friends too, many were now in the Armed Services but we couldn't ask where. We always sang 'Stille Nacht'. Albert did come home for Christmas in 1944 and we were so pleased to see him. Everyone thought that the war would be over soon. Munich had been bombed heavily and I lost both my parents in the raids. The meal was rather subdued and when our few friends had left Albert said that he wanted to say something. 'I hate to say it,' he said, 'but we have been betrayed and will soon lose the war.' 'Are you sure Albert?' asked Papa. 'Absolutely certain.' he replied, 'and when the Russians get here heaven knows what we should expect. So I've arranged some papers for you, Mama and Papa to take a ferry from Hamburg to Malmo. You must hurry but these papers should help you to get through.' 'But what about you and Mitzi?' Mama asked. 'Listen and listen carefully.' Albert said, 'From now on you do not know us. If you are questioned you do not know what became of us. This is a life and death matter for me and maybe for Mitzi, just promise me you'll do it.' he said. 'Yes, we'll do it' said Papa, 'and we won't ask why. We'll get packing tonight and thank you.' That night as we lay in bed he took my hand and said, 'My darling, they do not need to know what has been happening and what will happen, but you do. If you are to come with me you must be told everything.' I lay there beside him listening to his heartbeat, I loved him so. 'Tell me then, tell me.' I said.

'Right.' he said. 'I have papers in my bag for an Alfred Brenner and a Frau Magda Brenner. That's us. They have provided us with a new identity and tickets for a flight to Buenos Aires the day after tomorrow.' He paused and then continued, 'I've tried not to bother you with my army duties.' he said, 'but now you have to know. Well, after Dunkirk I served on the Eastern Front with Hitler's elite, the 'Waffen SS.' We had some dirty work to do there I can tell you, but nothing prepared me for my next assignment. I was wounded, as you know, so they sent me to Poland, to a place called Auschwitz, a prison camp. 'Arbeit macht zu Frei' it said at the gate but no one was set free. Most prisoners died there.' He paused. He could see that I was shocked, 'Then did they die by accident or disease?' I asked. 'No my liebschen.' he said grimly, 'Prisoners were worked to death and then killed, or just selected to be gassed when they arrived. I was a guard. I'm so sorry, I'm so sorry. I thought it was my duty and I only acted under orders do you see?' He grasped my hand so tightly that I thought it would break.' Yes dear I understand,' I whispered, 'I understand and I do love you so.'

Sue shivered. She remembered what she had said back in the office when she teased Charlie about following 'orders.' She looked at the frail old lady and smiled. 'It must have been really hard for you to accept this mustn't it? After all you weren't under orders were you? How did you feel about it?' Frau Gieseling looked at Sue in a rather puzzled way and then replied. 'No my dear, it was easy. I loved him you see. I loved him' Sue paused and wondered, 'So this was love was it? 'Love is blind is it?

Meanwhile Charlie had his thoughts too, 'So love is loyalty after all.' he whispered to himself. Then Sue spoke again. 'Thank you so much' she said. 'You've been very open and honest with us. Did you ever think that he might be the victim of Nazi hunters or maybe the Israeli Mossad then? Had there been any sign up to now' 'No, none, Frau Riedler would have told us if there had been. She's part of the 'organization' you know.' Charlie didn't want to say yes, we thought as much so he just said, 'Do you feel up to finishing your story now then? It will save us coming back tomorrow won't it?' He also didn't add that they would avoid the watchful Frau Riedler.' 'Yes I will' she said, 'Just give me a moment to go up to my room and I'll be back soon.' Obviously they couldn't stop her but what if Frau Riedling came back? Sue spoke up, 'Would you like me to come with you?' she asked politely. 'Oh no 'she replied, 'I just need my tablets. I won't be long.'

They need not have worried. She soon returned and continued her story.

'We lived at a place called Uberaba in the Sacremento valley on the Rio Grande It was more than 500 miles from Rio and rather isolated but we became happy there as a family, we even bought a large kitchen table and had our own parties at Christmas. We always sang 'Stille Nacht,' There were quite a few foreigners there, including some Germans, but no one asked questions. Albert had found that everything was arranged for us when we got there. They had remembered everything. He started as an assistant engineer with GM and worked his way up to be chief by the time we left. We had begun to feel safe you see, so we returned to Germany. We'd been there for more than fifteen years and felt rather homesick so we returned, but they arranged a job for Albert in Stuttgart with Mercedes Benz. He specialised in overseas technical specifications so had to travel abroad sometimes, but they always arranged identification papers when necessary. We had a lovely home and once again I made sure that we had a large kitchen table where our new friends could gather at Christmas and of course everyone sang 'Stille Nacht.' I suppose that I felt secure, but Albert was often looking over his shoulder at strangers and that's why he wanted to stay close to home except for business. I know that stories appeared from time to time about Nazi hunters, Eichmann and Bormann but that was nothing to do with us was it? Albert was only a soldier, he had a uniform and a position in the Army and he followed orders as I have told you. What should he have done then? You tell me!' She was getting flushed and reached into her bag for a tablet. Sue handed her a glass of water and said, 'You're right, We weren't there and we can't judge and we won't judge, but others have and are still doing so. It's them we must find out about and we will. If they had anything to do with this we will find them.' It was Charlie's turn to speak now and he did so in rather measured but sympathetic tones. 'I think that's all for now Frau Gieseling. This is a very difficult time for you we know but we can assure you that what you have told us will remain confidential. We shall continue to search for your husband and also follow up on the details you have given us. Thank you again.'

Back at the office Charlie looked shell shocked. 'What's this all about Sue?' he said, 'A visitor goes missing in Bath and now we're dealing with 'them'. The 'Boys from Brazil,' that she keeps referring to as 'they,' who organized everything for ex

Nazis, giving them a new life and identity. These were war criminals weren't they? Is that what this is about? The whole case might be much more serious than we thought.'

Sue was more cautious. 'No Charlie, let's not jump to conclusions nor to judgement either. Don't forget that he might turn up soon. Amnesia or something. And if he doesn't there could be any number of reasons why he went missing. Maybe just an accident, and maybe we'll never know.' Charlie looked at her and smiled, 'Yes, of course you're right but I think I'll speak to the Inspector in the morning to give us some ideas. I do know one possibility even though it's unlikely. That chap who's always in Sally Lunns with his mates, you know, the old codgers. Ziegler, that's him. I heard that was in Auschwitz so we might need to question him do you think? And should we need to get in touch with Interpol or the Foreign Office, and do you think there's any connection with that other missing person case, you know, the Howard one? She's dealing with that as well isn't she? This could be a really tricky case couldn't it?' He paused, 'But Inspector Chan will not be beaten by the 'Black Hand Gang' will he?' Sue laughed at the way he had diffused the tension. 'Never!' she said, 'With Losie Lee at his side he will solve the case!' Charlie was very pleased with her support. In fact he was rather pleased with her all round, and he'd had begun to notice that she was rather an attractive looking woman. But this was Police business.

More 'Howard' clues at Sally Lunns

Now that it had become a murder investigation Lockhart decided to pay Sally Lunns another visit, taking Sue along. He was keen to get on with it before Jean Curtis got more leads than he had, and he was very pleased that she'd been sidetracked on that other case. As they headed for the door he turned to Sue and said, 'Pity about this, some of my favourite watering holes in this street, won't ever feel the same again' She thought it was typical that he was thinking about himself again. They met Lorenzo inside and he told them to 'feel free' to go through the paperwork. Before they went up Sue noticed a man sitting in the corner. 'Excuse me' she said, 'Is that man a regular, I mean, could he have been here on that Thursday?' 'Quite probably' replied Lorenzo, 'regular as clockwork. That's Professor Bob Hunter from the University, quite famous, in his own way. He does TV documentaries and things. You can ask him if you like.' 'Well it might be worth a shot,' said Lockhart as they went over to his table. 'Sorry to trouble you Sir,' said Lockhart, 'we are making enquiries about the Peter Howard case and wondered if you remembered seeing him on the day he went missing.'

They were all rather taken aback by his immediate answer, 'Yes I did, and I was thinking of coming in to report it but I got tied up in a matter about Aztec Gold up at the Uni and it slipped my mind' he said with an apologetic smile. 'Well sir' said Sue, 'What exactly do you remember?' 'Well, just that he was here but, as he was leaving he seemed to bump into someone who was coming in or just passing by, I couldn't tell which.' 'I don't suppose you saw who it was?' Sue asked hopefully. 'I did as a matter of fact. It was that Colonel Lambert, you know, the one with the loud voice. He shouted something and then they went off. That's all I saw.' 'One last thing Professor' interjected Lockhart, 'Did they go in the direction of the Leisure centre and did they go together?' 'I'm afraid you've got me there old boy, can't say I really noticed. That Aztec Gold was getting me really wound up at the time.' 'Never mind' said Lockhart,' You've been a great help anyway, thank you Sir.'

They left him at his table and went into the office. 'We'll have to follow up on that one,' said Lockhart, 'let's look at some of these files.' They sat at the desk; perhaps there were some other clues that might be worth pursuing, especially, he thought, credit card receipts and the like. There might even be a paper trail, showing who was there that Thursday so he and Sue started to go through a mound of disorganized paper and receipts in every drawer and, it seemed, on every floor space. There were receipts going way back, some more than a year, but after about half an hour Sue shouted out, 'Eureka! Sir. You'll never guess what I've found.' Lockhart was irritated by the way she expressed herself. 'I've told you before Constable, we're not in the guessing business. Evidence, evidence, that's how we work. Anyway, what have you got?'

Sue savoured the moment before she spoke, 'Well, I think this counts as evidence Sir, I'm sure of it' she said coolly, as she passed over a receipt before she continued. 'That's a Barclay Card receipt for a Mr D Grearson for £ 13, and a Sally Lunn receipt for a table for two, one coffee, one Sally Lunn Bun and a mineral water, and this is the invoice also for £13 and timed at 4.30.' It was Lockhart's turn to be stunned, 'Well, what do you know? Crafty devil, well, well, well indeed. Looks like Grearson's got some explaining to do doesn't it?' Sue was quick to reply, deliberately giving him some of the credit because she had noticed that he would take it anyway, 'Yes sir, you're right sir but do you think we might run a check on his card before we speak to him? See what else he's been up to maybe?' Lockhart looked at her with approval, 'Good idea Sue.' he said in his 'friendly' voice 'We'll make a good officer of you yet.'

Although it was late Sue decided to check the data base when she got back to the office and, typing in the necessary passwords and codes, she soon had access to the Grearson Barclay card account. There were numerous dining bills, some shopping receipts, the Sally Lunn Bill, a subscription to a bowls club and a weekend at the Hotel Miramar in Bournemouth for a Mr and Mrs Grearson dated 20th March. Sue turned each receipt over carefully asking each one the same question. This one was for a subscription. 'Now what are you hiding you bad little receipt, what are you keeping secret?' she looked again and again, turning it over and over, and then it popped out at her. The subscription receipt 'gave in,' and she could now see clearly that it was dated Thursday 1 April and was from the Bath Bowls cub at the Leisure Centre where the body had been found. 'Game and Set maybe' she chuckled, 'Now what about Match?'

Denis Grearson in the spotlight

The next day they went to see Grearsons. Sue had told Lockhart about her latest discoveries and he couldn't wait to see what Grearson had to say. They arrived at about eleven am and Lucy Grearson them offered coffee around the large kitchen table. 'Sorry to trouble you again' began Lockhart, 'We are just following up a few leads about Howard. Just formalities you know, come to think of it we needn't bother you both, perhaps you could show Sue your lovely conservatory that she was admiring as we drove in.' It was his usual ploy and Sue was ready, 'Oh yes Mrs Grearson, will you please?' Mrs Grearson responded at once 'Of course, yes, of course, it's just through here. Bring your coffee won't you?' They walked out of the room and Lockhart waited for a moment before coming straight to the point. 'I might as well tell you now Grearson, that we have reason to believe that you haven't told us the entire truth, and I strongly advise you to do so before we go further.' He spoke in his most officious tone. Grearson made as if to speak but Lockhart put his hand up, as if in a traffic policeman's stop sign, and continued. 'We have found out that you were at Sally Lunns last Thursday and that you weren't alone, we know that you went to the Leisure Centre to pay a sub. And we also know that you spent the weekend of 20th March in Bournemouth at The Hotel Miramar. Now, is there anything that you would like to tell me about all this before we call Mrs Grearson in?' Denis Grearson had gone a deathly shade of pale white with some red blotches on his face, he was shaking and his top lip quivered. 'No, no please don't do that. She doesn't need to know does she?' 'Maybe not, if you've nothing to hide,' said Lockhart coldly, 'but you must answer some more questions first. OK? Then I'll decide whether Mrs Grearson needs to know or not. After that the matter will be between the two of you of course. Now answer me this truthfully. Who was with you at Sally Lunns?'

Grearson was silent for a moment but Lockhart did not let up. 'Shall I call Mrs Grearson to ask if it was her then?' he asked rather menacingly, getting up as if to go to the door.'No, no that won't be necessary. I'll tell you but it mustn't come out, it mustn't come out please, please' Grearson pleaded. 'Can't promise but I'll try' responded Lockhart, 'Now who was it?' Grearson could hardly speak, and then he croaked rather than spoke the words as if he was choking, 'It was Diana, yes Diana Lambert and at the Hotel if you must know' and, saying this, he slumped into a heap, his head between his arms on the kitchen table. 'I'm finished, I'm ruined, my life is over. I'm so sorry, so sorry' he mumbled and wept and wept, his shoulders shaking nervously. Lockhart went over to him and touched Grearson's elbow rather sharply. 'Time for all that later.' He said, 'Go and freshen up now so Mrs Grearson won't know what's been said. I'll go and get the Constable and then we'll leave. It's up to you then.' Lockhart walked into the Conservatory smiling, 'That's all settled then' he said, 'nothing to worry about Mrs Grearson, we're leaving now'.

They walked out together to the car and, before he started the engine he turned to her with a grin and patted her knee. She pulled away sharply but he just smiled mischievously and said 'You'll never guess, you'll never guess not in a million Sundays' She knew he was playing with her but she still asked, 'What?' Lockhart spoke slowly and dramatically, 'Our Mr Goodie Goodie Grearson has been having it off with, with, with . . .' He paused for the most dramatic effect, 'the lovely young Mrs Lambert'

Sue was not as surprised as he was, having made her earlier observations at the house but she didn't let on. Let him have his moment she thought. 'Do you think that we should tell her that we know?' she asked. 'Not yet' said Lockhart, 'this all seems a bit muddy to me. What do you think all this has got to do with Howards' murder? Probably Grearson did it. I reckon Howard saw them, Mrs Lambert and Grearson together, but Grearson also saw him, followed him and killed him. You know Grearson, any whiff of an affair and his marriage and his carefully cultivated reputation would be over. Perhaps he warned him, but then got wild and killed him. Mmm quite possible don't you think?'

Sue kept quiet, she thought that this theory had too many holes in it, not least the knife, where did that come from and why the beating up afterwards. She ventured another suggestion, 'How about Lambert himself sir? There's something about him that is so, well, so honourable, if you see what I mean. What if Howard told him about his wife's 'affair,' Lambert would not want anyone else to know would he, so maybe he killed him to keep him quiet?' Lockhart snorted, as if he wasn't entirely convinced about her suggestion. Sue sniffed, as if she had a cold, but she didn't like his notion either She actually thought there might to more to learn about Peter Howard himself, and she hoped to do that the next day when she planned to see Lorna.

Lorna Howard confides in Sue

Sue had telephoned ahead to make the appointment and she duly arrived at eleven o'clock. Lorna greeted her ay the door looking rather tired and wan. 'Sorry,' she said. 'I've been up all night. Please come through to the lounge, I've just been going through some old photograph albums and things.' As she said this she steadied herself against a chair and Sue moved forward to help her. 'Are you all right?' she asked, 'Perhaps you need to sit down for a moment. Let me get you a glass of water,' 'Oh no thank you,' Lorna replied, 'I really am fine, just a little tired that's all. Please go through to the lounge and I'll bring us some coffee.' Sue thanked her and as she went in she noticed that there was a photo album on nearly every table and chair. Some were labelled, and some were not, there was, 'Holiday in St Malo' and 'Sarah's Wedding' and 'Our New Home' and many others. Sue did not like to pry but here before her eyes there seemed to be a lifetime of memories. It seemed churlish to intrude on Lorna's grief but she knew that she must. 'We can leave this you know, if you like,' she said sympathetically. 'No,' replied Lorna, 'I'll tell you when I've had enough and you can always come back again can't you? Just let me tell you in my own way.' Sue agreed, 'Well, first of all tell me about Peter's friends and work colleagues. Anything that comes to mind and anybody he didn't get on with.' 'I'll try' said Lorna 'but you wouldn't say that if you knew Peter. He got on with everyone, just everybody even strangers. 'She stumbled for a moment before going on, 'that is except that affair up in Manchester with a chap called Carson. It was all about time off and expenses and Peter had to get him dismissed. He did make some threats at the time but we didn't hear any more about it when we came here. Of course we have been quite close to our neighbours Alan and Alma Johnson and then there's the Lucas family, next but one with their four children. We often see them about. We play Bridge with George and Sue Hamilton, then there's the Grearsons, nice people but a bit on the religious side for us, and the Lamberts and your boss, the Lockharts of course. There's probably a lot more, but come to think of it, there was a rather unexpected visitor recently.

His name's Roy Black and he's an old acquaintance of Peter's. It was one of those really weird coincidences that don't seem to have any explanation. It was Roger Hunt who 'found' him. Now Roger, who's also a Times associate of Peter's, was travelling on the Underground in London minding his own business, when a chap sat opposite him and opened up 'The Times'. Roger was trying to read the headline when he noticed that the man had one finger missing on his left hand. 'I've only seen one other like that in my life,' he thought and that was Roy Black, the American who was injured at Pleiku in the Vietnam war. He'd gone on to become a Press Officer for The White House. It couldn't be him could it? But just then the newspaper was folded and the man looked up and smiled. 'It's Roger isn't it?' he said. 'Yes it is and you're Roy aren't you?' 'Sure am, always will be. Still reading it you see,' he replied and laughed. They shook hands and, when Roger told him that he was still in touch with Peter, he made Roger promise to give him his number. Well, to cut a long story short, he came to stay with us soon after and they had a right old time drinking and chatting into the small hours. I thought I heard them arguing once but Peter said I was dreaming.

Anyway, Peter didn't like to argue.

The Ellsberg affair 1965

Lorna loved her husband and maybe he didn't like to argue, as she said, but his job as Foreign Editor at 'The Times' had brought him into conflict over many contentious issues over the years, none more so than the 'Daniel Ellsberg' affair. This had been the reason why Peter and Roy had fallen out so long ago, when Peter was staying with the Blacks on a visit to Washington. It had all begun with a news headline on 8 Aug 64.

*   *   *   *

'Hey Peter, look at this in the article in The New York Times,' said Roy addressing his comments to a rather sleepy Peter at the breakfast table. They had had a long night of it and he wasn't quite ready for chat. 'Can't it wait?' he pleaded rather hopelessly, because he knew that Roy would never give up, not in Vietnam as a decorated war hero, nor on anything that he felt strongly about. 'He's done it, the old man's finally done it,' he said in a triumphant and approving voice. Peter was waking up. 'OK, all right, you win, I'm in love with you,' he sang in a rather dull monotone. 'What are you getting so excited about? Pour me a coffee would you, there's a good chap.' 'Sure thing pardner, there you go.' said Roy, 'There, see for yourself.' and he handed the paper across the table.

The headline read, 'PRESIDENT GETS TOUGH' and it went on, 'Following an attack by North Vietnamese troops on the 'US Maddox' in the Gulf of Tonkin, President Johnson has now obtained emergency powers under the aptly named 'Tonkin Gulf Resolution.' to deal with critical decisions without recourse to Congress. Our readers will recall that we recently warned that (The entire Allied position in the Western Pacific would be in jeopardy if the Vietcong were to make headway.) We have been proven right yet again.'

Peter read the article carefully and then looked at his friend,' I don't see why you think this is such a good idea,' he said, 'don't you think that it rather overrides the system of checks and balances in the Constitution?' 'Constitution-Monster-tution!' replied Roy with a laugh, 'I don't think the founding fathers had the Viet Cong in mind when they drafted it do you?' Peter thought for a moment because he didn't want a row with his friend, so he simply said, 'Well, let's see how it turns out then. Do I see waffles over there?' They finished breakfast and, as usual, fitted in a round of golf before they went to their respective offices. The agenda in both was the same but from very different perspectives. The White House Staff was 'cockahoop' that the 'Pres' had managed to 'put one over' on the Congress but in the Washington office of the 'London' Times there was a different atmosphere, as Peter found out when he was called into the Editor's office. There were four other people there, three of whom he knew but the other was a stranger. 'Come in Peter' said Ralph Steadman, the Editor, 'You know Sam, Yvonne and Martin don't you?' Peter waved and said, 'Yes, of course, hi everyone.' He sat down and waited.

'Peter,' began the Editor again, 'Peter, you may think you've had some tricky stories in the past but I can tell you this is the trickiest and maybe the deadliest, so I don't need to remind you about the need for absolute secrecy. No bar talk with those pals of yours from the White House, Pentagon, or anywhere else, I'm sure you understand.' He smiled, Peter smiled back and nodded, 'Of course, yes I understand.' he said, 'just tell me what it's all about.'

The Editor paused and then said, 'What do you know about the 'Tonkin Resolution' then?' Peter was taken aback, it was only that very morning that he'd heard about it, so that's what he told the Editor, 'What's more,' he added, 'Roy Black seemed very pleased about the whole business.' The group in the room seemed to suddenly take notice, especially the stranger, but it was the Editor who spoke again.'I don't think anyone here is surprised about that,' he said, looking round,'but here's another question. What do you know about the 'Pentagon Papers' then?' Once more Peter was on the back foot. He told them that he was sorry but he hadn't heard of them at all. The Editor listened to what Peter had said and then went on. 'Well, that's why we're here. We've got to decide what to do with a very, very, very hot potato and that's why our guest is here, to serve it up, without sauce and garnish if you see what I mean.

So let me introduce Dr Daniel Ellsberg from the University, Vietnam Vet. and consultant with the Rand Corporation on Macnamara's exhaustive appraisal of US foreign policy since the 1950's known as 'The Pentagon Papers'. Daniel, this is Peter Howard from our HQ in London, Peter meet Daniel Ellsberg. Now I'll hand over to you Daniel to fill in the missing parts of this story. Daniel.' The Editor sat down and sipped his coffee and Ellsberg began to speak.

'It was sometime ago that a study was commissioned to look into the various geo-political and military aspects of US Foreign policy since the '50's and I was given responsibility for a section of it.' he said, 'the trouble was it turned out to be a 'can of worms' if you follow me. It seemed that behind every major military decision there had invariably been a party political imperative. In other words, getting elected or re-elected was more important than battle casualties. There were many instances of this behaviour in the files and now we have a new one, the 'Tonkin Resolution.' Half of the Senate is up for re-election in two months time and they are likely to approve the President's 'special measures' if only for that reason. The resolution gives the President a blank cheque for executive war and it's passing through without a whimper. You'd have to go back to Fort Sumter or Pearl Harbour to find such a significant event in US history but there's more.' Ellsberg paused and took a long drink from a glass of water. 'It's been suggested, suggested mind, either that the attack on the US Maddox was provoked by the cruiser itself, or even more extraordinary, that it didn't even take place at all, but was just a ruse to escalate the war.'

The Editor looked at those in the room and said. 'Any comments?' Peter was the first to speak. 'Well where do we come into it, I mean, if it's true what do you expect us to do about it on your word?' Elldberg did not seem put out, 'Look,' he said, 'I've taken my suspicions to all and sundry, on an unofficial basis of course but no one will put their head over the parapet at present. That's why I've come to you. I want you to publish the papers. To publish them in full.' It was the turn of Yvonne, who was the Diplomatic Editor to ask a question. 'Do you mean you've got them, the Papers I mean?' 'Well, no not yet but I am sure that I can get clearance to review them all again. There are copies in the offices at the Rand Corporation and I can get access.' he replied.

Yvonne continued her line of questioning, 'Would I be right in thinking that these are classified top secret papers protected under the Official Secrets Act?' she asked with a smile. 'Yes you're goddam right they are,' he replied, 'and I know what I'm in for if they find out. Treason they'll call it, but what else can I do? The country is sending young men to die when, to put it simply, it's not necessary. Rather than pull out now and admit we can't win they'll send more young soldiers out there rather than lose their reputations. I know that they'll get me in the end but I know that I'm doing the right thing. Nobody else will so I must, it's up to me.' There was a silence in the room because everyone appreciated how high the stakes were. If they knew that the Papers were vulnerable the CIA would stop at nothing, including murder to protect them. Everyone knew that, and it was some time before the Editor spoke. 'Thank you for coming to us Daniel. We won't decide just yet what to do, but I'd rather like to see a few copies from the file to strengthen the case. Perhaps we could meet again in a week.' This being agreed the meeting broke up, and Peter went back for an evening of Bridge with the Blacks.

A few days later Roy was late getting back from work and when he did he looked terrible. Mrs Black was out for the evening so Peter got him a stiff Scotch and sat him down. 'Trouble at work?' asked Peter. 'You could say that,' replied Roy, 'The CIA have cleared my office and I'm out of a job from today. Security lapse, they said. Me! No way, I've never blabbed to anyone not before and not now. I'll be seeing the Chief in the morning, they won't get away with it, I'll fight to the death if I have to.' He took another large slug of whisky and then said, 'I'm bushed Peter so I'm going up. See you in the morning.' Peter waved and said, 'Right, I won't be long myself. I'll just wait for Hilary to come home.'

The next day was an ordinary day for Peter at the office but, as he drove home, he was wondering how Roy had got on with his boss. Some mistake probably, storm in a teacup maybe. He was wrong. As he walked into the house Roy and Hilary were sitting in the lounge and there was an ominous silence as they both looked at him.

'What's up folks?' he asked in his customary way, 'What's going on?' Roy looked at him coolly before he spoke, 'What do you know about Daniel Ellsberg?' he asked.

Peter just sat there. He couldn't think what to say. Should he lie? Yes he must lie because he'd been told to keep the matter secret, but before he could say anything, Roy continued, 'Ah, I see.' he said, 'Now tell me if you've ever heard of the Pentagon Papers.' Peter felt a creepy feeling of deja-vu come across him and he was silent once more. He was tongue-tied, his mouth was dry and he didn't know what to do or say.

'You bastard,' said Yvonne,' you fucking bastard, after all you two have been through together. Benedict Arnold was a saint compared to you. Get out of my house, get out, get out now!' and with that Mrs Black ran out of the room in tears. 'Better do as she says old man,' said Roy, 'I wouldn't want to vouch for your safety here when she's in that dangerous kind of mood.' He stopped, as if thinking very deeply about something, and then he spoke slowly and deliberately. 'I don't have moods,' he said, 'but I can tell you one thing for sure, that I'll never forget what you have done to us and, By God if I get the chance I'll get my own back somehow, no matter how long it takes.' Peter tried to speak, he wanted to explain that this all had nothing to do with him, but Roy was gone and all future attempts to put the record straight had been rebuffed.

A year or so later Peter left 'The Times' and took a job in Africa. Roy was unemployed for many years until he got a job with a US arms manufacturer and they hadn't met since, not until now in Bath, that is.

Footnote

The US government tried to stop the publication of the Pentagon Papers for years. CIA operatives raided the office of Ellsberg's psychiatrist to try to undermine his credibility but eventually the Supreme Court ruled that it would be unconstitutional to deny their publication. Ellsberg himself was tried on conspiracy charges but the Judge declared a mistrial partly on the grounds that the burglary at the psychiatrists was linked to the break in at the Watergate Democratic Party HQ. By then it was 1972.

Lorna's African tale

When Sue arrived the next day Lorna looking refreshed and she immediately invited Sue into the lounge. 'Sue,' she said, 'I just wanted to finish off something I was trying to tell you last night, about Peter. You didn't know him of course but he was an absolute darling, in fact, I would say he had the sweetest disposition you could wish for. Got on with everyone, but it was more than that. It was if he had a gift, a gift to make others happy. He made me happy, so happy. Do you think everyone can be like that if they really try? Why doesn't everybody do it? What makes people behave the way they do? Don't people care about how they hurt others? Do they even think about it?' With this last outburst Lorna finally gave in and began to cry. Sue moved across and held her in her arms and it seemed like an age before Lorna broke away and said, 'Thank you Sue but we'd better get on with it don't you think?' 'Yes I agree' she replied, 'the sooner we get some more info the sooner we'll find out what happened and why I'm afraid but I can leave it a few more days if you like.' 'No, no, let's do it now, I need to know that I'm doing something, anything really.' Lorna responded and so they talked for some time about Peter's job at the Newspaper, his boat and his recent interest in bowls. 'It's been really good for him you know. He hadn't played before but the club gave him tuition and he's come on very well, at least so he says', Lorna smiled at her own little joke and Sue joined smiled sympathetically. 'Had he been a sportsman then, I mean in the past? 'she ventured, wondering if there might be leads in that direction. 'Well, actually no, not since we were in Dar. We both played tennis there but of course Peter was away a lot on business then. More coffee?' Sue was taken aback for a moment but soon recovered,' Oh yes please. Did you say Dar?' 'Yes I did, we all called it Dar, for Dar-es-Salaam you know, we were out there in the late 60's during the UDI crisis for about 5 years'

Sue was pricking up her ears. Three African connections and she didn't believe in coincidences. This was better, much better. Was there a link she wondered. 'Sorry to go on Lorna, may I call you Lorna? I only know a bit about that from school. In fact I don't even know what UDI means, it was all a bit before my time if you see what I mean. I' d be really interested if you've got the time to tell me about it.' Sue had tried to sound persuasive and it worked. 'All right Sue, now that we're on first name terms it seems less formal. Come into the lounge and I'll tell you the whole story, and show you our photograph album. There's also a small book that you might find interesting. Yes here it is, here you are' she said, handing Sue the book, 'Why don't you have a read while I make some coffee?' Actually Lorna was glad to have something else to think about, because she could not bear the thought of Peter not being there for her, and with her, as they'd always been. Sue said 'Thank you,' and, taking the book, she began to read. The chapter was titled 'UDI.'

UDI in Rhodesia 1965

'The background to UDI began in the wider world of African affairs. It was Harold McMillan's 'Wind of Change' speech in South Africa that crystallised the situation on the African continent, stating, as it did that African affair must soon be handled by African nationalists, in majority governments. This had already become the case in many African States but the situation in Southern Rhodesia remained unsettled and a white minority ruled there albeit as a 'self governing colony' under British control.

The Government in Salisbury (S.Rho.) under Ian Smith, wanted independence but the British refused this, using the term 'NIBMAR' (no independence before majority rule) to make the position clear. There had been abortive attempts at an agreement in 1961 but the African majority still only had a few seats in Parliament, mostly because qualification was by wealth. There was deadlock and so the Rhodesian Government declared their independence on 11 November 1965. Ironically it was Armistice Day. The British PM Harold Wilson met Smith on HMS Tiger in December 1966 but again they could not agree. The country most closely affected by this was Zambia, which was dependent on Rhodesia for transit of her copper exports and fuel imports. The border was closed, and the British government and others had to come up with strategies to transport fuel 1500 miles by road to landlocked Zambia via the port of Dar-es-Salaam in Tanzania. It became known as 'The Hell Run'.'

Sue had finished this small section by the time that Lorna came back . . . Lorna smiled and said, 'I hope that's all a bit clearer now. Good book I think, but it doesn't tell the whole story, not at all, nor how bad it was for some of us. Here's the coffee, get comfy and I'll tell you all about it.' She sat down and for the next hour she told Sue all about their time in East Africa, Tanzania, Zambia and the Smith regime and the Unilateral Declaration of Independence for Rhodesia that they had got caught up in. This was her story and Sue listened spellbound without a word. She began, 'It was 1966 and Peter had been working for The Times . . . .

*　　*　　*　　*

It was 1966 and Peter had been working for 'The Times' in the City for some time. He specialised in Foreign Affairs and things like that. Well, one day he had a telephone call from an ex colleague called Clyde Walker who apparently was then working for Mercedes Benz. Would Peter be interested in a job in East Africa and, if so, would he attend an interview in London in the next week. Well, it was a bit of a bolt from the blue, but he was intrigued and thought a change might do him good. Clyde had said it was all highly confidential and of course that really got Peter hooked. Anyway, to cut a long story short, Peter went up to London the next week. The offices were on the Embankment near Cleopatra's Needle. I know that because I went with him and then met up with Lucy Dalton at Claridges before an expensive trip to Harrods. I was to meet Peter at the Harrods tea room about six but he didn't turn up until seven. Unlike him I thought, so something must be up. I was right. Peter came in looking pleased but also rather thoughtful so I asked him how it went. He told me that he had been offered a job as Director of Operations in Dar-es-Salaam with a six figure salary, all expenses, two Mercedes cars (one for me) and a house on the coast. I remember that he smiled shyly when he had said it, or perhaps it was more a guilty expression, as if he had been caught with his fingers in the Cookie jar. He was a very modest man and I suppose he didn't think he was worth all that. My response was different because I had great faith in him all round. Crikey! I remember myself saying 'I hope you grabbed their arm off!' His response puzzled me a little because all he said was that he wanted to think about it and let them know. 'Anyway,' he said, 'It's getting late and I'm starving, let's order dinner shall we?

I knew when not to press him and he didn't broach the subject for a few days, then, on the Friday he said that he'd booked lunch at the Club on Saturday. He often did that when he had something important to discuss and it seemed he had almost made up his mind. I think we should go, he had said, but before I tell them I'd like to tell you more about what we're getting into. I didn't quite like the sound of that but I waited for him to go on and he did, telling me at some length that Clyde had been seconded to a transport consortium involving Mercedes Benz of Stuttgart and a local transport group named Mariakos, formed to transport oil from the Tanzanian Coast at Dar-es-Salaam to the Copper Belt in Zambia.

You know that Zambia is landlocked so, since Smith's UDI, no fuel has been allowed to pass through Southern Rhodesia. And that's where we, I mean they, come in, he had said with a smile. An International Petroleum Finance Board (The PFB) has been created to organize the delivery of thousands of gallons every day by any means. As well as us (them) there are teams from Russia, Jugoslavia, China and Italy under the AGIP logo. Most of them have subcontractors as does Mariakos; some Africans or Arabs maybe with only one truck. I couldn't help myself suggesting that it all sounded a bit like Dunkirk and he had agreed. In that sense he said, the Mariakos team were a bit like the Royal Navy, being the biggest fleet, except they had German trucks of course, he had said with a smile. Thirty 2620's and Twenty 1618's, six Datsun pickups to monitor the route and even an overhead spotter plane operated by a Safari Company under sub contract. He seemed very proud of his new friends already, and I was impressed as well, but I still waited for more. I knew Peter and he usually kept the best, or sometimes the worst, until last.

'There is something I haven't told you yet and it's something we'll have to be prepared for.' he said. He sounded serious now and I waited for him to go on. 'To put it bluntly it may be dangerous out there. We will be breaking Smith's sanctions and he won't like it. I've been told to expect trouble, incidents, bribery, 'accidents' and maybe more. It may not be safe at all and I will be away quite a lot; in Zambia visiting Lusaka, Ndola and Kitwe but also maybe Nairobi, Mombasa or even Beira and I'd be worried about leaving you alone in Dar-es-salaam. Frankly I can't guarantee our safety and nor can the Company.' He paused and looked at me intently, 'But I can't bear the thought of going without you.' he paused again and held my hand, much as he had done when he proposed, 'Shall we?' he said. 'Dance?' I replied 'Yes, of course darling, we've always been together and we always will be. Let's do it!'

And so we did it, and Peter had been right when he said trouble. It seemed like nothing but sometimes. Fuel rigs off the road; he called it spillage, but there were always doubts about theft. Drivers could be tempted to siphon fuel off and sell it to locals they knew or sometimes the whole load to an organized gang, maybe even terrorists. It was also known that the Rhodesian Army would send guerrilla groups into Zambia to hi-jack petrol, using it fuel the illicit trade in Diamonds from the Marange Mines in Rhodesia over the border into Mozambique. Of course we had some wonderful times along the coast at Bagamoyo where our house was, with beautiful beaches as far as the eye could see; and scenic trips to Zanzibar as well. Unfortunately Peter was away a lot but I had some lovely neighbours, the Pedersens, a delightful Swedish family whose children frolicked naked on the beach. To tell the truth we did sometimes, but only when it was dark.

Although our house was on the beach, more or less, it was only a few hundred yards to scrubland where I would often see Wilde Beast, Zebra and all kinds of buck including Impala from time to time, and, yes, the occasional pride of Lions. In fact I ran out of petrol once about a mile from home and wondered if I might end up as a Lion dinner. I kept a small animal sanctuary, all sorts really, some that just came and others that people brought to me wounded, often fatally. There was one that I'd like to tell you about; she was a tiny Impala that I found in the bush. Parents dead I supposed and so was she nearly, poor little thing. Well I brought her home and nursed her for a few days and showed her to Peter when he came home. He took an immediate liking to her, and she to him, in fact when he was there she ignored me and always went to sleep on his lap. I called her 'Bimba, this was half way between Bambi and Bibi which is the Swahili word for wife, because that's how she seemed sometimes when Peter was home. In fact she made such a fuss when we went to bed that sometimes we had to let her in to get some peace and quiet. It was quite extraordinary that she always seemed to know when Peter was coming back, if he'd been away. The day he was due back she'd be there at the front door waiting but, if he'd been delayed for any reason she waited at the gate, as if she knew he would not be home yet. Yes, that side of it was idyllic but there was a very dark side as well. This is what Peter told me about the Hell Run.

'Kenneth and John Theuri were getting ready for their Safari,' he said . . .

* * * *

The Hell Run 1968

Kenneth and John Theuri were getting ready for their 'Safari' as they called it. Last week they had modified their old farm truck, which was used for carrying Sisal.

It was now a sleek looking tanker and they had spent the weekend painting it in the 'MARIAKOS' livery of red and white. They had a contract, and now all that had to do was to collect the fuel from the Docks and deliver it to Ndola in the Zambian copperbelt. Yes, that was all, but Kenneth was worried. The brothers came from Kisumu in Kenya, up near Lake Victoria and had come to Tanzania as drivers at the 'Zarvos' sisal plantation. They had soon put their wages toward their own truck and this was it, their pride and joy, but Kenneth was very worried. 'We don't need it' he said to his brother, 'we're doing fine aren't we? We've still got the Zarvos deal and we could get another one if we wanted it. I've heard that the Papadopolous farm is looking for transporters. We'll lose all that just for a few shillings now. And it's dangerous. It's not called The Hell Run for nothing you know, I think we should back out of it don't you?' John was the elder brother; he looked at Kenneth with affection but spoke sternly, 'Kenneth, my dear brother, have you forgotten all the sacrifices that our family made for us back in Kisumu? Even when the fishing was very, very poor, we were always fed while Mama and Joogoo had nothing. We came here so that we could send money back to them and how much have we sent? Nothing. It's always next month or next week. Just think how much we could have sent if you didn't like your Tusker Lager beer so much! No. This is the chance of a lifetime; we'll make enough money to buy a house for them and one for us, full of Tusker if you like!' He laughed and Kenneth laughed as well. He loved and respected his brother a lot. 'OK you're right as usual. Shall I drive first?' he said as he jumped into the driver's seat. 'I suppose you should, from there' John agreed, and then they were off, down to the Docks, paperwork done and out onto the Highway.

Their truck was in good order. It was old, but fortunately it was a Mercedes Benz, and the German engineers at Mariakos had given it a good service. The supervisor was Keit, a very experienced man from Munich but his two assistants were novices. Muller and Friederichs. Both came from Stuttgart and they had a rather superior Teutonic air about them, very different from Keit. Both were Mercedes trainees and considered this job to be somewhat of a lark, but they loved their trucks, treating them much as a Tank Commander would in the field. Nothing was too good for their charges and the subcontractors benefited from this efficient handling as well. They gave the Theuri truck a birthday such as it had never seen and the brothers were grateful. 'Just look at it, just listen' John had said, 'Isn't she a beauty? Just listen to that engine. Purrs like a cat!' and they were to be glad of all this attention as they began the 1500 mile journey to Zambia.

Only the first 30 miles to Morogoro were tarmac, and after that it was all, that red-brown 'murram' track that threw up dust everywhere, especially from passing trucks. There were escarpments and mountain ranges, where they had to edge forward inch by inch, where the road had slipped away into a ravine, and there could be flash floods and wandering wildlife on the road. It was no picnic, and they were very relieved when they reached Tunduma on the border, having passed through Iringa and Mbeya without incident. They pulled over into a makeshift transport café where everybody, except them, seemed to be drunk. A party was in full swing but they could hardly keep their eyes open, in fact John was already asleep before they stopped. They had been on the road for 20 hours with only a very short stop, and they were only half way there.

Kenneth was exhausted but couldn't switch off. Every time he closed his eyes he saw the road twisting and turning in front of him. A Zebra ran out in front of the truck, barely missing the front wheels, another truck failed to dim it's lights and he swerved just missing a deep culvert and then Googoo and Mama were there, fishing in Lake Turkana with a boat overloaded with Samaki (fish). He twisted and turned but just could not settle. Eventually he gave up and, getting out of the cab quietly, so as not to wake John, he went down to the bar. 'No harm in a couple of Tuskers' he thought, 'They'll probably help me to sleep'. He approached the bar, 'Jambo B'wana' he said in the familiar Swahili that tended to be Lingua Franca in East Africa. 'Jambo' came the reply 'Habari yaako?' (meaning 'how are you') Kenneth replied that he was very well thank you 'M'souri sana tafadhali, Tusker please.' The barman responded at once, taking a bottle from the shelf and handing it over the bar. 'You're new aren't you?' he asked. 'N'dio' Kenneth replied, 'Our first time.' 'Good luck then' said the barman. 'Don't worry about us' said Kenneth, 'Me and my brother John can handle just about anything.'

He sat down and soon he was chatting to a group of drivers who were in the bar, all complaining about the dangers of the 'Hell Run' as they called it. Another group were in the corner and he noticed that there were two 'Msungus' (White men) amongst them and before long the two groups had merged, and the two white men seemed to be buying all the drinks. Kenneth got drunk, very drunk as the others discussed the route and their families and homes. He heard their voices in a daze all talking loudly about their wives and children; 'Janet, Simon, Mbeya, Livingstone Memorial, Marange Diamonds, Suzy the Ridgeback, the Dinga Mine a dam called Keeba or something and a Rose Farm' all muddled up before he nearly passed out. It was nearly 3 am when he flopped back into the truck and went to sleep.

Dawn was breaking, that beautiful sweet smelling time of the day when it was cool and refreshing, with just a little dew on the ground as the dawn chorus welcomed the rising sun. John was refreshed. He climbed out of the cab and splashed himself in a bucket of water. Then he moved around to Kenneth's side, knocked on the window and peered in. Kenneth was dead to the world but soon woke when John playfully splashed his face with cold water.'Wakey, Wakey Kenneth!' his brother called out, 'let's go and get some grub at the bar.' Kenneth had woken but he didn't want to be seen in the bar again, in case they remembered him, and John found out about his drunken night. 'Not hungry' he called out, 'you go, I'll just freshen up.'John was gone for about ten minutes but he came back with a package of Biltong, dried meat that was so useful in the Bush. 'Help yourself' he said, handing the package over and although Kenneth felt sick at the thought, he pretended to find a piece to chew so that John would not put two and two together. 'Right, we're off then.' said John, 'I'm feeling good today so I'll drive if that's all right with you.' Kenneth was grateful but just said, 'OK, you usually do first thing anyway.' and slumped into his seat hopefully, but unrealistically, for a bit more sleep.

They crossed the border at 8am and passed without incident through Chunga and Chusali making good time, but a few miles before Chilonga they spotted a blockage ahead. This was not at all unusual, as trucks often ran off the road, so they slowed down to be directed into a small track by two men, one of them Kenneth recognized as one of the men in the bar. They pulled over but, as they began to dismount, they noticed that they were surrounded by a group of maybe twenty men, some in army uniform. The white man spoke curtly in a strange accent 'Right you two get walking, we're taking the truck now.' John had grown up in Colonial Kenya and he knew when not to argue with a 'Msungu' especially with a gun in his hand. He lowered his head and mumbled 'N'dio Bwana, N'dio B'wana' and began to shuffle away. Kenneth however was still full of booze and ready for a fight. 'Big man, Big man!' he taunted the man with the gun,' Take the truck, but I know who you are and I remember what you said last night. You won't get away with this. You'd better watch out B'wana!' He turned to follow his brother and everything went deathly quiet for a moment.

It seemed that even the birds stopped singing. And then a shot rang out. Kenneth looked surprised for a fleeting second, and then slowly crumpled to the ground at John's feet with a bullet in his back. 'God, My God, No, No! He's been shot. You've shot him! He's bleeding, get me some help, help me, please help me!' John held Kenneth in his arms and shouted desperately to the group of men, but they were already climbing on the trucks. Soon they had disappeared in a cloud of smoke and dust leaving the brothers behind. John held his brother's head in his lap, 'You're going to be fine' he said, 'Just rest someone will be along soon.' Kenneth lay still as if dead, but suddenly he grabbed John's arm and looked at him intently 'John, John my brother' he croaked. 'Yes Kenneth I'm here, I promised Mama and Googoo that I would take care of you and I will, I promise' John spoke with a tear in his eye but held Kenneth closely. 'John, John,' Kenneth spoke again but weaker this time, 'Come closer, closer, yes, yes that's it,' his voice was fading and John pressed close to listen. 'Keeba, Keeba, Keeba farm, Marange diamonds, Dinga mine, lovely white rose, Janet, Simon' he whispered before he passed out. John thought he was dead but he was still breathing, just.

John waited for hours before a truck came but it was getting dark and it didn't stop, then another and another, but none stopped and it was nearly dawn before John spotted one of their own Datsun pickup with the red and white Mariakos livery. The driver was George who stopped immediately sensing that this was a real emergency. They soon had Kenneth in the back and John cradled his head as they bumped their way to the nearest hospital at Lukulu where he was rushed immediately into Accident and Emergency. John and George waited for about an hour before a doctor appeared. He was a very distinguished looking Sikh in a soiled white gown. He looked at them in a sad way, 'I am so sorry' he said, 'Your brother did not wake up. He died a few moments ago. We did all we could. I am so sorry.' and with that he walked away. John gasped and then slumped into George's arms weeping bitterly. He couldn't see, he couldn't move and couldn't think. He felt dead as well.

Of course they had to stay while arrangements were made but after a few days they were back in Dar and, because the matter was so serious, John made a personal report to Peter. He was offered a bonus and money for a new truck, which he accepted, but he opted to buy a Datsun pickup instead saying but he did not want to continue as a truck driver. He told Peter that he had some 'unfinished business' to attend to. There was no further explanation and Peter thought no more of those words until later.

John spent the next few months organizing a 'trip'. He would tell no one. He was setting out to find his brother's killer but he had no other plan. He did not even know what he would do if he ever tracked him down. He was not an educated man but some research at the library had established that there was a 'Kariba' (not Keeba) dam on the border between Zambia and Rhodesia. He took a big book down from the shelf and read.

'THE KARIBA DAM is jointly owned by Zambia and Rhodesia and was built with funds from the World Bank. A power station has been carved out of the bed rock on the southern (Rhodesian) side of the Zambezi river and it supplies up to 70% of Zambian electricity. Close by is the all important rail link between Zambia, Rhodesia and South Africa which crosses the gorge at the Victoria Falls in a dramatic high span. This link carries 95% of Zambia's imports incl fuel, and all of her copper exports.'

John was impressed and he knew that this had all changed now since the isolation of Rhodesia, but as this was the last thing that Kenneth had said, as he lay there mortally wounded, John guessed that it might be the most important. He decided that he would go to Kariba the very next day and take it from there.

His journey took him over the same route that he had travelled with Kenneth and tears filled his eyes again as he passed through Tunduma, but he did not stop at the bar this time. Onward through Kabwe and around Lusaka until he arrived on the shore of Lake Kariba and rested. He slept through the night and awoke to a beautiful dawn over the Lake but he could not rest. He was driven, and his first task was to find a job so that he could test out some of Kenneth's last words such as Livingstone, Farm, Dinga mine, White Rose, Janet, Simon, Marange diamonds: what could it all mean? After a few days asking around, he was lucky enough to get a job as a labourer on a farm run by an Afrikaans family named Meintjes. He had worked there for nearly a month, keeping his eyes and ears open, but still wondering what to do next, when he got a really big break. A truck pulled into the yard as John was working and, as he looked up he got the shock of his life. There, on the side of the truck, painted in big red letters was a big sign. It said 'WHITE ROSE FARM, KARIBA.'

A few questions to his workmates revealed that the farm was only two miles away and that night John decided to go there. It was unusual for him to drink but he took some bottles along just in case he needed some courage. He parked his pickup in a small clearing near the farm and waited for nightfall. He drank one Tusker, then another and another until finally he decided to approach the barns at the back of the farm. As he walked carefully through the sheds he saw a panga lying on the ground. This, he thought, was a handy size for protection, being about four foot long with a very sharp blade used for cutting grass, so he picked it up and moved closer to the house. Dogs started to bark but they seemed to be chained up. Just then a light was switched on in the house and a voice called out, 'Who's there, is it you Simon?' John was scared but he was also elated. He had come to the right place. Kenneth's last words had been Keeba Dam, White Rose Farm and Simon. His elation was turning to hatred as he looked at the house more closely. There was a porch just by the front door and he stepped on to it carefully, but as he did so, the door opened and a woman stood there with a shotgun and two small boys by her side. 'What do you want Kaffir?' she said 'Get off my land now. You don't scare me!' saying which she pointed the gun straight at him.

John said that he could not remember what happened next but, crazy with grief and drink, he lunged at the group with the Panga that he held in his hand. When he drew breath there were three bloodstained corpses on the veranda. He stumbled aimlessly back to the pickup choking back more tears and drove back to Dar without a stop.' Lorna finished her tale with a sigh. 'There's more to tell' she said 'do you mind if I finish it tomorrow, I'm rather tired right now?' Sue agreed and arranged to visit the next day. She wanted to hear more.

Simon of White Rose Farm

There is a part of this story unknown to all except Simon. Peter did not know about it at the time so he was not able to tell Lorna either. We rely here therefore on a statement given to the Police by Doog Moss, a friend and neighbour of Simon's in Kariba. It is included here in his own words to fill in a few gaps in Lorna's story.

Simon told me that John Theuri had left some evidence behind. The police found the bloodstained Panga with a good set of prints and beside it was John's note in his own handwriting, 'Kariba Dam, White Rose Farm? Simon?' It meant little to the Police who put the killing down as some sort of grudge, but the grieving husband and father, who had had to hurry back from an important mission with the Rhodesian Security Forces, noticed something else that chilled him to the bone. He said nothing to the police: this was to be his case and his rules and only his rules would apply from now on. He had noticed that John's note was written on an old invoice for petrol. The name on the invoice was 'Mariakos' and this meant a lot to him. He had little faith in the local police at any time. They were OK if they had good 'white' officers with them but after all what could you expect? In truth he would have been disappointed if they did manage to solve the case because he had plans of his own he told me. The next few days were all about the funeral arrangements and then the day itself. Many friends and colleagues attended, many crying and trying to comfort him as well. Actually, any tears or emotions that he displayed were an act because he was cold inside, so cold, so icy and yet so resolved to take matters into his own hands. Only then would he allow himself to grieve. However, he managed to see the day through and thank his departing guests, before settling down on the verandah with a very large Gin and Tonic. The only other person in the house was Fatumah, the children's Ayah but she was weeping so bitterly that he decided not to ask for refills but just to get the bottles and ice for himself. He sat there for a long time watching the sun go down creating rainbows in the spray of the Victoria Falls, which he could just see through the hills. He blinked and began to feel tired, very tired, and soon he was in deep fitful sleep and he was dreaming, dreams seemingly so real and frightening that he was afraid to wake up in case they were. This was the dream he told me.

The Kariba Courtroom Dream XXXX

XXXX . . . A man was in the dock accused of murder of an African driver. He was being cross-examined by attorneys at law in gowns and wigs. The prosecuting counsel was a big African 'Mama' who insisted that murder was murder. Self-defence had not been an issue, murder is wrong and he, the accused, should know that, she had said. She continued, 'Are you a human being?' 'Yes' he replied. 'Do you know how humans differ from others in the Animal Kingdom?' she asked. 'Yes, I think so' he answered, 'We can think and we can plan, and enjoy music and the arts, we can . . . .' He paused but before he could continue she intervened 'Stop!', that's not at all what I meant.' she said, 'Please answer this question. Do you know right from wrong?' 'Yes I think I do, yes I'm sure I do,' he replied.

Now it was her turn to pause before she approached the stand. 'Then you know that you are guilty, I do not have to tell you so or prove it because <u>you know it.</u> Guilty. Guilty. Guilty!' saying which she turned away and began to conduct the people in the courtroom as if they were a choir; first one side, then the other as in a response. They sang out louder and louder. 'GUILTY, CRUCIFY HIM, GUILTY, CRUCIFY HIM,

Louder and louder went the singing until, very slowly, the defence counsel got to his feet and raised his arm to signal for quiet. There was an immediate hush as he began to speak. He took his time He was an experienced lawyer who had been brought in from Pretoria and, when he spoke, it was in a strong Afrikaans accent.

'My colleague makes much of guilt,' he began, 'but where does guilt really reside in this case? Surely it is with the heinous murderer of this unfortunate man's wife and family? Now, you might ask, what proper measures might a man take to defend his home and those who are dear to him? I put it to you that any measure would not only be a legal act but also a moral one. This man has suffered intolerable provocation and is obviously not guilty.' and, with that, the counsel sat down with a flourish. The judge dismissed the jury, and everyone waited anxiously for them to return. They were soon back, with a unanimous verdict of Guilty. The judge stood in sombre fashion and placed a black cap on his head. 'Msungu Bwana' he pronounced, 'You have been found guilty of murder by this court; but I find you guilty of a greater crime, that of ignoring your conscience; and, for this crime, I sentence you to eternal damnation.' He sat down, and there was an audible gasp of surprise and horror from the courtroom.' XXXX

Simon was still asleep, or was he? No, he was half asleep and half awake. His waking side did not want to wake up in case it had not been a dream at all but a deadly reality. He turned and turned, in and out, in and out, until finally he awoke in a cold sweat. 'Thank God' he had muttered to himself, 'Just a dream, a stupid, stupid dream, who cares about dreams?' He got up rather unsteadily and walked wearily to the shower room before crashing out on his bed for a long, long sleep. In the morning he was feeling refreshed and determined to find his first victim. Dream—or no Dream. Judge—or no Judge.

'This is a truthful account as told to me by Simon' signed Doog Moss.

Lorna concludes her story

Of course none of this drama in Kariba was known to Lorna, but she did have more to tell Sue when she called on the following day as arranged.

'Naturally I didn't know about all the details at the time' she continued, 'much of it came out later, and I'm still in the dark about some of it. Back then I had become quite worried when I didn't hear from Peter for a few days. We have always been so close you know,' and, saying this she choked back a tear, so close, so close. Bimbi was getting anxious as well. She wouldn't come in and she waited at the gate for days and days, sometimes scratching the ground with her tiny antlers in frustration.

Eventually we heard that there had been another 'incident' at the Mariakos depot in Mbeya. Peter had been shot at but escaped with a flesh wound. Fortunately he was soon home, but we began to consider our options after that. Peter tried to get in touch with John Theuri but he was too late. John's body was found floating in the river with his hands tied and a bullet in the back of his neck, as in an execution. We came home soon after and tried to forget about the whole affair, and we have done really.' she paused, 'until now. There can't be connection can there, with all that back then can there? That's all so long ago and this is Bath not Dar!' 'No I don't suppose so, we just need to be sure that's all', said Sue reassuringly, 'I'm off now, thank you and I'll be in touch soon.

Sue's gets on with it

Sue was at home sprawled out in front of the fire with her notes all around her and she was determined to make some sense of the affair. She decided on a process of elimination. Lambert first. She had noted that the Mau Mau crisis in Kenya was some ten years before Lorna's troubles in Dar so she was inclined to dismiss him on that score but there may have been some old scores to settle, and he hadn't properly accounted for his movements on the day. Furthermore there was that funny business about the East African Safari diamonds that Charlie had written about in his report. She dug out a copy and read through it again. This time she noticed something unusual that no one had commented on so far. Why was the note of instruction from Pretoria all written in lower case except for the word KEY who was to be the contact on Lake Tanganyika. Lockhart had told Charlie not to worry about all the small details but Charlie had been trained well and he knew that small details might make a big difference. As for why Lambert couldn't find out more, Sue thought there were very many vested interests and political intrigues around at that time which might ensure that the full story would never be known. She began to make notes but there wasn't much to go on. 'Pressure. Threaten him with Mrs Lambert! Where did he go on the Thursday when Howard went missing?' Now, what about Grearson? Was he a man with a guilty conscience about an affair, or maybe a murder? And now there's Carson, and Black, the mysterious man with the missing finger. Did they have anything to do with the murder she wondered? She screwed some of her notes into small balls and tried to loop them into her waste bin. 'Damn, this is getting nowhere' she muttered. 'I need some light relief!'

She decided to give Adam a call. She needed loving tonight, all night. She made the call trying to sound rather offhand. 'Oh Hi Adam. I was wondering if you were at home.' she said. 'Hello Sue, yes I'm here, how are you doing?' he asked, seeming rather concerned, 'Is everything all right?' 'Oh yes,' she replied, 'Fine, just fine but

I've over ordered a Pizza and there's a bottle of wine here that I shouldn't drink all by myself.' Her voice tailed off, and there was a momentary pause before he said what she was longing for him to say, 'Shall I come over then?' She said,' Yes, why don't you' and that was only the first time that she said it. The night was full of passion, but a loving passion, such as she hadn't known before. She felt like saying, 'I love you Adam' but thought of the old song, 'Saying something stupid like I love you' so she held back her words, but whispered an unintelligible sound in his ear to let him know that she did. He responded with a bite on her ear lobe and she smiled.

By the following morning she was refreshed and ready to start again. What about Howard himself and why did he get himself killed? She smiled at herself. Nobody gets himself killed does he? They are, well, they just 'are', murdered. But there must be a reason. Another love affair maybe but no; Sue had seen Lorna Howard's despair and listened to her touching account of their life together. No, that can't be it. So? What then? Africa, Africa. The answer's there, but just where? Where?

She decided to give Lockhart an opportunity to go through the options. 'Well I think you've got enough there to check out their alibis.' he said, 'be persuasive but insistent, you know, threaten them with their wives, or me if you like.' He laughed at his own little joke, 'I'll check out the alibis for Carson and Black myself. You never know, there might be something important.' Here he paused and looked at her gravely, 'but take some advice from me Susan, take it as an order. I'd forget all about the Dark Continent if I was you. Take it from me, the answer's here in Sunny Somerset not up the Limpopo!' He said all this with a smile, but she ignored his attempt to be familiar again and said, 'Thank you sir, I'm sure you're right. I'll question them tomorrow.'

The next few days turned out better than expected in some ways. Firstly, Lockhart had discovered that Carson was in Pentonville Prison on a fraud conviction, but unfortunately Black was still unaccounted for. Secondly both Lamberts' and Grearsons' alibis checked out. The stuffy old Colonel had been to a massage parlour and Grearson at the Golf Club.' In some ways better but, having eliminated their wives (unless with accomplices) there were no other suspects on the Lockhart side. She began to wonder how the other team under Inspector Curtis was doing but no, NO! Africa was her baby and she was sure that the Dark Continent did hold a secret, up the Limpopo, the Nile or the Zambezi, she didn't care, she was determined to find it. How come Howard got himself killed and why? Think, think; if there was a connection was it a 'Mariakos' matter? Someone had finally caught up with Howard after all those years, someone who would have never given up, someone, maybe, who had lost his wife and children in that bloody murder at Kariba. Was that it? Lockhart had told her not to bother, but Sue had a mind of her own. She decided there and then to go to the Library to review the newspaper accounts at the time and, if she got into trouble, she'd put it down to experience, but she had to find out. She soon found them on microfiche.

The lead story in The Salisbury Times on 8th Dec.1967 (The voice of the Rhodesian Nation) was much as Lorna had said, but a name was given to the murdered family. It was Lock. A Mrs Janet Lock and her two sons, Samuel and Stephen of White Rose farm Kariba had been murdered by intruders while Captain Simon Lock was away from the farm, serving with the Rhodesian Security Forces. The police were making enquiries and 'an arrest was imminent', the paper said. Sue looked again and froze, 'Lock!' she muttered under her breath. But this was a 'Simon' not a Stephen. Could this Simon Lock be Stephen Lockhart? And then it struck her that the mysterious 'Lake Tanganyika' diamond contact had been called KEY! Surely not this as well! Or was this just one more silly little coincidence? However, it did seem to her that some of those pieces of the jigsaw that she had noticed could be beginning to fall into place. Lockhart had known about the David Shepherd East African paintings at the Lamberts, he had spoken of the 'Limpopo' river and 'watering holes' He was a Yorkshire man hence 'White Rose Farm' but most strange of all, macabre even, were the names of the Lockhart boys who were killed, Samuel and Stephen, the same names of Lockhart's sons here in Bath. Sue shivered. She knew she was in above her head but who could she turn to with these suspicions, because that's all that they were? She was shocked, she was scared and she really didn't know what to do next. She was too tired to call Adam so she decided to go home and crash out on the settee. She went straight to sleep and didn't wake for twelve hours.

Team work?

The next day was another review meeting, this time with Lockhart and Curtis both there. The Superintendent laid down the order for the meeting. First it would be the Howard case and then, if they had time, that awkward 'Gieseling' affair. He obviously thought that it was low priority, in other words, not a murder enquiry, as yet. 'Jean' he said, 'will you start please, Howard case only remember.' She said 'Thank you sir Clean bill of health on my side I'm afraid, except a Mr Lawence Gooding who had a small business venture with Howard. Put all his money into a dodgy enterprise renovating canal boats and lost his shirt. Blamed Howard, it was only last year but we haven't tracked him down yet. Family all in the clear we think and there weren't any other social or business problems that we could discover.'

Now it was Lockhart's turn and he began briskly. 'Well, what have we got so far then. Any missing persons over here then?' he said sarcastically. There were three other officers besides Sue reporting to him and Sgt Tom Martin spoke first. 'Report on Mrs Howard Sir. I could find nothing. Wrong MO unless she had an accomplice.

Not likely Sir. Everyone says how close they were.' Lockhart sighed as if all that was a complete waste of time. 'Who's next?' he said impatiently. 'May I Sir?' It was Tom Blandish, who proceeded to give a more detailed forensic report concluding that it had seemed like a very professional job adding, rather dramatically, that the beating had taken place after death. 'Crime passionelle, then.' interjected Inspector Curtis but Lockhart was having none of it, 'It could be lots of things Inspector Maigret,' he said rudely, 'I suppose that you could be right, it doesn't have to be a man does it? A strong macho woman could do it easy couldn't they?' he said, and looked over at Jean rather meaningfully.' Now what have you got for me Constable?' he said turning toward Sue. She looked at him closely. She hesitated. She was seeing him in a totally different light for the very first time. She knew him to be a surly Yorkshire man but now, was he a cold-blooded murderer as well? Could she keep her cool or was she going to give the game away by some carelessness at this stage? Luckily she was able to pull herself together and speak confidently with a smile. She told him about the Lambert and Grearson alibis because she thought it wise to leave the door open in that direction for the time being. She did not want to alarm Lockhart nor give him an inkling of what was on her mind.

The Superintendent continued. 'Good, good, so far so good but do try to make some more positive progress won't you? Working as a team all right? Good, good that's what I like to see.' Of course he failed to see the dark looks that Lockhart was giving to Jean, and she ignored them.

'Now. What about that other case Jean? What's that all about?' he said.

Jean thought that this was an opportunity for Charlie to shine so she just said, 'PC Charlesworth can update us Sir. He's been handling the case up to now. Over to you Charlie.' Charlie stood up. It was his first time in a serious meeting and he felt exposed, but also confident. No Charlie Chan jokes today he thought. Actually his presentation was very simple and easy, until near the end of what turned out to be a very long story indeed about the Gieselings, Frau Riedler and the 'Boys from Brazil.' He was just getting to their resettlement in Germany when the Superintendent interrupted, 'Sorry Charlie,' he said, 'but what's all this got to do with a missing person? I mean, have you any evidence that there's a connection between all this cloak and dagger stuff and a man who is, to put it bluntly, just missing?' Charlie looked despairingly at Jean and she didn't let him down. 'Actually there's a lot of evidence that he was on the Nazi Hunter lists under one name or another, but as far as we can tell, they hadn't managed to track him down so far. Maybe they did but we can't be sure.' she added. The Super was mollified, 'Mmm good, good remember we don't want an International incident here do we? Just let's be sure of our facts shall we? Anybody like to make a comment?'

There was a brief silence and then Lockhart spoke up. 'Seems to me sir that they've done a very good job. Well done Charlie and well done Jean of course. They really might be on to something here you know sir and I've begun to wonder if the Howard case might be part of the same picture. I'm going to do some checking in that direction just to be sure sir.' The Super didn't know whether to be pleased at this apparent harmony in his ranks, or frustrated that neither case might be as 'open and shut' as he had hoped. 'Right, good' he said as usual, 'Let's meet back here two days from now then.' He then picked up his files and left the room. They all did but Sue was last to leave. She was wondering about Lockhart's change of heart about Jean Curtis and her thoughts about 'crime passionelle', and what made him say that the cases might be connected. Weren't these options just too much of a convenient smokescreen for him she thought.

Sue 'checks out' The Hotel Miramar

The next day Sue went to see Lockhart. She knew that she must confirm her suspicions soon or be found out so she had decided to feign 'women's problems' and ask for a few days off. Due to her, she said and a weekend break would be very much appreciated Sir, she had said. This tactic fitted neatly with Lockhart's idea of the 'weak woman' so he had agreed. 'Back on Monday mind' he said, 'don't forget we've got a case to solve.' Many a true word thought Sue, but said, 'Thank you Sir.'

She had decided to have a weekend away with Adam. She couldn't help but be curious about the Hotel Miramar where Diana Lambert and Denis Grearson, had been, so it had to be Bournemouth. They drove down in perfect sunshine and were soon booked in under their own names. When she had suggested Mr and Mrs Smith Adam had frowned and said, 'This is the 20th century you know and we've got nothing to hide have we?' They went up to their room and she tumbled him immediately on to the bed and climbed on top. 'Come on Mr Smith, come on, do it now, come on, do it now, please pleeeeze!' He kissed her warmly and stroked her eager body but, after a few moments he stopped and said, 'Look Sue we've got all day and night and we should be making the most of the sunshine shouldn't we?' Sue sighed and curled away from his hard, warm body. 'Yes I suppose we should but you never know if there will be another time do you?' she said reluctantly. 'Don't be silly' Adam replied with a grin 'Come on, race yer!' and soon they were soon down in the gardens at the back of the Hotel overlooking the sea.

A band was playing for a wedding and Adam was listening intently. He was a part time jazz musician and couldn't resist the sounds of Jazz. He'd been known to walk down dusty streets and into dark alleys to try to track down a sound that he'd heard from far away. Sue tried to get his attention, 'Look, over there! Isn't that a beautiful Yacht, yes, and look, look Adam, they're waving, they're waving at us! Come on Adam, don't be stuffy, come on, wave back!' Adam ignored the boat and he ignored her except to say, 'Shussh, Sh, hhhush. Listen to that tenor sax. He plays just like Getz with that cool sound of his and listen, they're playing Girl from Ipanema your favourite.' He was oblivious to anything else, so, catching the eye of the waiter she ordered another cold beer. She couldn't decide whether to drink it or pour it over him. He could be so frustrating. Fortunately it was the band's interval time and she managed to persuade Adam to take a stroll down to the pier. It was a lovely afternoon and they held hands and cuddled on the pier benches, first one then another, up and down both sides until Sue had forgiven Adam and couldn't wait to get back to their room for an afternoon 'rest'. They walked into town and thought about going on the Merry Go Round but good sense prevailed.

It was tea-time but Sue cleverly avoided going into the hotel from the back because she knew that the band would 'capture' Adam once again, and she wanted him to herself this time. She guided him through the front door to reception and ordered tea and sandwiches for their room, Number 98 it was, 'What a pity!' she thought with a smile. They went into the room and this time he was eager, seeking out her body as she arched towards him so warm and so ready for him to take her. The knock at the door barely disturbed them. 'Room service!' called a voice. They stopped and listened for a few seconds, but their momentum did not allow for a long pause 'Thank you. Please leave the tray outside!' Adam called out in a strangled voice, almost in desperation at a very critical moment. They didn't surface until 8pm, nearly too late for dinner but Sue decided it had been worth it, definitely. The night was still young, and so was she.

Later, as they were having dinner, her thoughts turned again to the stolen weekend of 'Mr and Mrs Grearson'. She never discussed 'work' with Adam but the scenario added a certain 'frissance' to her weekend. While he was thinking about how to please her, she was wondering what it had been like for 'them' the 'Grearsons'. 'Adam' she said, as they were having coffee and after dinner mints in the dining room, 'Adam, I've been wondering, what do you think it would be like if we were married?' He looked shocked, scared even. 'What? What did you say? Married? What a time to bring that up, when we're away for a dirty I mean a romantic, weekend. Anyway, we said we wouldn't discuss it until we both felt the time was right didn't we?'

Sue laughed and laughed, so loudly that everyone in the dining room turned to stare. 'Oh dear Adam, you are so funny and so sweet. I didn't mean to each other. I meant to somebody else, that's what makes it a 'dirty week end' isn't it? This isn't a dirty weekend for that reason, but what if it was? Would you feel different, act different, be more passionate perhaps? Take me by surprise, be more, well, more imaginative maybe?' Adam sat still, looking at her intently before he spoke, 'I thought you were happy with me. I mean us. You were this afternoon, I mean in bed and all that. You certainly behaved as if you were anyway. What's changed now then? Is there something you want to tell me? If so tell me and get it over with?' He sounded very cross and Sue realised that she had made a mistake, and maybe one that would be difficult to recover from. She couldn't tell Adam that it was a sort of vicarious pleasure that she was seeking, without explaining all the details of the case, because once she started he would not let up until she had told him everything. That's really why she never told him anything and now she'd blown it, and maybe her hopes of a passionate night. She was right. Up to the room, a giggle at the door, she showered and then lay back on the bed just in a tight T-shirt and pants and waited. Adam came in from his shower and just flopped into the bed beside her. 'It's been a lovely day' said Adam, 'I'm feeling quite bushed, let's meet up in the morning?' 'Good idea' said Sue, and they did, but only at breakfast. There was no more loving. It had, almost literally, slipped through her hands again.

Sue and Kath

After the meeting and her weekend away Sue decided that she might share some of her problems and ideas with Kath Hartley another young PC from the station. The two young women police officers decided to get together the next day, and where else but at Sally Lunns. 'Funny isn't it,' said Sue, 'how everything seems to start and end here.' 'Yes,' replied Kath, 'The Alpha and the Omega of Bath, that's Sally Lunns all right.' Sue smiled and said,' How's your case load going then? Mine is really stuck. I've got some ideas but no proof, as yet. The trouble is that I can't find a motive for the life of me, unless . . .' she stopped and then continued, 'well nothing really. I don't really know how to say this but I think that Lockhart's involved, one way or another.' Kath was silent and looked at her friend seriously and said 'Watch it Sue. That man's dangerous.'

'That's what I'm worried about. I've just got to get some more evidence that's all.' replied Sue, 'Anyway, how are you getting on with Charlie?' 'Fine, he's a bit of a laugh you know. Calls me 'Losie Lee' to his Charlie Chan you know. Trouble is that I think that he fancies me, and that won't do, in the office I mean.' replied Kath. 'Well don't do it in the office then! Incidentally he's tried that 'Losie Lee' lark with me too' said Sue with a laugh, 'Just look at that young couple over there. Can't be more than fourteen can they but look at them. Bet they're having it off already, just look at his hands and her eyes.' Kath smiled, 'Yes I can see them but tell me Sue when did you first, you know?' 'Do it?' replied Sue, 'Funny I've forgotten, it was all so long ago.'

The girls hooted with laughter just as a young blonde waitress arrived in a smart white blouse and dark skirt. She had a badge on her ample breast and it said 'Mitzi'. Kath ordered a Bun with Stilton but Sue couldn't take her eyes off the waitress and she couldn't speak. 'What is it Sue, what is it?' asked Kath feeling rather concerned. Sue seemed to come to, and then said, 'The same please.' in a rather hollow tone.

'You look like you've seen a ghost.' said Kath, 'Are you sure you're all right?' Sue still looked pale but she turned to Kath and said, 'Do you believe in re-incarnation or spirits or deja-vu?' Kath didn't know what to say so she tried again, 'What's this all about Sue?' she said. Now Sue smiled and her cheeks were rosier as she sipped her coffee. 'Of course you don't know do you, what we've just seen?' she said, 'Well, we've just seen Mitzi Gieseling in her Jungmaedel uniform just as she was in 1936. That's her, here today in Sally Lunns. Spirit Ghost or Messenger, that was her all right.'

Kath thought that this was all a bit silly so she tried to change the subject. 'How do you get on with Jean?' she asked. Sue did not reply but gazed expectantly to the serving hatch. Soon a white blouse and skirt could be seen coming from the kitchen and she leant further forward in anticipation. The figure entered the room and came directly to their table. 'Two Buns with Stilton.' she said and placed them on the table. Sue looked up and smiled. The girl was very dark and her badge simply said, 'Anna'. 'Thank you' said Kath, as the young girl turned away, but Sue hadn't finished, 'Miss, Miss,' she said in a rather faltering tone, 'I hope you don't mind me asking, but has Mitzi gone to lunch or something?' Anna looked bemused, 'I'm very sorry madam,' she said, 'but we don't have a waitress called Mitzi, I'm sorry, you must be mistaken. Enjoy your meal.' Sue sighed as if she knew that this was the case, but a shiver ran right down her back and her arms and legs tingled rather uncomfortably. She realised that there were some things better left where they stood and this was one of them, nevertheless she broke the ice. 'I don't expect you to understand but I think that Mitzi is telling us that love never dies, and she will still be here until we find out what happened to Albert.' Kath smiled, 'You may be right and you know more about it than I do' she said, 'but I need a drink. Miss! Miss! Bring me a double brandy please. Quick as you can!' 'Me too!' Sue chimed in, and both girls fell about laughing until the tears came into their eyes.

Sue investigates

Sue had been discomforted by the 'Mitzi' affair but now she faced discomfort of a different kind. She was more scared than anything else. She'd always been a little afraid of Lockhart but this was different. She'd never liked him, but he was her boss. Up to now she had been loyal and co-operative, maybe not always obedient, but that was her way. Now she was out on a limb. Say nothing and wait for others to investigate? But they wouldn't would they? She was the only one who could make it stick but she needed confirmation of the name connection otherwise it was all supposition. Was Stephen Lockhart of Bath the same person as Simon Lock of Kariba and, if so, when and why did he change his name? There was only one thing for it, she would have to go through his files to see if there was a paper trail of some sort, but even as she thought this, a shiver ran down her back. If it was he, he was a vengeful and ruthless killer and Sue knew that she would have to be very, very, careful. She would wait until this coming weekend when she knew that Lockhart would be away with his family, She would arrange to work on Sunday and use the opportunity to look in his files.

The days dragged by, but it was soon Sunday and she was in the office, alone for now. She didn't have much time before somebody else might come in so she moved quickly to the filing cabinet in Lockhart's office. She knew where his keys were, in the desk, yes, there 'Now, which key for the cabinet? Yale, Yale, that's it, now turn, turn, click, that's it I'm in! Now, first file, second file, which one? Let's see now. Not staff or Holiday Club but Personal, yes Personal. Yes, <u>Personal SL</u>, yes that's it.' Her hands were shaking as she opened the file. 'No it can't be. Damn! It can't be, Damn!' But it was. The file was empty 'Damn it's empty, Damn, Damn, Damn!' Sue was nearly crying with frustration. 'But, hang on a minute.' she muttered as she stopped in her tracks, 'There's a note, let's see now, what does it say?' She read the note. It said simply, 'Taken home to update.' She sat back. She was exhausted. 'What to do? What to do now?' she thought, but then she noticed a bunch of keys at the bottom of the drawer, two bunches in fact. 'Office keys and House keys I shouldn't wonder. Now if I can get into the House tonight I can return the keys before he gets back. Well, in for a penny, in for a pound I suppose. There's only one thing for it now. There's going to be a break in!' She laughed at the thought, but realised that this would indeed have to be her next step. However, she had decided on one other tactic before she went down the 'Burglary' route, and that was to check out the Register of Births, Marriages and Deaths in the Bath Central Library.

An initial search on the computers was not forthcoming so she asked for access to the 'micro-fiche' records and there she found what she was looking for, a birth certificate in the name of 'Simon Stephen Lock-Hart, born Sheffield in 1936'. She realised of course, that this did not prove anything, but now she felt more confident than ever. Easy to drop half a hyphenated name she thought. The problem was that it was all supposition and just that gut feeling she had. She remembered the old black and white movie 'Double Indemnity' in which Edward G Robinson spoke of the 'Little Man' in his stomach who told him that something was wrong. Perhaps she had a 'Little Woman' down there as well she thought, because she just knew that something was not right. However, she could not take her suspicions to anyone without some evidence, and the only way to get it was to see what was in the files at his home. Once more she had to wait for an opportunity when he would be away, not just from the office but from his house as well. She knew that he sometimes took his family to Budleigh Salterton, where he had a cottage, and usually he and his wife collected her brother from Bradford on Avon, before setting out the next day for Devon. It was the kind of routine that Lockhart was comfortable with, and he'd usually bore all his colleagues with the details on his return to the office so, when he said that he was off to Devon again for the next weekend, Sue decided to make her move. 'It's now or never' she sang softly to herself.

She would be on her own. She knew that. She thought about leaving a note with her suspicions in case something went wrong. Yes, that would be a good idea, and what about a Will? She shivered and decided against both. She would sink or swim and trust her instincts. She knew that this was the right thing to do. She just knew it. This was her moment. That moment, given to all in so many different scenarios, that moment when it is possible to say, yes, or no. A fleeting moment perhaps but one on which a life or lives may depend. She thought of Herr Gieseling back in pre war Munich. Was that his moment after which it was too late? She wondered about Denis Grearson. When might he have said no? And what about Lock-Hart if he was involved in all this? Sue felt tired again. She needed to rest and, she decided, she would try to do what seemed right for her, and not dwell too much on the motivations and conscience of others.

The Burglary

It was Saturday and Sue was in her bedroom getting ready. 'Now, what does one wear for a burglary?' she thought, 'Black perhaps? Trousers? Yes. Mask? No. Too dramatic, but a Black Hat, which covers face and hair, seems like a good idea; and a scarf. Yes. Crowbar? No, I don't think so. Gloves? Yes, and trainers. Good, I'm ready or as ready as I'll ever be.' She paused as she looked in the mirror at her disguised appearance, holding a glass of Scotch in her hand. 'Not bad, not bad at all.' she said, holding up the glass to this mysterious mirror image. 'Cheers! Skol! And good luck Susan. You won't let me down will you?' Midnight came soon enough as Sue tiptoed out of her back door and started to jog across the back fields to where the Lockharts lived. No use for a car, too noisy, too noticeable, and she was a fit young woman anyway. She skirted around a small industrial estate, in case there were security guards around, and soon she was approaching Park Gardens and the Lockhart home. She checked her watch. It had taken her 14 minutes.

'Excellent' she thought, as she stopped to view the house from a safe distance. There were no street lights and that was fortunate for her purposes; but there was a party going on a few doors down. She thought about waiting until the noise subsided but decided that, on balance, it would be best to go now, straight up to the front door with an excuse if she was seen. But what excuse? She hadn't thought she'd need one so didn't have one ready. 'I'm going anyway,' she decided, and walked confidently up to the front door. She tried the first key. No it didn't fit. Now the second, 'Yes, Yes, I'm in' she whispered to herself, as she squeezed inside the front door listening for any sound. Her mind tracked back to think of some excuse again if she was spotted, but then she stopped and nearly laughed out loud. 'Stupid. Stupid. What use would any excuse be when I'm dressed up like a cat burglar!' she thought.

She decided that it was time to move and, as all seemed quiet, she tiptoed up the stairs guiding her way with a small torch and not risking any main lights. She had already decided that, if she was going to find anything, it would be in the study and she looked around on the landing. There were four doors, two open, one the bathroom, and the other a child's bedroom, so she moved towards one of the others and opened the door. Yes, it was the study. A computer, a desk, files of many kinds, and bookcases on every wall. She shone the torch around, picking up the labels on each cabinet before opening each one carefully. She checked every file in all the cabinets but could not find what she was looking for. 'Damn, damn, damn' she muttered under her breath, 'Where are you?' She shone the torch around again and this time it picked up a box-file labelled 'Lock', tucked in amongst some history books in a bookcase.

She took the file down and opened it carefully. Inside were five folders, each marked with a letter of the alphabet. These were Y, C, K, M, and B. She opened the first one in the torchlight. The file was entitled YORKSHIRE and it contained old family photographs, certificates, letters, school reports and other miscellaneous papers in the name of Lock-Hart. Sue put it down and picked up the next. It was marked CAREER, and inside were official papers from the police and the army as well as photos and other papers. The file included a section marked 'Rhodesian Security Force code name KEY' and a comment, 'Decided to call myself Lock for security reasons.' Good old Charlie she thought for making such precise notes. She picked up the next and her heart nearly jumped out of her mouth. The title page was KARIBA. She hardly dare open the next. She had a good idea what it might be but she scarcely dared to hope. She picked it up carefully, read the first page, and there it was, in black and white, the incriminating word, MARIAKOS!

She wanted to study it straight away but, before she did, she looked to see what was in the fifth file. The title page was BATH, and inside were details and photos of Lockhart's 'new' family in Bath. Sue sat at the desk wondering where to start when she heard a noise. Was it the sound of the front door opening? She listened again, yes, there it was again; a noise, this time the click of the front door shutting. 'Oh God, he's back, he's come back!' she whispered to herself, 'what shall I do now? Oh no! Is he coming up?' She strained to listen for any sound, and there it was again, another sound, and this time a definite creak of a stair. 'Hide, Hide, Quick, but where? Put the file away quick, quick, that's right. Now hide here, yes here, under the desk, tight but, yes, it's a squeeze but I'm in.' These were Sue's thoughts as she lay there petrified as the footsteps got closer and closer. They seemed to go into one of the bedrooms, and then into the bathroom, because she heard the sound of the chain. Then the door of the study opened and light flooded in from the hallway. Sue bit her lip until it bled, she was shaking in her cramped hideaway but all she could see were a pair of legs and shoes moving into the room. 'What was he looking for and why now, Why now?' she thought.

The legs moved around for a while and then sat down, exactly where she was hiding under the desk. There was a musty smell of sweaty socks and trousers, and it was as much as she could do to stop from being sick there and then all over those shiny shoes. What then? They stayed there for what seemed like a lifetime, before they got up and walked out of the room. Sue listened raptly and, yes, they were going downstairs, and was that the sound of a car starting up? Yes it was, she was sure of it but she couldn't move. Fear and cramp had left her immobilised, and she had to wriggle painfully to escape from her hidey-hole. She stood up painfully and shone her torch to locate the file but it was gone. Sue was speechless. She slumped onto the floor in a crumpled heap and began to sob. 'Why me? Why do I always cock things up?' she cried, 'Why? Why?' She stretched out and looked at the light on the ceiling, then she absentmindedly shone the torch around the room. Posters and plaques, Ferrari models and then, there, over there in the corner, yes the Box file!

It was the Box file with the distinctive label L. It had been moved but it was definitely the same one. She staggered over and picked it up. It was empty. It was empty! Sue shivered, 'It can't be, not again, not again!' she muttered, 'Why move it then? Why move it? Logic Sue. Logic. Come on, why move the file? Yes, because he wanted the contents, but why? And did he want all the contents, or just some of them? Yes, that's it. He wanted the family photos for the holiday and that must mean that the other files are here somewhere. Now, let' s get looking. I'm going to tear this place apart until I find them!' Sue felt sure she was right, it was one of those feelings you get sometimes when you know you are right, and she was. The files were there in a heap on top of the photo-copier.

She discarded the Y for Yorkshire file that was still there. The B for Bath file was missing, as she had guessed, and now she held the vital K and M files in her hands. Of course she must read them, but what if she was wrong and he did come back. Photo-copies of course, and there was the copier right here. She began her work and it took nearly an hour to copy both files. She put the originals back, placed the copies in her bag, and got ready to leave. Then it struck her that she needed the originals if charges were to stick. She would have to take a chance that the files might not be looked at for awhile so she must take the originals, and leave the copies in the files. This she did without delay, arranging the files carefully so it would not seem that they had been disturbed. She crept downstairs and out into the night. She was soon home.

When she got inside the door she suddenly felt tired, not sleepy tired but emotionally drained. She flopped immediately into he favourite chair and was asleep in seconds, and then wide-awake in minutes, totally refreshed. Now she opened the files and, fortified by a large tumbler of malt whisky, she began to read and make notes. It was all there, much more than she had dared to hope for. Lockhart's campaign of revenge for the murder of his family had been planned down to the last detail. Not just the planning, but the recording and outcome of each incident, was there. It was a plan but it was also a testament to the justification of each murder. Somehow Sue had known that it would be like this. She had noted, over many months how indifferent and dismissive he had been as the two cases evolved. It seemed that he lacked any compassion, because 'to care' in these cases would have meant an admittance of guilt, if only to himself and this he was not able to do. He did not deploy his conscience, if he had one, because, in his eyes he was the agent (or angel) of righteousness in all that he did. Sue took out her lap top and began to type, slowly at first as she noted each incident and date, and then faster and even faster as if the story would escape if she did not pin it down. When she finished she placed her report and the incriminating documents in a folder. She sat back with a sigh of relief. Now she felt that she could sleep for a fortnight, but she put her alarm on for 7am.

The Denouement

On Monday when she went into work she was pleased to hear that Lockhart would not be coming into the station until the Tuesday. This gave her the chance to hand the file and her suspicions over to Jean Curtis. She knocked on the Inspector's door. 'Oh come in Sue' said Jean, 'May I help? I hope you haven't come to spy for your Lord and Master.' she added with a smile. 'Not exactly.' said Sue, 'I just thought you might like to see this before I hand it over to the Super.' And with that she placed the file on the table. It was not just the K and M files, because there was also a full analysis and rationale prepared by Sue, which pointed the finger directly to Lockhart for Peter Howard's murder.

Jean read the Kariba file quietly, looking up occasionally at Sue as she did so. When she had finished, she picked up the file marked M for Mariakos and began again. This file contained a detailed account of Lockhart's plans and action since the murders in Kariba, starting with the 'assasination' of John Theuri, and the unsuccessful attempt on Howards life back then. There followed some press cuttings of 'unsolved murders' in the Salisbury newspapers with red ticks in the margins. There was also an article about the 'Tragic Death in Dar-es-Salaam' of the former Director of the PFB (The Petroleum Finance Board) in a boating accident off the coast; also marked with a red tick in the margin. This was followed by a section marked, 'Howard the Criminal,' which contained full details of the murder plan right down to the time, place and weapon of choice. It concluded, 'Revenge is Sweeter than Wine!' and there was yet another section, simply labelled 'KEIT.

Jean leafed through the file and looked over at Sue. 'We've solved Charlie's puzzle as well.' she said. 'This file says how Keit was 'executed' in Bath by knife and then his body dumped in the river and weighed down by bricks.' Sue was puzzled. 'I know that Keit was the Mariakos engineer. But why in Bath?' 'Well, Lockhart's file is very detailed as usual,' said Jean, 'Quote 'Saw Keit in Sally Lunns, by sheer chance, calling himself Gieseling. Keit, the Mercedes engineer who I discovered was the one who spiked our car in the Safari, and stole our diamonds, which were so important for the war. Remember this was Keit, the blockade breaker with Mariakos. Great pleasure in knifing him after I told him who I was. 'Any last words?' I asked him, 'Nein.' he said, 'I deserve to die. All my life I have wondered how I might atone for my part in the war. It must have been possible to refuse orders at some time or even to desert. God help me and thank you.'

I did as he asked and then bagged him up and dropped him way down in the river. Funny though, he didn't really know about or have any part in the Kariba killings and he said he didn't know what happened to the diamonds. I wonder if people do tell the truth at the end, no point in then lying is there? Any way he's dead now. <u>CLOSE KEIT FILE.</u>'

Sue looked at Jean and said, 'Poor Keit or Gieseling. You know I felt quite sorry for him. He was thinking about Auschwitz wasn't he? Was he a victim or, having chosen his path, was he then ultimately responsible for his war crimes, even under orders?' She paused, 'and do you think that free will always means a free choice? Perhaps it's like a cat with nine lives. We get chances too but don't we ignore them usually for convenience or maybe pride. And then suddenly our number's up and it's too late to turn the clock back. His was.'

Jean sat quietly listening to Sue and then said, 'Maybe some of us get a better deck of cards than others but it's up to everyone how they play them isn't it? I'll just finish reading the file. Just wait a moment.' Then when she had finished she just said, 'Well, well, well. This is excellent. I only hope we can make it stick. He'll deny it all you know. He'll say you made all this up and cobbled together some unconvincing copies to back up you story. I do hope you know what you are doing.'

Sue smiled confidently and, speaking very quietly, she said, 'Look again Jean. Those aren't copies. They're all originals and they're all in his handwriting.' Jean did look, and so did the Superintendent, and so did Internal Affairs when they came to interview him. The case was over.

The next day Sue had coffee at Sally Lunns. She also had a large Sally Lunn Bun to celebrate. She had managed to persuade a rather good looking young Lawyer called Jeremy to be her date, 'and maybe more' she thought. They chatted for a while and then he said, 'I hope you don't mind me asking, but aren't you supposed to be going out with Adam. I mean aren't you two an item?' She paused for a moment and then tapped his hand, 'Adam who?' she replied with a big smile. She was feeling confident and even a bit frisky until, by chance, she saw the newspaper headline in the Bath Chronicle which was being held and read by the man at the next table. It said, 'CHURCH MOURNS SUICIDE OF LAY MINISTER DENIS GREARSON'. Suddenly Sue felt sick. 'Sorry Adam, I mean Jeremy, got to go.' And with that she hurried out into the street, leaving Jeremy, the young lawyer, feeling decidedly peeved.

Meanwhile Lucy Grearson was reading this letter. It was tear stained because she had read it over and over so many times. Adrian was beside her and holding her hand. She felt guilty herself, as she read the words, because she knew that Adrian would not understand. Matters were often very black and white for him, but she understood Denis's torment.

Dear Lucy, 'I believe in God the Father Almighty, Creator of Heaven and Earth, and of all things Seen and Unseen.' But I do not believe in a vengeful God who would condemn my decision to take my own life. God gave me my life and I know that only he should take it, but I pray that he will understand that, just as I have shared my life with you and with Him, it is the case that I can no longer be with you both, as it was before. I love you so much, and I love God, but I am unworthy. 'Lord I am not worthy to receive you. Only say the word and I shall be healed.' But I have heard no word, because I know that the word must be my word. I must forgive myself before I can be forgiven, and I cannot. I am so sorry my love. DG

If you know Bath you have probably been to Sally Lunns. If walls had ears this place would have many such tales to tell, tales of love and deceit as well as murder, guilt, atonement and even amusement. She will keep your secrets but can you keep them from yourself? Sue had such a secret that she could no longer keep from herself or to herself. She picked up the phone and dialled Adam's number. A voice answered 'Hi Sue, I'm here' Her words came tumbling out 'Oh Adam, Adam, thank God it's you, I love you Adam, I love you I really do! I just had to tell you!' His reply was immediate. 'I love you too Sue, so much, all of me for all of you. I'm coming round right now. Let's go to Sally Lunns to celebrate!' Sue flopped on her sofa. This felt like love all right. She felt sure that there would be no re-appearance of Mitzi Gieseling in her Jungmaedels uniform at Sally Lunns this time. Mitzi could rest in peace now that the case was solved. And then Sue remembered what Frau Gieseling had said when asked how she felt about Albert.

'I just loved him you see' she had said, as if that explained everything.

And Sue decided that it did

FIN

PART 2.
CROQUET AT CHATEAU CHEVALIER

Contents

Summary

This story continues to follow the fortunes of Constable Sue Parker after she solved the case set out in Part One of 'Bath Buns at Sally Lunns.' She is now a Sergeant and she has to take on a baffling new mystery in a Medieval Chateau during a 'management motivation' weekend. There are just too many motives and suspects when a suspicious death occurs, and to cap it all she is still trying to sort out her love life.

Introduction

What would you kill for? Money perhaps or could it be love? Revenge is another good motive, as are many disputes in the world of Politics or Religion. All of these motives are explored in this story set in a medieval castle near Bath, which is actually more of a folly than the genuine article. During a weekend organised for 'management motivation' the police are called to investigate the suspicious death of a VIP at the hotel.

Leading the case is <u>Sue Parker</u> whom you may remember from the 'Bath Buns at Sally Lunns' case a few years previously. Soon afterwards she was promoted to Sergeant and now reports to Inspector Jean Curtis instead of the disgraced Inspector Lockhart. If there ever was such a thing as an open and shut case this was not it, because, as she began to investigate, it soon transpired that the VIP had enemies, and many of them were at the hotel. And now she had MI5 to contend with.

So, have you ever ridden a Quad bike?

Pity, because it might have been useful if you had attended this Bank Holiday weekend, where competition and fun shared the headlines with murder and international intrigue. Let's begin by catching up on Sue as she tried again to mix business with pleasure.

Sue Parker

Sue had moved to Bradford on Avon where she shared a lovely apartment overlooking the river with he friend Chrissie. Her romance with Adam had gradually 'fizzled out,' especially after she was promoted to Sergeant and the Government 'cutbacks' took hold. She'd had a 'fling' with Martin (Corcoran that is) but that didn't go anywhere either. There was just no time for a social life, let alone a love life, and she knew of a number of marriages that were under pressure as well. Anyway she was still young, 29 in fact, and she enjoyed her spare time on her terms such as going to the gym on a whim. She had become a steward at the Bradford Arts Centre and this appealed to her eclectic sense for music. She had grown to enjoy jazz since meeting Adam (Damn him!) and so she tried to go to concerts as often as she could. Apart from that she spent her weekends with Chrissie (if that young lady wasn't out with another new boyfriend) or other friends from University or elsewhere. Oh, and she was saving up for a new car and then (of course) she was planning a holiday in Barbados. Surely that was enough to be getting on with.

It certainly didn't suit her to get a telephone call late on the Monday about a death at the Chateau Chevalier. She knew the Chateau quite well because Martin had invited her to some of his 'business weekends' with his management training company 'Muck&Brass'. She rather hoped he would not be there this time. Or did she? That was then and now was now wasn't it? She was off duty, but the Inspector said it was urgent, he was sending round documents and she should go as soon as possible. Of course her car wouldn't start. ps Buy new car!

Sue had become a 'career policewoman' and it didn't quite match her character in some ways. This dedication to duty came at a price, namely her love life. She had never seemed able to balance these two and love had lost out all too often. This had been the case with Adrian and Denton and she remembered that weekend at the Hotel Miramar in Bournemouth with Adam when things seemed to go badly only to be revived when the 'Sally Lunn' case had been solved. How come we 'drifted' after that, she thought?' And History had repeated itself with Martin. How close we had been and now look at us, strangers. Sometimes she wanted to forget and sometimes she desperately wanted to remember every little detail, every gentle touch and every kiss and especially that week in Guernsey.

She remembered a special morning. It was a Saturday morning . . . .

*   *   *   *

Sue in Guernsey

It was Saturday morning at the St Pierre Park Hotel, Rohais in St Peter Port when Martin called out from the bedroom 'Come on Parker, get your skates on! We've got a busy day today!' Sue could 'barely' hear him from the shower but she soon put a dressing gown on and stepped out. It was one of those nice white fluffy ones that Hotels sometimes supplied. 'Do we have to?' she pleaded. After all they had only arrived yesterday on the Condor ferry from Weymouth and last night had been, well, let's say last night had not been especially 'restful'. 'Must we?' she repeated, rather plaintively, 'Don't you see anything that you like?' she said, at which point the gown fell magically to the floor and she stood, her back arched before the open French window with the breeze fluttering her damp hair and the sun shining behind her silhouette. 'Oh Crikey!' Martin gasped and moving very quickly, soon had her pinned on the bed. 'Now, now' she said with a giggle,' 'I thought you said we were going out!' And they did, but it was a little later than planned.

That particular day they had decided to experience the 'La Valette Underground Military and Occupation Museum' which was in fact a series of underground tunnels built as a hospital and store chambers during the Nazi occupation from 1940-45. Other days were set aside to explore the Islands, including Hern, Sark and Alderney, as well as the famous 'wrecks' all around the coast. And then there were St Peter Port and St Sampsons to explore, and Sue wanted to visit Le Tricoteur where the traditional Guernsey sweaters are made. (Presents of course). 'I wonder why people pack so much in to a holiday,' Sue said as they drove to the tunnels, 'Why don't we just go and find a beach and I could wear my bikini. You'd like that wouldn't you Martin?' But Martin drove on, 'Yes I would but No we're going on,' he said, 'You know you'd regret it if we didn't see what we came for wouldn't you?' 'Depends what we came for.' she said as she snuggled up to him in the car. When they arrived she suddenly felt rather frightened, the tunnels looked so dark and deep and forbidding but in fact they now had proper lighting and air conditioning, which was a far cry from when they were built by slave labour, much of it from Eastern Europe. Sue felt very comforted by Martin's arm around her all the way through (so there were compensations) but she was pleased to walk out into the sunshine after about 45 minutes. Sue was interested in the occupation and had often wondered what it had been like for the residents of the Island and, as they came out she noticed that the warden wore an impressive badge with an impressive name, 'P. Sauterez'. She knew a bit about Guernsey and she knew that this was a very traditional name going back at least 800years, so if anyone could shed light on the war years this man should be able to.

'Excuse me M'sieur,' she said, 'you can tell that we are visitors but can you maybe tell us what it was like under the Nazis and, well, was there much resistance?' 'No, there wasn't much, too dangerous, too isolated, not recommended or supported by London and liable to be heavily punished.' he replied. 'There were just a few raids and these all failed so what could we do? Nobody cared about us then. The Germans left us starving and the allies neglected us to such an extent that it took the Red Cross to bring in food supplies, but even that wasn't until much later.' Sue wasn't happy though and would have argued with the warden some more but Martin took her to one side. 'Sue,' he said, 'Don't let us have an argument with the warden please. He's only doing his job you know. We weren't there were we, so how could we know what it was like, for them I mean?' Sue felt hurt and upset, 'Doing his job? Following orders you mean? Now where have I heard that before?' she said, 'And why were the Maquis in France and other resistance groups prepared to take risks and the Islanders here didn't?'

Martin realised that he had touched a raw nerve, 'You're right of course,' he said,' But we'll never know will we so let's just try to enjoy our holiday please, please Sue, let's forget it for now.' She smiled and took him by the arm, 'I'm sorry Martin,' she said, 'I didn't realise I'd feel like this. I lost my Grand Dad at Dunkirk you know and this has brought it all back to me.' She turned to him with tears in her eyes and wept on his shoulder for quite a few moments. 'Well' he said, 'you'll be pleased to hear that I've made a decision. Back to the Hotel for us, and a visit to 'Le Mirage' Health Spa for a relaxing Jacuzzi.' 'Yes, I agree, that's a great idea' she replied,' but I'm placing you under arrest just to make sure!'

The Spa was indeed all it was cracked up to be. The dinner was great followed by coffee and mints in one of the many lounges. However the hotel had been booked by a conference of boxing promoters and their young charges, some of whom were to take part in 'trial combat' in the main hall. 'Can't get away from it,' Martin had said, 'M&B would be quite at home here. I'd better leave them a card.' 'Right,' said Sue, 'and then you're coming with me. Don't forget you are under arrest and you must do exactly what I say.' It was quite early, only about nine when they arrived at number 68. 'Nearly,' she said with a smile, 'Now, go into the shower and freshen up I command you.' She commanded, and then he commanded, on into the night until sunrise. Sue sneaked out at some point and put a sign on the door outside. It said 'Do not disturb.'

Sue gradually and reluctantly came out of her reverie and looked at herself in the mirror. 'Well Sue,' she said, 'That was then, and now is now and I've got a job to do, Martin or no Martin.'

A week is a long time at Chateau Chevalier

Saturday. An astronaut and a pond

Two days before Sue got her phone call the M&B 'management training' weekend at the Chateau was already well under way having started on the Friday. Two events had been organised for the Saturday, firstly a Quad Bike race and secondly a Courtly Love Ball. Nothing had been left to chance with many professionals on hand to advise, guide and help the contestants. However the unexpected could always be expected and there were soon reports that an Astronaut had crashed and now lay belly up in a pool of croaking frogs and toads. If it had been dawn it would have been their version of the Dawn Chorus, but it wasn't, in fact it was just getting dusk. He seemed almost to be one of them, as he lay with his legs and arms splayed out, his helmet and goggles at one extremity and his boots and gloves at the others. He lay just as he had fallen to earth. He was winded and it was some time before he had the strength to call for help.

'Help! Somebody please help me. I'm stuck. I can't move! Help!' But no one came and other machines now whirled around him as dusk began to fall, their lights now glistening on the pool that was his prison. He continued to lie there surrounded by the many curious amphibians that seemed to give him their vocal support in his hour of need. 'Help!' 'Croak, croak' 'Help' 'Croak, croak' 'Help!' 'Croak, croak.'

But still no one came until eventually one of the machines stopped and a voice called out. 'Is that you sir?' 'Yes, thank God, who's that? Get me out of here whoever you are. I'm stuck fast.' he replied, gasping for breath. 'It's Mike here Sir. I'll have you out in a jiffy,' came the reply and, sure enough he soon found himself being lifted out of the mud to the sound of much squelching and, it seemed, many objections from his new found friends as they croaked their disapproval. And then he was out and on the bank, much relieved and feeling a bit silly.

'Thanks Mike, I'll buy you a drink when we get back to the Mother Ship!' he said with a laugh, 'Beam me up then Scotty!' Mike Mc Dougal laughed, 'Right you are Captain Kirk, just hop in and we'll have you back in no time.' Mike's 4X4 started with a splutter leaving the crashed Quad Bike of 'Astronaut' 'Brig' Brotherton in the pond.

They were soon on their way back to the hotel, and as they arrived the 'Brig' looked a forlorn figure as he walked into the hotel bar. 'Get me a drink for God's sake,' he called out to the assembled company, 'Can't you see I'm desperate?' They were all there, all the teams, and not all were sympathetic. Some were curious but many, even his team-mates, were amused. 'What's it like up I space? Tell us about Deep Space Nine. What happened to your rocket boosters?' Titters of laughter filled the room as more jokes continued until eventually someone placed a drink in his hand. He smiled and raised the glass in a toast, 'Just you wait until tomorrow' he said, 'some of you buggers will be lucky to survive! You're not going to get me so easily next time.' This brought a round of applause and more drinks until it was time to change for the 'Courtly Love Ball' that was scheduled for the evening.

The weekend begins. Friday. The reception & the Orangery

The whole weekend had begun the previous day and this was not without drama either as a case of food poisoning had to be investigated.

The Courtly Love Ball and the Quad Bike race were just part of the activities that were to take place at the Chateau Chevalier near Bath that week in a 'management motivational' weekend organised by 'Muck and Brass,' a company that specialised in challenging activities during the day and recreational ones in the evening.

The competitors had arrived on Friday and had been entertained by a small jazz band on the substantial patio. Canapes and 'Champers' were served and a light buffet was also available. The new arrivals were encouraged to take part in a friendly game of Croquet as a bit of a warm up for the more serious croquet competition that would be held on the Sunday. Actually it was the buffet that Roger Brotherton was referring to when he jokingly said that 'you won't get me so easily next time'.

That evening both he and another contestant, Miss Bea Brughal had been taken ill with suspected food poisoning. A doctor was called but he could not be sure that it was in fact the food, or the drink for that matter. Nobody else was ill so the doctor took precautionary blood samples and promised he would let them have the results in a day or two. They had been packed off to bed and the evening continued into the small hours for some. Others took the opportunity for a wander around the Chateau or a browse in the library.

Tom Spooner and Tamsin Albany had been chatting all evening and Tom had finally managed to separate her from her brother Lance. She liked the look of him and she had had more than too many glasses of champagne so when he said, 'How about a stroll?' she just giggled which he took to be affirmative, which it was. They strolled out into the warm moonlight and she said, 'Aah, isn't it lovely? What a beautiful evening, it reminds me of . . .' But no more words came, as his lips reached out for hers and he held her tight, one arm around her waist and the other against the nape of her neck as he pressed her to him. He shivered momentarily and then slowly, very slowly withdrew from their embrace and held both her hands in his. He smiled and said, 'Would you like to go to the Orangery for a bit of privacy, it's only over there?' He pointed to the attractive Victorian looking glasshouse across the lawn. Tamsin looked at him and bit her lip.'Well I don't know. What do you take me for.' she said and paused for a few moments, sizing him up and down, and down and up and then, with a loud laugh she broke free and ran across the lawn, 'Catch me if you can,' she cried out, 'Last one to the Orangery is a cissy!' They tumbled through the door and onto a rather conveniently placed heap of straw just inside. They lay side by side and then he kissed her again.

Muck&Brass Events timetable

Martin Corcoran had worked for Muck&Brass PLC for some time. It is one of the leading management training and motivational groups in the country and they are especially expert at combining outdoor challenges to competing teams during the day, whilst retaining an air of civilised 'Olde Worlde' costumed activities as well. This was their programme for the weekend at Chateau Chevalier near Bath.

M&B PROGRAMME

Muck&Brass welcome you to a weekend at Chateau Chevalier that will test and stretch each of those taking part. Your aim is to win the event. There are 4 teams of 2 women and 2 men competing as a team. Each team and each member has been given a 'nom de plume' for the weekend and these are given below. Firstly here is the weekend agenda.

Friday from 7pm. Welcome reception and informal croquet.
Saturday Prep for race. Quad Bike race 4 pm. Courtly Love Ball 7pm

Sunday Optional Church service. Croquet competition 3pm Freetime
Monday Group meetings. Paint-balling combat 3pm Pool relaxation.
Tuesday Award ceremonies breakfast and farewells.

The teams

Team A Hi-Flyers (Garvey Lonsdale Ins. Inc.) - Astronaut (Roger 'Brig' Brotherton) - Skydiver(Anne Lomax) - Cloud Niner (Deidre Spencer) - Sunray (Tom Spooner).

Team B Royalty (Royal Crescent Assoc Bath) - Richard the Lionheart (Simon Stewart) - Berengaria of Navarre (Sheila Stewart) - Henry III (Lance Albany) - Eleanor of Provence (Tamsin Albany).

Team C United (Dublin College of Tourism) - Manchester (Sean Lifferty) - Newcastle (Maggie O'Meara) - Dublin (Tam Collins) - Belfast (Bea Brughel).

Team D Bedrock (Community Workers Group) Fred (Brian Martin) - Wilma (Jan Tooley) - Barney (Wilf Woodside) - Betty (Anne Day)

Enjoy your stay. Be punctual. Play fair but play to win.

Sgd. Pam Tockington, Martin Corcoran and Mike McDougall. (For M&B)

Saturday The Quad Bike race.

After the social get together on the Friday it was down to some serious business from the word 'Go' on the Saturday morning. Teams were advised to have a good breakfast and a very light lunch because the afternoon promised to be a 'bumpy ride' for some, to put it mildly. To begin with they were led down to a very large paddock area with large barns on all sides. A few weeks back this area had been host to a Veteran and Vintage car rally called 'Formule Libre' after the 'free-formula' racing of earlier decades. There had been no racing on that day but some evidence was still around including a complete 'Hispano-Suiza' (under a dust sheet admittedly) that it's owner had not taken away. Tam Collins wondered if they had forgotten about it and perhaps he could claim 'Treasure Trove!' because he had seen it first. Everyone decided that this was unlikely but there were some brochures and documents alluding to possible connection with the Marquess of Bath. 'Plenty of room for his wifelets' joked Jan Tooley. 'And their chicklets of course!' she added.

However, the sight that greeted them had to be 'seen' to be believed'. There were Quad Bikes of all shapes and sizes in the courtyard and in every Barn. 'Muck&Brass' had made sure that the event would be properly organised by enlisting the help of the regional QB racing association as well as a leading retailer of QBs namely 'Comanche Bikes' of Stroud. This accounted for the many different varieties on show and M&B

had been rather foresighted in organizing an official 'SW Area' competition on the previous Wednesday. The track and the bikes were therefore tried and tested, but the St John's Ambulance was there as well just in case! Indeed it was to be another 'Formule Libre' event as competitors, under the guidance of a dedicated group of QB experts to each team, began to choose their mounts.

M&B had thoughtfully included handicap criteria so a large unit was not necessarily an advantage especially for Sean Lifferty who was only five foot three in height. He chose the smallest on offer, which was the 'Yazuka ATV50' looking very smart in Blue and Silver. It was said to have a max speed of only 30 mph, but Sean decided that might be enough in what looked to be slippery conditions. The others made their selections. The field eventually comprised a mixture of the following; Adderly 300XS (beautiful in Green), ALX 320CF SuperMoto(shiny red), AUK 250 TerraBike (sinister in Black), Comanche RLX 450 (a deep orange) and lastly the Yamaha yfm 250r (in Royal Blue), chosen by all of Team B of course. There was much excited chatter as the teams returned to the Chateau for lunch. They had to be back at the courtyard by 3pm to don their racing outfits and some were already exhausted at the thought of it. Nevertheless they were all there and the laughter increased as each 'insect like' figure appeared from the changing rooms. For this and the other competitions each team was given a coloured 'shirt' chosen by them. A chose Red, B chose Blue, C chose Green and D chose Orange. There were to be two timed races with one rider from each group setting off together followed by the next group after 3minutes. They were to do two circuits of a two-mile track across fields, sand dunes and bogs. The first 4 were chosen by ballot and the order reversed for the 2nd race.

Engines revved and smoke billowed out from the assortment of engines as the official QB President raised the starting flag. They were off!! A running commentary might have sounded like this, 'And they're away with Orange up front followed by Blue and Red but Green has already been overtaken by the second wave of riders and oh dear there's a Blue rider in the ditch, no, the bikes up again, now they're heading down the Belling Straight and I hand you over to . . .' But there was no second commentator, not even a first, so beyond sight from the starting line it remained a mystery until they came round for the first time, their numbers and colours clearly showing as they were timed for the first lap, and then for the second and last before they had to re-organize and start again in reverse order. 'After Laps One and Two' announced Martin Corcaran to the riders, 'Red Team is leading. Well done Hi-Flyers keep it up. Now you other teams get cracking, there's only a few points in it.'

Engines revved again and smoke billowed out again as the QB official raised his flag once more. This time there was a mad dash for the first bend and it seemed that there might be an accident but all first starters got away cleanly as did the following ranks. They were soon coming round again with Red still apparently in the lead starting the last lap. Moments ticked away and then they appeared again, all racing for the line as over they went. 'Mmm' said Pam Tockington, 'Looks like Red to me.' But Martin was looking worried. 'I only counted 15' he said, 'what about you Pam?' 'Don't know' she said, 'Mike, how many?' 'Yes 15' he said, 'There's a bike missing! I'll get out there and see what's happened right away.' saying which he jumped on his own BLX 4x4 and set off with screeching tyres. And that's how he found 'Astronaut' in the pond and that's how Hi-Flyers lost the race to 'Bedrock' with 'Barney' (Wilf Woodside) the individual winner. A rather sour note was introduced after the race when the officials reported to M&B that Brotherton's brakes may have been tampered with. On reflection, and because it wasn't proven, Pam and Martin decided to keep it quiet so as not to spoil the weekend.

The 'Brig' a VIP Indeed

He had had an unlucky start at the Chateau but 'Brig' Brotherton wasn't one to let adversity get in his way. The team from Garvey Lonsdale Inc. was taking part because Brotherton's 'Venture Capital' department was the most profitable in the GL group and this was their reward (bonus if you like) from which he hoped to gain some more approval from the Directors. Profits over the last few years had been outstanding and much of their success did indeed lie with the leadership of Brotherton. Affectionately known as 'Brig', an epithet referring back to his army career, he had however, long since retired from active service. Nevertheless he continued to hold an honorary post as Colonel of the 'Far Sight Rangers' a group loosely attached to, but not part of the official Territorial Army. 'Don't like to be tied down' he would say. He was thought to be influential at Westminster and held many directorships in the City as well as being chairman of the Windsor Hunt. His home was in Datchet where he took pride in his small stable of Horses and Hounds. He was married to Lucy and they had three children at University.

You may have gathered that he was very, very competitive and so he was annoyed that it was his performance that lost the team the first event. 'Can't understand it,' he said, 'That bike was going like mad, I was driving like a master and was well in front and then Wham! Out of control and heading for that nasty ravine. Only just managed to pull it back, but still ended up in the pond. Wondered where I was at first.' Now he laughed, 'You meet a nice class of amphibian in a pond you know.' he added. His colleagues felt a bit relieved because a grouchy 'Brig' was quite capable of spoiling the weekend for them all. 'Never mind Sir' said Tom, 'We can easily catch up tomorrow and the next day.' Tom Spooner was the youngest of the GL group and, as we have seen already, he could take the department's meaning of the word 'Venture' to another level as he did last night with Tamsin in the Orangery, and hoped to do so again that evening when he planned to be a Troubadour at the

Courtly Love Ball. However being rather young he could also be indiscreet, and it may not have been a good idea to tell Anne Lomax that there was a rumour going around that 'Brig' was going to leave Garvey Lonsdale and his wife, and move to Provence with Deidre Spencer.

Anne and Deidre were both PA and 'Secretary' to 'The Brig'. He used them but they used him as well. He gave them both the same job to do and then 'rewarded' the one who did it best. Nothing was ever said about these arrangements. Anne drove an Audi R8 V10 and Deidre owned a lovely 'Gites' in Provence, both, one might say if one looked into it, well above their formal status. Naturally they were both there for this weekend and it was well understood that teamwork and 'sharing' were to be the order of the day. There hadn't been much of that on Friday as 'The Brig' had gone down with that mysterious food poisoning, or something. Now, with the Quad bike race over, the girls had arranged to meet in the Jacuzzi before the Courtly Love Ball later that evening.

Anne was the first to arrive wearing a fairly 'adventurous' pink bikini. She slipped into the foam and stretched out languidly, accidentally brushing the toes of the man who was already there. It was Mike McDougall, the organiser from Muck and Brass who had found the 'Brig' in the pool earlier in the day He grinned and said, 'Lucky I found the old Brig today wasn't it? He could have lain there for hours couldn't he?' 'And died,' thought Anne,' that would have solved things.' However she just smiled and said,' Well I hope he appreciates you and gives you a reward.' Then things seemed to change somewhat, as if her voice had awoken something in him. She felt his leg stretch out and find hers rubbing it in a gentle circular motion. 'I'd rather have a reward from you.' he said. Now Anne was no prude, quite the opposite in fact, but she did have a sense of time and place, and this was neither. 'Not much I can do for you I'm afraid.' she said drawing her knees up to her chest, 'and haven't you got work to do?' This was one of her favourite brush off lines and it usually worked. However, it looked like Mike couldn't take a hint and might even try again, when Deidre arrived in a low cut one-piece blue swimsuit. Anne used the opportunity, 'Hello Dee,' she said, 'Mike's just leaving. He's got work to do.' He looked very disappointed but gave in gracefully, and, not so gracefully, left the Pool with a cumbersome splash. 'Jacuzzi Joy Rider' Anne said, and both girls burst out laughing.

They lay contentedly for quite some time with the water bubbling around them and, in the way that things are when one is close to someone else, it's nice to feel them close. Gradually then, in the pool, their svelte young bodies slipped into a gentle, somewhat erotic embrace more focussed on a loving glance and 'feather touch' than anything else. 'Seems we're practising for tonight,' laughed Deidre, 'but I don't think M&B will have accounted for the Island of Lesbos.' Once more they laughed out loud as Deidre took a shower cream and rubbed it carefully across Anne's shoulders and breasts. 'Mmm that's nice,' Anne said, 'Now what do you think that we're in for tonight. After the Ball I mean?' They often talked like this, compared notes, made plans because as well as being 'rivals' they were also active collaborators in the 'Brigs' fun and games. 'Who knows?' replied Deidre. 'I'm game for anything.' 'Yes I know you are.' said Anne, and gave her a big splash, which was returned with some vigour, followed by more and more splashes and laughter. 'Now, Now, girls.' said a voice. They stopped and looked up. It was Brig.' Starting already/' he said, 'Can anyone join in. Or is this girls only?' The girls giggled and continued splashing, 'Well, it's never stopped you before.' said Anne as they continued to splash, this time with him in the middle.

After about ten minutes they set out to return to their rooms but the 'Brig' stopped them as they passed by his suite. 'Just come in for a minute. I'd like your opinion on my costume for tonight.' he said. The girls weren't fooled but they went in and sat down on the bed to wait for him to appear in his resplendent outfit. After a few moments, there he was, the epitome of Henry VIII, dashing and daring and it wasn't even six o'clock. He dashed and he dared, first with Anne, and then with Deidre in the middle. 'Phew. I think we've broken the rules of Courtly Love.' he said.

So what is courtly love? Well, it began in the ducal and princely courts of Aquitaine, Burgundy, Champagne and Provence at the end of the eleventh century in poetic form and gradually took on certain conventions over time, such as heroic deeds of valour and endless subterfuge. The lady in question had to seem to be pure and virtuous, and sex had no part to play. If it did, the rules would have been broken and, well, just think about mediaeval torture and forms of execution! Get the idea? Painful.

Team B (Royalty) were really looking forward to the Ball. As we have seen, their 'nom de plumes' had already been chosen to associate with that era. You may have also noticed that the team members were also related to each other in connection with the disputed 'Royal' house of 'Stuart-Albany' linked by some to the Merovingian dynasty. It was indeed no accident that M&B had organised such an event. In fact they had been lobbied for some time to do so by the Chateau itself, and the event had been funded from others who shared the same interest.

In short, those involved were involved in nothing less than a revival and survival of their historical and religious claims. Not outwardly perhaps because, after all, this was to be a 'Courtly Ball' to be enjoyed by all. No, it was more the beginnings of a resurgence of their claims, not only here but elsewhere in the country as well, especially where their 'Lodges' were under threat as was the case at the Chateau which was owned by the 'Royal Crescent Association' the 'Royalty' team itself. Not everybody knew this but plans for demolition were already well under way, with planning permission secured, architects employed and in which legal/insurance companies such as Garvey Lonsdale were prime movers.

Saturday The Courtly Love Ball

As guests arrived there were a number of professional 'troubadores' with a variety of lutes and other instruments to entertain. There was also the solitary figure of a 'love sick' poet addressing all who would stop and listen. There was a fairly unappetizing meal laid out with not much cutlery (use the bread you fool!) and plenty of Mead and some wine. Fortunately the organizers had fresh water to hand, which of course would not have been the case in earlier times. Participants still wore their team colours because they were going to be judged on the 'Stages of Courtly Love.' However, to be strictly accurate we should note that the whole concept of such a phenomenon in the 'real' world of the fourteenth century is challenged by many historians. Nevertheless some eminent writers such as Barbara Tuchman have felt able to enunciate eight characteristics, and these were presented on a card to all the men so they would know how they were going to be assessed. The ladies were given a different card reminding them of their unquestioned chastity and listing the 'Four Loves' as set out by C S Lewis in which they might express themselves during the evening.

Men
Stages of Courtly Love
Attraction only by eyes or a glance
Worship from afar
Declaration of passionate devotion
Acceptance of virtuous rejection
Renewed wooing with oaths of eternal loyalty
Moans of approaching death from lovesickness
Heroic deeds of valour
Endless subterfuge and artifice to secure objectives.

Women The Four Loves
Affection
Friendship
Platonic love
Charitable love

The cards were distributed and the evening began. It was a little bit like 'The Apprentice' where Alan Sugar's minions evaluated the hopeful contestants on this or that task. We mentioned Tom Spooner as a Troubadore earlier. He was now dressed in a charming off the shoulder dress (sorry, smock) and drooling over Tamsin Albany who studiously avoided his gaze of course. A more 'courtly' suit was being pressed by

Brian Martin on Sheila Stewart who looked every inch the epitome of her character, Berengaria of Navarre. He'd done the moaning bit and was now considering what heroic deed of valour to perform because she had given him a small token of a 'friendship' namely a monogrammed sweet smelling handkerchief. In another part of the room it seemed rather odd, given the rules, that Jan Tooley was to be seen hovering around the 'Brig' with fluttering eyelids. He was flattered but, as Eros wasn't on the agenda for now, he soon took up his manly heroic role and she one of implied 'Affection'. They were observed gazing at each other for extended periods of time and talking earnestly about who knows what.

Their interest in each other did not escape Hi-Flyers Anne and Deidre either, as they both tried to ward off various predatory men who didn't seem to know, or care about the rules. Overall the evening was a great success. There was much laughter about some of the antics including some indiscreet ploys of the men, but it was all taken in good part and most of the women retained their virtue. It had been observed that Eleanor of Provence (Tamsin) did not appear to be taking her vows seriously and talk of a chastity belt was mooted, again to peals of laughter. It was agreed that Sunray (Tom Spooner) would be put on the rack in the morning, until he told everyone where 'they' had been after 9.30. This again led to much amusement with one exception, 'Brig' Brotherton. He was keenly aware that the Quad Bike race had gone against them and was disappointed that they were unlikely to do well at the Ball with one team member missing, 'awol' perhaps (and one from Royalty of course). The Brig 'dared to win' in SAS jargon and lack of effort was a capital offence in his eyes. In other words, in the morning he would 'tear a strip' off the young rascal.

Talking of virtue, if one had stood outside the Brig's room for any length of time after midnight one might have heard a certain amount of giggling, so it may not be surprising that he didn't appear for breakfast on the Sunday morning. Nor, as a matter of fact did Anne Lomax or Deidre Spencer but perhaps they were just out for an early morning gallop.

Sue acts the part at Dillington House

Sue was going through her papers. She knew that she would have to attend the scene sooner rather than later but for some reason she was putting it off. Of course it was Martin. Did she want to see him again or not? Not only that, but she had noted that a 'Courtly Love Ball' was on the programme and this reminded her of how they had met only two summers ago at Dillington House near Ilminster in Somerset. That particular weekend a play entitled 'Poles Apart' was to be performed and the Press had advertised for persons with 'absolutely no dramatic experience' to take part, not just as extras but in the lead roles also. They had got off to a really bad start and it took some perseverance on his part to improve matters. The play had been written by the director and was set in Tudor times in England. This rather charismatic writer/ director was redefining old ways in the theatre and his aim was to heighten the drama and the unexpected. (He was Russian of course, small dark and brooding with a slightly hunched shoulder but attractive in a kind of hypnotic way. His name was Sverdlov but he insisted that his 'family' as he called the caste, should address him only as 'Master' or less formally, as Dimitri. Another change to usual practise was that nobody (except him) saw the whole script and the cast were only given 'their' part each day. Direction came from a narrator who sat in a sort of rocking chair seemingly oblivious to the drama enacted before his eyes. These first scenes were rehearsed only once before the performance on the last day, but to add further tension the cast were only given their script for the last act as they came on stage for that last act. This ensured an added element of surprise as the actors themselves only then became aware of their final role.

Actors were told that if they wanted to be in the final acts, they must not communicate in any way about the play during meals and in the evenings. This made it all rather mysterious and that suited Sue very well. She felt that novelists and playwrights often touched on the human condition in a way that bare statistics could not. She hoped for some illumination and hopefully inspiration from this weekend. This in turn she thought might help her to give more attention to the unusual and unexpected in her work. Her friend Jill had planned to go with her but a bereavement caused her to cancel and Sue therefore had a large timbered, 4 poster bedroom all to herself. After unpacking she lay back on the soft downy mattress and thought, 'Yes, this is the life. I could get used to this.'

Dillington House is set in beautiful surroundings just outside Ilminster. It is reached via a long driveway to a car park and thence to stables and a coach house. There is a new addition to the buildings, built in 2009 and this is 'The Hyde' which offers further accommodation and the theatre. The house has medieval origins but was largely updated by Lord North who was Prime Minister under George III. Rooms abound on the many floors, many with tapestries and formidable paintings of the great and the good. There are a number of terraces, a walled garden and an arboretum. Just the place for a weekend of drama and relaxation, Sue thought but there wasn't much time for reflection as all cast members had been invited to drinks and a buffet supper on the terraces prior to introductions by the Conference centre management team and the Director of the play. Sue got talking to a small group of women from the local U3A but they were as mystified as she was about what the play was about, but soon enough the director clapped his hands for silence and began to speak.

'Fellow Thespians,' he said, according them a respect such as they had never heard in their lives before. 'Fellow dramatists,' he went on, (not quite so good but fair enough), 'I welcome you here today at Dillington House to take part in a breakthrough in drama. You may think that a bit strong but please reserve judgement until the final Act of the performance on Sunday. As you know from our initial contacts with you, the plot will only be revealed gradually and not totally until the final curtain call. Tomorrow we meet after breakfast for assignment of roles and costuming. Remember, your role must be kept secret until it is revealed on stage. Now are there any questions?'

As usual there was a sort of embarrassed silence, with everyone wanting to ask the same question but nobody daring to, until a voice did speak up from the back of the group. The speaker was a young man with a ready smile and, as he stood Sue noticed that he was, in her words 'a bit of a hunk.' 'Sir,' he began, 'my names Martin sir, maybe I'm the only one who is curious but what does the title mean? 'Poles-Apart,' I mean, can you give us a clue please?' 'I'm afraid not,' the director responded, 'but you'll find out in due course. For now please take this booklet and read it overnight. It may fill in some gaps for you but make sure you get a good night's rest. We have a busy day tomorrow. We meet at 930 for getting your character assignments and costumes.'

With this he left the room and the crowd soon broke up apart from a few stalwarts who made their way to the bar. Sue was tired and ready for bed as she headed down the corridor to her room only to be 'waylaid' by him, yes, that man, Martin. 'Fancy a drink?' he said. 'You're Sue aren't you?' He held out his hand, 'my names Martin.' he said. 'Yes, I know,' she replied, 'you asked that question back there, but he wasn't telling was he? Maybe the info's all in here.' she said as she waved her booklet under his nose. 'Fancy a drink then?' he repeated. Sue looked him up and down. Yes or No, which would it be? The coin in her mind came down heads and she just smiled briefly, 'No thanks, busy day tomorrow, see you then,' and she was gone, on her way back to her room, stopping only to give a 'maybe' smile over her shoulder. In her room she began to read.

POLES APART

Margaret Plantagenet was born in 1473, two years before the Battle of Bosworth brought about a new Tudor dynasty. With the accession of Henry VIII as 'Defender of the Faith' it seemed as if old factional and religious rivalries might be at an end but matters were soon to change. The play will conclude in 1541, some 8 years after Henry's divorce from Catherine of Aragon and his marriage to Ann Boleyn had been declared legal. Early resistance to this 'The King's Great Matter' had been snuffed out in 1535 with the executions of Thomas More and Bishop Fisher followed by the 'Dissolution of the Monasteries' from 1536 and the defeat of the 'Pilgrimage of Grace' one year later in 1537. In 1541 Henry had been married to Anne of Cleves for one year (after three years with Jane Seymour) but it only lasted another year (Marriages to Catherine Howard and Catherine Parr followed after 1541.)

So, in 1541 it was Henry and the Protestant Anne of Cleves who were King and Queen. Henry had removed his strong and somewhat challenging advisers over the year starting with Wolsey, More, and even Thomas Cromwell. What's more there was a male heir waiting in the wings, the future Edward V1 who was only age four in 1541. The future for Protestantism seemed sound at that time and it might be fair to say then that the Catholic cause was in some disarray. Our story follows such a Catholic family in these troubled times, a local Somerset/Wiltshire family with royal connections to the Plantagenets and the Duke of Clarence and his wife Isabel Neville who was herself the daughter of the famed Warwick the Kingmaker and the Yorkist cause All well and good but this heritage could be dangerous too as they had naturally taken the 'Yorkist' (Richard III) side in the only too recent Wars of the Roses in which Henry's father, Henry Tudor (Henry VII) had defeated Richard at the Battle of Bosworth.

'It was a time to lie low perhaps but one is not always given that luxury.'

Act One   1473   A room in Farleigh Castle
Act Two   1485   Bosworth Field
Act Three 1509   Court of Henry VIII
Act Four   1528   A nunnery in Wales
Act Five   1540   Salisbury Cathedral cloisters
Act Six   1541   The Star Chamber

*   *   *   *

Sue put the leaflet down with a yawn and was soon asleep, or was she? She sensed a figure beside her bed. A man in Tudor doublet and hose was standing there with a sword at his belt. She gasped and made to scream but the figure put a finger to her lips in a signal for silence. She pulled the sheet down over her bare body but he removed it gently and smiled. As he did so the hose, doublet and sword disappeared and it was now a proud naked man who knelt and took her toes in his hands. She shivered with fright or was it anticipation? No matter because she suddenly awoke with a start as a rowdy crowd passed by her door. 'Phew, narrow escape.' she thought, 'but I'm sure I've seen that face before and if so. Mmmmm.'

The next morning Sue and the others were given their parts to play, hers being revealed as Margaret Plantagenet herself the leading role, and rehearsals begin without much preparation.

In Scene One she actually played Margaret's mother Isabel Nevill to demonstrate the family resemblance, as well wishers gathered around the 'birthing' bed. Cries of 'It's a girl!' and 'Isn't she lovely' were heard whilst the less favourable comments of George Plantagenet were whispered in dark corners outside.

Scene Two. Bosworth Field was a chance for Martin to show what he could do as he tried to persuade the doomed King Richard to flee. He is playing the part of William Pole, a member of the Nevill family.

In Scene Three Henry VIII is crowned. Sue (Margaret) and the Plantagenets are at court cheering with everyone. He promises to be the 'Defender of the Faith' as old rivalries are quietened.

Scene Four follows Catherine of Aragon as she takes refuge in a nunnery after the divorce. Sue (Margaret) is there to console her.

Scene Five Margaret (Sue) is now married to Sir Richard Pole and is Countess of Salisbury. She meets others in the Cathedral cloisters to discuss how to respond to the Oaths of Loyalty pronounced by the King.

Scene Six. The King meets with the Star Chamber to discuss the fate of those who refuse his ultimatum. Margaret has to sit behind a curtain as she listens to their deliberations. She hears the King's voice, and then a voice that seems strangely familiar. It is Martin's voice (William Pole her husband's cousin) and he has this to say. 'The woman is a malcontent, a Papist and she deserves to die.' Margaret swoons as the death sentence is proclaimed. She is to be executed at the Tower of London. (A dark curtain descends and the only sound is that of the executioners axe.)

End of Play

The bar was open and everyone was congratulating Sue, but she was shell shocked at the enormity of the part she had played. 'Cheer up,' said a voice. It was Martin. 'You look like you've seen a ghost.' he said.' How about a drink?' She was cross, 'Drink, drink is that all you can think of after what I've just been through.' she said, and at this point the Director came over and kissed her on both cheeks. 'I've never seen a more realistic performance.' he said, 'you should consider acting as a career.' She smiled, 'I thought that I was in a pressure job,' she said, 'but acting takes so much out of you. I just couldn't do it.' Martin intervened again, 'You took it all too seriously,' he said, 'It was only a play.' 'Not exactly,' said the Director, 'these events, but for a little artistic licence, did take place and I can see that Sue senses it. The only real creation on my part was the betrayal of Margaret by her cousin, hence, 'Poles Apart.' The penny finally dropped for Martin, 'Oh I see,' he said, 'sorry I've been a bit dim. Come on Sue let's get that drink.' She looked at him seriously before giving her reply. 'No Martin, I know now that I can't trust you, and it's made me think how

99

some people who love and trust others can so easily be betrayed as well and that's an important thing to know in my job.' With that she turned on her heel and left the room. Martin was bemused and headed for the bar muttering, 'It was only a play.'

Authors note. *The Director was right. Margaret Pole was executed at the Tower of London in 1541. Her son became Cardinal Pole and was instrumental in the return of Catholicism under Mary Tudor.*

Sue was cross with herself for reliving that episode and taking up time that she should be spending on the case, but deep down she thought that lessons learnt then could well be useful now. With that thought she set out for the Chateau with a spring in her step.

The Masons (Sunday morning)

Back at the Chateau it had been suggested that Sunday Morning might be a good time for the group to come together in some form of prayerful contemplation, but whatever kind of 'Church service' was available at the Chateau, the management knew that they might upset somebody. They were well aware that there were probably some Catholics in the 'Dublin' group whilst the 'Royalty' group represented those that had been persecuted by them in the past and feared their intentions now. None of this might come up in day-to-day conversations, but in a 'Church' or 'Prayer' setting they were sure that someone was bound to say the 'wrong thing' and spoil the weekend for future bookings or worse.

Furthermore the Chateau management were not entirely without their own preference, as they were unofficially connected to the local Masonic Lodges themselves. Actually they were their own Lodge, as one is entitled to be in the Masonic tradition. This is known as the 'appendant' tradition in which certain autonomies are permitted. Nevertheless there is usually much in common with other Lodges especially in their attitude to religion, which we referred to earlier (naturalistic deistic) in which, although a Supreme Being is recognized, that 'Godhead' is not specified or identified. A Christian may interpret the figure as Christ, a Moslem as Allah and a Hindu as Shiva or some other spiritual being. It seems that everyone of religion is welcome, but it does tend to leave atheists, agnostics and humanists out in the cold.

Another problem for the Masons concerns the disquiet of some around alleged Right Wing political links with Judaism/Zionism and with the 'English Defence League' who themselves are alleged to have links with the 'New World Order' groups in America on the Republican 'Right' such as the 'Tea Party' group supported by Sarah Palin (The Republican Vice Presidential Candidate) and others. Acceptance and persecution of the Masons went hand in hand over the centuries with religion and politics at the forefront of persecutions. In Hitler's Nazi 'Weltanschaung' (New World Order) for example, the Freemasons were identified as a '<u>political</u>' threat. In prison camps, where up to 200,000 died, they had to wear an inverted 'Red Triangle' for identification, placing them in a similar category to the Jews, who had to wear the 'Yellow Star.'

Given this minefield of potential misunderstanding or mishap the management (quite wisely) decided to give every guest a copy of the local Sunday morning services in the vicinity and left it at that. As they expected, some left for a while and others stayed for croquet practice. This was the best outcome in other ways because the Chateau kept it's 'Appendant Lodge' identity very secret, not only for commercial reasons but because, with some other like minded Lodges throughout the World, they provided a 'home' for the Merovingian tradition with all that that entailed, in other words they claimed to jointly possess the Holy Grail.

Sunday pm Croquet

M&B PLC was accustomed to dealing with diverse groups and (to date) they had not had any major difficulties, so they prepared for the next event with their normal professionalism. This was to be the Croquet competition in the afternoon. Identification of teams would not be too difficult because there are 4 colours of ball available in formal croquet and these matched up with the 'team' colours except for the 'Green' team who had to settle for Black. A handicap system (bisques) was also available to distinguish novices from those who had played before. Once more it was an opportunity to dress up, this time in the style of Beau Brummel or Jane Austen perhaps. This accorded with the dates of it's introduction to England under the name 'paille maille' when London's Pall Mall was famous for street games played by the King. As before M&B took no chances with the rules (which can be very complex) by inviting representatives of the CA (Croquet Assoc) to coach and to referee the games. It is said that the game can be 'viciously competitive' and M&B wanted to keep the 'vicious' out of it.

It was a lovely sunny day and, although there was rivalry, there was also much laughter and good humour as 'roquet' and 'croquet' shots sent the opponents ball into the long grass. Overall winners at last were the Hi-Flyers, an outcome that persuaded the 'Brig' to let Tom Spooner off with a warning for the time being as he took him aside in the bar that evening. 'You did a good job today Tom,' he said, 'and as you know I shall be submitting my report to the MD when we get back. I don't know what he'll make of your earlier 'antics' but I will have to tell him or you can be assured that somebody else will. Do well tomorrow and he might overlook it but don't forget we're here on Company money and it's not a social junket. 'Play hard, work harder' that's my motto, and here's some more advice, 'Don't sh-t on your own doorstep!' Comprenez?' Tom mumbled, 'Thank you Sir,' as he glanced around for Tamsin, 'You can rely on me Sir. Je comprends OK.' he added, wishing he could stop the report altogether, but how? Maybe the Brig might become 'hors de combat' again. This time permanently.

The 'Brigs' Plans. The VIP shows his hand.

Monday had soon come around, and the day's planned event filled some guests with much excitement and others with fearful trepidation. On this occasion the 'Brig' was feeling confident being ex Army himself, but he wasn't so sure about his team or of the strength of the opposition. As it happened, the organizers had set the morning apart for Group meetings so he decided to give his group a taste of 'what's what' in a slide, map and video presentation; strictly 'Hush Hush' of course.

M&B had organized advice, charts and referees through the European 'Millenium League' for the afternoon so most groups were having an easy morning but not the 'Hi-Flyers.' This was to be the Brig's big moment and he didn't want any slackness. All teams had their own 'prep rooms,' usually with doors left open, which allowed for the light banter of passing rival teams. Not this time! The door was locked, curtains pulled (In daylight) and the scene was set for the 'Brigs' presentation which rather reminded Anne and Deidre of Churchill's 'We shall fight them on the beaches' speech, although they wouldn't have dared to say so. In any case he was routinely oblivious to any criticism and this was no exception. He was on a mission, having spent much time preparing 'for a battle' as he put it. And this is what he said.

'Good morning Hi-Flyers. I don't need to remind you that we are the A team, and not just because they say so. We are the A team because we are the best, and this afternoon we will prove it, together as a team. You'll get a handout from M&B later and that will give some pointers about the rules and pitfall to look out for but I'm more interested in strategy and tactics this morning. I'm going to give you the benefit of my vast experience so that you can take it with you to the 'battlefield' this afternoon. Don't think that what I have to say is irrelevant, far from it. It's planning, strategy and tactics that will be all important later. I may have told some of you that I have been involved in quite a few of these events through my work as 'Logistics Adviser' to the MOD.

MilSim (Military Simulation) is not new to me, far from it and, I can tell you, more training of this kind might have avoided the cock up on 'Bloody Sunday' in Derry. Yes, I was there and it's one of the reasons that I need 'minders' from time to time. The Irish haven't forgotten, some of them may be here today, but nor have

I, and it taught me a lot about how to deal with opposition. Act first, I say, and ask questions later. You'll see what I mean in a minute when it comes to the changes we'll be making in government soon, 'hush hush' you know.

I'm not saying that some mistakes were not made in Derry, but the enquiries have concentrated on that day alone instead of placing it in context. The 1st Batt. Paras have even been compared to General Dyer's troops at Amritsar in the way that they behaved. Just think of it, at Amritsar in 1919, the so-called 'massacre 'took place in a closed sports ground where the crowd were cornered and could not escape. The shooting that did occur was intended to disperse the crowd, but there's no doubt that the force used was not proportional in that case, especially as 379 people were killed. Now take 'Bloody Sunday' on 30th January 1972. The locations were in open spaces with firing and cross firing from both sides. I'm sorry to say that 13 'innocent' people probably were killed by mistake, but that's not to say that they were not involved in, or at the very least supportive of the demonstration, which was also illegal at that time. But here we do have a similarity with India in 1919, because both were 'illegal gatherings' according to the law.

Not only that, but in the months leading up to the incidents, there had been much provocation and even killings of British troops, most notably to my mind, that of Major Hanky who was shot in Derry a short while before Jan '72. It wasn't so much the shooting, which was bad enough, but the fact that the so called 'innocent' bystanders prevented the emergency services from helping him, causing a heightened level of resentment and suspicion amongst the troops. Lastly, I would say this.

The Army were called in, in 1969 to take over certain functions of the RUC (Royal Ulster Constabulary) who had been finding it difficult to cope. This led to two problems that affected the situation in Derry that day. Firstly, that the Paras were trying to act as policemen, not soldiers.

It was not a role that they had been properly trained for and some might have panicked I suppose. The second point is this, that the Army were supposed to operate alongside the police in the command structures but, according to what I have been told, the Police Chief was not there to help. Some said this was because he had thought that it was foolish to try to prevent the demonstration at all, so he opted out. I've got no time for all this. I say that the only thing some people understand is force.

Today will be a picnic compared to 1972 but the principle's the same, 'Get them before they get you.' I may as well tell you now about another reason why you can be sure that we'll win later on today. It's because I know how to win at all costs and I'll tell you now in confidence about the big changes you'll here about in the news in a few days.

I'll be leaving Garvey Lonsdale at the end of the month to take up a new position in Government as 'President of the National Council.' That's a new group that's going to replace the Cabinet, so we can bypass parliament if we need to. I'll also be appointed

'Director of Internal Security,' a post that will combine all Army and Police Units in a new force called the ISF that I've been preparing for with the 'Far Sight Rangers'. Most people thought that this was playing at soldiers, now they'll know differently. So I know what I'm talking about when it comes to putting down opposition.

You'll remember that provision for such a force was included in the Queen's speech earlier this year after that wave of violent protests over the abolition of all government funding for those public services that remained after the purge. Some complained but most couldn't care less. We'd actually started all this way before then, soon after the first coalition Government in fact. Remember the 'Freedom to work' law? Well what that did was to destroy Union power once and for all. Large Unions were broken up, tax funding was withdrawn and new ballot thresholds all made them a toothless talking shop.

As you may know that measure had been tacked on to another Bill (The Law for removing the People's Distress) last year. The Lib-Dems were supine as usual and, although some Labour politicians spoke up. We got them with our anti terror legislation, 'fomenting public disorder' etc if you remember. Anyway Labour had not repealed our Civil Contingencies Act of 1994 so who were they to talk? There was one who called our measures 'Nazi Tyranny' and gave us all a lecture about Hitler's Enabling Act of 1933. Another wrote to The Times under the pseudonym 'Otto Wells' who was leader of the Social Democrats in Germany at that time, 'We pledge ourselves to liberty and justice Blah, Blah, 'he wrote. Well anyway, our 21st century hero's in gaol now.

I'm confiding in you today because I want you to trust me and follow my lead. This isn't just a game I'm telling you, but maybe a preparation for battles on the streets and if it comes to it I'll be ready then. Will you?'

He finished his diatribe with a flourish, as if he was actually at a Nuremburg Rally and stopped for a drink of water. His small audience clapped politely. 'Why don't you tell him that there's only three of us here?' whispered Anne with a chuckle. 'You tell him' said Deidre, 'but have you forgotten about them?' and, as she spoke, she gestured to the back of the room where four smartly dressed men in suits sat listening intently and smiling broadly. The 'Brig' had introduced them earlier as 'Special Advisers' for the afternoon but were they more than that?

'Now let's get down to cases' said Brig. 'First, let's look at this film about Bloody Sunday. When it's finished I'd like to hear your impressions then we'll move onto some of my own slides to show how it should be done. Then we'll scout the 'terrain' from the maps and when we've finished we'll be really well prepared for later. Any questions?'

'No sir' came a triple response, almost with a resigned sigh. They all knew that they were in for a long stay, so he might as well get on with it but Tom was thinking, 'He's off his head. If he's serious surely someone's going to try to stop him before it's too late.'

Monday Paintball combat

At 3pm all teams were given a briefing in the area where they had been introduced to the Quad Bikes. On display were their coloured 'vestments' as before together with a set of goggles and a 'paintball marker.' (This was actually a gun given a less frightening description). 'Pods' were included which could hold up to 200 rounds of Paintballs and this was considered adequate here. Fortunately the coloured Paintballs matched those of the competing teams so a 'kill' could be easily identified. Once more there would be referees on hand although all would be made aware of certain protocols such as 'Die when you're dead!' In other words don't cheat. There are many different forms of this activity but here it would be 'woodball' variation (a defined wooded area) and, to make matters really complicated there would be three half hourly combats in which each team would be allied to each of the others in turn. Imagine the confusion! 'Aagh I'm dead. I thought you were on my side.' Still, it made for a very interesting afternoon as bodies littered the woods until told they could go back to base to start the next round.

Murder in the woods

As expected the Hi-Flyers had been the ruthless killers that the 'Brig' had envisioned and were well in the lead at the finish. But where was he? 'He's probably in another pond,' someone joked but just then they saw a small group of marshals walking towards them with a stretcher, 'God, I hope he's all right.' said someone else as the stretcher was placed down in front of them. 'I'm afraid he's dead.' said the Marshall in a rather matter of fact way. 'Stand back please. We'll have to call the Police straight away. He's been shot you see.' Taking no heed of his advice the small crowd pressed forward, 'Look,' said a voice, 'He's been shot by his own team. It's Red. The marker's red can't you see?' There was a moment's silence and it was some time before another voice spoke out. 'It's not the colour of a red marker. It's the colour of blood. See? Blood Red. Real Red Blood' A woman fainted and then a man fainted.

Sue puts MI5 in their place

Following the discovery of the body, uniformed officers had already cordoned off the immediate area where it now lay. However that was only the start, because they had sent back a message for more posts and rope to secure the whole wood in which the Paint Ball combat had taken place. Sue knew Sergeant Tompkins from the uniformed branch, well. 'OK George' she said, 'can you organize the forensic boys when they get here. It'll soon be getting dark and, if it rains, we'll lose what evidence there is. Thanks. Now, who found the body?' Two marshals stepped forward. 'He did' said one. 'No, you did.' said the other, and then, in unison, 'We did.' 'That's all we need' thought Sue, 'Tweedledee and Tweedledum'. Let's hope they remember where they found it. Fortunately they did, so George sent off them off with a couple of officers to mark out that exact position. Now Sue called him over for a quiet word 'Will it be OK if the rest of us go back to the Chateau before forensics get here George?' asked Sue, 'They've been waiting here for hours and it's getting chilly. I can keep them all together in the Main Hall or somewhere and under close supervision until their clothes have been tested, for gunpowder residue you know. That'll mean two teams of the forensic boys and girls, one in the wood and one in the house. These few hours could be crucial don't you agree?' George did agree but added, 'You'll be lucky to get one before the Press is swarming all over the place.'

Sue smiled and nodded, 'Right, ladies and gentlemen, sorry this has taken so long. I'd like us all to walk back to the Chateau now and gather in the main Hall. We must stay together and no one can change clothes, at least not yet. Loo breaks will have to be supervised for a while. Just try to be patient. I should think that you might order some refreshment when we get there. Any questions? No? OK let's go then.' It was about half a mile to the Chateau and legs were weary when they got there. They were greeted at the door by the M&B staff and the Chateau manager. 'So sorry about all this, so sorry, please come in. We've laid on some drinks and a small buffet in the Hall where they are waiting.' said Sylvester (The manager). Sue was perplexed, 'Who's waiting?' she said. 'I don't know for sure,' he replied, 'Very official, white gowns etc. Forensics, I think they said.' Now Sue was gob-smacked. 'Who the heck was this Roger Brotherton anyway', she thought. 'Seems like he must be a very important person. I see trouble ahead, trouble and more trouble. Yes I've got a nasty feeling that this case is going to get a lot of attention if he's such a high profile character. We'd all better mind our P's and Q's'

That wasn't all she had to look out for because it seemed that matters had already been organised in the Great Hall when Sue walked in. The 'team members' had been ushered down to the far end of the room and were already being inspected and 'dusted down' by the forensics team mentioned by Sylvester. Sue strode immediately to a table set nearby where one woman and one man sat at a desk seemingly co-ordinating the data from the other officers in white. She came straight to the point. 'My name is Sergeant Parker. I've received instructions to investigate a homicide here and I've already ordered a team of forensics experts from Bath. Might I ask who you are and what you are doing here?' The woman stood up and smiled graciously, 'Yes we wondered when you might get here Sergeant. As you know speed is of the essence in these enquiries. We've just made a start that's all. Your people can have a go when they get here of course.' Sue was startled, 'My people!' she exclaimed, 'So who the heck are you and your people? You can be sure that the evidence is contaminated by now so I don't think there will be much for them to do here. Anyway I'm sending another team to the scene of the crime.'

The woman smiled again, 'No need Sue, we've taken care of that as well.' This time Sue was nearly speechless. 'What!' she exclaimed. 'Stop. Stop right now and tell me who you are and what's your authority here today? And how do you know my name?' This time the man got to his feet. 'Sorry Sergeant I thought that Dr Ford (he nodded to the woman beside him) had already explained. We were told you'd be in charge. We're from the Home Office and we've been called in by that lot over there.' He pointed to another table set back in a darkened recess which, until their arrival, had been the home of a giant Grizzly Bear who now seemed to supervise proceedings. Sue made a Beeline (or should it be Bearline?) for the table at which sat a group of three men. As she approached the tall one in the middle stood up and held out his hand.

'You must be Sergeant Parker. Yes, your reputation goes before you. My name's Franks, this is Oliver and that's Dussault. We're from MI5 and he's Interpol but don't tell anyone will you?' He laughed and then said, 'Please sit down. I suppose you're wondering what this is all about.' Sue sat down, quite taken aback but already resolved not to let these groups interfere with 'her' investigation. 'With respect Sir,' she said, 'I don't think that you fully understand the position here. This is a murder investigation on our patch, the Bath and North Somerset Police. I would politely ask you to fit in with our enquiries not the other way round.' Dussault raised his arm as if to say something but Franks waved him aside. 'Let her finish Jules, she does have a point.'

Sue was encouraged by this, and one might say, even emboldened. 'Thank you again Sir' she repeated, 'I have realised that the victim may have been an important man, and if that is to figure in my enquiry I shall find out through diligent enquiry and examination, and if I need you help I shall ask for it. However I do recognize that you have a job to do and if you think you have some information about the murder, about the murder only mind, I would like to share it. Meanwhile I plan to set up at least eight interview tables here in this room and I'd be obliged if you would find alternative accommodation for your enquiries.' The three men looked at each other in a rather shame-faced way until Mr Oliver broke the ice. 'That's telling' em Sergeant.' he said 'And so shall it be!'

His colleagues laughed as well and the situation seemed immediately less threatening. 'We'll move out in the morning,' said Franks. 'They'll probably find us a conference room or something. And of course we'll let you have copies of all our forensic evidence as soon as the Home Office are done. Deal?' He held out his hand and Sue took it with a smile.

Her colleagues were waiting patiently. She had worked with 'Charlie' Charlesworth before and he was now officially in the Detective branch at the Station. On duty that day had been Senior Sergeant Martin as well as Constable Tom Blandish, so they were there as well. Unfortunately Martin was leaving the Force (voluntary redundancy) at the end of the month and Sue supposed that is why she was given the job. 'Right' she said, 'From tomorrow eight o'clock sharp I want you here with brain firmly in place. Not you Sergeant, I know that the Super has something special for your last few days, and hopefully we'll all be there to drink it!' He smiled and said 'Right Sarge.' 'One more thing,' she added, 'I expect Inspector Curtis will be here in the morning to see how we're doing. Ideas welcome at briefing 8 am sharp here as I said. I' m also going to ask if we can borrow Kath Hartley from Newbridge Station. You all know her from when she was here with us. OK?' Everyone nodded in agreement, especially Charlie who decided there and then to renew his 'Kath' campaign, which hadn't got very far last time.

Before Sue left for the evening she decided that tomorrow she must find Martin, whom she had now discovered was indeed part of the M&B team that weekend at the Chateau. She had been there before of course as his 'guest' and the accommodation, including its' bedrooms were not unfamiliar to her. She thought that it would be best to have a chat, as working colleagues so that any embarrassment or difficult moments could be avoided. Until tomorrow then, now she needed sleep.

Tuesday. Interview preparations

It was Tuesday morning and Sue's team were all there for the morning briefing. 'Thank you for being here on time and no hangovers I hope.' she began. 'The Inspector's given me approval to borrow Kath so that makes 4 of us. That's very convenient because there are four teams competing here this weekend. I suggest we take one each. Individuals mind, not as a team. Jean says that she'll try to find time to interview the M&B and Chateau staff, as well as any other guests that might have been staying here at the time. She'll be here at eleven to help us to get started. Unfortunately we didn't put a travel embargo on them, so some of them might have left or will be leaving soon. They'll need following up perhaps. So, does anyone want to say anything before we start? No? Then let's remember that we'll find our killer through meticulous police work, motive and opportunity, but, if you have a hunch, follow it and look out for any signs of uneasiness or indifference. These can be just as helpful.

I'll take team A, Garvey Lonsdale, one less with Brotherton off the scene, but that will allow me to co-ordinate as well. Tom, you take B, that's the Bath 'Royalty group, and Charlie team C, the Irish. I'll ask Kath to take D when she arrives. That's the

'Flintstones' of course. Set up your tables well apart and don't discuss your findings with each other here or privately until the process is completed. Then we'll bring all our leads or blind alleys together. OK? It will be up to you to organize interview times but it's all got to be done by tomorrow evening.

That might give us time to eliminate most people and allow them home before the weekend. Even so we may have to call some back, even from Dublin Charlie, so you'd better get your skates on. It's 9am now, get your tables set up and let's have coffee at 10. You can book your first 'victim' at 11 if you can find one. Make it a short sharp hour and then see them again if necessary. I'll see Jean at 11 and then make a start on mine. Lunch to suit you but take it here please, even with the 'guests.' You might learn something you never know. That's it. Good Luck everyone.'

From 11 am the tables were busy, as Sue had hoped and by lunchtime it seemed that the process was going well. Inspector Jean Curtis had arrived at 11 am as promised, taking Sue into the Library straight away. 'The Super called me in this morning,' she said, 'He seems to think that this case could hit the National Headlines so watch out for Press and TV. Now you know who he was don't you?' Sue had to admit that she had only guessed at his importance so Jean told her about his role as Government adviser and also a little about the conspiracy theories that abounded in Whitehall and elsewhere, namely that a 'group' of like minded politicians and businessmen had effectively been preparing a coup d'etat that had been imminent and now might have been forestalled. Sue kept quiet, then said, 'A motive maybe but was it the motive?'

Constable Blandish 'Castle Historian' (Team B)

Constable Tom Blandish was the first to get going, but not with interviews. He wanted to do a bit of personal research on the group assigned to him, the 'Royalty Group B Royal Crescent Assoc Bath.' The names they had chosen intrigued him. Mediaeval-crusader style they seemed to tie up with the 'Chevalier' name with which he was already familiar. Tom was a bit of an amateur historian. No matter where he went he was always nosing about in archives and dusty old corridors looking for the unexpected. He said that that is what made History so interesting. He was fond of saying that historical enquiry was like scientific enquiry. It required an hypothesis based on the evidence at any one time, but the evidence itself must be capable of absorbing new evidence which itself might modify any prior hypothesis.

Frankly he didn't believe the 'historical hype' (as he put it) surrounding the Chateau. The owners had taken liberties with the Chateau and it's historical record and Tom wanted to find out the truth. He had taken a stroll around the grounds earlier and now he sat in the library leafing through old documents and books.

The Chateau brochure itself gave a potted history in the introduction and this is what it said.

CHATEAU CHEVALIER SOMERSET
The Chateau was built by the 'Knights Templar' in 1200 AD.

Authors note. *After their return from the Holy Land they had built a series of Castles to protect their fragile foothold in the Lebanon. (The most important of these was the 'Krak de Chevaliers' which, as well as being a strongpoint, could actually house a whole village.) Naturally, on their return they duplicated a successful formula here and elsewhere.*

Tom had already observed the many suits of armour that lined the reception areas and corridors as well as the numerous paintings of gallant Knights in armour slaying the unfortunate Saracens. The walls were not without adornment either, with heraldic shields and weapons adorning every corner all giving a distinct impression of a bygone age. To be fair there was a small note at the back of the brochure which stated that the Chateau had 'of course' been modified and modernised over the years whilst remaining true to the 'Templar Tradition' This puzzled Tom even further because he did not know of any Templar 'building' tradition.

In fact, the only 'tradition' linked in most people's minds with the Templars was their claimed protection of the Holy Grail for which they were persecuted so badly. Putting that thought aside for one moment however, he began to compare the Chateau in his mind to two other castles in the vicinity, which seemed to declare their provenance much more openly, one a genuine Castle and the other a 'folly.'

The first of these was Farleigh Hungerford near Trowbridge built from about 1370AD but now a ruin cared for by English Heritage. It's history under the Hungerfords and later owners has been systematically recorded including the fate of Margaret Pole, born at Farleigh in 1473, later Countess of Salisbury. This was the very same lady that Sue had 'played' in the Dillington House drama 'Thy will be done.' some years before.

The second 'Castle' that Tom had in mind was a different kettle of fish altogether. It was 'Eastnor Castle' which sits in beautiful splendour near the Forest of Dean. Like the Chateau it is a most imposing building and, on entry there were, just like the Chateau, suits of armour and heraldic devices everywhere. (no Saracens mind!). The whole atmosphere is one of mediaeval grandeur but, 'surprise, surprise', the brochure proudly proclaims that it was built in 1870 as a rather extravagant 'folly' by the owner at the time. Eastnor was, like the Chateau, also a venue for corporate functions but, unlike the Chateau, it claimed no genuine mediaeval heritage. It was getting late as Tom closed the books and wandered up to his room but he was still bothered, in fact a recurring question kept him awake all night.

'What was behind the 'Templar' tradition espoused by the Castle and was it possible that a threat to it could actually lead to murder?' Finally he could stay awake no longer and he drifted off to sleep, dreaming of Scheherazade and the Arabian nights with a smile. This happy state of affairs was not to last however because he was awake after only a few moments. There was only one thing for it and that was to open up the laptop and Google a bit more history, and this is what he found.

The Merovigians, Templars and Masons

The Templars were the protectors of the ancient royal house known as the Merovigians who claim to still exist in the Stuart-Albany line.

The <u>Merovigians had</u> vied with the Carolingians for power in early mediaeval Europe but were assigned to obscurity by the success of Charlemagne in seizing spiritual as well as temporal power (786-814).

However, the ousted Dynasty and their supporters did not, and do not accept this state of affairs even today. Indeed they might have disappeared altogether, were it not for their extraordinary claim to 'possess and protect' the 'Holy Grail' thought to be the 'Cup of the Last Supper,' the 'Facecloth of the Crucifixion' or even according to some of the more outrageous claims, to be the family 'Bloodline' of Christ.

As long as they maintain this position they can claim to represent the legitimate authority of the Christian Church. It is this belief that they protect today, and it has guaranteed them the enmity of the Catholic Church over the centuries, classing them as 'heretic' along with other sects such as the Cathars and Albigensians.

<u>The Knights Templar</u> were their protectors in the Middle Ages who, despite leading Crusades and building castles throughout the Holy Land such as the 'Krak de Chevaliers' were nonetheless eliminated by the French King Philip1V and Pope Clement 1V in 1307. The Grand Master Jacques de Molay and his followers were lured into a trap in Paris and many were killed. The Order was disbanded and their very substantial properties sequestered by Church and State.

<u>Freemasonry</u> has also been linked to the Templars but the experts disagree about this, because the Order itself was not established in the main until after the year 1717 (in England). Having said that however there are persistent claims that the Runic imagery of the Masons echoes that of the Templars. Evidence is cited from early rune stones such as the Kensington (Minnesota) stone of 1362 and the Larsson papers from Gotland Island in 1449. But, if this is the case, it seems to be at odds with Masonic tradition, which specifically allows any religion that recognises a 'God' of any sort, and not solely a Christian God which of course has always been at the heart of the Templar tradition . . . It may just be the antipathy of the Catholic Church to

both which has brought them together in some circumstances, but many still believe in a deeper connection. XX

Tom put the laptop down with some satisfaction. He liked to be well informed and he liked to be well prepared. He had found out that, if they were so inclined, members of the 'Royal Crescent Assoc' might well wish 'Brig' some harm if he threatened their stewardship of the 'Grail' at Chateau Chevalier, with development plans.

Tuesday. News of attempted murders

Soon after Sue had been briefed on the importance of 'The Brig' she and Jean got a message that they were wanted in the manager's office for an important announcement. When they arrived, the officers from MI5 were already seated. Franks smiled and said, 'We're as puzzled as you are about this Sergeant. We're waiting for Mr Lowrie here to give us the low down. Go ahead Sir, don't keep us waiting in suspense.' He smiled at Lowrie in encouragement and he responded with a sigh. 'As if we didn't have enough trouble,' he said, 'but I must tell you that I've just had two disturbing reports that I think you should all know about.

The first concerns the 'food poisoning' scare last Friday that you may not have heard about yet. Brotherton and Bea Brughel were very ill that evening, and the toxicology report has just come back to us. We have been told that a copy has gone to Police HQ so you'll probably get formally advised very soon. You see it wasn't a bug. No it was arsenic, a very high dose for the 'Brig,' and a lower one for Ms Brughel.

But that's not all. We also have information that Brotherton's Quad Bike was sabotaged. You also may not know that he ran off the road on Saturday during the race. Comanche Bikes of Stroud, who provided the bikes, confirm that the brakes had been sawn through with a very rough hacksaw. They are thinking of suing us, and probably M&B as well. So you see we have three attempts on Brotherton's life. I thought you should know that's all, especially as one was successful.'

It's not surprising that there was a moment's silence before anyone spoke and then it was Franks. 'Well Mr Lowrie, you can see we're all taken aback and now we'll need to look into all three of course. Might we use your office privately for a short while to discuss our approach with that of the local police?' Lowrie said it would be OK, he had other work to attend to anyway and then he left. Sue spoke up straightaway, 'This might make it a more complex case of course but don't let's forget that we are looking for a killer and insofar as the attempts are part of that, we're interested in those too.' 'In other words, business as usual' added Jean.

'Not quite I'm afraid.' responded Franks, 'We have reasons to believe that there is more than one group, person or persons who might have wished him harm. There may be a number of potential killers out there and we'll be following up the links that we have already. However I'm sure we'll work together well. Official secrets allowing of course' he said with his customary smile. Sue and Jean looked at each other and said, 'Right' simultaneously. This somewhat disguised the fact that both women were determined that their enquiries should take priority 'official secrets' or not. 'Let's call the team together now' said Sue, 'they ought to be in the know in case some of the facts add up don't you think?' Jean agreed at once but Franks paused before he nodded his head. 'OK then but please tell them to keep 'stum' and not talk to the Press won't you?' he said, 'This could be a very delicate matter and we could all get our fingers burnt. It's my understanding that the Home Secretary is taking a keen interest in all this.'

Jean and Sue got up to leave, 'You can rely on our discretion Sir.' said Jean as they left the room and then, under her breath to Sue, 'The phrase grandmothers and eggs comes to mind doesn't it Sue?' They both laughed as they set off down the corridor to the Hall. But Franks had been right in one respect. One or two journalists had already got wind of a 'story' and were waiting to question them. 'What's this all about?' shouted one as they walked in. 'Who was this Brotherton?' shouted another. 'Have you made an arrest?' added a third.

Sue walked to her desk and put her hand up for quiet. 'We'll be issuing a statement very shortly,' she said, 'and we'll keep you updated as we make progress. We'll try to hold a News conference regularly but in the meantime we request that you all leave the Chateau grounds. As you know it is still the scene of a crime and evidence could be disturbed. You'll be invited to the Chateau in due course but please do not wander in the grounds. I hope that's clear. Any questions?' There was much mumbling and then one dissenting voice, 'Mike Romsey from the Bath Chronicle. Does this mean we have a Police State already then?' he said. Once again there were murmurs from the other journalists, but Sue was tactful, 'Just doing our job Sir.' she said with a smile, 'Any more?'

By mid afternoon interviews were well under way, except for Toms' Team B because he had taken time out to do some research. Meanwhile Kath Hartley had arrived and had begun her questioning of Team D completing her task with a report by 10pm. This was the report.

Interviews

Team D report (Community Workers)
PC Kath Hartley

I interviewed all members of the team separately, then in two's and then all together to try to flush out any inconsistencies or embarrassments. It soon became obvious that they were there with some malicious intent toward Brotherton. Although they called themselves the 'Community Workers Group,' they are in fact a hard line split from the more formalised Trotskyite opposition to the government. They didn't deny this but said that they were there just to keep an eye on him and maybe gain some inside information. I got the impression that it was Anne Day who was the leader of group, quiet and resourceful, one could imagine a ruthless streak, but if she had been involved it would probably have been as an organiser not a perpetrator. Jan Tooley had been seen in close conversation with him at the Ball and maybe that was a lead of sorts. Was she looking for weaknesses perhaps? But in short they all had opportunity and motive. However perhaps only Wilf Woodside had the skills to cripple a Quad Bike and shoot straight. He had been in the Royal Engineers. I see Brian Martin as the weak link in their group. He seemed altogether more idealistic than practical and I intend to interview him again to maybe get some insight on the others. Sgd PC Kath Hartley

Team C (Dublin College)

'Charlie' Charlesworth had been buzzing around Kath since she arrived but had to be satisfied with her response when he cornered her in the Great Hall. 'Look Charlie, we've a job to do here and I haven't got time to mess about and nor have you. I'll have a drink with you, one mind, when it's all over and not before. OK?' Not OK thought Charlie but he had to make the most of it. He'd do a good job on Team C and she'd be impressed and so would the Sergeant and Inspector. Let's see, I think I'll call Bea Brughel first. She got poisoned on that first day so is there something she can tell me about that I wonder.

Bea Brughel

Charlie began, 'Hello Ms Brughel, my name's Constable Charlesworth and I'd just like to ask you a few questions about last weekend. Is that all right with you?' She nodded. 'Now, what did you make of the poisoning incident on Friday/' he went on, but she stopped him there and then. 'What poisoning are you talking about. Do you mean food poisoning? Yes I was quite ill with it.' Charlie paused for some effect before he spoke again. 'No. Arsenic poisoning. You and Brotherton were given arsenic on Friday. Your small dose was hardly threatening but his was.'

She went very pale and he thought that she would faint. 'They wouldn't' she muttered under her breath. 'Can you say that again Ms Brughel, did you say 'they wouldn't.' Who wouldn't do what?' She composed herself and complained that she felt a migraine coming on and could he see her later. 'I'm afraid I'm babbling.' she said, 'I just need to lie down for awhile, please excuse me. Thank you.' And she was gone. Charlie felt excited if thwarted. 'They', she had said,' they' her own team (?) had poisoned her in order to kill Brotherton and cover their tracks. Yes that's what it meant he was sure of it. He had solved the case already and wanted to tell Kath and everyone else at once, but he was a good police officer and he wanted to nail one, two or all of the other three red handed if he could. It was time to call Lifferty who seemed to be their leader.

Sean Lifferty

Sean Lifferty was in his late fifties, slightly gnarled at the edges but with a ready smile typical of the Irish. 'So how can I help the 'polizei' he began with a grin. Charlie smiled, 'Well, first of all, can you tell me why the Dublin College of Tourism, as you call it, has come all this way to study management. I should tell you that I've checked with the Irish Tourist board and they've never heard of you, so who are you and what are you doing here?' The 'Old Blarney' seemed to have deserted Lifferty for a moment but then he was ready. 'To be sure,' he said, 'no, we're not an official college, we're just a group interested in promoting Ireland in whatever way we can, be it for ordinary travellers or for those who want to know a bit more about our History and Politics. Historical and Political Tourism, that's us.' Charlie looked at him closely and then said, 'Would you say that your group is involved in any way in current Politics then, or do you concentrate on O'Neill, Cromwell or the Battle of the Boyne?'

'You know your history,' replied Lifferty, 'no to be truthful we are involved in current affairs as well. How could one not be as a Republican Irishman? But we're spectators not murderers you see that's what we are. To be fair we wouldn't be against a warning, if you get my meaning. Or a punishment, say for 'activities against the Irish people.' You'll find out soon enough that Brotherton commanded a unit of the SAS on Bloody Sunday and he must have thought we'd forgotten about it. But no we never forget and I wouldn't criticize someone who wanted to punish him for it.' Charlie was quite surprised by his frankness, 'Do you have someone in mind then?' he asked. 'No, not especially, you're the policeman aren't you?' came the reply. 'All I can say is that I had nothing to do with any of it. You'll have to ask the others for their stories.' Charlie realised that he would get no more out of Lifferty so he thanked him after asking for a detailed record of his movements on the days in question. This was more to make comparisons with other peoples' stories than to implicate him. To be honest each day had been so fluid, anyone could have been anywhere at any one time and Charlie knew that he would depend on contradictions to make headway.

Tam Collins and Maggie O'Meara

Charlie interviewed these two together working on his theory that there may be some hesitation or apparent disagreement in their stories, maybe even some anxiety but they were both as 'cool as cucumbers' and their stories dove tailed precisely, maybe too much so Charlie thought. Anyway with nothing doing there he thanked them, resolving to apply gentle pressure to Bea Brughel later. Then he had a brainwave. He would ask the Sergeant to give permission for Kath to approach her informally, maybe at tea time on the patio thus putting her at ease and more likely to respond. 'If the Sarge agrees,' he thought, 'I'll be well in with her and also with Kath. Softly softly catchee monkee Inspector Chan.' He added to himself. Chan was his idol, and Charlie had tried to develop an oriental inscrutable demeanour, usually before a mirror in his bedroom, but Kath had enjoyed the joke before. He had called her 'Losie Lee' and hoped to do so again. Mind you, he'd tried that tack with a number of girls before including the Sarge when she was a constable. Without wasting time he found Sue at her desk and gave her his proposition and as he had thought she was very impressed. 'Good thinking Charlie,' she said, 'I'll have a word with Kath, keep on with the others, you know, just going over things, just to get the record straight, that sort of thing and keep well away from Ms Brughal please, and well done Charlie.' Now all he had to do was to sit back and wait for Kath to come running into his arms, he thought, or maybe not quite yet.

It was teatime and as usual Bea Brughel sat alone on the patio. One might say that she was' in the group' but not 'of the group' and this benefited Kath as she approached. 'On you own today then?' she said, 'mind if I sit?' Bea looked quite pleased and said, 'Yes, of course. Aren't you with the police?' 'Yes' Kath replied, 'but not on your patch. Mine's quite boring really, delegates learning about community service or something. I like to get away from police talk, shop as they call it. Tell me are you actually from Dublin? I spent a magic week there with my ex boyfriend a few years back.' Bea replied with enthusiasm. Yes she lived in Dublin and looked after her widowed mother. This was supposed to have been a holiday this year and now it had all gone wrong. A tear came into her eye and Kath moved closer to hold her hand. 'Tell me.' she said, 'Tell me what's gone wrong and why you're so upset.' 'Can I talk to you really, can I? I'd feel much better if I could. Can I?' 'Of course you can,' said Kath, 'but let's meet quietly in the Library, say at 4 o'clock. You can tell me more then. Will that be all right?' 'Yes, Yes, four's fine. See you then.' and with that Bea got up and walked away waving to her team colleagues who were all seated at another table as she did so.

Team A Interviews (Garvey Lonsdale)

Sue had much on her mind with the general organization necessary such as liaison with MI5, keeping the Press at bay and keeping in touch with Sergeant Tompkins as his men scoured the scene of the shooting trying not to trip over MI5 staff doing the same thing. She had also agreed to check out the other guests who had been at the hotel that weekend, some of whom had gone home by now. This left the M&B and Hotel staff to be considered and she had asked Jean Curtis for some help on this.

Tom Spooner.

Nonetheless she had said that she would deal with Brotherton's own team although she thought it unlikely that they were involved. After all, why wait for a weekend away when there must have been many other opportunities if any person in the team was looking for one. She tackled Tom Spooner first, a young man somewhat out of his depth in the world of high finance she thought and, according to reports, a little too randy for his own good. Yes he had fallen out with the Brig over his 'irresponsible' behaviour but that was as far as it went. Sue felt that he was telling the truth and was unlikely to shed any light on the case but she also knew that a casual conversation may sometimes yield unexpected results. She decided to put him at his ease and 'fish'.

'I'm tired Tom,' she said, 'do you mind if we have a coffee in the Library away from all this?' 'No, not at all,' he replied, 'Good idea, let's have a bit of a break.' But 'Break' wasn't what Sue had in mind, no, let's try again; fish, trawl, entice, persuade, remind; these were the items on her agenda. 'Good, here we are,' she said with a twinkle in her eye. 'I'll pick up the coffee tray you sit down over there and take your jacket off. It's really hot in here.' He sat down on the comfy leather settee as she suggested and removed his jacket with a flourish. ('Mmmm is it true what they say about Policewomen?' he thought to himself.) Sue knew that she was an attractive woman and that Tom seemed to be, well, a bit susceptible to female charms so she sat at the other end of the settee with her legs crossed demurely. 'Will you pour please Tom, no sugar for me, I have to look after my figure don't I?' He looked at her and looked again as her white blouse revealed curves under her jacket, 'I wouldn't say so, no I wouldn't. You look just right to me.' She smiled 'Well Tom I do believe that's the nicest thing anyone's told me for a long time. Still, no sugar please.' They drank coffee and chatted for a while and then Sue thought it was time too 'seed' the pond. 'Tell me Tom, what was the Brig really like? I mean I know that he was your boss and all that but you must have heard something about him mustn't you, sports, army, social life, family?' Tom was keen to please and had already edged a little along the red shiny leather settee toward her.

'Well, as a matter of fact I do know a lot about him but it goes way back. I grew up in Datchet and went out with his daughter Jenny when we were at school together. We were kids, about fifteen I suppose and we had just started going out. I know that she liked me but she wouldn't let me kiss or touch her. This went on for quite awhile until I got a bit fed up and tried to press close. She pushed me away with a cry that I hope I'll never hear again, 'Don't, don't,' she cried out, 'Filthy, Filthy just like Him!' and with that, she ran away sobbing. I didn't see her again, heard she'd been sent to a 'finishing school' in France, but I often wondered whom she had meant by 'Him'. Soon after Brotherton offered me a job.'

Tom had now edged even close but Sue didn't move. She hadn't finished with him yet. 'Well Tom that's quite a story, tell me, what do you think happened back then?' By now he was emboldened and placed his hand on hers in a confidential way, 'You can't get me like that,' he said, 'but to tell you the truth I think I ran away from the possibilities and I suppose I put them to the back of my mind.' Sue withdrew her hand gently taking time to pat Tom's gently (good dog?). 'Thanks Tom you've been very helpful and very nice. Let's wait til this case is over before we try any more of that.' she said as she got up to leave. 'I may have to see you again soon so don't run away will you?' Tom nodded and slumped back in the settee. 'Women!' he thought to him self, 'Why do I bother?' Sue however was on her way, under sail, small fish caught now let's go after the Big Fish. Could Brotherton have been involved in 'something' back then and if so, had it been covered up? Next up were Anne and Deidre.

Anne Lomax and Deidre Spencer

Sue decided to interview the two women together in order to find out more about the Brig himself, as a person and as a leader. She began, 'I'm sure you are both very upset about the tragedy this weekend and I'll try not to keep you long, but please, I do need to know more about the Brig and who his enemies might be. Can you help me?' Anne spoke first, 'When you knew him,' she said, 'you knew that he could be the most generous man on earth. It must have been a political thing. He certainly made enemies there although of course we only knew of his business affairs.' Sue waited and looked at Deidre expectantly. 'Generous yes but kind also so kind and loving, I mean kind and caring. I do know that there were those who opposed some of Garvey Lonsdales development plans including, strangely enough, this place here, the Chateau. He had actually been warned off anonymously last year you know.' Sue had noticed some anxious glances but decided to say nothing for the time being. She had also noted Deidre's 'Freudian Slip', when she changed 'loving' to 'caring' in an instant. Sue was always on the look out for those little nuances that made all the difference. Here there were plenty but what to make of them? She decided to thank them for their trouble and immediately call Tom Spooner back. He was an insider and might well know what was going on if anything.

Tom-again!

'Thanks for coming Tom.' she said, 'Now there is nothing for you to worry about but I think that you can help me, in confidence of course. Tell me Tom, was Deidre having an affair with the Brig?' Tom paused for a moment before he replied. 'They both were.' he said, 'sometimes separately and sometimes together if you see what I mean. That's partly what this weekend would have been about if he hadn't got sick on the Friday. I imagine that Saturday night was a real steamer in his room. Sorry, am I shocking you?' No. Sue assured him, she was not shocked. But she was, a bit anyway. 'So were they both equal in this ménage a trois. I mean whom did he prefer generally in your opinion.' she said.

'I can't say for sure but Deidre told me that he couldn't wait to get away from his wife and all this, and settle in Provence with her. Most unlikely in my view but she believed it because she wanted to. I heard that Anne had threatened to tell his wife about the three of them if he did so. But that proves one thing doesn't it? They wouldn't want to kill the 'golden goose 'would they?' Sue was impressed at his logical thinking, perhaps she had misjudged him and then it struck her, the most important question of all. 'Well Tom, do you think that Mrs Brotherton had any idea about all this. Do you think that Anne may have already told her perhaps or she just 'knew' as wives usually do? And do you think that she knew what happened with Jenny and chose not to say anything?' Tom thought for a moment before he replied. 'All I can say is, I'm not a woman. You work it out.' Sue smiled and said, 'Yes you're right Tom I'll have a word with my woman's intuition and see what she comes up with. Thanks anyway.'

Sue had already mentally added another suspect to her list but surely this would be a real outsider compared to the others, but motive. 'Yes'.

By mid evening Constable Tom Blandish felt ready to take on Team B having done a copious amount of research about them. He was not one to be caught out easily so he was confident that he would make progress when he asked Simon Stewart to join him in the Great Hall.

Team B Interiew (Bath 'Royalty')

'I might as well tell you Mr Stewart,' he began, 'that I know all about your links with the Chateau and your ancient Merovigian claims. I know therefore that you would be very hostile to any plan to develop this site, which has special significance for you. So tell me, what plans did you have for Mr Brotherton when you arrived and how has it worked out for you?' Stewart laughed, 'Well, that's a fine start and good evening to you too. Yes, we are proud of our heritage and the role that our safe houses bring to our sacred objects, but murder? No Sir. I suppose though that we were here this week as sort of guardians, together with the Chateau management of course. Having said that we did warn Brotherton off last year and maybe he did need a reminder. But not murder. No Sir.'

Tom felt he was getting somewhere so he pursued his questioning. 'So you did intend to give him a warning, maybe even a scare then but it all went wrong and he ended up dead, that's it isn't it?' Stewart now stopped and looked seriously at Tom, 'You can bring charges if you like but I'm saying no more and nor will any of my team. In fact I've told them not to talk to you without caution. Is that clear?' Tom was taken aback and tried to retrieve the situation but it was too late. Stewart was gone.

Bea goes missing

Kath went to the Library at four o'clock as arranged to meet Bea Brughel but by five there was no sign. Furthermore she did not appear for dinner and Kath began to get worried. Sue agreed that they should ask her team partners and also the management if anything was known of her movements that afternoon but no one could shed any light on the subject.

Team C was Charlie's responsibility so he was the first to suggest that they tried her room and, with the manager's permission, gain access to she if she was there, hurt or something, but she was not. Everything else was there Charlie noted. 'She can't have gone far' he said, 'Look, her clothes are still hanging up and her case is still there. She might have fallen during a long walk, or worse, been 'got at' by her so called friends. In any case we need a search party out there at once. We may have left it too late as it is.' But Sue was carefully pacing the room, looking carefully here and there, under the bed and even in the laundry basket. Then she stopped and turned to Charlie. 'Do you have a handbag Charlie?' she said in a flat monotone. 'No Sarge I don't. You know I don't.' he replied feeling rather ruffled. 'Well, she does, all women do and it's not here is it, money, cosmetics, passport, all gone. Why Charlie? Why?' The penny had finally dropped. 'Sorry Sarge' he said, 'I suppose it means that she's run away for some reason or other and I think we all know why. She didn't feel safe talking to us so she left.' Charlie's perception had been correct but his tendency to rush things had left him looking foolish. There would be no kisses from Kath just yet. Sue decided to leave it at that for now but to be sure she would ask Sergeant Tompkins, still in the grounds, to keep an eye out. Not for a suicide because who needs a handbag for that, but just to confirm no foul play on the premises. Meanwhile she would put out an APB to Airports and the Irish ferries. 'That's all we can do today' she said, 'let's all go home and get a good night's sleep.'

Sue's Dreams and Realities

It was 11 pm by the time Sue got in and fortunately Chrissie was already in bed, this time without a partner, so she flopped thankfully on her bed and drifted into sleep. Then she was awake with a start then asleep again, a deep, deep dreaming sleep this time. She was standing by a door to a luxury bedroom and there were three figures on the bed. A little girl sat on a wicker chair in the corner of the room. She couldn't see very well so she edged closer. It was the Brig with two naked girls sprawled across him and they were moving in some kind of rhythmic pattern that she felt bound to follow. And then she was on the bed naked, she was one of them and it looked like being her turn when she suddenly awoke in a cold sweat. She made a dash for the bathroom and under a cold shower. She felt soiled even though it was just a dream.

'Sleep well? Nice dreams?' said Chrissie in the morning. 'You can say that again.' replied Sue. "Well I heard you murmuring something in the night, at least I think I did.' said Chrissie 'Well that makes a change, it's usually the other way round nest ce pas?' said Sue. Both girls burst into laughter and then Chrissie spoke again. 'Don't forget it's your 30th today and we're having a party here tonight?' 'Would you let me? Sue replied.

As she drove to the Chateau that morning she was restless. Maybe it was lack of sleep or that very disturbing dream or both but she had made up her mind to see Martin the minute she got in. It was no good putting it off any longer it just had to be done. She found him alone in the M&B office, 'Hello stranger,' she began, 'Have you been avoiding me?' He looked up at her rather ruefully from his desk. 'Yes I suppose I have. Sorry. I thought it might be best but now I'm not so sure,' Sue suddenly felt a tremor through her body as she heard his gentle voice again and when she spoke it was with a tremor that she could not control. 'Well I'm sorry too, but I'm sure that we both have work to do now. No doubt we'll see each other from time to time, won't we?'

She moved toward the door but Martin barred the way and Sue couldn't help herself falling into his arms as he held them out for her, cradling her with such comfort as he used to do. 'Sue Sue,' he said, 'what a fool I've been, please forgive me.

I still love you, I'm sure that you know that I do.' She trembled in his arms, 'Kiss me Martin. Kiss me now. Yes, like that, now hold me tight, very tight.' And this is how they remained for quite a few moments until there was a tap on the door and Pam Tockington walked in, 'Oh I see you know each other.' she said. Sue and Martin did not move but, almost in unison, they said, 'Well we do now!' At which all three burst into laughter causing some amusement also to Mr Franks of MI5 as he passed the door.' Sue said 'Shush. Careless talk and kisses costs lives you know.'

Wednesday. That's the ticket Charlie!

Sue was back at the Chateau early having called a 'Round Robin' meeting for all officers at 10am but at first she had arranged to meet up with the Inspector Jean Curtis to see how M&B and Chateau staff had responded to questioning. Like Sue, Jean was a very conscientious officer but she had little to report. 'It's like this Sue,' she began, 'nearly everyone had opportunity and many did have a motive. This 'Brig' was not a very popular man as you've probably found out for yourself. But as to murder, well, I would only grade that possibility at less than 10%. I've excluded M&B entirely. They're the only ones with no motive as far as I can see. Lowrie and his staff at the Chateau were not fond of Brotherton and his plans for redevelopment, but a scandal on their own doorstep? I don't think so. Brotherton's 'men in dark suits'? Well, who knows but remember they weren't here until Sunday, ruling them out of poison and Quad bike although that doesn't rule them out for Monday of course. I've checked on all the other guests including Shiekh Abdullah and his entourage, or should I say, harem. Nothing doing there I'm sure of it and his staff occupied a whole wing. There was a Rev Tyler from Devizes with his wife. They've gone home but local police advise me they are the salt of the earth. No Sue, the killer is one of the 'team members' but which one only you can tell, or maybe God! Before I wind up, and I'm sure you've thought of this, it's my instinct that we have three uncoordinated attempts by three different person or persons unknown with differing agendas. Not helpful I know but that's how I see it.'

Sue was inclined to agree and so was MI5 whom she consulted before her 10am meeting. Franks was blunt. 'It seems to me,' he said, 'that interests of National Security have only been threatened by Team D the so called 'Community Workers Group.' We've had our eye on them for some time and of course you can never dismiss radical Irish groups. We know about them as well. Be sure we'll be keeping an eye on both but as to the murder, that's 'your patch' didn't you say?' He was smiling that irritating smile of his but Sue would not be drawn. 'Yes sir it is and we have a number of promising leads.' she said. Now Franks laughed out loud. 'Before I joined MI5 I was in the Met you know and 'promising leads' was code for 'getting nowhere' then.

Nothing changes does it?' Sue smiled graciously but was seething inside at his smug inference. 'We'll keep you informed Sir.' she said. 'I've called a Press conference for 2pm but I'd be grateful if you'd leave to us, the local Plod. I think we can manage that.' Franks agreed and said they would not attend.

At 10 am the police team all gathered in the Great Hall and one by one they made their reports. Kath said that she had had one outstanding lead in Brian Martin (TeamD) who she thought might be a weak link but a further interview had revealed nothing new. There had been no sign of Bea Brughel since she went missing and this was important because she might still have some incriminating evidence against her own team(C). Teams A and B were hardly clean but neither were they specifically implicated in any way and nor were other personnel or guests.

'Well,' said Sue, 'thank you all for your input. Needless to say we can't leave it like this. We'll just have to go round again looking out for those little inconsistencies and weaknesses that transpire from time to time. As you know we have a Press conference at 2 pm. Please leave it to me and don't be drawn to answer any questions. Is that clear? Thank you but before we go I've asked Sergeant Tompkins to tell us how his search at the scene of the crime has been going. He's already told me that the fatal bullet was from a pistol, not a rifle, and there was only one cartridge near the body. In other words 'The Brig' knew his killer, as there were also powder marks on his tunic. This could still point to any of our suspects so we're not much further forward yet. Anything to add Sergeant?'

Tompkins was a career policeman. Thirty years in the force and now likely to face redundancy he was and always had been an excellent officer. He had refused a 'safe' office job preferring to be out there 'where the villains are' he would say. He now spoke carefully and deliberately, 'Thank you Sue,' he began, 'No there's not much more except this travel voucher and ticket that we found in the bushes today. It's in Brotherton's name as you can see. He must have dropped it during the Paint Ball exercise. Nothing else new I'm afraid.' Sue took the voucher and placed it in an evidence bag. 'Thanks Sarge' she said. 'Now does anyone else have any questions?'

No one spoke for a while but then Charlie raised a tentative hand. He didn't want to feel like a fool again but he did have a question, or rather, an observation. 'Sorry Sarge,' he said apologetically, 'but didn't Brotherton get here by car?'

There was a stunned silence in the room and then other voices clamoured in, 'Yes, by car, by car, that Lexus in the car park, yes I saw him . . . .' Sue looked at Jean and gradually it dawned on her, it wasn't Mr Brotherton at all but Mrs Brotherton who had travelled by train to the Chateau. She opened the evidence pouch again, yes it only said 'Brotherton' and was for travel on the Monday, the day of the killing when the 'Brig' had been there for three days. 'Well, well well' she exclaimed, 'Well done Sarge and Charlie. Listen everyone. I'm sure that the ticket was for Mrs Brotherton from Windsor to Bath on Monday. She's our killer I'm sure of it, I'd already found out that the 'Brig' was having affairs but I hadn't figured it had come to this. There could be no other reason for her to be here without announcing her arrival or departure. Obviously she had to buy another ticket for the journey back and we can check on that. There can't be too many Bath to Windsors on any one day. What a relief!

Of course that wouldn't account for the attempts on Friday and Saturday but we could speculate 'til kingdom come about those. I can't wait to see Franks' face when he finds out but he won't, not yet anyway, nor will the Press until we've seen Mrs Brotherton and I'll arrange that now with the Windsor police. Well done. Let's give ourselves a round of applause!'

They did for quite a few moments and Charlie used his new-found approval to sidle up to Kath. 'What a turn up.' he said almost expecting the usual rebuff, but no, she pulled him close and whispered in his ear, 'Well done Charlie Chan, Losie Lee velly implessed.' And what's more there was a kiss on the cheek before she ran off. Charlie was back!

The news conference went off without a hitch. Sue was able to say, with some truth now, that they were 'following important leads and making real progress'. She was also able to circumvent the odd question about specifics with the reassurance that they would be called back in a couple of days with more details. 'The pack' went off muttering and Sue breathed a sigh of relief as they left.

A car was waiting outside reception. It was an unmarked police car that would take Sue and Charlie to Datchet. She had decided to take Charlie partly as a reward for his perseverance but also because she felt that four legs would be better than two if there had to be a local search. She needn't have worried. They met up with a Police Sergeant, Madge Drew, at Windsor and made their way to Datchet. It was getting dark and it was raining as they knocked on the door of 'Brittania' a formidable looking mock Tudor residence at 23 Castle Street. The door was opened by a very striking looking woman in her late fifties. She was dressed quite formally in a black suit and white blouse.

Sue spoke first holding out her warrant card, 'Good evening,' she said, 'My name's Sergeant Parker from Bath and these are my colleagues. May we come in please?' 'Yes of course, I'm Lucy Brotherton and I've been expecting you.' she said, 'mind the case in the Hall. As you can see I am quite prepared but do let's have tea first, or would you prefer coffee? Come in and take a seat in the dining room won't you.' She went into the kitchen and soon reappeared with a tray of drinks and biscuits. 'There you are,' she said, 'help yourselves. It must have been a long journey.' She paused and folded her hands neatly in her lap holding a white hankie with which she brushed the occasional tear from her eyes. 'I don't expect you to understand of course but I just had to do something this time. I'd overlooked so much in the past, and I shouldn't have done you know, I shouldn't have done. My daughter you see . . .' she continued, but Sue interrupted and said, 'Don't say anymore just yet Mrs Brotherton, we may know something about that already but let's leave it until you make your formal statement at the station shall we?' From then on it was too easy to be true. Lucy Brotherton admitted everything under caution and there was little left for them to do but to take her to Windsor Police Station for the night and a potential hearing in the morning. As they left she held out her hand and said, 'Thank you Sergeant you've been very kind. Goodbye.'

Sue was moved and had to choke back a tear, 'Good luck Lucy.' she said thinking back in her own mind as to how the case had gone. It had just seemed so obvious that there were those at the Chateau who wanted to punish him for his past actions, or to stop him from future ones. And she remembered talking to Franks of MI5 when she had questioned whether the security issues were 'the' motive. Everyone was looking for 'a' motive but it turned out that Lucy Brotherton had more than one. 'Why didn't I see that earlier?' she thought, 'Why hadn't I remembered that human nature is a very fragile balancing act in which there often seems to be a 'last straw' a 'tipping point' after which all bets are off.

When that point is reached no amount of rational argument can prevail. You might say that the 'die is cast,' and any act, including murder, is easily justified, almost celebrated as a kind of inevitable catharsis. People in that position are 'driven,' and in retrospect there hadn't been signs of that in the other suspects. If Mrs Brotherton had been at the Chateau I might have spotted that she neither displayed a guilty conscience, nor a demeanour of indifference. I remember now that that was at the core of 'Bath Buns' case as well, and I'll have to be a bit more wary next time.'

As they drove home Sue was quiet in her thoughts and Charlie knew better than to intrude.

They were soon home and 'Oh Gosh!' thought Sue, 'I've got to change. I've got a Party to go to and it's not just any old party. It's my 30th and I've asked Martin to come and to stay over. That'll teach Chrissie to hold the 'love limelight'. 'Get your skates on Parker,' she whispered to herself, remembering Martin's words at the St Pierre Park Hotel last year. It was going to be all right this time. She just knew it was. She wasn't going to give history any chance to repeat itself. She had her man at last.

And she still had handcuffs if he resisted.

FIN

PART 3.
TROUBLESOME TALK AT
RIVER WALK

Summary

You may remember Sue Parker as a Police Constable and Sergeant involved in two cases set in Bath, namely the 'Bath Buns at Sally Lunns' affair and the case of 'Croquet at Chateau Chevalier.' Now she had been temporarily transferred to Frome as Acting Inspector and as usual she was determined to make a success of it, and her life generally. Her latest romance with Martin had not worked out and work was taking priority again. She had not been at her new desk for long however when a very strange, seemingly motiveless case came to her attention. Who could possibly wish to harm an old lady in Frome? Surely the answer would be simple and local, but not a bit of it as once more Sue was propelled headlong into a world of International intrigue and murder.

Sue Parker (Sue hasn't given up on love yet. Or has she?)
Madeleine is found dead in the passenger seat.
A Handbag? (A lady never forgets her handbag does she?)
Friends and Relatives (The police get busy with interviews)
The Bowls Club (The Merclots make an effort to join in.)
The Church (They are Catholics in non-conformist Frome)
The Conservative Club (Could sainthood be in order?'
The Theatres (They help out whenever they can)
How to make bowls boring (You just have to ask the Chairman)
Bruce gets a move and Sue gets a date.
Polonium 210 (Madeleine is found to have poison in her blood.)
The Buck (Sue gets a promise in a country pub)
MI5 & a Russian trade delegation. (Background chatter)
Weymouth (Sue thinks that she is followed)
Rats in the Belfry! (Sue confronts her worst fears)
From here to eternity?(Chesil Beach and a French Lieutenant)
The Diaries 1 (Madeleine begins her story)
The Spanish Civil War (Paris, Poum and Colonel Lopez)
The Intruder (The man wore a dark coat and leather gloves)
The Diaries 2 (Bruce helps out)
WW2 The Resistance (Lopez and Tawney are rivals)
The Diaries 3 (Sue is warned about her safety)
The Diaries 4 (Madeleine reviews her life and faith)
Weymouth revisited (Panhard Pods are the vital clue)
The Yarkov papers (A communist cell is revealed)
A Spy Ring in Frome?
Love and poison (Go together with smoke and mirrors)
Eros or Venus? (Sue gets flowers and a proposal)

Sue Parker

Sue Parker was now 'Acting' Inspector assigned to Frome Police Station. Frome is a pretty market town about 12 miles from Bath but, as Sue liked to be close to her work, she had moved to the rather pleasant village of Bell Dinham. No shared flat this time, no boy friend and no pets, rather isolated in fact but close to work, and to the excellent local pub the 'Buck'. Superintendent Masterson was very affable, one of the old school, one might say, and he was very welcoming as was his wife Madge who was a Local Councillor. Sue was given a staff of 4. 'Cutbacks, cutbacks,' said the Super, 'but they're all good men, oh and women of course.' 'Didn't I hear that 'afterthought' back in Bath with Inspector Lockhart.' thought Sue, 'So much for an enlightened 'modern' police force. I'm going to have to make my mark as soon as possible so they can see what a woman is capable of. I hope I get a simple case soon'

A death in the family

As it happened she got an opportunity to do impress the 'Super' sooner than she expected when the team were called to a 'sudden death' just outside Frome at a place called River Walk just a few yards from the riverbank. It was not in her nature to try to impress but she knew that it was important to get a good start, and this seemed like an easy open and shut case. She couldn't have been more wrong. With hindsight she might have made a simple diagnosis, 'nothing suspicious' perhaps and this in itself might lead forensics to settle for 'death by natural causes', but no, there was something not quite right, she knew it, but not what it was. This was her strength, although it could be a weakness at times, especially with the opposite sex. She just would not let go, 'She's got a bee in her bonnet' her mum used to say and it was quite true. Sue was indomitable. This time it was all about a handbag. What had happened to that?

The person who had been found dead was a Mrs (or Madame) Merclot, a 92 year old French lady who lived there at a small farmstead called 'Volets Bleus', (meaning French shutters). She had been found, seated in the passenger seat of her car by her husband. The car was still in the garage with the keys in the ignition. Her husband said that she often went out to the car prior to a shopping trip and waited for their driver Bernard.

Actually it wasn't a purpose made garage but one of four sheds without doors all connected in a row at the back of the house. Between the house and the sheds was a large gravel space with lavender and sunflower pots as well as a couple of rusty old bicycles. Perhaps the Merclots might have an allotment somewhere. They

129

obviously sold fruit and vegetables because two of the other sheds were full of boxed and unboxed potatoes, Brussels sprouts, apples and other items.

In the last shed stood an ancient French Panhard van with the name **MERCLOT** / Marchand (greengrocer)Clement Avenue **BOULOGNE** on the side. Mr Merclot had told the police on the phone that his wife had planned to go shopping but, when the car didn't leave the garage for some time he realised that their driver was late so he went down to see if she was all right. He said that he thought that she was asleep, as she seemed 'really peaceful' but when he tried to wake her she had just slumped off the seat and he could do no more.

An ambulance and squad car had arrived within minutes and, because she was new, Sue had decided to go with the Sergeant and Constable who attended the scene. There was some debate as to whether the body should be moved before a forensic team arrived, and Sue made a decision that nothing should be touched until some preliminary and exploratory work was done. She could see that her colleagues thought that she was being overcautious but she made a joke of it, 'Well you can't shut the garage door after the car has bolted,' she said. They all had a bit of a laugh and it eased the tension somewhat. 'Heart attack probably,' said Sergeant Capstan, 'but I suppose it's best to wait as you say Ma'am.' Bruce Capstan was one of those who had been bye-passed with Sue's appointment but actually he was not one to hold grudges. He was a 'nice bloke' everyone said. The other officer was a young policewoman, Jenny Harding and she reminded Sue a bit about herself a few years back.

Soon enough a forensic team and the Coroner both arrived on the scene and went about their business whilst Sue had a word with Mr (or Monsieur) Merclot in the house. 'Is there someone who can come over and sit with you?' she asked him. 'Non, No, not really. I have many, how you say, acquaintances here but no one I would call an 'amie'. All our very close friends and family are far away and I would not want to bother these local people. We didn't know many of them that well anyhow.' Sue knew that she would have to be patient, 'You must be very shocked and upset' she said 'Do you mind if the Constable makes us a nice cup of tea?' 'No not at all, bien sur, of course, mais oui that would be very nice.' he replied. Sue gestured for Jenny to 'do the honours' and then continued with a few more questions. 'Tell me Sir. Had your wife been unwell recently? Had she been seeing the doctor for any particular reason?' Merclot paused for a moment and seemed to be choking back a tear. 'Yes,' he said, 'in fact she had only been given a few months to live. The cancer was terminal you see.' Sue gave him a chance to recover and then said, 'I am so sorry, and now all this, I am so sorry.' Just then Sergeant Capstan came into the room and signalled Sue for a word.

'Excusez Moi,' Sue said, 'I must have a word with my sergeant.' She got up and went to the door and after a few minutes returned to Merclot. 'Tell me Sir,' she said, 'Did

Madame usually take a handbag to go shopping?' He replied quickly with the hint of a smile, 'Bien Sur, of course, zat is ze French custom and, I think the English custom also n'est ce pas? Sue nodded, 'Yes indeed it is but there was no bag in the car. Did you perhaps pick it up when you ran in to call the police?' 'No I did not.' he replied, 'That's very strange, well, what do you think has happened to it Inspector?' Actually this was the first time that a person involved in a case had called her 'Inspector' and it felt good. She started to feel a little more 'Inspectorish' and continued, 'Sir, can you describe the handbag? It's vitally important that we get a description out to the local police forces, as it may be that we are looking at a burglary or 'mugging' that has gone horribly wrong. Also there may be credit cards in the bag. The sooner we find it the better. In the meantime please put a 'stop' notice' on all cards that she might have had. Incidentally can you think of anyone else who might wish her harm in any way? For example had she had any rows recently as far as you know?' Merclot looked shocked. 'We have been married for more than fifty years,' he said, looking at her sternly, 'In all those years I have never heard a bad word against her. You can ask anyone. Anyone. Everybody loved her and I loved her so much.' He bent his head and started to cry, 'So much, so much, why did all this have to happen? If only . . .' He paused and could not go on, and Sue could see that she should stop, so she patted his arm to demonstrate her sympathy and said, 'That will be all for now try and get some rest. Give the details to Constable Harding please and we'll just finish off in the garage. Thanks.'

Sue walked back to the garage and as she did so Capstan called her over to the car and the body of Mme Merclot lay beside it being studied by the coroner Dr Grimsby. 'Look Sue,' Capstan said, 'if you're right about a mugging or something, why are there no signs of cuts or bruises. As you can see, none and no sign of a struggle either. Strange don't you think?'

A Handbag?

Sue was puzzled also but, as the coroner was there, she decided to ask his opinion. 'No injuries,' he confirmed, 'probably a weak heart just gave up. We'll know after a proper examination. Nothing more I'm afraid.' Bruce Capstan looked up at Sue, 'Do you think that she just forgot her handbag?' he said. Sue looked at him and laughed, 'Don't know much about women do you Bruce?' This was the first time she had called him Bruce and she wondered if she had been too familiar, but he soon put her mind at rest. 'No Ma'am,' he replied, 'I don't think I do.'

Back at the station Sue arranged for details of the missing handbag to be circulated and for known local 'villains' to be interviewed. She had Tommy and Ronnie to do that. These young men were her 'Eyes on the Street.' Tom Thompson and Ron

Radford seemed to know everyone and everywhere in Frome. Both had trained in Birmingham but recalled to Frome when qualified. They had both been educated at Frome Community College so they were familiar with the rival gang cultures and North versus South elements in the 'criminal' community, but they returned empty handed after a couple of days. It did transpire however that one of the credit cards had been used to draw £250 in cash a day later at Barclays bank in Radstock, a few miles away. Tommy and Ronnie were immediately sent to that area to liase with the local police and Sue had to wait impatiently for information.

Friends and Relations

The next day, with Tommy and Ronnie still out on the street Sue held a meeting with Bruce and Jenny to go through the possibilities of the case. Sue began by asking their opinions before giving her own. She had found this to be a useful tactic to encourage their input and convey the message that she valued their opinion, but of course it could backfire if they got the impression that she was a passive observer rather than a dynamic leader. She began, 'Thanks for being here with me this morning. You know that I'm new here so I'll be depending on you for some time. I want us to work as a team and don't be afraid to come to me with hunches. I'm a great believer in a 'police nose' one which sniffs the air and senses when something doesn't seem quite right. Back in Bath I had an Inspector who kept on about evidence, and that's right of course but don't underestimate intuition, sometimes that leads in the right direction. Of course it can't just be unfounded guesswork, rather a theory based on matters maybe only loosely connected to the case in hand. Sorry if I'm teaching you to 'suck eggs' but what I'm really saying is that I value your opinions as well as your detailed police work. So let's begin. Bruce you're the senior officer so I'll give you first crack.'

Capstan stood up but Sue beckoned him to sit. She wanted this to be an informal but very serious meeting. 'Well Ma'am he began. There are certain things that we know about. Mrs M had a weak heart. Her handbag was missing and it had been used a day later in Radstock. My guess is opportunistic burglary gone wrong. Maybe somebody just routinely stealing veg. Sees Madame slumped in seat and nicks hand bag. We're looking for casual burglars.' Sue was glad that Capstan had widened the case to include a 'no intent' scenario and now turned to Constable Harding, 'What's your first assessment then Jenny?' she asked. Jenny thought for a few moments and then replied, 'Yes Ma'am I think Bruce has got a point but we can't overlook the possibility that she was harmed in some way and it hasn't shown up yet. And in any case we know that she had cancer but nothing was said about a weak heart. That doesn't preclude that possibility of course.' Sue was pleased with this response too and added an hypothesis of her own at this stage. 'Good and thank you both. In addition to those two possibilities there's another one isn't there? For example I'd like to know if the 'dear old lady' had any enemies, or anyone who might wish her harm. M Merclot had said 'Non' but I think we need some backup on that don't you?' They nodded and in the rest of the meeting they set out strategies to deal with all the possibilities discussed so far. Jenny would join Tommy and Ronnie on a widened general local enquiry while Sue and Bruce would divide the Merclot's local friends and clubs to see if they could find out more about the 'famille Merclot' in Frome.

The Merclot's had a living daughter who lived in Boulogne but apart from that there were no relatives in England. After talking to M. Merclot they established that their lives revolved around a few major interests and locations. Sue discussed these with Bruce and they agreed to split them up and then meet up each evening to discuss progress. Bruce would take the Frome Keyford bowls club where they were both members, and incidentally had introduced 'boules' some years back. He would also take the local Conservative Club where, once again, they were both members. Sue would take the Catholic Church, once again in which they were both members and officials in addition. Their other main interest was in both the Mermaid and the Memorial Theatres, often as volunteers. The last item that M. Merlot mentioned was their 'weekend retreat' namely a small flat in Weymouth to which they 'escaped' from time to time. At other times it might be let to afford them some extra income.

The Bowls Club

Bruce had made an appointment to see the Committee and the bowls club and the outcome was that everyone agreed that Mme M was very popular.

'She often made cakes you know,' said Dai Davies the secretary, 'You know those French Fancy ones.' 'And he would always bring a bottle of home made wine for the raffles' added Mo Gentry, the Treasurer. George Everitt, who was chairman said, 'Why don't you come up at the weekend to ask a few of the members. We're playing at home to Frome Trinity.'

This was the first time that Bruce had heard about two bowls clubs in Frome and he was somewhat surprised for such a small town. Everitt explained, 'Many years ago the workers at Butler&Tanner's printing works went on strike and played bowls for their amusement in the public park. There was already a bowls club in Frome, our club 'The Keyford' and this club had many businessmen and managers from Butler&Tanner, so the workers might not have been welcome even if they had wanted to join, so they formed their own club which was called the 'Trinity'. When the Merclots arrived they looked at both and decided that our club was more suitable for them. They're both Conservatives you see.' Bruce didn't see exactly but he got the drift. The Merclots were social climbers.

The Church

Meanwhile Sue made an appointment to see Martin Scott, the Deacon at St Mary's the local Catholic Church. He more or less confirmed the general opinion that the couple were very popular and helpful in the Parish. They had both taken on different roles from time to time, being Eucharistic Ministers, collection counters and hymn book monitors etc.

Sue had not noticed the Church before because it was tucked away behind the hospital and did not even feature in the book that she had borrowed from the library namely 'Frome Past&Present' FromeRotary Club (2000)

In that book there were a number of other churches shown with photographs, namely St John the Baptist, Rook Lane Congregational. Wesley Methodist Church, Christ Church, St Mary's Innox, St Michaels Gare Hill and Mells Church. It seemed that Frome was strongly non-conformist or High Anglican so Sue had wondered why a French Catholic family had ended up there. She confided her interest to the deacon who said that he wasn't sure but he thought that they had been offered work by a well known local figure Field Marshall Tawney on his large Estates near the town after the war.

According to rumour the Merclots had been very active during the war with the French Resistance and Major Mike Tawney (as he was then) had been their British contact. Some said he had been in love with Madeleine but that was taken to be gossip by most people because she and her husband were always together and, not to put too fine a point of it, they were not in the same huntin' shootin' and fishin' class as the General and his wife and six children. And to cap it all the General's family were Methodists continued Scott, and he died last year. She's still alive though, younger you see, probably in her late Sixties now.' 'Well thank you very much indeed Deacon,' said Sue, 'Perhaps I can get back to you if we need some more details. Thank you very much indeed'

Sue wandered back to the Police station, wondering, just wondering mind, if the crafty old General had brought his mistress back and tucked her husband in the 'back seat'. No! Surely not. Or just maybe. 'Am I looking for a love torn geriatric woman in her sixties as a suspect then?' she thought and chuckled to herself, and then burst out laughing, 'Don't be daft Sue,' she chided herself, 'You must have love on the brain.'

The Conservative Cub

Meanwhile Sergeant Bruce Capstan had moved on to the Conservative Club. 'Lovely couple, they'd do anything for anybody.' said the Secretary who happened to be on the bar at the time. 'Isn't that right Mrs Chew, isn't that right Dr Manson?'

Everyone was agreed they were a great couple, often in the club helping out or having a drink. Bruce thanked them and left. 'Looks like sainthood is in order.' he thought to himself.

The Theatres

It was the same story when Sue visited the two Theatres in town. Regulars, supporters, helpers and benefactors, the Merclots were all of these things. Really? And when she caught up with Bruce he told her that his story was very similar. There seemed to be absolutely no grievances against them and no enemies either. 'So where do we go from here?' he said. 'Back to the drawing board, that's where.' she replied. 'Well what about a drink first?' he suggested out of the blue. 'No can do,' she said, 'First of all we're on duty and secondly I don't mix business with pleasure. Sorry.' Bruce looked quite pleased, 'So it would have been a pleasure then?' he said. Sue smiled, 'Maybe, if things were different and I wasn't your boss and we didn't have a case to solve and . . .' 'Stop' he cried out, 'You'll see they might be different sooner than you think.' Now Sue was puzzled, 'What do you mean Bruce?' 'Can't say,' he replied tapping his nose, 'Need to know basis, top security.' They both laughed.

When Sue got home she flopped on her settee and dozed. What had he meant she thought and what if? Now she tossed and turned and couldn't sleep, after all he was single and 'quite' attractive. 'Damn men!' she thought as some of her past loves appeared in her dreams but Bruce was there as well, try as she might to 'dream him out!'

How to make Bowls boring

The next day was Saturday but Bruce was still on duty. He had gone to watch the local 'Derby' between the two Frome bowls clubs and couldn't help finding himself interested and involved, taking sides with Keyford of course. George Everitt, the Chairman whom he had already met made a valiant effort to enrol him in the club and took some time out to explain the basic principles. 'Without complicating it too much,' he said, 'the game can be played in teams, maybe 16 on each side divided into 4 lots of 4 playing on 4 different rinks. Got it?' Bruce nodded so Everitt continued, 'That's just an example but that's how we're playing today. In addition there may be singles, doubles or triples at other times. Got it?

Bruce nodded again. 'Now, the yellow or white ball is about the size of a cricket ball, and the aim of the game is to get as close to this as one can. It's called the 'Jack.' The team that wins the toss will roll the Jack up the Green to a distance that suits them and it then be centralised. Variability in this is called 'long' or 'short' jacks. Got it?'

Bruce was forgetting already but he nodded just the same and the Chairman continued. 'Good, good, now each player may have from 2-4 bowls, or woods as they are sometimes known and each team player plays in a pre agreed sequence against their 'opposite number'

So the game begins with the two players designated to go first, these are called the 'leads'. Team A lead player bowls followed by Team B lead, then it's Number 'Two's' and then Number 'Threes'. The fourth member of each team has stood, so far, at the 'jack end' as Skipper or 'Skip' as it is known. He's there to guide the others and when they are done he has his two woods to bowl. Got it?'

Bruce sighed and wondered if there was much more but he said yes just the same. 'Good' said Everitt, 'When that's all done a count is made regarding the nearest woods to the Jack. The nearest wood is called 'The Shot' and if that wood is followed in closeness by other woods from the same team they are counted as well, so it may be 1 shot only or maybe 2 shots or 3 or 4 depending on the closest of the other team's woods. That's all there is to it really. We 'roll up' or practice on a Tuesday afternoon. Do try and come along.' Bruce had almost forgotten why he was there and, to be quite honest, he felt like a cup of tea.

Fortunately it was teatime and he did get a chance to talk to some of the members. 'Used to be a good player did Claude, reliable too, usually skip. Madeleine used to be lead, very accurate.' This wasn't really what Bruce was after, but eventually some members spoke about her and how they would miss her and how terrible it must be for Claude. Bruce had got his answer and it was the same as before. The couple were Salt of the earth.

Door closed. Door open.

Sue had spent her weekend in the garden, shopping and ironing and then it was back to work on the Monday and when she arrived she was immediately called into the Super's office. 'Ah, Sue, come in come in sit down do,' he said, 'Coffee? Yes, help yourself. Now how's the case going?' Sue wasn't one to beat about the bush so she just said, 'To be honest Sir we haven't a clue, if you get my meaning. There just doesn't seem to be any coherent leads to follow so I plan to visit M. Merclot later today to see if he can help further. My three juniors are being very thorough and Sergeant Capstan is excellent so we'll just persevere with good police work until we get a break sir.' The Super looked thoughtful for a moment, then up at Sue and then down to a paper that was on his desk. 'Very good Sue I'm sure you're right. Something may turn up soon but I'm afraid you'll have to carry on without the Sergeant. He's being transferred as of today to be Acting Inspector at Warminster. I'm sorry but it's out of my hands as you can see.' He waved the piece of paper at her and looked rather glum. 'I can see that there's no point in objecting,' she said, 'so who's to be his replacement?' The Super looked even glummer, 'Nobody I'm afraid, it's the cutbacks you see, all of us are having to make do.' he said, 'You'll just have to do the best you can and do come and see me if you need any advice won't you.' 'Yes sir, thank you sir but it's boots on the ground I need not advice at this stage.'

She walked out feeling really down. It had been the beginning of a good team of officers and now she was down to three. 'Blast!' she said, but as she reached her office, Bruce Capstan was seated there, 'Sorry Sue,' he said, 'Couldn't say too much before in case it didn't come off. Hope you don't mind.' Sue smiled, 'Of course not Bruce, you deserve it and I wish you luck.' Now it was his turn to grin. 'Does this mean we can have that drink now?' she was thoughtful for a while weighing up 'things,' but then she made up her mind, 'I believe it does Bruce. Yes I'd like to. 'The Buck' at Bell Dinham then, say at 8.30?' 'Yes Ma'am,' he replied.

Polonium 210

As Sue was getting ready to visit M. Merclot she received a message that she was wanted in the 'Super's' office. 'Come in Sue,' he said, 'glad I caught you. There's been a bit of a complication you see.' Sue waited. She'd had enough trouble for one day. 'Before I go on I must tell you that this is a matter of utmost secrecy and may involve your friends from MI5 again.' He paused for effect and continued, 'Well to cut a long story short it seems that Mme Merclot was poisoned, but not just any old poison. It was 'Polonium 210', very nasty and very difficult to trace. Could take some time to filter through the bloodstream so a victim may have dropped dead at any time especially if they had other medical conditions.'

Sue didn't know what to think or what to say but eventually she spoke up, 'Sir, that Russian spy, Litvinov or something wasn't that how he was killed?' 'Yes you're right Sue, Alexander Litvinenko in London in 2006.

That's why this case has suddenly become high profile and what we do, and how we do it, will come under very intense scrutiny.' 'May I suggest Sir,' said Sue, 'that I continue with the case as if we didn't know this detail. It may help to catch someone off their guard, although I must say I can't think of who.' The Super nodded appreciatively, 'Yes, that's a very good idea. Go and see the old man this afternoon as planned and get him to agree that you can go and have a look at the Weymouth flat. Tell him it's just for background.' 'Right Sir,' she replied, 'I'll get on to that now.'

Once more she went back to her office and collected her papers. This case was taking a rather sinister direction and she felt a little uncomfortable.

Small town cop and Polonium 10 didn't seem to go together.

She arrived at 'Volets Bleus' about 15 minutes later and M. Merclot was waiting for her, 'Asseyez vous, please to sit down.' he said, 'I've made us some tea. I can still remember after all these years even though Madeleine wouldn't let me near the teapot.' Sue said thank you and then went through all the details of the case to date (except the poison, after all could he be a suspect too?). She then asked if he could think of anything to add about life in England, and before in France. Was there anyone that he could think of who might wish her harm. The answer was a firm 'Non' again but he did offer another avenue of enquiry. 'Inspector,' he said, 'this is very difficult for me because it was so personal to her, but I think I should tell you that she always kept 'un agenda', how you say, a diary. She kept them every year since we were married, more than fifty years ago and she stored them in a large Tea Chest in the attic. Do you think that they might be useful?' Sue tried not to look too excited, but she was, 'Well thank you Monsieur,' she said.' Would you mind if I borrowed them for a while? I suppose they will be in French so we'll need to get them translated if anything relevant turns up. I promise that we will not interfere with her private personal thoughts in any way.' 'That's good,' he replied, 'because no one else had read them, not even me, but they're not here, they are at our flat in Weymouth.' Sue was pleased at this turn of events, 'Two birds with one stone' came to mind, a search of the flat and the diaries. 'May we get them then Sir and would you like to come with us?' 'Bien sur, of course but I do not need to go. I can see that you have police business to attend to. Wait, I'll give you the key.' Sue thanked him and left with a little spring in her step. Diaries eh? Who would have 'thunk it' and a date to go to at The Buck'. 'Things are looking up Parker.' she whispered to herself.

The 'Buck'

8.30 at 'The Buck' and Bruce Capstan was waiting pint of bitter in hand. At that precise moment Sue was into her third change of outfit, and this was just for a drink! Bruce was a patient man and although he knew that Sue lived less than half a mile away he was content to observe the comings and goings in the pub that night. 'The Buck' is very well known in the local area due, in no small part to the joint landlords Jimmy and Louise. They seemed to know everyone and if they didn't they soon did, if you follow. The upcoming weekend was their annual Cider festival and the place was beginning to fill up. The pub has a large camping area at the back so serious 'soider' drinkers often plan to camp at this particular weekend. At other times there may be Jazz (incl the local Cat's Eyes trio) or Folk-Rock of different kinds. There is a small Restaurant adjoining the bar and although the bar itself is narrow that somehow adds to it's friendly atmosphere. Upstairs there is the 'Barn,' which is used for meetings and other activities, such as the 'book reading' club that Louise started. Outside there's a mini garden and 'Gazebo'. All in all it's a favourite watering hole for punters of many different persuasions.

And here she was, dressed in a red polo under a smart hacking jacket and blue jeans. 'Hi Sue, what'll you have then?' asked Bruce. 'Hello Bruce' she replied, 'White wine Spritzer please, is that OK?' 'I'll ask,' he said, 'Take a seat and I'll be right back.' She noticed that he did not take his glass for a refill even though it was half empty. 'Cautious Cop,' she thought, 'Like me, doesn't take chances.' Then she chided herself, 'You're out for a drink Sue not a study in human nature!' Bruce returned almost at once, 'Cheers' they said simultaneously and then, almost without a pause they both said, 'Nice pub this.' causing them both to laugh which was a good start. 'I thought about resigning you know,' he said, 'when you wouldn't go out with me before. I thought, maybe she will if I'm not in the force. But then I thought, what if I resign and she still won't. What then? So the move to Warminster was great for me. But would you have done?' 'What?' she said. 'Gone out with me if I had left the force?' She thought for a moment and then said, 'No, probably not, because it would show that you were impatient, and I don't like that in a man.' 'Well thank goodness for Warminster then.' he said, 'and I've got a diploma in patience you know. Perhaps I'll demonstrate one day.' She smiled at the way the conversation was leading but she didn't mind.

They chatted happily until Jimmy called time and beyond, until Louise had to come and budge them from their comfy settee. 'OK, we're going' said Bruce, 'Pity though, have you got a spare tent?' This caused more laughter and when they got outside Sue said, 'You could have asked me first.' 'Just joking' he replied. 'Oh, that's a shame,' Sue said, giving him a peck on the cheek. 'We'd better book up next time!' She then walked briskly to her car and drove away with a wave. Bruce was almost speechless. 'Wow!' he thought, 'This is looking promising.'

MI5 and a Russian Trade Delegation

As the Super had anticipated, MI5 officers were in his office early next morning and Sue was called in. 'Good morning Inspector.' said one, 'My names Franks, you may remember me from the Chateau enquiry a few years ago.' 'Yes, of course,' she replied, 'just let me know if I can help you in any way.' He shook her hand, 'And this is Christine Long who'll be in charge of the case here.' 'Pleased to meet you.' Sue said and waited. 'Well, let's all sit down shall we?' said the Super, 'I've organised coffee but perhaps one of you would like to tell us what this is all about.'

Christine spoke first. 'I am the MI5 co-ordinator for Russian trade delegations when they visit this country. Well, you may or may not know that the Russian Vice President is due here in 10 days time to sign a joint manufacturing and distribution agreement for the new electric 'Volta' car at the new car plant just off the M5 at Bath. Thousands of jobs may be at stake at the factory and in the local sub manufacturers. It's important, and it's also important that we keep him safe. He is perhaps the only one in the Kremlin really committed to the new round of disarmament talks that are to follow in London.' Coffee had arrived so there was a slight pause before Franks continued. 'To be quite frank we did have some low level 'chatter' that he might be a target and of course we have taken sensible precautions but Polonium 210? Well, it's the first we've heard of it being used since Litvinovsky and it just seems to be a real coincidence.' 'But we don't believe in coincidences' added Christine. 'Basically we want to know everything that you know, when you know it.' Franks smiled and looked at Sue. 'And I haven't forgotten what you said to me, or warned me about, last time. We recognise that this is a murder enquiry and we'll try not to get in your way. We'll be staying at the 'Frome Flyer' so I suggest we meet there from time to time or as matters develop. OK?'

The Super said, yes that would be fine and shepherded them out. He returned to Sue looking very worried. 'I hope you can find some leads pretty soon Sue,' he said, 'I can see the Home Office down here next.'

The next week saw another visit to Frome by Jenson Button (another Frome Flyer) and erstwhile World Motor Racing Champion, so Sue and all the force were out and about not only with security, but also with attendant social functions. She had also met up with Bruce on a couple of occasions, most notably at 'The Bear' at Rode where they kissed by the tumbling stream. 'Let's go away' he had said, and she didn't say no.

In fact she wondered if she might combine her visit to Weymouth over a weekend and enjoy some sea, sand and sex as well. They spoke on the phone the next day and she was wondering how to put it when he said 'How about Weymouth?' This remark was out of context and out of the blue but she took her chance. 'Well, as a matter of fact Bruce, I have to go to Weymouth to get some papers and thought about doing it this weekend. I'm planning to stay at 'The Heights,' that stunning Hotel on Portland Bill. Perhaps you could book another room and then we could meet up for dinner and a stroll maybe.'

Bruce sounded very pleased, 'Thank goodness I'm not working this weekend. I'll give them a call. By the way you didn't say anything about breakfast did you?' She smiled to herself but replied in a mock-shock tone. 'No I certainly did not, what do you take me for?' There was a bit of a silence and then she laughed and she could hear him laughing too.

Weymouth

There was work to be done. Sue had to visit the Merclot's flat that was at No.29A East Street, Chickerell near the 'Old Turks Head Inn' before she could enjoy a bit of leisure time. Furthermore she had become more aware of the potential importance of the diaries. Once she had retrieved them she wanted to put them in a very safe place, in the main safe back at the hotel. She parked in the road outside and approached the flat cautiously, looking over her shoulder. Was she imagining things or had she been followed all the way from Frome? Or was it possible that someone in Weymouth had been alerted to her arrival? But why? She didn't know anything did she, except, of course the existence and location of the diaries.' Yes, that's it, if I am under surveillance it's the diaries they're after.' she thought, then paused for a 'reality check 'Paranoid, that's what you are Sue,' she chided herself, 'Ever since you heard about the Polonium, don't be daft girl, just get on with the job.'

Rats in the Belfry!

Although they had travelled down together she had left Bruce back at the Hotel (Room 22), hers' was 29, same floor but a few doors away,' just right'. She had not wanted to involve him in the case since his transfer, but she jolly well wished he was with her now! She approached the front door and tried the key. It stuck. She tried again and this time it worked. Once she was in she took a good look around. Neat lounge and connected kitchen, modern furniture with a 'green-blue' colouring scheme including pictures of marine life and sea birds. All as expected and one large bedroom, a very small study and a bathroom completed the accommodation. The study had a desk and quite a few papers lying about. There were bills and cards for tradesmen etc as well as some boxes which seemed to contain memorabilia of one sort or another, photos, letters, Christmas/Birthday cards and the like. Sue thought for a moment about the contents but decided to make that 'Plan B'. She could always come back. She opened the door of the bedroom, and here she did get a surprise. Not only was it furnished in matching pink and cream with roses and hearts adorning the bedspread, but there were also a number of erotic, almost explicit, prints on the walls. 'Phew,' thought Sue, 'so it's true what they say about the French. I think I'll call myself Mademoiselle Sue back to the Hotel and see what happens.' Her little giggle relieved the tension for a bit, because she had yet to climb into the attic.

She didn't like confined spaces at the best of times and this was certainly not one of those. There was a trapdoor and one of those collapsible ladders, which she put into position before ascending step by step. Then, just as she reached the top there was an almighty noise of fluttering and squealing that almost overwhelmed her as she wobbled at top of the flimsy ladder. She reached out in the dark to find a switch, Ah, there it was, but when she switched it on there was no light, none at all. 'Stupid, Stupid Sue,' she cried out, 'Who forgot to bring a torch then? And you won't catch me going up there with no light, amongst the fluttering birds and RATS!' She climbed down. She was shaking so she went downstairs to see if she could find a drink. No, the water was off. She put her head in her hands peeking through her fingers until she spotted the Drinks Bureaux. She staggered over to it and gently opened the door revealing a half full bottle of Grant's Whisky. 'Medicinal purposes.' she assured herself as she took a long swig. She looked inside to see what else was there. She wasn't a whisky drinker but after all this was an emergency. Then she saw it. Not a drink, but something far better. It was a torch.

Once more she was at the top of the ladder, once more the birds and rats took flight in a noisy hubbub but she had the torch this time. She shone it into every dark recess but could see nothing from where she stood. She would have to venture into the attic itself and look around every corner and this she really didn't want to do. She was scared. No, more than that, she was terrified but she was also a 'brave girl.' She remembered that that was what her Grand Dad used to say when she was a little girl, when she hurt herself. He had been brave in the war. He had been awarded the DSO before he was killed at Dunkirk and, amongst other things she felt that she could not let him down. So, 'Up we go, careful now, we don't want to fall through the floor do we.' she thought to herself. She advanced steadily across the space and shone her light into every corner, and then she saw them. Eyes reflected in her torch beam, dozens of them, just staring back at her. It was stalemate. 'Who's going to blink first?' she thought, then laughed, 'Is that a joke Sue?' she wondered. She then shone the torch into another corner and there it was, an ancient and somewhat battered valise (case) such as would have been used on the Titanic. It was of a dark brown colour with wooden strengthening struts and leather binding, but when Sue tested it's weight she found it to be surprisingly light, and, thank goodness it was unlocked. She lifted the lid gingerly in case it was the home of another family of rats, but no, there in the case were a few neat packages tied up with string. 'The diaries!' she exclaimed. She then took each package, of which there were six, marked in approximate decades, to the hatch and let herself down taking the diaries with her, and leaving the 'field' to the victorious resident rats.

She returned to the Hotel, looking over her shoulder as she made her way in with the bulky parcel of diaries. She left it in the main safe and made her way up to her room where there was a message from Bruce which said, 'Join me on the Terrace when you get in.' Well, that would all have to wait' she decided, 'What I need is a hot bath and a lie down first.' She spread-eagled herself on the bed 'just for a couple of minutes' but the next thing she heard was the telephone. She picked it up slowly in a sleepy haze and listened, 'Hello Sue, it's Bruce here. Are you all right? It's nearly six o'clock and the sun's going down. Can you hear me?' 'Yes Bruce I'm here and I did get your message but I just dropped off when I got back. Sorry.' She wanted to tell him that she'd been frightened in the loft and outside, but thought better of it. It was her case and it was police business. They had other 'fish to fry' she hoped. 'Never mind,' he said, 'Shall I see you in the bar, say about seven then?' 'That'll be great' she replied, 'I'm going to have a bath now and I'll put on something special just for you.' There was a pause and then he just said, 'I want to kiss you.' and hung up. Her knees went all weak for a moment, 'Now now, Sue don't get carried away,' she thought, 'it's probably the Scotch.'

From Here to Eternity?

They had a drink and then dinner and then took a stroll along Chesil beach, that long tongue of sand that connects Fortuneswell and Chesil Cove to Weymouth. The beach does not stretch to Portland Bill itself and they thought that they might drive that extra distance past the Mesolithic sites on the next day. But now was now, they were on the beach and even though it wasn't quite a scene from Hollywood's 'From here to Eternity' it wasn't bad for Dorset! Bruce wasn't quite a Burt Lancaster either, but he was strong and assertive yet gentle. She sighed as the waves lapped their toes and then suddenly a freak wave took them by surprise and soaked her dress. It would have also drenched her underwear if she'd been wearing any. 'I'm soaked' she said, 'Let's go back shall we?'

'Good idea,' he replied, 'May I stop by your tent a bit later?' She pretended to think about this for a while then answered. 'Knock three times and ask for Mamselle Sue, and if you can find a uniform from the Foreign Legion I'd be very very, very grateful if you see what I mean.'

Bruce laughed and picked her up, swinging her around so that her dress billowed out. 'I'll try.' he said.

It was an hour later when the knock came on Sue's door. She went across and asked, 'Qui est la?' the reply came, 'Ici le 'French Lieutenant' J'ai perdu my way. I should be on the Cob at Lyme Regis. Please have pity on me.' She smiled and opened the door. Bruce stood there but not in a uniform of the Foreign Legion. No, he was wearing a Breton striped shirt, shorts and a hat that said 'Kiss me quick Sailor'. 'Best I could do' he said as he took her in his arms, once more picking her up and carrying her gently to the bedroom. She would remember that night forever. She had enjoyed sex before but this was making love as she had always imagined it would be. She tried to stop a small cry and a shiver but could not.

The Diaries 1

The diaries were taken back to Frome and a professional translator was called in. They were ready within days and Sue called the team in to look at them. She decided to split them up, taking, what she thought were likely to be the most informative for herself. These were the decades just before and just after the war and, in addition, the most recent decade. She felt that if there were to be any clues, they would probably be found there.

However that still left a lot to be covered by Jenny and the others. 'This is urgent,' she said, 'but don't rush it. We must not miss anything that might shed light on the murder. Old scores, rivals, money and anything that might link her to the Russians, unlikely as it might seem.'

It was late and, despite the risk to security, she decided to take her share home. However, she did not suggest that the others could do so. It was far too risky for that, and she would allocate time at the Station for them.

The Spanish Civil War

Home then, in front of a blazing fire that was not needed, but cheered her up, she began to read. The first diary began in 1936 and the translators had thoughtfully asterisked 'very personal passages' and placed them in an addendum at the end of each period. Madeleine Merclot had provided an introduction and it soon became obvious that there was only one important matter on her mind, even as a teenager, the Spanish Civil War.

This was what she put in her diary.

*   *   *   *

'Non Intervention.' she wrote, 'This phrase will haunt and shame politicians for years to come. Blum (the French PM) is a coward.' (Although she conceded that to a degree, he was a prisoner of his own right wing.) Her view of Baldwin (The British PM) however was much more extreme, 'A wolf in sheep's clothing.' she had written. 'He chooses not to intervene because he would rather see a Fascist government than the properly elected left of centre one that Spain had before 1936. While Nazi Germany and Fascist Italy send aid to Franco and the rebels, France and Britain do nothing and the Government has to depend on it's own resources in the country, due to the League of Nations cowardly policy of non-intervention. Thank goodness for Russia, it's the only country sending aid and assistance to the properly elected Government.

But now we have a chance to help! It's October now and winter's on it's way, but Madrid is under siege and volunteers are flocking to the cause from all over the world. I have heard that George Orwell, the British author, was in Barcelona in August. He is in the 'International Brigade' and in the same group, the 'POUM' that are organizing our papers and everything. I am proud to say that Claude and I have signed up and we leave tomorrow for Paris, Perpignan, Valence and onto Albacete, inland from Alicante where the Brigade is being trained. We will join the 'Commune de Paris.'I will be a nurse and Claude a soldier. I am so proud of him. God willing we will lift the siege and send the Fascists packing'.

*   *   *   *

From then on the diary related day-to-day events as they unfolded and, as she turned the pages, Sue seemed to find herself there, with Madeleine and Claude Merclot in Paris, back in October 1936, not as a reader of a diary, but actually with them as if recording a narrative for a friend.

*   *   *   *

The diary went on to tell of their stay in Paris. The last time had been in May when they had gone to see the 'Quintet of the Hot Club of France' with Django Reinhardt and Stephane Grappelli. Madeleine tended to love classical music especially the later French composers such as Ravel, Debussy and Satie, but she was only too happy to go with Claude to the concert. She loved seeing his face light up when he was enjoying himself. He too was aware that it wasn't exactly her 'cup of tea,' so he took the trouble to give her a special card that he had made himself in which the 'story' of Django was outlined. It began,

To my Darling. If Django plays 'All the things you are' it will be because I made him do so, because you are all things to me. Je t'aime.

The card then opened out into a heart shape on which Claude had copied a brief outline of Django Reinhardt's life and career. This is what it said.

'One of jazz's most exotic legends, guitarist Django Reinhardt was the first non American Jazzman of originality. Born 1910 in a caravan in Belgium, he was a gypsy and his playing was a fusion of Jazz and Tzigane traditions. He was forced to give up the violin after a caravan fire mutilated his left hand leaving him only the use of two fingers. His distinctive style is immediately recognizable and, as well as his own group with Grappelli, he has recorded with many well-known American Jazz Giants, most notably Coleman Hawkins. He has a very wide repertoire, but look out for his own composition 'Nuages' (Clouds)'

145

Madeleine remembered that day as if it was yesterday, but this time they took the opportunity to do some sight seeing instead. 'Look Claude, isn't it wonderful,' said Madeleine gazing up at the Eiffel Tower. 'Come on let's go up in the lift.' They paid their francs and soon enough were overlooking the City. 'It's a sight to behold.' said Claude, 'Look over there. You can see for miles down the River Seine.' 'All the way to Perpignan.' said Madeleine. Claude laughed and hugged her tight. 'You are a funny little Bunny,' he said, 'I rather think that the Seine flows into the Channel not the Med. But don't let it bother you we're travelling by train not by river boat.' She held him tight, 'I do love you' Msieur Claude Clementine' (remember, he was a greengrocer) she said kissing him warmly and stroking his face. 'You will be careful won't you.' she said, 'Out there when we get there.' 'Oui Madame Lapin' he replied, 'but first we've got to find the 'House of Syndicates' in Mathurin-Moreau Avenue. There we'll be given our papers, probably with false names to get us over the border into Spain. Come on we haven't got much time.'

Eventually they found it and, as he had said they were given the documents that they needed after a long wait, because the place was bulging with men and women from all over the Globe. It didn't mean much to Claude at the time but his papers were issued by the 'POUM' organization. This group was prominent in the International Brigades but they weren't the only one. On this particular day there were at least 500 volunteers, mostly from France and Belgium but also from England, America, Canada, Hungary, Poland and many Germans. However, although there was an air of 'camaraderie' it seemed to Claude that organising an army with so many different languages, customs and skills (or lack of skills) would not be easy.

The Albacete Camp confirmed all his worst fears. Their barracks were in an old shed where 'Fascists' had been shot only recently and their blood was still on the floor and walls. On the parade ground some officers tried to gauge their skills. 'Who has shot a rifle before? Who knows how to read a map?' Chaos, but somehow the commitment of all involved overcame some of these difficulties. There was a women's Militia Unit, and they were easily recognizable by the dungarees that they wore. However Madeleine was a trained Nurse, so she was billeted in somewhat better accommodation at a former convent. This was where they met quite frequently until it was time to advance on Madrid.

Their favourite place was a Lemon Grove just behind a statue of the Virgin Mary. She put her head on his shoulder and sighed, 'I hope it will always be like this,' she said. He laughed, 'What? Insects and Thorns? Ouch! I think I've sat on one!' 'No, silly,' she replied, 'Here, us, together, the smell of lemon blossom, and you. Promise me something Claude.' 'Of course ma cherie,' he replied, 'What is it?' She looked at him closely and held his hand. 'You know that I love you with all my heart and soul, but please remember that others will depend on you when conflict begins. Do not think of me, but of the cause for which we are fighting. Do your duty and pray to 'Our Lady' to keep you safe.' He reassured her that that was his intention but he did confide a small matter that was bothering him. 'I'll be fine,' he said, 'but, well, you probably remember that when we signed up it was through the agencies of the 'POUM.' I've found out since that, although they are anti Fascist they are also anti-Stalinist. They really don't get on with the Red Brigades. They just want a return to the elected Government but the Red Brigades are a different matter entirely. They would like the war to end in a Communist Government for the whole of Spain. They are Soviet backed and each Battalion has more than one political commissar. But what's more important is the fact that they have modern weapons and professional officers. I very much doubt that the 'Poum' amateurs, like me, will get very far once battle begins. I think that we'll be very vulnerable.'

Madeleine looked crestfallen. 'So what does this mean for you then my darling?' she said. 'Well,' he replied. 'It seems to me that our objective here is to win the war, not to fight future political battles. So I think that I should transfer to the Red Brigade. I'll be safer and I'll be able to contribute more with a full magazine of ammunition instead of a pot-luck one or two rounds.' 'Yes I think you're right,' Madeleine replied, 'but now you must make me another promise. It's this. You must promise me that you won't get involved in any attacks on the Church or the Clergy. Promise me. Promise me.' 'Of course I do my darling,' he replied, 'I'm Fighting Fascism not the Church.' But even as he spoke he knew that there were many who thought that the two were hand in glove, especially when it came to the dreaded 'Falange' and the 'Carlists'.

When they reached Madrid there was an air raid warning, and they saw German Junkers and Heinkels raining bombs on the City. Then there was a cheer as a Russian fighter took up the chase, and another cheer when a plume of smoke could be seen from one of the bombers. Then the loudspeaker struck up with the voice of 'La Pasionara' evoking the 'No Pasarin' (They shall not pass) slogan that the City had adopted.

Almost immediately the Merclots were split up. Claude to his new Brigade and Madeleine to the main hospital where she was soon busy with the wounded and dying from the fighting near Madrid at Aranjuez and Maqueda. But by now the Fascists were closing in on Madrid itself. The situation was desperate and on November 15th the Luftwaffe Condor Legion pulverized University City as Legionaries and Moors broke in only to be repulsed. There was to be another week of fighting before the siege was lifted, but on the last day Madeleine got a message that Claude was seriously wounded and in the Hospital. She immediately ran to his ward to discover that he had been badly shot up and had lost a foot.

'My darling, ma cherie. What have you been up to?' she sobbed as she ran to his side. 'Ah! Madeleine!' he cried out, 'thank goodness you are here.' They clinched in a really close embrace before she looked at him seriously. 'I've got to get you out of here,' she said, 'There are too many cases of gangrene for my liking and typhus is a definite possibility. I'll speak to Matron. After all we are just volunteers. Then I'll arrange for us to get back to Bordeaux where you can recover.'

Claude smiled and held her hand tightly. 'I'm afraid not,' he said, 'that may be the case in the 'Poum' but don't forget I'm in the Red Brigades now.' She looked at him sternly, a look he had seen many times before when her mind was made up. 'Well, you're the wounded soldier,' she said, 'You'll just have to leave things to me won't you?' He was silent as she continued, 'Now, what's the name of your commanding officer?' Claude laughed, but it hurt and anyway it was no laughing matter. 'General Miaja is in overall command' he said, 'but my battalion is commanded by Colonel Juan Lopez. To think of it, I just about saved his life last week, so he owes me one. Here, let's see if there's a way. Take this note to the barracks and ask if he will see me.'

She did and sure enough, within a week they were in an Ambulance bound for Soria, thence to Pamplona and over the Pyrenees across the French border into Bayonne. Another few days and they were home. 'Welcome home darling' Madeleine said, handing him the biggest bunch of flowers he had ever seen. 'Thank you precious,' he said, 'But I wouldn't be here without you, and Colonel Lopez of course.'

'So how did you persuade him?' she said. 'Well I just said what you told me before, you know, loyalty to the cause and all that. His reply was very warm as he shook my hand, and all he said was that, with a war brewing in Europe, no doubt I'd get a chance to serve again.'

*   *   *   *

The diary for 1936 finished here and Sue slowly came out of her reverie as she leafed through the pages again. It was incredible, it was a story out of romantic fiction but she had also detected the 'hard edge' that she was looking for. It seemed to be the case that Claude Merclot, at least, had had some contact with a Russian backed Red Brigade during the Civil war. 'Had it stopped there or was there still a connection?' she thought to herself. She was so fascinated that she wanted to continue with the next year, but her eyes were heavy and she was soon asleep.

The Intruder

Sue was in the middle of one of those very deep sleeps when dreams sometimes link up with reality. In her dream a man was walking down the street and knocking at each door, but when somebody came to the door he just walked away and went on to the next house. Each time he did this, the door of each house creaked as it was opened so, in her dream she was anticipating the next creak as the mysterious man knocked again. Yes, there it was, but much louder this time, and much nearer. 'Oh God! He's here in the room, I know it.' she cried out, leaping out of bed immediately. She was right. The man stood by the door. He didn't move and nor did she, she was petrified. The man was wearing a long dark coat and black leather gloves. She couldn't see his face because it was too dark, but she saw him rub his hands together, as if undecided as to what to do next. 'He's going to kill me, he's going to strangle me' she thought, but when she looked again the man had gone.

She wanted to call Bruce but she knew that she must report the incident anyway, and she didn't really want everyone to know about her new love affair. Not yet anyhow. A squad car arrived within 6 minutes and a dog team within 15. There was no trace of the intruder. Had she been imagining it all? If not, the officers asked, could she think of any reason, apart from burglary as to why she was a victim. Of course she couldn't tell them the background to the case, so she just said no and they left promising to send forensics the next day. She managed to get a few hours sleep before they arrived. They found a man-sized footprint outside her French Windows, which she had already admitted, might have been left unlocked. 'Have you had any male friends visit recently?' the officer asked quizzically. Sue was able to answer no truthfully, because Bruce hadn't been to her house yet. She had hoped to invite him next weekend 'if she was still alive!' But she wished he was herewith her now. 'We'll take a moulding Miss and check our records. You'll be informed in due course. Thank you and don't forget to lock all your doors.' the officer said, 'Can't be too careful you know. Probably teenagers out for a lark.'

'Oh yes,' thought Sue,' teenagers in a long dark coat with leather gloves? I don't think so.' Anyway it was 10 am and she was late for work.

There had been a development in the case overnight. The handbag had been found at Mells. It was empty. Sue called her team into her office to discuss progress including the bag. She opened the conversation by asking them if they thought that the location was significant in any way.

Silence. She prompted, 'Well, Mells is nearer to Frome than Radstock isn't it.' she asked. 'Yes, 'replied Jenny, 'and that probably means that the man who was in the garage probably went to Radstock to cash the money to draw attention away from Frome, and he chucked the bag away on his way back, ergo, we're looking for a Frome resident.' Sue smiled, pleased that Jenny had spotted the clue and also pleased that she would gain confidence from her suggestion. 'Well done Jenny,' Sue said, 'that's what I think as well, although of course it's not certain. OK everyone, now I've arranged with the Super for you to work on the diaries here at the Station. There could be some important evidence so please be careful.

Let's meet tomorrow, say at four o'clock here to compare notes. Thanks.'

'Shall I or shan't I' thought Sue. 'Shall I take the diaries home again or not? Or maybe would it really be OK to tell Bruce the whole story and work on them at his place? Business not pleasure mind.' And that's what she decided to do. She had felt very vulnerable at home so she gave Bruce a ring and asked if she could bring some 'confidential papers' to work on, and could she bring a toothbrush. He was delighted.

The Diaries 2

When she arrived she told Bruce about the new developments in the case. He was very considerate and just said, 'Let me know if I can help. I'll make some coffee and sandwiches. You get started.' She gave him a big hug and a kiss and said 'Thanks Bruce, I knew I could depend on you.'

She sat down and opened the diary file once more. From 1934 up to 1939 they were mostly about family and business issues. The drama of Spain seemed well behind them, but 1940 changed as war came to their own doorstep. Madeleine spared no detail in noting how they survived and sue could not put it down until she was finished. Madeleine recalled that 'Lopez's words back in Madrid had been prophetic . . . .

WW2 The Resistance

Lopez's words back in Madrid had been prophetic because within a few years German troops had swept all before them in Europe, and held Boulogne and many other French towns in a grip of terror. Claude could not serve in the army because of his amputated foot so he was allowed to continue his grocery business. This was very helpful because it gave him access to German Barracks and passes for travel. Helpful, because Claude and Madeleine were secret organisers of an 'Escape Line' for Allied airmen, who had been shot down. Their task was to retrieve them, hide them and then send them 'down the line' usually to Switzerland but sometimes through Spain to Portugal. Another route was that into 'Vichy France' the semi autonomous region in the South. Air crew were moved to Marseille via Reims, Dijon and Lyon. Officials in none of these could not really be trusted, but some could be bribed.

The Merclot Vehicle was a Panhard with folding seats that were called 'sofica'. It had been modified with two 'pods' beneath the floor in which two airmen could hide. Others had to make do by hiding in Straw, Potatoes or Brussel Sprouts as Pilots and Navigators etc were delivered to their destination. Although they were an independent group with about a dozen trusted helpers, it was inevitable that their activities would cross over with other Anti-Nazi operations in the region.

They had been sent a British liaison officer, Major Tawney to help them with logistics and radio support. Soon he had become invaluable to the operation, but he too was subject to surveillance. On one occasion he was picked up by the Gestapo and only got away without interrogation when Madeleine swore that she had been 'with' him at the time in question. This story was not believed, until she ripped off her blouse and showed the Gestapo officers a series of love bites on her breasts. They were highly amused but their Commander Obersturmfuehrer von Stuck insisted that Monsieur Merclot should also see them. Tawney's fate would depend on his reaction and Claude played his part to a T. 'You bitch, you f—ing bitch, I'll whip you to kingdom come when we get home' he shouted, grabbing her by the hair as she wriggled to escape. Tawney was released later that day and he was very grateful. 'I'll never forget your bravery and if ever you need help after the war, just ask.' he said. Meanwhile it was back to business.

There were one other group that the 'Escape Line 'had to be aware of and this was the 'informal' French Resistance known as 'The Maquis.' Unfortunately, as in Spain, members were a disparate group of activists who did not always get on. It was actually made up of individuals and several groups with opposing political allegiances such as the National Front, the Liberation, the Combat, the Franc Tireur and the AS (Secret Army, Org. of Army Resistance). Here as in Spain, an important ingredient was the input of the Russian Comintern, who sent Commissars to help organization and supply. The Allies helped by parachuting supplies not only to the FFI (French Forces of the Interior) but also to the FTP (Francs-Tireurs and Partisans), namely the Communists.

Unlike in Spain, the Merclots did not owe allegiance to any one group although they did receive advice and equipment from their British liaison officer Tawney. They might not have got involved with this rivalry and infighting at all, were it not for a surprise late night caller at their cottage. They would not usually open the door until they heard a familiar voice or a password but this was different. 'It's Juan,' the voice said, 'Juan Lopez from Spain. Let me in please I've been shot. Help me please.' Of course they both rushed to the door and took him in. He was bleeding profusely but Madeleine soon attended to his most obvious wounds and Claude made him some warm soup. It soon became apparent however that he had broken his leg and could not walk.

He told them that he was attached to the local Partisans for a 'special operation.' There was to be a parachute drop of ammunition and supplies at Lumbres near St Omer, about 12 miles from Boulogne the next day but he had information that it was a trap. Pro Nazi elements in the FFI had found out about it and planned to ambush the 'drop' with their own activists, forces from the Luftwaffe Police, the Gestapo and, for good measure, the local Gendarmerie. A message must be sent by hand to the area because all forms of communication had been forbidden as the day of the 'drop' approached.

'Mon ami,' Lopez said, speaking in French, 'Mon camarade. I don't know how to say this but it's true. Only you can save the loss of a British plane and it's crew as well as of dozens, maybe hundreds of lives if the Gestapo take prisoners. I am asking you to help us, and the cause of freedom. I am begging you to go there, to a farm that I will describe for you, so that the mission may be called off. We have tried to stop the plane as well. But if it does arrive it will not drop unless it receives a signal. I know that your heart is in the right place, not just for those lives, but because it is still possible that the war will be won against Nazi Germany only to hand over to neo Fascist elements that still exist here in your beloved France as well as in Britain. This is a battle to be won but there will still be a war going on. This is your chance to finish the job you started in Spain.'

Claude looked at Madeleine and she nodded. 'You must go ma cherie.' she said, 'but please be careful. I don't want to nearly lose you again.'

That evening they loaded up the Panhard with a mixed load of vegetables to deliver to the farm of Gaston de Luc at Hazebrouck, not far from Lumbres. Unfortunately of course, M. de Luc did not know that he would suddenly have a surfeit of potatoes and carrots, and Claude hoped that his surprise would not be evident if there happened to be 'unreliable' persons there. In fact, apart from a few very close collaborators, it would not be untrue to say that nobody could be trusted, even family.

Claude expected to be stopped on his way over and so it turned out.

'HALT!' shouted a uniformed German soldier as he approached a number of light armoured vehicles at the side of the road. 'Papers please. 'Danke' You are M. Merclot. Marchand from Boulogne?' Claude knew that if he showed fear they would spot it, but if he was too confident, they would also be suspicious. 'Oui m'sieur Sergeant.' he replied. 'So why are you here in Cassel? It's not your area for groceries is it 'Claude now had to bluff. 'Well, not exactly.' he replied, 'But my brother has a farm at Bethune and he has to supply a large 'epicier' (grocer) with vegetables by Friday. I'm helping him out that's all.' The sergeant asked him to wait while he approached an officer seated in the front of the leading vehicle.

He soon came back and asked Claude to step out of the car. 'The lieutnant is not satisfied.' he said, beckoning to a group of soldiers nearby. 'Search this vehicle' he continued, 'and make a good job of it. We know that contraband arms are sometimes carried on these road and even RAF pilots. I'd like to get my hands on one of them!'

The soldiers were thorough, very thorough. They tipped all the vegetables out but found nothing suspicious until one of them spotted the small catch that led to the concealed chambers. 'Sir!' he called out 'Look, a secret chamber.' The Sergeant immediately called more soldiers to surround the vehicle with rifles at the ready.

Then he called the officer who strolled over looking very relaxed. 'Well, what do we have here Monsieur?

Un 'chambre secret' if I'm not mistaken. Well done Sergeant. I will report on your vigilance. Now Monsieur, tell us, what is in the chamber and don't lie or it will be the worse for you.' Funnily enough Claude was amused at this turn of events but he could not show it. Instead he just said, 'Legumes Lieutnant, legumes seul.' (only vegetables). 'I think we'll see about that,' said the Lieutenant, 'Ouvrir la casse!' he ordered and immediately the lid was prised open to reveal . . . . Celery. Claude would have laughed out loud if he dared but he just kept quiet. The officer turned to the Sergeant. 'Dumkopf!' he said and walked off. The soldiers walked off as well and the sergeant slunk away to his vehicle leaving Claude to clear up the mess. He didn't mind, in fact he started to whistle 'Colonel Bogey' to himself as he picked up the vegetables.

The vegetables were delivered, the message was delivered and Claude returned home safely. Madeleine welcomed him with a warm kiss and (another) bunch of flowers. Lopez kissed him on both cheeks, greeting him like a lost brother. Claude smiled and told them the whole story.

'Do you know,' he said, 'that's the first time that our 'pouches' have been searched. Just think how many airmen we've carried in them in the past.'

'You are a brave man' said Lopez. 'We will need men like you in the future.' Claude smiled, 'That's what you said last time.' he said.

*   *   *   *

The diary for that year finished there, and Sue sat back deep in thought.

Just then she felt warm hands on her shoulders, and warm lips on her neck, and warm breath nuzzling her ears. She shivered and let feelings run all over her. Then she sighed and said, 'Take me Bruce. Take me to bed and take me; now.' He picked her up gently and led her to the bedroom. She lay very still, just enjoying the preliminaries until suddenly she welled up with emotion, and took charge of the next stages of their lovemaking. And that's what it was. Sue had fallen in love . . . (again!)

The Diaries 3

The next day she read the next batch of diaries in her care, but this time at the office. Nothing unusual cropped up nor were there any references to the wider political or social issues in the world. It was a sort of French Mrs Dale's (or Merclot's) Diary.'I'm worried about Jim' (Sorry, Claude).

This only left the last five years to cover, but Sue expected more surprises. Something had occurred that had resurrected old memories and loyalties. She believed in her instincts and she was often right.

(Authors note. Mrs Dales Diary was a long running radio show on the BBC, well before the Archers, and TV's Come Dancing etc.)

She wasn't quite ready to see the Super with a report yet but he wanted to see her. Franks and Christine Long were there from MI5 and started they ball rolling. 'We think that you're in danger Sue,' said Christine, 'and the Super wants you off the case. Take a holiday or something but get as far away as you can. These people are ruthless and will stop at nothing as you've found out for yourself. We should handle it from now on. We have 24/7 protection organized for the Vice President when he gets here, but we still don't know if there is a credible threat linked to what's happened in Frome. It's best if we take the heat out of the situation here.'

Sue looked at the Superintendent and, if looks could kill, he would have died on the spot. 'Is that your decision Sir?' she asked politely. 'Well, no, not exactly, taken under advice, that's what, under advice, what's best you see, for all concerned that's what.' he replied rather miserably.

'Then can I take it Sir that you will not stand in the way of my application to go back to Bath with immediate effect?' she said in a rather offhand manner, which disguised the fact that she was seething inside. 'Oh no. No need for that, plenty to do here, plenty.' Sue looked him straight in the eye, 'I think you've misunderstood me Sir,' she said 'as I see it, I have a murder case to solve. Threats or no threats, Russians or no Russians and with respect, MI5 or no MI5, and that's what I'm going to do unless you arrest me,' she paused, 'Sir.' she concluded. The Super looked helplessly at Franks and Long. 'I think that concludes our meeting,' he said, 'Inspector Parker won't be going anywhere.' Franks shrugged and said, 'Right but we can't be responsible for her safety. Let's just agree to keep in touch as we go along. Thank you Sir, and thank you Sue. I must say that I'm not surprised at what you said. Good Luck.'

Sue's next task was to review the 'Diary Studies' with Jenny, Tommy and Ronnie. They all seemed to agree that their assigned 'years' did not seem to reveal anything sinister but were 'normal' diaries in the sense that they covered family celebrations and social life just the same as the last batch that she had looked at. She had decided to go to Bruce's again to review her last few years because she wanted, as well to have time to consider what the 'Diary Studies' were revealing overall, if anything. She had identified a context but it went way back, more than fifty years, and she didn't believe that that was all there was to it. This time she decided to look for names and places and she thought that Bruce might be able to help in cross referencing etc. Was there another reason for her decision? That was for her to know.

*   *   *   *

The diaries 4

When Madeleine began her diaries of the last five years it was obvious that she was aware of he own mortality. She had her 90th Birthday in 2008 and the entries often contained little phrases about prayer and life after death, as well as little sayings such as 'All things are possible to those who believe.' in which she found much comfort. She had remained a devout Catholic despite Claude's reservations from time to time. They had generally agreed that the Church could be a force for good in the world but Claude's experience in Spain had convinced him that the Church were too often on the wrong side when it came to matters in the socio-political sphere. He found the Church too conservative when he thought they should be radical. 'Just as Christ was.' he was fond of saying, but he continued to go to Mass with her every week with his private prayers for a more 'enlightened' Church. Madeleine shared his pain and his anxiety but she placed more emphasis on simple faith and prayer. That does not mean that they argued, indeed they had always given each other room to 'breathe' and their love had remained true.

All this was evident from the diaries but, as she read one page and Bruce another, it soon became obvious that the Merclots did not share as much as they used to. The year 2005 had many references to their outings, friends and little gifts that they took delight in, but from about 2009, although the gifts remained, and she always mentioned them, there were fewer recordings of their joint social life. It could have been that this was an age or sickness issue but actually Madeleine mentioned the absence of this closeness that they had shared for so long. 'What has happened to Claude,' she wrote, 'he seems so far away sometimes, and when I ask him if he is troubled in any way, he always kisses me and tells me not to worry.' Later in the diaries she mentions names that Claude has mentioned in passing, names of people she had never met. In other passages she dwells on the fact that he has started to go to Weymouth without her on a regular monthly basis. She recalls that a couple from Weymouth had stayed with them in Frome a few times and she thought they were very nice. They were Frank and Zelda Robinson who were great Theatre Goers and lovers of classical music as was she. She confided that she would like to meet more of the Weymouth 'crowd'.

Claude explained that most of his time there was taken up with the 'All England Bowls Committee' who met in Weymouth monthly. He said that she would have been bored and, in any case, they continued to go together quite frequently as well. Her diary recorded her acceptance of these situations and his reasoning, but there was a sense of loss there also. Claude had been ill and had had a heart bypass and it was obvious that she did not want to tax him with her concerns, especially when he admitted that he had also kept in touch with what he called a 'Left of Centre Think Tank' that was based in Dorchester.

'You know how I feel about these things,' he had explained, 'and you know that our life in Frome was always a cover for my real sentiments. We never fell out about it because we love and respect each other too much. We have never had to choose one way or the other and that's the way it should be. If you ask me to do something for the Church you know that I will always do it and vice versa. Don't worry, I'll try to find more time for us in the future because you know how much I love you.' She had smiled and agreed that they could both try to be more understanding and supportive in the future.

There is then quite a gap in the diary record and, when she returns to her writing, it is to report that she had been diagnosed with cancer which is 'Inoperable' the Hospital had said, but 'Don't worry' she confides to her diary, 'It is not spreading at present (2009)'. That was the last entry.

*   *   *   *

Weymouth revisited

Sue admitted to herself that there didn't seem to be much in these entries to go on except a feeling of unease that everything was not quite right. She told Bruce that by 2010 Madeleine had only been given a few months to live and asked him what he thought about the whole thing 'Well I know you'll think that I'm up to something and have an ulterior motive,' he said, 'But I wouldn't be surprised if the answer lies in the Weymouth flat. It's something that you didn't find. Something that you probably didn't even look for, and if I'm right we'd better find it before 'they' do, whoever they are.' Sue felt warm and safe. She was with Bruce and what he had said made a lot of sense. 'Let's go tomorrow,' she said. 'I agree,' he replied, 'Lucky for you it's my day off. Now say thank you.' She did not reply but got up slowly and walked towards the bedroom pausing at the door.' Thank you, Bruce. Now you say Please, Sue.' she said.

As planned they travelled down to Weymouth the next day arriving at the flat at about 11 am. Sue still had the key so she opened the door and stepped inside but as she did so she had an uneasy feeling. Someone had been there before them on that very day. Sue knew it because a fragrance filled the room. 'It's Chanel Number 5' she called out to Bruce who was looking under the stairs. 'What is?' he said as he poked his head out.

'The perfume. A woman has been here and only recently, but she's been careful not to disturb things. Looks like we're on the right track. Now, what was she looking for? What are we looking for?' Sue pondered. Bruce didn't reply. He had disappeared under the stairs for a moment so Sue started to go through all the drawers and cupboards that she could see. Nothing and Bruce said 'Nothing' as well. They sat down and in a comic, one would have seen 'puzzled thought bubbles' coming out of their heads. Still nothing until Sue had a brainwave. Now if Madeleine had stored her diaries in the attic, wasn't it likely that Claude would do the same but not quite the same because he told me where to find her secrets, but if I'm right, I fancy he didn't want me to find his.'

Then it dawned on her. The 'Panhard Pods' from Spain! Yes, that was it. The documents were under the floor boards just as the airmen and celery were carried. 'Bruce. Bruce.' she called out, 'I've found them, I've found them.' He came dashing in from the kitchen, 'Where? Where are they and what is 'them'?' Sue laughed and explained. 'But I haven't actually found them yet. I just know where they are.' There was nothing to say to Sue when she was in this mood. It was better to go along with her even if she was mistaken. But she wasn't. Bruce lifted the corner of the carpet and there they could see a small 'catch'. They pushed back more of the carpet to reveal a trapdoor, which opened when they slid back the catch.

The Yarkov papers

Inside was a small chamber of a kind that Sue had seen before on historical trips to pre-Reformation Catholic 'safe houses' or Convents. Such a chamber was where the priests' 'Things for the Mass' (cross, candles, breviaries, rosaries, chalices etc) were hidden. At that time, saying Mass was punishable by death so everything had to be hidden away. Sue reckoned that that was another reason for the chamber. She put her hand inside carefully and brought out a number of folders handing them to Bruce as she did so. The 'pod' was now empty and she stood up. 'Right Bruce,' she said, 'Let's see what we've got here.'

The documents turned out to mainly the minutes of meetings of the 'Left of Centre Think Tank' that Madeleine had mentioned in her diary. Claude was the secretary and, far from being a 'think tank' it was a Communist 'cell' which had been re-activated in the last few years after decades of inactivity. Items on the agendas included strike agitation as well as bribery and 'where necessary,' force. Names and lists of contacts were all there, as was a special red file marked 'YARKOV VP CONFIDENTIAL'

The missing link

Sue and Bruce read the file carefully. It began with a simple justification for the 'elimination' of Yuri Yarkov the Russian Vice President on a visit to the UK to open a new 'Volta' car plant and to sign a 'Peace and Disarmament' accord in London. The proposed signing of the 'Accord' was perceived by the Russian Government as the act of a traitor to 'Mother Russia,' and a direct challenge to the President and the Politburo. It had been agreed by them that Russia needed to stay strong and independent in the face of rising Islamic Fundamentalism as well as resurgent Neo Fascist groups in the world such as in France, Holland and the UK, not forgetting the United States itself. Disarmament at this time, it went on to say, would betray the sacrifices of past generations. The VP did not agree with this and had made his views known, He was thought to be formulating a new power base to challenge the leadership, the report said and he must be stopped before he could sign. The 'weapon' of choice was to be a new refined form of Polonium 210.

Sue froze. The 'Missing Link' was right there in front of her eyes. It seemed that the sleepy Somerset market town of Frome was at the heart of an International Conspiracy. She continued to study the files to see what else would be revealed and there was plenty, and all in meticulous detail. The documents listed a series of logistical plans and timings with names and responsibilities of those involved. It was a goldmine of information and Sue could not wait to pass it on to MI5 because she recognized that it was their responsibility. However, the murder was hers, and she had noticed something very important from the file. Prominent amongst the names on the list were Frank and Zelda Robinson who, Sue remembered, had been mentioned as visitors to Frome in Madeleine's diary. Had they been visiting even more recently she wondered?

Back in Frome she presented her findings so far, in a report to the Superintendent leaving him to liase with MI5. She then made an appointment to see Claude Merclot to clear up some 'loose ends.'

Love and Poison,

He welcomed her with a somewhat nervous handshake. 'Come in 'Madame Inspectrice' he said. 'I have made Coffee. Instant I'm afraid, not quite up to Madaleines' standard. Here you are.' Sue thanked him and, after the initial pleasantries and with an apology, she told him all that she had discovered in Weymouth. When she finished she waited for his reaction, but he just sat there and waited for her to continue. 'It seems therefore M'sieur that your wife was given poison here and, as far as we know, you were the only one here with opportunity but I cannot think what your motive was. Please tell me so that I can close the case now.'

Merclot gave her an amused look. No, it was more one of pity. Then he spoke, 'Tell me Mam'selle, have you ever been in love?' he asked. Sue was surprised by this question, it sounded too personal but she realised that it was the beginning of something that he wanted to tell her, so she answered him. 'I think so. I suppose I have, I'm not really sure. I think I'm in love then something comes along and changes it, and sometimes I don't even know why.' He sat back in his chair and smiled.

'Yes.' he said 'You are a young woman with a career to think about, and perhaps you do not have time for love, but I can tell you this. When a person is in love, it is because they are loved. Not in return for being loved, but because love is created by and thrives on love. In other words, without mutual love, a singular love will die. I am telling you this because that is how Madeleine and I were with each other. We were so blessed and I hope you will accept that I could never have harmed her.'

Sue thought back to Frau Gieseking in the 'Bath Buns' case when she had just simply said 'I loved him you see.' as if that had explained everything. And here was that sentiment again, closing down her options in the investigation, but somehow ringing true now, as then. Claude displayed no twinges of conscience, nor did he seem removed from the situation. Sue decided to change tack, 'Well let's put it like this M'sieur.

I think that you can explain more than you are telling me at present, and I beg you to help me to see that Justice is served in this case.' Once more he adopted that quizzical look, as if Sue was a babe in arms.

'Justice.' he said, 'Don't talk to me of Justice! Love and Loyalty will outweigh Justice any day. If I ignore Justice I am a poor citizen it's true, but if I ignore Loyalty and Love, I am a very poor human being indeed.'

Sue wondered where all this philosophical heart searching was leading, but she sensed that Merclot was about to tell her something crucial.

'Come,' he said, 'Suivez moi (Follow me)' and he led her into a lovely conservatory at the side of the house overlooking the River Frome and the fields beyond. 'Madeleine and I would sit here to watch the Sun go down. C'est un bel endroit n'est-ce pas? he said, (This is such a beautiful place isn't it?) and what I am going to tell you now is for you alone. I will not repeat this in a Courtroom for reasons that I will explain, but I think that what I say may unlock a few doors for you, if not all.

Now, I ask you to cast your mind back a few weeks, and imagine that you are a 'fly on the wall' here at 'Volets Bleus' as Madeleine welcomed her guests for the weekend. I'll tell you the story in the third person as if I was just an observer and that might make it less stressful for me and perhaps easier for you to understand. He began, 'A car drove into . . . .

*　　*　　*　　*

A car drove into River Walk in Frome and entered the yard at the back of a rather charming little farmhouse called 'Volets Bleus (Blue Shutters) hooting it's horn as it did so. Four people climbed out and the lady of the house walked, somewhat unsteadily to greet them, waving two large bunches of flowers as she did so. 'Bienvenue! Welcome!' she called and embraced her husband, presenting him with one bunch and the third guest with another as they stepped out. This was Madeleine Merclot. She was an old lady and rather unwell but she had so looked forward to seeing her husband again. He had spent the last two weeks in Weymouth where they had a small flat. He had said that his 'affairs' would take a little longer than usual, but that he would bring his friends, Frank and Zelda Robinson with him for the weekend. She was looking forward to meeting them.

There would be a third guest too, the famous Russian concert pianist Alexei Basmanov, who was giving a series of concerts in the UK. Last week he was in Bournemouth, and next week he would be in Bath and Birmingham. In between he was attending a symposium on 'Twentieth Century French Piano Masterpieces' at the Bradford on Avon Arts Centre, which is only a short distance from Frome. Madeleine was very excited about her visitors. She loved to gossip and to 'catch up' but, above all she wanted to talk to Basmanov, and if possible to attend the symposium. She had some CD's but she had not met him before. 'Claude is such a caring man.' she thought, 'He knows how I love classical music, especially Ravel and Debussy, and now this. What a treat!'

There was some time spent that evening talking about this and that, but Madeleine got tired very quickly because of the strong pain-killers that she was taking for her terminal cancer. She apologized and went to bed early, leaving the other three to talk and drink, and drink and talk. Not much was said about their plans concerning Yarkov because much had been settled already. They were all essentially 'carriers' of the Polonium that would be delivered by Basmanov to another contact in Bath. How it was to be given to Yarkov was not their concern Claude then confided in them that he was very worried about Madeleine. She was in such pain, he said, that he thought that she would not make the symposium. 'If only I could die,' she had said to him, 'my pain would be gone and I could meet 'Our Lord' at last.' Claude knew her very well when her mind was made up. She had made him swear things before in Spain and elsewhere and now she exacted another commitment from him.

'Promise me,' she said, 'that no matter how ill I become, that you will not 'assist 'in my death in any way. I am content to suffer as 'He' did on the Cross. I know that you would not do so anyway, but promise me please.' He had done as she asked and now he was regretting it, he confided to his friends. To hear her suffer was more than he could bear.

The next morning and the next Madeleine was up early, cheerfully making breakfast for them all, but each day she got tired earlier and earlier. On the Saturday night everyone was awoken by her cries of pain, and they all wondered if she would be well enough to go to the symposium on the Sunday afternoon. She made her intentions quite clear after breakfast by reappearing just before lunch all 'dressed up' for a concert, as if it were to be her last. 'You look wonderful ma cherie,' said Claude and everyone agreed. At the symposium Basmanov was amazing. Not only did he play the piano like a Genius, but he was also so informative about the 'Impressionist' composers. Madeleiene enjoyed herself immensely, but when she got home she collapsed on the settee and they had to help her to bed. During the night even this semi-coma failed to disguise her pain and Claude was increasingly worried. 'They'll take her away.' he confided to his friends, 'To a hospice or somewhere. She would hate that.' 'Well, we must not let that happen,' said Frank.

Madeleine did not get up that morning, so Zelda took her some tea before the others all came up to say goodbye, Madeleine apologised for being such a poor hostess, but they all assured her that she was a very wonderful and brave woman. She then seemed to doze off again as they tiptoed out. Claude saw his guests to the car and they thanked him for a wonderful weekend. Zelda was reassuring, 'I don't think that Madeleine will suffer much longer Claude. It seems that her time is nearly up. You must be as brave as she has been when her time comes.' she said.

Madeleine seemed to make a bit of a recovery over the next few days, so much so that she decided that she would make her normal shopping trip with Maurice their driver. She often went out to the car early to settle in and read the paper before he arrived. In the meantime Maurice was preparing to have a shower and went to the airing cupboard for a towel, but the door would not open. He pushed and tugged but it was stuck, much as a door can be sometimes if a stone is wedged under it. He found a knife and gently moved an object that was indeed wedged there, but it wasn't a stone. It was a tiny cork. Now where has that come from?' he thought, 'Where have I seen a cork like that before?' Then it dawned on him. It was a 'pipette' cork, as used in a laboratory or for poisons. Then another realisation dawned on him. His guests had possession of at least four such pipettes and, heaven forbid was it possible that one had been used on Madeleine and the cork had rolled away where they could not find it? He dashed out to the car where Madeleine was seated peacefully.

'Darling!' he called 'C'est moi, Claude. I've come to see if you want another coat. It's a bit chilly out here.' She did not respond, and, as he touched her she rolled gently over with, what he thought, was a smile on her lips. 'Madeleine! Maddie!' he sobbed, but he knew that she was gone.

He knew that he must call the emergency services just the same, but as he reached the house he realised that he must do something else as well. It was difficult for him to accept, but it seemed that Madeleine had been 'put to sleep' out of love. Not his love, because he had determined to suffer with her, but the love of the others for them both. There was no other reason. He decided at that point not to cause them to be implicated in any way, and that is why he set about a rather convoluted cover up.

The cover up involved taking the handbag out of the car to make it look like an opportunistic robbery that went wrong. Maybe one that inadvertently caused a heart attack. This notion would be strengthened when a card from the bag was used for cash in Radstock. Claude would attend to this over the next few days and then jettison the bag. He had no reason to suppose that there might be an autopsy and, even if there was, he knew that the 'new' polonium was virtually untraceable.

*　　*　　*　　*

He had finished his story and Sue sat deep in thought. They had been so lucky she thought, to have shared so much love. In one sense they '<u>were</u>' love, if it can be defined in any meaningful way. She remembered that there had been a 'Courtly Love Ball' at the Chateau Chevalier a few years back. In that setting four definitions of love had been 'borrowed' from C.S. Lewis and the four Greek words for love namely,

Storge-Affection / Phileo-Friendship/ Eros-'in love'/ & Agape-Charity.

She was certain in her mind that Madeleine and Claude shared a love based on Eros, a sense of 'being' in love. Eros does not mean erotic, although that probably was present also. Lewis used another word for this 'sex drive,' namely 'Venus.' although he did not class this as 'Love'.

She was less certain about why Claude had defined the actions of Frank and Zelda as being ones of 'love' but then she remembered that Agape was the' Love that brings forth caring regardless of the circumstances' and, in Christian terms, this was the greatest love of all.

The Robinsons may have been ardent Communists with the murder of Yarkov on their minds and much else besides, but they had behaved in an altruistic, not to say, 'loving' Christian way on this occasion.

After awhile she 'stepped' out of her reverie and spoke seriously to Claude. 'You know that this makes you an accessory to murder,' she said.

'Only if you can prove it all in Court,' he replied, 'remember I told you that this conversation 'never happened' so you'll need independent verifications of some kind won't you?' Sue was miffed. 'For such a lovely old man, you're a right cunning bastard.' she thought but she did not make her feelings known. Instead she made the formal announcement of a police officer when arresting a suspect. 'M'siur Merclot,' she said, 'I should take you into custody at this point but I'm not going to do so yet. You will probably be questioned again under caution quite soon. Is that clear?' He replied 'Oui, Mamselle Inspectrice.' with a smile.

Over the next few days MI5 were in and out of the office and the Superintendent was jumping around like mad. Sue's discovery of the secret chamber and it's contents had come too late to arrest any of the conspirators all of whom were back in Russia by now. Paradoxically Yarkov had reneged on his promise to sign the Disarmament Accord and he had returned to a hero's welcome in Moscow, shoulder to shoulder with the President. 'Smoke and Mirrors,' thought Sue, 'Was this what was intended all along and were MI5 duped from the start?'

Eros or Venus? Who cares?

There was still the 'murder' to be solved so another interview was organised for M. Merclot, this time by a different and 'independent' Police body. There being no reply, the officers went in the front door, which was open and there was Claude sitting in his chair in the conservatory, dead. By the time that news got through to Sue she was having dinner with Bruce. She put the phone down and felt strangely upset. 'Merclot's dead.' she said, 'they say it's a heart attack.' Bruce put his arm around her and said, 'That's that then. You're out of it now. Just don't mention the Polonium or the whole thing may start again.'

This broke the ice and immediately she was in his arms laughing and crying at the same time. He said, 'Look I've got a 'Madeleine' present for you.' He opened a bag that he had been hiding and there inside was a beautiful bunch of flowers. 'Oh thank you Bruce, thank you. That is exactly what she would have done. She always gave flowers when she wanted to show how much she loved him' she said. 'Now open the card Sue. Don't forget the card' Bruce said. 'Wasn't she such a wonderful woman.' she repeated. 'And so are you Sue.' he said again. 'Open it.' Now she did so, her hands shaking as she read Bruce's words in French.

'Je t'aime ma cherie. Mariez Moi s'il vous plait.'

There were no bees buzzing in her bonnet this time
as she simply said,
'OUI M'SIEUR, BIEN SUR'

FIN

PART 4.
FLOTSAM AND JETSUM

Summary

Another case for Sue 'Parker', Somerset Sleuth.

Readers may remember Sue Parker from a previous_novel 'Bath Buns at Sally Lunn's.' You will know therefore that she was a very resourceful police officer but having made her way up to Inspector, she was happy to get married and retire. She was only 45 at the time and Bruce (Garmston) her husband continued in the Force until he became ill. They were not given much time to enjoy joint retirement but they did manage a number of memorable holidays together. After his death Sue moved to Salisbury to be near friends and it was on holiday with them, one New Year's Day that she became unwittingly involved in a case just as intriguing and threatening as before. It all began on a windswept beach near Portsmouth.

Force Niner
Sue thinks it through

The Luvvies
Where's Bernie?

Double Jeopardy
Just routine

Sue's cruise
John Doe

Newshound
Hello again Sue

The Odessa File
Love from a cold climate

Déjà vu Sue
Silver Linings

FLOTSAM AND JETSUM

Force Niner

Sue Parker had moved from Bath to Salisbury and was celebrating New Year on holiday with friends at Hayling Island near Portsmouth. Whilst she was there she planned to meet up with her old friend from the Bath police station, Glynis Edwards and her husband Jack.

Jack Edwards was not a seafaring man. Indeed, if he'd known even just a little bit about the sea, he might have been more helpful to the police as they began an investigation into the body that he found washed up on the beach at Hayling Island on New Year's Day. He might even have provided those vital clues that only exist momentarily on an ever-changing shoreline. However he was not a seafarer and such niceties would have to be left to the police and the meteorological experts later. For example, did it seem to be part of the natural <u>flotsam</u> of the sea, floating with other similar objects from who knows where, or could it be <u>jetsam</u>, something that had been jettisoned overboard from a sea vessel either accidentally or deliberately. And maybe it was not even the result of an incoming (Flood) tide but an outgoing (Ebb or Rip) one.

It is tempting to draw an analogy here with the vicissitudes of fate, in which waves of good fortune and misfortune might buffet an otherwise sanguine life. Sue had had more than her share of bad luck, but then again she was an optimist and counted her blessings 'one by one' when she was in a difficult spot. She was not one to sit and mope and she often thought about prayer, but somehow found it difficult to make a personal connection with any established Church. Notwithstanding that, one of her favourite expressions muttered under her breath was 'Thank you God', and she really meant it. He or she was to be thanked, but never to be blamed when things went wrong, and Sue always took responsibility for her own errors of judgement, be they personal or professional. However, she'd also come to realise that others might operate on a very different wavelength, in which moral considerations had no part. This had been helpful in her police work in the past, and now it was to matter again.

Nautical terms such as 'Flotsam or Jetsum' would have been a mystery to Jack because he and his wife Glynis had spent most of their life in Bath and had only recently retired to the Portsmouth area to be close to their grandchildren. There must be many nautical folk living in the Portsmouth/Southampton area but the Edward's were not amongst them, and most of the 'locals' were now retailers or retirees such as Jack and his wife. He had been 'something' in the Civil Service and she a secretary at Bath police station. For them retirement was just a dream about a bit of peace and quiet, and maybe a bit of 'messing about in boats'. As retired couples do they had soon adopted new routines, one of which was to walk the dog at 9 o'clock after they'd had breakfast, and this was Jack's job. 'C'mon boy. C'mon!' he would say every morning, 'C'mon Nelson, time for a walk, Force Nine or not.' He'd heard that expression many times but had no idea what it meant, except that it sounded vaguely nautical and hinted at intrepid seafarers braving the storms as he was about to do, except that he hoped to stay very clear of the sea. However, he could not always depend on Nelson to do so. The dog loved the sea and the sand and the pebbles, and would tug at the lead if it seemed that Jack was heading away from the waterfront. Nelson had been a 'rescue' dog, a Labrador-Alsatian cross with a thick black coat and a rather haughty demeanour. Jack used to say that he acted as if he really had been that important Admiral but he loved him to bits, so every day they headed for their familiar stretch of beach and Nelson was let off his lead.

Even though it was a blustery New Year's Day morning, Jack had been up and about since 7.30, and decided to take Nelson out earlier than usual. 'A Force Niner out there,' he called out to Glynis but she was still in the bathroom so he called out again to say that they were leaving. There was no reply once more so, with Nelson jumping up and down with excitement, he gathered the lead and they set off for the beach.

When Glynis appeared a few moments later she went into the kitchen to prepare breakfast, but there was no sign of Jack or Nelson. He usually had his eggs and bacon before he took the dog out, so this was upsetting her morning routine and she wasn't pleased, not pleased at all.

However, unaware of the trouble they had caused, Jack and Nelson were soon walking on the beach that was the dog's favourite spot for digging, splashing and chasing sticks. Inclement weather was no hardship for this old 'sea-dog' but Jack's glasses steamed up with the effort of the walk. Nelson usually rang rings around him but today the dog seemed to have some sympathy with Jack's hangover and just strolled along, nose to the ground. Then he noticed that Nelson had stopped and was sniffing a large bundle on the seashore. 'Nelson. Nelson!' he called, 'leave that, c'mon boy, c'mon. You don't know where it's been.' he added with a laugh. But for once Nelson ignored his master's voice and stayed still, one paw raised over the package as if on guard on the HMS Victory. There was nothing for it then but for Jack to walk over and put Nelson back on his lead, but as he got closer he could see that Nelson was serious this time, his tail still and not wagging as usual. 'What is it boy?' he said, 'Whatever have you got there?' Now Nelson did move away, as if pleased to hand over the responsibility of this bundle to someone else. Jack took the opportunity to fix the lead back on and gave the object a prod for good measure. It was soft and felt rather like a part deflated balloon that might burst under too much pressure. All this he deduced from his toe poke because now the penny had dropped. It was a body. There was no doubt about it, it was a body, a large one at that, probably a man he thought because all that could be seen at first was a black coat with hat and boots to match and that was enough for him. He stooped momentarily over the body and saw that it was a white male before looking out to sea wondering if a boat lay at anchor there. If so it would have been difficult to see through the strong blustery wind and spray. He took another look, this time to the shops along the seafront but could see nothing there either. He was puzzled but most of all he was surprised, this was the last thing that he had expected to see that morning. Satisfied that there was no one else around to deal with the problem he made up his mind. 'Come on Nelson.' he said, 'we'll have to hurry home and report this won't we?' Nelson wagged his tail in agreement and they set off.

Soon they were back, staggering through the front door and out of the winds that seemed to insist on following them. Nelson was off his chain in a flash and heading for a 'bikkie' reward in the kitchen as Jack took off coat and boots and scarf and gloves and deposited them into the heap of 'stuff' in the hall. Glynis appeared from the kitchen, 'Where do you think you've been?' she asked, 'You might have told me you were going early Jack, and I'm very surprised at you Nelson, you of all people.' (She should have said 'dogs' of course but Nelson was 'family.') 'Just what have you been up to?' she continued, 'You've been ages, hope you don't mind having your bacon hard.' She always said this even if he was only moments late. It was her way of keeping (or thinking that she was keeping) some control over Jack whom she considered to be a somewhat wayward child. 'That dog's got more sense than you have.' was another one of her sayings but Jack took it all in good part. 'Yes, of course, sorry dear, you see, we've had a bit of a shock, haven't we old boy?' He patted Nelson on the head as the dog padded in from the kitchen wondering where his 'treats' were. 'Yes we have. Yes we have.' he continued in a tone much as one might address a toddler. 'Sorry Glyn but I've got to nip upstairs for a mo' he said, 'I'll be down in a tick.' saying which he hurried up the stairs as if on a mission. 'That'll teach you' Glynis thought, 'mixing the hop and the grape, even if it is New Year.' She was sympathetic but after more than 10 minutes, she'd had enough. 'Come on Jack' she called out, 'you and your stomach. Come on, breakfast's getting cold.' Jack could see that there was no point in arguing, so he dutifully hurried downstairs and sat down in front of a really big New Year's Day breakfast, with all the trimmings, while Nelson gnawed at a bone under the table. Glynis had one of those rather formidable looks about her and he was wondering when and how to broach the subject of the body. Fortunately she took the initiative as she poured a glass of orange. 'Eat up. Eat up.' she said. 'You're definitely looking off colour. Anybody would think you'd seen a dead body.' Jack nearly choked on his toast. 'You won't believe this Glyn, but that's exactly what we have seen. I've been trying to tell you for ages. I was going to dial 999. That's best don't you think?' he said.

'Never know with you do I Jack Edwards?' she replied, still wondering if her husband was having another one of his 'flights of fancy' as she called them. When some of 'his' friends came to the house they often played a board game called 'Diplomacy,' that was set during the First World War. Players had to maximize the power of their allotted country be it, Germany, France, Russia, Austria-Hungary or Great Britain, and tempers could get frayed from time to time. 'You all behave as if this is real,' she would say as she served drinks. 'Heaven help us if they update the thing.' Fortunately there had been no updating of the board game but she suspected that he played 'War Games' up in his computer room anyway. However, this time she had to admit he did look serious. 'Well you'd better do it right now if you're sure', she said, 'Yes, dial 999 and I'll put your breakfast back in the oven. We don't want it getting cold do we?'

Jack was relieved; it gave him time to think. He made the call and agreed to be available for more questions later. Then he sat down for breakfast only half listening to Glynis as she outlined plans for the day. The truth of the matter was that he was still puzzled and rather unnerved by the events of the morning. It just didn't make sense.

Sue thinks it through

Readers may remember Sue 'Parker' from her adventures in Bath as a Police Officer, including the 'Bath Buns' affair and, as stated in our introduction, she had now moved to Salisbury. She and her friend Rebecca had chosen the Warner's Holiday Hotel on Hayling Island for their New Year break because it gave her a chance to 'catch up' with her old friend from the Bath Police station Glynis Edwards who had retired there. The hotel had been fully booked with visitors from far and wide for many months and amongst these was Sue's group, the 'Luvvies' from Salisbury. Their title actually owed more to a love of all things theatrical rather than members of an acting group. It also hinted at the word 'Love' because a stipulation of membership was a single status, in other words it was a 'singles' club if not an all out 'dating' one. Still, members did meet and fall in love and others hoped to do so, especially Rebecca who was always on the look out for a new male friend. She'd had quite a few romances over the years but somehow never a 'Mr Right.' Sue wasn't even looking although it had been 10 long years since she lost Bruce. 'I'll know, when my love comes along.' she always sang to herself if friends tried to fix up dates for her. It wasn't that she felt constrained by the ties of her marriage, because she remembered how Bruce had explicitly asked her to find another love 'when I'm gone' if that would make her happy. In fact he had said that it would make him happy from his heavenly cloud. In musical terms he had said that she should 'Look for the Silver Lining' because that's where he would be, up there looking out for her. When she sometimes heard the song by mistake it brought floods of tears because, although she was not religious in the formal 'church going' sense, she actually did believe in a 'Heaven' up there beyond her knowledge. She also knew somehow that it was the 'religious' part of her that informed and guided her when she might have been 'in a spot,' which was not unusual for her. Of course her police work had dangers and dilemmas but sometimes she thought civilian life contained as many, if not more traps for the unwary. Choosing the 'right' option was never easy and a wrong one could bring disaster. Sue was not persuaded by the powerbrokers of Christian churches over the centuries, but she did think that the notion of some kind of redemption made sense.

She argued that for there to be forgiveness there must already exist some idea of sinfulness and, although this is amply provided in the 'Old Testament' story of Adam and Eve, yet ideas of such 'sinfulness' must have pre-existed that story as well. In other words, she argued, people recognised that they were inherently prone to sinfulness and that story merely reflected their situation, hence the 'need' for a just God who would ameliorate their predicament through prayer. The Christian view took this a stage further by their acceptance that Christ died on the cross for those very sins, which were thereby redeemed. These 'testaments' make sense to those who have faith. But what of those who do not?

Sue's experience had taught her that there were notions of right and wrong in any society, and it wasn't just a case of being legal or illegal. No, there was always a drive, almost a longing to do the 'right' thing and where did that motivation come from? She wasn't a theologian but it stood to reason that if one acknowledges that there is a 'right' thing to do, then that is good. Conversely a 'wrong' thing is bad. Now, Sue thought bad might be accepted by some as 'just the way it is' but in acknowledging that such and such is 'bad' it falls short of being good and if one's drive is to be 'good' then one might need to seek forgiveness or redemption. She reasoned that failure to do so results in a sort of sick feeling described by some as a poor conscience and this is to be avoided at all costs. For her that inner sense of right and wrong, was often on the face of it, all that stood between her and her adversaries in crime and she believed that, despite the predisposition to evil given in the Bible, she thought that everyone had a drive to be 'good' and that their failure to be so due to greed, anger or revenge etc. would show itself sooner or later.

In other words they would give the game away by the actions they take or fail to take, and Sue was ever watchful. However there were also cases in which a suspect would not feel guilty because they believed their actions to be fully justified. In such a case Sue would look out for a different kind of behaviour, one in which perhaps the person or persons showed signs of a bravura that was often disguised as indifference. But Sue was retired.

Surely she wouldn't need such deep thinking again? Or would she?

The Luvvies

When she moved to Salisbury Sue decided that she would join a number of social groups to have a good time and one of these was the 'Luvvies.' The Luvvies group for the New Year visit was 8 in number, 4 'Guys' and 4 'Dolls' with Malcolm and Maureen their titular leaders, or 'Skips' as they termed them from Malcolm's knowledge of bowls. A 'skip' is a sort of captain of a rink for the day, not a captain of the whole team, and this he thought suited them very well. He was happy to delegate but Maureen tended to think of herself as the one and only captain, let alone skip. It was this approach that led her to, let's say 'interpret' the rules as it suited her and one of the ways that it did suit her was to bring her 20 year old son Bernie along to this and that function. She said that he would be 'lonely' if she left him at home and as most other members did not have children under the age of 30, she was given some licence, and others also recognised that he was rather immature and a bit of a 'mother's' boy. 'It can't be easy for her.' Sue said, 'She's a divorcee and he really is a bit of a wimp, what else could she do?' Janet, Jerry & Ron made up the group.

The other guests came from a variety of locations, some local and some far distant, some in two's, three's or four's and some, like the Luvvies in larger groups. Warners Holidays operate an adult franchise, so there were no children on site, and hence quite a number of retired couples. At this New Year festivities there were three groups larger than Sue's, one from Glasgow and they called themselves, 'Scotland the Brave.' Every year they left Scotland to experience the delights of Hogmanay as celebrated throughout the world. Last year it had been Moscow when Gordon, their leader had been expelled for being drunk and disorderly. Fortunately this was on their last day, but Gordon always maintained it was because he asked a soldier on guard duty why he was killing innocent civilians in Chechnya. The others warned him not to say too much about Culloden or those 'Hanoverian Sassenachs' for their visit to England this year.

The second large group were from Japan. They were a mixed group of managers from the Nissan factories in the North of England, together with visiting executives and their wives from Tokyo. Led by Mori Hirosaki they knew how to enjoy themselves 'British' fashion with just a hint of the Orient in the formalities of dance. Nevertheless the girls wore short dresses and the men wore casual jeans. There was nothing of the 'Empire of the Rising Sun' about them, but that alone could not guarantee their safety from some hostility by another group at the resort.

This was the third group from New Zealand named 'The Battle Hill Memorial Society.' They had come to England to team up with surviving relatives from those who had fought the Maori Wars in 1846, especially those who had died there, namely Seaman William Roberts, Private Thomas Tuite and one other, whose name had been lost in the records. Jenny Ward who led this group had the doubtful distinction of having lost a family member fighting 'For King/Queen and Empire' in every British conflict for more than a hundred years. Apart from Rugby and the Admiral's Cup Sailing, there is nothing that binds New Zealanders more than a love of the 'old country.' It was this that had brought the 'Battle Hill' group together but it was not solely a one-battle memorial group. Over the years they had found much comfort in their loss with others who had experienced the same over many different theatres of war from the Boer War, First and Second World Wars and beyond. Wherever NZ forces were in peril, the 'Battle Hill Group' was there for them, and although this was supposed to be in the spirit of reconciliation, this charitable outlook was not for everyone. For this reason they avoided a tour of the Far East where emotions still festered but now they found themselves neighbours with the Japanese delegation. Jenny knew that she'd have to meet up with Hirosaki as soon as possible if trouble was to be avoided. Fortunately he was of the same mind so they quickly organised a joint bowls match with a prize to be donated to the victims of the earthquakes in Christchurch and Tokyo. In no time at all the two groups were getting on well, and there even a hint of romance in the air with Mike McLeod of McLeod from Dunedin demonstrating the niceties of the Highland Reel to a bemused Tina Tanaka from Tokyo.

Naturally not everyone had such distinct reasons for being at the Warners Holiday Resort. Altogether there were more than 300 guests and most were just out for a good time. The Luvvies planned to spend the first few days making the most of the excellent facilities at Warners including a pool and Jacuzzi, a bowling alley and a large games room. They arrived at about midday on New Year's Eve and while others explored the place Sue went out to meet Glynis and Jack to spend an afternoon with their grandchildren. It was fun on the beach despite the blustery weather, but she was back in time for the evening meal and 'entertainment.' The evenings at Warners are really the highlight of the day for most people when there is full waitress service for a 'three course' meal followed by floor-shows and wild and not so wild dancing to follow into the 'wee small hours.' It was natural that a certain amount of drink led to a certain amount of conviviality and the Luvvies soon made friends all round, including some from the groups mentioned as well as others.

Furthermore the group were soon on friendly terms with the receptionists Beatrice and Marie, the shop manager 'Gloria', and the room service staff as well as 'their' waitresses, Anna and Paula, young girls, probably less than 20. As is customary among the young they had tattoos that caused some speculation among the 'Luvvies.' Names such as Boris, Zani, Eva, Sergei and Nashi all seemed to have some romantic connection, and Ron wondered whether they had more hidden, 'you know where.' This caused some mirth at the table, but Ron was ever hopeful that he'd strike lucky one day and gave himself licence to flirt outrageously. 'I love these Polish girls,' he said, 'I love their accents and they seem s ss ss ss so . . .' he hesitated as he had a slight stammer, but before he could speak again, Jerry interrupted with a smile. 's-so sexy do you mean Ron?' he said, and at this the whole table fell about laughing, except for Ron who was a bit embarrassed and Bernie, who never seemed to realise what was going on anyway. 'I don't think they're Polish' said Sue, 'their accent is sort of Russian but not quite, and anyway, Russia's not in the EU. I'd say they're from one of the Baltic States, probably Estonia. I've been there on a cruise as some of know, and as I'm interested in languages I made a point of listening out for differences, inflexions in speech, if you see what I mean, not that it matters a lot. Don't forget I'm presenting a slide show on our Baltic Cruise later and I'll be talking about the different dialects then. It's a shame though,' she continued, 'cheap labour, all the hours God sends and minimum wage if they're lucky.'

That was too much for Maureen who thought that Sue should be kept in order, 'Now, now Sue,' she said, 'we've been through all this before haven't we? Remember that old lady at last year's Turkey and Tinsel who didn't want immigrants in her street and you said she should be ashamed. Well, as we all know she felt faint and had to leave the table. Then she went home and her son claimed compensation and I got a rather nasty letter from Warners. We're probably lucky to be here at all, so please leave your social conscience at home if you please.' This was like a 'red rag to a bull' to Sue who had volunteered to work at her local CAB (Citizen's Advice Bureau) when she had retired from the Police Force. The CAB not only operate a policy of 'zero tolerance' but also one of 'challenge.' She was about to explode when she felt a tap on her shoulder. It was Malcolm. 'Dance?' he said. His smile was a knowing one and Sue got up graciously. 'Thanks, I'd love to.' she said. Janet glanced at Rebecca with relief. A nasty situation had been diffused and 'next up' was a Line dance. 'Come along Sue,' said Rebecca, 'This one's great!' Sue sat back, 'I can hardly dance, let alone Line dance.' she protested but all in vain. Rebecca held one arm and Janet the other as they propelled her to the dance floor. The 'caller' was friendly but firm. Sue recognised him as one of the other waiters at table. 'Look, It's Franco!' she said. Rebecca smiled and said, 'Yes, your Italian stallion. Fancy him do you?' Sue just laughed and gave her a nudge as they all lined up.

'Watch me.' Franco began, 'and then do the same when I tell you to. Left foot tap, right foot tap, turn around and bow to the facing rank. Right foot double tap then left foot double tap, turn around and repeat, now, let's have some music maestro please.' Sue turned to Rebecca in bewilderment, 'Did he say double tap first or . . .' but then the music started and it was too late. They were whizzing around the floor, right foot, left foot, turn around and around and around until Sue felt quite dizzy. And then it was over and they collapsed with laughter.

'I need a rest' said Sue, 'Let's go into the bar and have one.' 'And a drink,' said Janet, 'G&T's all round?' The others nodded and Janet headed for the bar returning after awhile with the drinks. 'Cheers and more cheers.' they said in unison. 'Guess who's on at the bar?' Janet asked?' The others couldn't see so they just said, 'Who?' 'It's Anna, and Paula that's who,' said Janet, 'Just back from waiting table and now they have to do the bar poor things. I bet they'll be on prompt at breakfast as well.' 'I wouldn't be surprised,' said Sue, 'and our dole queues get longer and longer. Still, you can't fault their service can you?' Janet smiled, 'Are you including Franco in that remark Sue?' It was common knowledge in the group that Sue was 'on her own,' and despite her protestations to the contrary, her friends couldn't resist a tease. Sue thought it best to ignore this latest innuendo. 'Another drink?' she said.

From then on the evening went very well as the wine flowed and eventually it was time for 'Auld Lang's Sine.' with everyone holding hands, everyone that is except Bernie who was nowhere to be seen. As a matter of fact he hadn't been seen for some time but nobody seemed bothered, least of all his mother who just said. 'Bernie just likes to do things his way. He can't be far away. He's got a mind of his own. He's probably in the Internet Rooms chatting in cyber space.'

Actually Bernie was not in the computer suite but he wasn't far away either. Unfortunately however he was trapped, and was desperately thinking of ways to escape before it was too late.

Where's Bernie?

Now some of the Luvvies group retired to their beds while others, including Sue headed for the comfy lounge bar again. She enjoyed this time of night when all the activity was dying down but she missed, oh how she missed Bruce at times like this. Actually it was not long before those who had joined her, peeled off one by one to bed and Sue was left alone with Eduardo, the pianist playing 'Georgia on my mind' for the fifth time that night. It was difficult to say who seemed more bored but the music seemed to carry Sue away into a reverie, a time when she was cruising with Bruce. The one she remembered best was to the Baltic, memorable maybe, because it was to be their last. They had cruised before and Sue always made a point of learning as much as she could about the culture of the places they would visit, as well as the language there. She'd always loved languages and had become known as 'Senorita Parker' when she was only thirteen. Her school had made a 'twinning' arrangement with a school from Barcelona and the Spanish department went into overtime to speed up Spanish lessons. But what a disaster! No one had mentioned the fact that the pupils there spoke Catalan, a very different language. It was 'all hands to the pumps' and Sue soon found herself teaching other boys and girls, some of whom were a lot older. Anyway this had given her a taste for languages and dialects especially. She'd learnt Fijian and Swahili and even mastered West Indian 'patois' whilst on a cruise there, and she'd also picked up Swedish, Russian and some local dialects for their Baltic adventure.

It was at this time that Bruce had told her to 'be happy' and to feel free and, although she had appreciated the sentiment it always made her feel sad. She was soon dropping off to sleep but suddenly awoke with a start. She had remembered that she was to give a slide show to a small 'Warners Travel' group entitled 'Sing for your Supper' about her experiences on that cruise, and she'd hardly done any preparation, so it was off to bed with a plan to rise early in the morning.

There were quite a few hangovers at breakfast and quite a few absentees also but Sue was there and so were Rebecca, Maureen, Malcolm and Janet. There was a lot of talk about the last evening and plans began to be made for the days ahead. The service was brilliant as usual. Janet only had to lift her cup and they were there. Anna held the teapot and Paula held the milk jug. 'Thanks,' Janet said as the tea was poured and the milk added, but like Sue she had a rather frugal appetite this particular morning, 'Nothing else,' she added, noting that nobody was having kippers or the standard fry up either. 'Just coffee for me' muttered a subdued Malcolm, 'Thank God this is only once a year.' Sue was also a bit dreamy, and maybe a little nostalgic too. 'You know what you need.' said Rebecca, 'There he is over there, Franco, your hero!'

At this point Marie, the receptionist came across to their table waving a note and said, 'Message I have for Mrs Garmston.' They all looked perplexed until Sue suddenly realised it was for her. She had reverted to her maiden name some years after Bruce died, but her accounts were still in her married name. 'So sorry,' she said, 'Yes that's me, I'm Mrs Garmston.' she paused and then for the benefit of the others she added as she rose to her feet, 'and I'm Ms Parker as well, Polygamist Extraordinaire.' This brought much laughter from her friends, but Marie was looking perplexed and rather worried. 'Phone call.' she repeated 'It important they say.' Sue shrugged, 'OK' she said, 'I'm coming.'

She passed Ron and Jerry making their way to breakfast as she headed for the phone, but soon she was back at the table looking rather shocked. 'What's up Sue, not bad news I hope.' said Malcolm. 'I'm not sure,' Sue replied, 'you see, they've found a dead body. That was my friend Glynis. She says that Jack found a body on the beach while taking the dog for a walk this morning. She wants me to go over.' There was a stunned silence and then Maureen gasped as if hit by a truck,

'Bernie! Bernie!' she cried out in anguish 'Where's Bernie? Has anyone seen Bernie this morning?'

Double Jeopardy?

Since receiving Jack's phone call earlier that day about the body on the foreshore, the Police had not been idle. A whole team of uniformed and other investigators had arrived at the beach and set up barriers to protect the 'crime' scene, if that's what it was. However, although most experienced officers expected no more than an accidental death at this point, Inspector Williams was taking no chances and set up an incident room at the 'Lamb and Flag' nearby. He sent Sergeant Dave Andrews to co-ordinate matters there while PC's Paul Pretty and Liz Cope would begin a round of local questioning and then, after a brief examination by the local coroner's office, the body could be moved to the hospital for a more thorough one. 'Open and Shut case' said the Inspector hopefully. He wanted to get back to his family for a New Year's Party in which he was to be dressed up as a clown. But as far as the case was concerned he couldn't have been more wrong, because just then the news came in of a young man missing from the Warner's Lakeside Village.

After her phone call from Glynis Sue had thought that she should at least help Maureen to check out Bernie's room and any other possible places where he might be. The Luvvies group split up and agreed to meet back at the reception in 30 minutes if there was no sign. Only then would Maureen call the Police. A key was obtained from reception and Marie accompanied them to Room 44. The door seemed to be stuck and Sue could feel Maureen nearly swooning as she held her hand tight. 'There's something heavy up against the door.' said Marie, 'I can't budge it.' Now Sue felt uneasy, 'Not another body' she thought, but just smiled at Maureen. 'Here, let me try.' she said, and with a heave the door gave way and she was in, followed by a pale Maureen. They just stood there, the three of them. It had been a case that prevented the door from opening and, apart from that the room seemed to be empty. 'I'll check the bathroom.' Sue said, 'Nothing there, I'm sure.' Fortunately she was right and turned to Maureen in relief. 'See, nothing, He's probably up and about somewhere while we're doing all the worrying.' Maureen didn't say anything but sat quietly on the single bed, collapsing slowly into the pillow with tears in her eyes. Then suddenly she was bolt upright and pointed to the pillow, 'It's perfume,' she said, 'perfume!! Dior if I'm not mistaken. Bernie doesn't even use deodorant. There's been a woman here.' She spoke in very certain terms but sounded incredulous nonetheless. 'It's impossible' she said, 'Bernie wouldn't go with girls.'

Marie looked tempted to smile as if she'd heard that one before, (and she had, many times) but Sue frowned and just said, 'Maybe he let a friend use the room, that's quite possible isn't it.' Maureen looked at her hopefully but still in disbelief, 'Yes. Yes of course, though as you know Bernie doesn't have many friends and he certainly doesn't make friends easily does he?' Sue knew that this was only too true and now she was getting worried. She made a quick call to Glynis to tell her what had happened and promised to call again later.

Back at reception they met up with the other Luvvie's search groups and Sue could tell from their faces that they had found no sign of Bernie either. 'Better call the Police,' she said, 'Here, let me dial the number.'

Now Inspector Williams had a dilemma on his hands. Did he have one case or two? No matter, he knew that the most important thing was to find the missing person. This could be a matter where time would be of the essence so he decided to concentrate his forces up at the Warner's complex, leaving Sergeant Andrews with only PC Cope behind at the Lamb and Flag. 'Just carry on with the routine stuff for the time being.' he said, 'the missing person could turn up at any moment. I've been told that it's a young lad so he might have just wandered off somewhere, but we can't be too careful. I'm organising dogs and divers just the same.'

The Warners resort on Hayling Island, or more properly the 'Lakeside Coastal Village,' is set in 32 acres overlooking Christchurch harbour. The village itself has everything for the adventurous or casual holidaymaker including outdoor and indoor areas for games etc. As one approaches they will see a driveway with the lake on one side and then a series of chalets much as in a World war two airfield. These surround a large building in the centre in which is housed the dining and entertainment area (known as the 'Chichester') as well as 'reception,' a shop and the casual 'Piano' bar.

Off to one side and at the back are various outbuildings including a games hall/ bowling alley as well as a leisure centre and pool. Other buildings are for staff accommodation and for maintenance activities.

The sheer size and watery location of the site meant that the Police had a big job on their hands and the Inspector reluctantly deployed the divers immediately. The lake was so close to the accommodations that it would have been fairly easy to topple in, he thought, in spite of the fencing. The next few hours were taken up in this painstaking search and it was beginning to get dark when the Inspector got a message on his mobile. This coastal area has poor reception in parts but he was able to hear the words, 'We've found him.' before it crackled loudly.' 'Hello, hello,' he called, 'Hello, hello, damn you, hello,' he called again, but it was in vain.

He was cut off and his attempts to 'return call' were futile. He had a mile to walk and he didn't know if they had found a dead body or a live one.

Meanwhile, given his instructions to 'hold the fort' Sergeant Andrews sent PC Liz Cope round to see the Jack Edwards. He thought that it was important to get a statement at an early stage before something was forgotten, and how right he was. Glynis opened the door and just said, 'Can you come back later please he's not in any fit state to see anyone. In fact if he wasn't my husband, I'd say he was drunk.' Liz was a young policewoman, much as Sue had been when she had started out, but she, like Sue, was very determined and would not be put off so easily. 'Just a couple of questions,' she said, 'just for the record. My boss won't take no for an answer and he can be a pain sometimes.' The ploy worked, as it usually did and Glynis relented, 'All right, come in here then, but don't be long.' she said. Jack was seated at the dining table but stood up and saluted when Liz walked in. 'Officer on deck.' he called out, 'Splice the main brace. Welcome on board Sir, I mean Ma-am.' 'Sit down you old fool,' said Glynis, 'and give me that bottle. You've had quite enough for one day.' Jack just mumbled something and handed the bottle over before turning to Liz. Suddenly he seemed quite sober as if he had enjoyed winding his wife up with his behaviour. Liz noted that he seemed able to change character on a whim. 'Was this just a game, or was it his way of disguising his true character for my benefit, and if so why?' she wondered. She thought that Jack Edwards might have some skeletons in the cupboard and they might be worth a follow up when she got back.

'Right constable' Jack continued, 'what would you like to know then? Mmm, Height well over 6 foot I'd say, probably about 16 stone or more and that's about it, except for a black hat, coat and boots. The boots seemed a bit unusual though, a big fur lining from what I could see, and worn over the trousers if you see what I mean, not under the trousers as I'd wear mine and,' he looked at Liz's feet, 'as you are I see.' Glynis looked at him suspiciously as if he'd been caught with his fingers in the cookie jar. 'Never mind about the Constable,' she said, 'Is that all you can think of?' 'Evidence, my dear, evidence, that's all I'm talking about and no Constable, I really can't think of anything else. You see we don't know much about the sea Glyn and me, but we know when there's a gale all right especially when the sea's up and crashing on the pavement and up over the road by the shops. You see I wouldn't know if anything was unusual I suppose.' Liz was pleased with her work. She thought that the boots might hold a clue when she got back to the station and then there was Jack Edwards himself a bit of a mystery man, a Jekyll and Hyde maybe or just an old fool. 'Thank you.' she said, 'thank you both. We'll probably be in touch later. Many thanks again.' As she left the house she could hear Glynis's voice once more. 'No wonder he drinks.' she thought.

However Glynis didn't have time to say much more to her errant husband before her phone rang in the hall so, picking up the half empty whisky bottle with a self-satisfied smirk, she left the lounge to pick up the phone. It was Sue, apologising for not coming over sooner but also to tell her that the missing boy had been found. 'Yes, he's fine apparently,' she said, 'a bit of a fuss about nothing it seems. They found him in a big basket of warm towels near the pool area. Apparently he can't remember much. He says that he'd had too much to drink, went for a swim and then flopped into the basket. I'll be over tomorrow if that's OK. It's too late now.'

But Bernie did remember, he remembered only too well, and it was not something that he wanted to tell the Police, or especially his mother.

Just routine

Inspector Alex Williams had been in the Metropolitan Police force during the recent street demonstrations in London. He had not liked what he saw, with, to his mind excessive use of force by some units and it seemed to him with the blessing of those in senior positions. When he made his feelings known 'Sergeant' Williams was suddenly offered a promotion to Portsmouth and had to think long and hard before accepting it. Something had told him that it was the wrong thing to do, that he should persist with his observations and maybe appear at the disciplinary meetings but the new post was Oh so tempting. It would give his young family a chance of growing up in the leafy Lee on Solent where there was yachting and other healthy sports activities as well as a more tranquil setting for Helen his wife. She had had to retire from teaching in the Inner City with a 'stress related' illness and life in London seemed to debilitate her.

On balance he had decided that it would be best to accept, but these factors weighed heavily on Alex in his new job as he set an almost impossible work schedule for himself and his staff. 'I'll show them that a good cop doesn't have to be corrupt,' he thought,' and one day I'll prove it.' Fortunately this did not make him unpopular amongst his colleagues who saw in him a 'really straight' police officer. He expected much of them, but no less than he expected of himself and he would delegate to those whom he trusted. He was a rare breed, a really 'Fair Cop.' But work did not always come first with him. That privilege went to his family whom he doted on, usually doing the school runs because Helen didn't drive. She in turn was a great support to him but deep down he knew that he had failed that crisis of conscience back in London, and he was determined to make amends should a similar occasion arise again.

For now, with the 'sideshow' over, he redeployed his officers to the various duties necessary in a case such as this. He was up early the next day having asked for a large screen to be sent to the pub. On it he wrote 'John Doe' and waited for the evidence to accumulate.

Fortunately he had an excellent Sergeant in Dave Andrews. The Inspector trusted him both for his diligence and integrity, a welcome change from some he had known in the 'Met'. Andrews was nothing if not thorough but life had taught him to be pessimistic. He had found that if he expected too much he was invariably disappointed. Others seemed to get by without the highs and lows that he had endured in his lifetime and he often wondered why. 'No matter', he usually decided, 'If I do my best at all times then if things turn out badly it won't be down to me.' Of course this made him something of a perfectionist and maybe a bit of a plodder, but these attributes can be very useful in police-work.

Now, given the task of organising a search he set about the job with enthusiasm and his usual meticulous detail. First, a fingertip search of the area for which he wasn't very hopeful, given the high winds and rain let alone the tide. He made a note, 'Body. Found at Hi or Lo Tide?' As for more evidence he decided to split his officers with himself taking the shops and houses on the shoreline, WPC Cope the Warners site, guests and staff, and PC Pretty the tourist and shipping offices where he would find details of the scheduled traffic to and from the port.

The Sergeant began each enquiry in the same way, a tap on the door and then, 'Good morning, I'm Sergeant Andrews. It's just routine.' he would begin, 'Just a few questions if you don't mind.' However it wasn't long before the Sergeant had that sinking feeling. 'No not a thing' or 'I've got better things to do.' were standard replies and he was getting nowhere, and of course many of the shops were boarded up for the winter anyway. He was surprised however that 'Dino's Diner' was closed. As far as he knew it had been open only a few days back, in fact he'd had a bacon sandwich and coffee there just a few days ago, and here it was shut.

It wasn't much better at the shipping offices. 'Just routine,' said PC Pretty but he could sense suspicion all round. At least he obtained some useful shipping timetables and charts to take back. WPC Cope started her questions in a different way, hoping to elucidate sympathy and co-operation. 'It's a lovely day.' she would begin, 'I do hope that you're having a wonderful holiday and I' m so sorry to trouble you.' Perhaps she didn't bargain for the stories that people began to tell her, all irrelevant to her enquiries, so the result was the same but it took longer. A change of tack was called for. For her next 'victim' she began, 'Just routine.'

Along the seafront the Sergeant had competed his task but, looking at his 'Denton's' local directory he decided to continue his enquiries into the back streets. 'Mmmm yes, number 21, Newsagents, Baljit Singh and Son.' he noted. There was a time when it used to be old 'Cap'n Scotts' place, famous for 'baccy' and licensed for rum he remembered, but how times change. As he entered the premises a small bell tinkled and he found himself inside a veritable treasure trove, everything it seemed, (except tobacco and rum) was on sale. He smiled at the small turbaned proprietor, 'Good morning Mr Singh,' he said, 'Just routine. I wonder if you can help with our enquiries.' Baljit looked at Dave rather suspiciously, 'Warrant card.' he stated. It was not a request; it was a demand as if he was world weary of the police and their enquiries. He too had a past, a lovely shop in Birmingham torched in the Handsworth riots with no convictions and hardly any compensation. 'Warrant card.' he repeated and smiled a little as Dave produced his. 'Can't be too careful,' he said, 'Now, how can I help you?' 'It's about New Year's Day, about 9 am. I can't say much just yet, but I'd just like know if you or one of your lads saw anything suspicious that's all.' Baljit turned to the back of the shop and called out, 'Imran, Imran come here a moment please.' After a short while a face appeared from amongst a stack of what seemed like Chinese New Year paraphernalia, 'Yes Papa, what is it? You know I have my homework. You always keep me busy, busy, busy. How will I be a great and successful business man like you if I can't study.' Dave smiled. He couldn't be sure if the young man was serious but one look at his face assured him that he was. 'I'm so sorry, little one,' his father said, 'but did you see anything unusual on your paper round on the morning of New Year, about nine o'clock?' The boy, who Dave could now see was aged only about 12 advanced into the room and looked at his father seriously.

'You are getting forgetful my dear Papa,' he said, 'I wasn't well, remember and you phoned Martin Drew from down the road to do it. Now can I get back to my calculus?' Dave was impressed, a 12 year old doing calculus and no doubt computers too, he felt more and more like a dinosaur every day. But one thing he did know and that was that young Martin Drew was a heap of trouble. He'd known him since he'd been the Schools Police Liaison officer and if there was any trouble you could bet Martin was in on it. Sometimes he felt sorry for the lad, life chances and all that, broken family and a mum who was always on the booze. 'Can't blame her either,' Dave thought, 'Six kids on her own. Can't be much fun.' Still he had a job to do and he was soon round at the Drew house knocking on the door. Eventually a young girl maybe not more than thirteen, answered the knock and without looking up from her mobile phone just said, 'Nah we don't want none.' and then slammed the door in his face. Dave was not put off by this, in fact it was 'par for the course' one might say, so he knocked again. This time Mrs Drew came to the door. 'Oh it's you.' she said, 'what do you want this time?' 'It's about Martin,' he began but she interrupted him, 'Why ask me?' she said, 'You've got him down the nick already. Picked him up 3 o'clock this morning. I should know, you daft buggers got me out of bed' Dave was stunned, 'Got him? Picked him up? What for Mrs Drew? I promise you I know nothing about that.' he responded somewhat in disbelief. 'Typical,' she replied, 'You Plods couldn't see your nose in front of your face.' And with that she too slammed the door. Dave stood on the pavement outside thinking hard. Wasn't Martin supposed to be doing Imran's paper round at 9am, so how could he if he was in the nick at 3am? 'What now?' he thought for a moment, and then decided, 'Well I'll just have to follow this latest lead and see where it goes to.' So it was back to the Station for him.

It didn't take him long to get an interview with Martin Drew up on a charge of burglary at that Dino's Diner that Dave had been wondering about. 'Oh hello Mr Andrews,' said Martin as if they were old friends, 'Come to get me out have you?' Dave smiled, you might say that Martin was a rather likeable villain but now he had business on his mind. 'Cut the crap, Martin,' he said, 'they tell me that you're up for a burglary rap, at Dino's no less. Bit small time don't you think, but what I want to know is, who did your paper round that you were supposed to do for Imran?

'Oh that' Martin replied with a laugh, 'I got young Eddie to do that. Mr Turban doesn't know who's who anyway.' Dave ignored the racist undertone here but just said, 'Well I'd better see him hadn't I?' 'Not so fast,' said Martin, 'why don't you ask me if I know something then?'

This took Dave by surprise but he could see the logic of it. Martin would have been facing the beach where the body was found, much earlier it was true, 4am not 9am but could he have seen something? 'Go on.' He said. 'Ooh not so fast Mr Policeman,' said Martin, 'What's in it for me if I tell you something?' Coming from someone else Dave might have listened but this was Martin Drew, arch young 'criminal of the year,' 'Sorry Martin,' he said, 'but unless you've got something concrete to go on I can't help you.' Martin held his hands up as if to say, well that's your loss then but there was something so cocky in his manner that Dave decided to try again. 'OK you give me something and I'll have a word about this burglary business. No one hurt was there?' he asked. 'Nah, I'm not a violent man Mr A, peaceful, me, out for a quiet life. Now let me think,' Light' Mr Andrews, have you seen the light?' He chortled as he said this, as if it was all one big joke. Dave couldn't help smiling at the cheek of the young man but he didn't like being manipulated either.

'Come on, out with it,' he said, 'now, or I'm leaving.' Perhaps Martin realised he had nearly gone too far so he just said, 'A light, a winking light from a ship out at sea and a person on the seashore, then a boat coming in and going out, and then two people and then one person walking away. I couldn't see any more, it seemed like the heavens opened and anyway I had a 'job' to do hadn't I? It was 2am already. You'll see me right then Mr Andrews?' Once more Dave was non-committal but he knew that this could blow the case wide open if true so he hurried back to the Lamb and Flag. 'I need a pint of bitter,' he thought, 'Duty or no duty, and when the Inspector hears this he'll want one too.'

Meanwhile Liz had had some luck over at the Warners' complex. She had interviewed a Mr and Mrs Guscott, both over 70 she imagined, and as she had asked for anything unusual, she had to listen to a few stories about the couple in the next cabin who were smoking when it was forbidden indoors, and the porter who seemed drunk, before she heard a story that had potential. It was Mrs Guscott who supplied the details. 'Well Miss,' she said, 'I hope you understand, you see I have to 'get up' a few times in the night, if you see what I mean and, after seeing in the New Year, Harold and me (she smiled across at him) well Harold and me came straight back here and we were asleep in no time. Anyway, as usual, I had to get up. I always check the clock and it was exactly One am. Well I didn't want to wake Harold, so after, you know, I stepped outside the door for a smoke and then I saw them, two of them heading for the swimming pool leisure area. Well, it's always locked at that time of night, but one of them had a key and they went in. I'd say it was a tallish man and a fairly short woman but it was dark and I couldn't see any more. I just went back to bed you see. Now was that helpful? Now would you like some tea?' Liz wasn't sure about the information but she said thanks just the same. Then she remembered that Bernie was found in the pool area. Was that just a coincidence, another couple perhaps, or had he been with a girl, she thought. Indeed had he been 'economical with the truth?'

PC Paul Pretty had completed his investigation on shipping offshore that night as far as he could, when he received a message from the Inspector at the Lamb and Flag to get round there as soon as possible. Apparently the other reports were in, as well as the forensics, and the Inspector wanted to bring it all together. He packed his bag with the voluminous sheets of 'arrivals and departures' and left.

Sue's cruise

Meanwhile time was running out for the holidaymakers at Warners, in fact they had two days to go. Bernie had been found safe and well so it was more or less back to the programme with Sue's slide show of her Baltic Cruise on the agenda. It was called 'Sing for your Supper,' and she explained that the reason for such a title would be revealed during the film. 'Delia of the Baltic?' someone shouted out and Sue smiled. 'Wait and see.' she said. It might equally have been called 'East meets West' she thought or more appropriately 'East beats West' as matters stood in 1988, but the political tide was turning as she had soon found out.

The small theatre room was packed (admittedly it was raining cats and dogs outside) as Sue began with the theme from the 'Onedin Line.'

As the slides came and went, she found herself transported back to that idyllic holiday whilst still managing to supervise the show. Actually she didn't have much to do because the music, the slides and her voice-over had all been pre-recorded, but she'd have to expect questions later.

However she knew that simple questions could not always be given a 'simple' answer. Some she would answer and some she would not, because it was on this cruise that she had become aware that the Baltic remained a political cauldron, and she knew that most people in her audience would be sadly misinformed with misconceptions of every kind about this. She therefore decided to present a 'tourist' rather than a political guide, with just a passing reference a rather more distant history.

It was actually following a chance meeting in Tallin, the capital of Estonia, that it had become clear to her that all was not as it seemed.

It was June 1988 and at last they going on a cruise again. It had been 3 long years since the last one to Jamaica and since then Bruce's cancer had been confirmed. He'd undergone extensive treatment month after month but one day the doctor held her hand and said, 'Why don't you take him on another cruise Sue, it can't be long now.' Of course she had known it but the shock was there just the same. 'I will.' she had said, 'and it'll be the best cruise of all, to the Baltic Sea.' Now they were on their way and she could hear Bruce's voice clearly, as she mounted the gangplank to board the 'Empress of the Baltic,' the flagship of the Swan Hellenic Line.

'Welcome aboard.' he called out from the ship's railing. He'd gone ahead to see to some of their luggage and now there he was waiting. She waved and in a moment she was in his arms again. 'Oh I do love you so much.' she said, 'I feel so safe in your arms. It's like heaven.' Bruce responded with a gentle caress and then stood back, 'Come on,' he said, 'let's go and find our cabin.' he said, 'then we can come back on deck and watch.' 'Yes, and wave to our adoring public,' she said. The days at sea passed by so slowly and yet so quickly, because Sue knew that he would not be with her for much longer, and she thanked God for each day.

Nevertheless he didn't give in to the condition that was slowly sapping his strength taking part in deck games such as quoits and dancing to the band at night under a starry sky. One evening he took her hand, looked into her eyes and said, 'Happy?' 'You know I am silly,' she replied and then without warning burst into tears. He tightened his grip on her hand and said, 'I'll never leave you Sue never. I'll always be a part of you but I want you to be happy when I'm gone also. In the future when you're wondering what to do just glance up at the clouds in the sky and look for the silver lining, that'll be me, looking out for you and loving you in all that you do.' Now Sue cried again, 'How can you say such a thing?' she said, 'I'll always love you and only you.' He smiled, 'Yes I know,' he said, 'but just remember what I've said tonight. Dance?' The band played 'True Love' and she held him so tight that he could not escape, now or ever, because she would never let go. She loved him so.

Once in the Baltic they spent a few days in Stockholm where Sue tried out her Swedish an unsuspecting waiter who seemed to take her efforts in good part. Then it was up to St Petersburg, on to the Gulf of Riga in Latvia and thence to Tallin in Estonia where nothing could have prepared them for what they witnessed. There had been no briefing from the ship's captain and they had not heard much recent news since boarding. They did know that muted calls for independence had been on the agenda in the Baltic States and Lithuania for some time, but as usual they had been diverted or suppressed. To be fair none of the cruise companies, including Swan Hellenic, drew attention to the fragile situation there, so holiday-makers Sue and Bruce included, set out confidently to explore.

It was the 'Old Town Festival,' so, once on shore Bruce and Sue had headed for the scenic areas of the City, and then taken a stroll beside the river until they came to a part known as the 'Song Festival Grounds' where the Festival was being held. It was dark and they could not get close because suddenly it became apparent that there were thousands of people gathered there with lanterns, torches and flags and all singing patriotic Estonian songs as if in one voice.

'I'm scared.' said Sue. 'Look over there, those sinister riot police in black with shields, they've got water cannon and probably tear gas too. It looks like they're going to come crashing in at any moment. I think we should leave right now.' 'Not so fast' said a voice from behind them, 'there won't be any trouble tonight. As you see, some of the riot police are actually talking to the demonstrators. It'll be OK. They won't move in to break it up tonight. Maybe tomorrow if it gets out of control. They'll be waiting for orders from you know where,' he went on, 'nothing to be worried about this evening.' he paused then added, 'Probably.' with a big grin. They turned around to see a man in a denim jacket and jeans, leaning nonchalantly on a lamp-post and smoking a cheroot.

'Allow me to introduce myself,' he said, 'Robin Watson at your service, freelance hack and everybody's friend. Just call me Rob. English are you? I can tell and so can they. See the cameras with the telephoto lenses? Well you are now on 'candid camera." He pointed to the long line of police and continued, 'Let me buy you a drink and tell you what this is all about. Seems like you've been out of touch lately.' 'That's an understatement,' said Bruce, 'we hardly bothered about the news on the cruise. Shall we go dear?' he asked turning to Sue, 'I'm not sure,' she said, 'but I would like to know what all the fuss is about.' 'Follow me then,' said Rob, 'I know an interesting cafe not far away but be careful what you say, they have eyes and ears everywhere.' Sue looked at Bruce as if to say, 'Are you thinking what I'm thinking? It all sounds very dodgy,' but he was in deep discussion with Rob as they made for the bar.

For the next hour they all drank vodka as Rob treated them to a geo-political history lesson of the region from the 1920's. 'These tiny Baltic States and their much larger neighbours had been the pawns in the power struggle between Russia and Germany. It was helpful then for Tsarist Russia to play the 'Pan Slavic' card, and even in World War Two it suggested a harmony between Russia and her neighbours that was not always there in reality', he said, 'now it was Russia versus the 'West."

He continued in a somewhat professorial tone pointing out that independence movements had not made any progress over the years but in 1985 they had been handed a real opportunity when Gorbachev introduced new concepts of 'glasnost' (openness) and 'perestroika' (restructuring.) in the USSR. An olive branch perhaps, to Satellite States as well as Soviet republics, reminding them of their common Slavic heritage within a greater Russian hegemony. 'But they didn't want a branch, they wanted the whole tree' Rob continued, adding that the Russian warm words of today might not be enough to erase the horrors of yesteryear. There then followed a flight of the 'border' states toward full independence. 'But some have moved too soon,' he said, 'the olive branch was not green but amber at best. No, the Kremlin doesn't like this at all, and they are quite prepared to take measures to prevent secessions.' *(It was too little too late however, because the Berlin Wall fell in 1989).*

Rob went on to say that he thought that that Bruce and Sue were very lucky to be here at this point in time, because it was Estonia that was bringing the whole drama to the world in what became known later as the 'Singing Revolution,' 'After all you can't stop people singing can you?' he said, then added, rather wistfully, 'Or can you? Oh yes you can, oh no you can't.' he added in a sing-song voice. 'You see, the fat lady 'Mother Russia' had not yet sung,' he said 'and if she couldn't have them, then no one else could. No, they couldn't join the EU, but they did; no, they couldn't join NATO, but they did. Russia now had but one card to play, and that was to ensure political victories at the ballot box or by other means, and the USA were determined to stop them.'

For the next few days he befriended them, taking them to see all the sights of the city but also behind the scenes where men and women met in dark corners plotting revolution and counter-revolution. Estonia, he told them, has more historical ties to Finland and Sweden than to Russia but after occupation by the Red Army in 1940, Tallin became the centre of massive Slavic immigration pushing the Russian population there beyond 40%, in contrast to the overall average of 25%. He took them to see the 'Hill of Toompee' a sight worth seeing with the magnificent onion domed Alexander Nevsky Cathedral on the top like some big icing cake, and standing in the middle of town like a throwback to a medieval age with cobbled streets leading down to the ancient city walls. Some say that the City is not unlike Zurich or Geneva, it has that sort of charm. Soon it would be time for them to go but Rob wasn't quite finished. 'I'm a journalist,' he said 'and I've learnt to be sceptical so when you hear the word 'Independence' I say to you 'Gin-dependence.' (He smiled at his own joke.) 'What I mean is, don't take the words on face value. These people demonstrating today are just as much pawns in the old game of diplomacy as any time in the past. Sure there are many who want closer ties with the West but there are others, especially here in Tallin, who don't and, as I said the CIA are not chary of a trick or two themselves. Perhaps the goose is well and truly cooked for the Russians here in Estonia and independence will come, but there are bigger fish out there. Take their 'bread basket' the Ukraine for example, or somewhere in the Black Sea such as Georgia. What's going to happen there I wonder? Both sides will take a high moral tone about non-intervention but it's going on I can assure you. It's alleged that whilst Russia might mobilise their own secret apparatus and youth movements such as Nashi, the West isn't far behind either with elements of the State Department, USAID, NGO Freedom House, George Soros and the 'National Endowment for Democracy.' You might also hear about activists like Gene Sharp later but don't be fooled. Just ask yourself who benefits when these States break away from the USSR? It's the West that's who.' he said. 'But come on you two, let's have some fun while we're young and alive.' At this, Bruce took her hand and she took Rob's as they ran to the next bar.

Sharp wrote his seminal work 'Politics of Non-violent Action' in 1973.

*   *   *   *

'Hello. Hello Sue.' came a voice, 'the film's finished. Did you drop off for a moment? It wasn't that boring was it?' At this everyone laughed and so did Sue. 'Well I hope not,' she said,' Now are there any questions?'

John Doe

As the officers all arrived at the 'Lamb and Flag' the Inspector greeted them warmly. 'Thanks for what you've all done so far,' he said. 'If it's OK with you I'd like to start with the forensics report. Professor Hartley has agreed to take us through it, and then he'll leave his assistant Sarah King here with us to answer any further questions. Professor?'

'Thanks Alex,' the Professor replied. 'I've given everyone here a copy of our report so I'll just take you through the basic details. Here it is.'

Report on one 'John Doe' body found on New Year's Day 2012
White male aged about 50. Height 6ft 3ins. Weight 15 stone.
Stocky build. Receding grey hair. Dentures (upper jaw)
Dressed all in black. Fur lined 'naval' boots
Appendix scar and old knife wound in ribs (LH)
Tattoos; A red rose, OK-Liberte, Dora (or maybe Bora?) UK. SJ88.
No papers or ID documents
No tracks on beach due to tidal movement
Blood Group 'O' positive

Time of death was between midnight and 9am 1/1/12.

Cause of death was gunshot wounds to the abdomen and chest. Four shots, the first two from close up to the abdomen showing scorch marks but the other two from a vertical distance of about 5 foot. He was lying down you see. The weapon was probably a Pistol with a silencer and now ballistics are checking the bullets. No cartridges were found.

*   *   *   *

Hartley finished his presentation and sat down. Then Alex stood up. 'Thank you professor,' he said, 'Now will everyone please address any questions to Miss King, and keep them short and to the point please.'

There were quite a few questions, and she was able to answer the 'Flotsam or Jetsam' one immediately. 'Had the body come in with the tide or was it going out on the tide?' she was asked. 'Neither,' she replied, 'He was killed on the beach or brought there. He had not been in the water. There were no water residues in his clothing at all' This caused a bit of a murmur all round but she was less helpful on the next questions. 'Do you have any idea about his nationality?' and 'What do you make of his tattoos?' To these she replied briefly with some amusement, 'I've no idea,' she said, 'that's your job isn't it? This truism resulted in a ripple of applause from the officers there, 'Quite right Ma'am,' said PC Pretty, 'but, from what you've said, would you agree that the assailant was quite a bit shorter than the victim?' Pausing only for a moment she nodded and said, 'Yes I would Constable. Two of the bullets, maybe the first two that made the scorch marks on his coat, penetrated his navel, not his chest as one might suppose if fired by someone of equal height. The second two bullets were probably fired when he was down. No scorch marks and from about 5 foot we think.'

Liz Cope then had a question, 'Do you think it likely then that the killer left the body, expecting it be carried out by the tide, but, maybe knowing nothing of tides, would have been disappointed?' she said. Sarah smiled warmly, 'Maybe,' she replied, 'but perhaps the body was just too heavy to carry. Have you thought that it might have been a woman?' Once more there was a gasp, almost as if she'd solved the case, but Sarah had her feet on the ground and she knew enough about police-work to understand that a case is never solved by conjecture. 'Or a short man,' she added with a laugh, 'But that's your job isn't it?' she said for the second time.

Alex thanked Sarah for her 'very interesting' contributions and then asked the others to present their findings so far. There were plenty of 'Ums and ahs' and a certain amount of head scratching as each told their stories and Alex seemed impressed. 'Good. Very good,' he said, 'Now let me see if I've got the details right. I'll talk through what you've told me and put it on the board where Sarah has put the forensics. Right, listen up.

'John Doe, Name unknown, no papers, big bloke shot in the stomach and then again for good measure. Yes I know, 'crime passionelle' but I don't think so. Dave's witness says he saw a signal light from a ship out at sea at about 2 am and then he saw a boat and then two people and then one. Liz was told that a man and woman had entered the pool area at about 1am. Any connections there I wonder? Paul's shipping itineraries might be useful if we can pinpoint a vessel in the bay around 2am, a ship that might have sent a signal perhaps, but to whom and why? Paul also studied the tides, and as Liz had suggested might be the case, the tide was incoming for another 12 hours after midnight, so there was little hope of a body washing out to sea on that particular night. If the body had been brought there for disposal, as Sarah hinted, they had chosen a bad night for it. That seems too careless in my opinion and I don't think that the killer was careless, ergo he was murdered on the beach, not carried there. Lastly Liz said that Jack Edwards was acting strangely when she interviewed him, as if he might know more, but was acting the fool to cover up. Then there was the strange diversion of Bernie going missing, at a time that seems to match the sighting of a 'couple' going into the pool area. That's quite a lot to be going on with. Comments anyone?' This was his style. He did not proffer an opinion until he had called for observations, making sure that all people present were included. He took all suggestions very seriously, and let his staff know that he valued their input, but more than that, that he valued them personally.

Paul raised his arm to signify that he had an idea. 'Yes Paul,' Alex said. 'What do you think? Something about the shipping?' Paul was a bit uncertain but he knew that the Inspector liked some input rather than none at all so he proceeded. 'It's about the tattoos Sir. It might seem too obvious but don't they point to somebody from Lancashire? There's the Red Rose, the Lancaster emblem, and then there's also a 'UK' tattoo.

I don't know about the others, maybe his initials or his wife's.' he said. Alex was pleased with Paul. He thought that he'd make a good police officer one day because he would offer an opinion whilst making it clear that he might have his own doubts, and there were doubts in this first scenario. 'Yes, thanks Paul' he said. 'And then there was the French word 'Liberte.' It might be good to check up on those ideas. Maybe his clothing or boots might offer a clue. Anyone else?' There was further discussion about other details and then Alex called the meeting to a close.

'Now I want you all to go back to the persons who gave you the information that you've presented here today. But there'll be a difference. I want you to go as a team to each one. What one might miss another might see, and that could be just that clue that we're looking for. I was intrigued by Liz's report on Jack Edwards. She thinks there's something not quite right and she has a nose for that kind of thing, so I'm going to see him myself to check him out. I must say I tend to agree with a school of thought in which the way people respond to questions, can be as important as the answers themselves. I'd like to see what he's hiding'

(He might have been talking about Sue Parker but they hadn't met. Yet.'

News Hound

The police soon released a statement to the Press giving some, but not all the detail that they had in their possession, calling on members of the public to come forward with any information they might have. There followed one or two articles in the local newspapers about the 'Mystery Man,' and the local radio offered a reward for an early lead but nothing was forthcoming. But, as is often the case, such a story might be picked up by one of the national news outlets if they found it interesting, or more likely by a freelance journalist looking for a good story, especially if there was sex or violence involved. The jury was out on this at present, but there was one London reporter who had another reason for following up the story. This was Rob Watson, a somewhat maverick reporter, known to go his own way but with an excellent reputation for his insightful articles on the 'Cold War,' of days gone by. (The very same Rob Watson that Sue Parker had met in Tallin those many years ago.)

As 'occasional' special correspondent for The Times and other broadsheets over the ensuing twenty years he had foreseen the break up of Jugoslavia, from the

Slovenian plebiscite in 1990 to it's bloody finale in Kosovo. He had written about a new 'Reverse Domino Theory' that would imitate that famous Truman Cold war phrase, but his warnings had been ignored to a large extent.

Many journalists and the general public had tired of the endless rounds of arms talks, and they could see little interest for British audiences in matters that seemed settled for good or ill. It seemed that he was often a lone voice as he wrote column after column about a brewing storm. No matter that he was proven right in many instances such as the Balkans and the Baltic States, he still found it difficult to get 'assignments' where he wanted to go, but now he knew that he was on to something. He booked a room at the Portsmouth Hilton immediately, and made appointments to see Harold Long the local editor and the Inspector the next day, telling them 'It's important and there may be no time to lose.'

He spoke from experience, remembering another tragic occasion when time had been of the essence, until it ran out.

After his meeting with Sue and Bruce in Tallin Rob had moved on to Berlin. Maybe he sensed that something momentous was about to occur, but in the meantime he was employed as a 'political adviser' to a UN Film unit in the making of a drama-documentary entitled, 'Berlin Bridges Not Walls.' The film depicted the trials and tribulations of a family split by the building of the Wall in 1961. They were divided physically and emotionally as well, and for some, their time and patience ran out.

As Rob travelled down to Portsmouth on the train, passing by many sidings, overhead gantries, flashing lights and pylons he was reminded of the watch-towers and searchlights in the last scene of the film that was actually never released. It had been overtaken by events and made redundant as the wall came down later that year. The scene had begun with Karl and Gudrun looking over the wall from the Western side.

BERLIN BRIDGES NOT WALLS.

Karl and Gudrun looked wistfully over the wall from their vantage point on a raised viewing platform on the Western side. Before climbing to the top their hands had touched and traced some of the graffiti that covered the wall as far as the eye could see; 'Reds Out' 'CND lives OK' an amusing one, 'Vopos Estate Agents' and a tragic one, 'Remember Mitzi Krueger born 8th June 1952 shot here on 8th June 1972 on her birthday.'

This was not the first time that Karl and Gudrun had been to the viewing area. However it was quieter than usual on that day as it was drizzling quite hard and that usually kept visitors away, but every time they came they were truly amazed and shocked at what they saw. The land before them was like a vast public square, maybe as big as Red Square in Moscow, but it wasn't a celebratory square. Instead the space was filled with barbed wire and tank traps with service roads on both sides and watch-towers every few yards. And then again, it wasn't a square either because it ran out of sight in both directions separating East from West. It was quiet, almost ghostly as if it was an organic thing that could raise itself when it needed, in order to devour those who would trespass.

'See, see!' said Gudrun excitedly waving her binoculars and handing them over to Karl, 'There, there,' and she pointed in the direction of a slow moving convoy that was advancing from their right. 'What can you see? What can you see?' Karl squinted, 'These aren't the best are they?' he complained, 'but it seems to be the change of the guard and if you're right, they'll take away 4 and only leave 2 for the night shift. Yes, yes, that's what they've done, and if it's the same for all the security towers, then Rudi stands a good chance tonight.' Gudrun suddenly went quiet and then said 'Let's go Karl, I can't stand any more of this, I really can't.' Karl leant across and kissed her. They had been married for two years and she desperately wanted her brother to see their new baby that they had named after him, 'Rudi.' He had been stuck behind the wall since it was built, and it was this news that had finally spurred him on to make an escape bid. 'It'll be easy,' he had said in a secret letter, 'Hans did it 3 months ago and the Vopos tightened up for a while. Now they're getting lazy. I'll send you the details, just make sure you are there on time.'

'Don't worry,' said Karl, 'it's going to be fine. Rudi's not stupid is he, and if things weren't quite right he'd call it off you know he would. He knows what he has to do. Wait for the search beams to pass, jump from his side, cut through the first set of wires, then the second and then he's here before the light comes around again. We'll have the grappling ladder ready as promised and he'll be over the top in no time. It'll be a piece of cake, then we'll all go to the Bier Kellar off Kurfustundam.' Gudrun smiled and squeezed his hand, 'Yes, won't it be lovely to see them together, Rudi and Rudi, I just can't wait, but let's have some lunch first to give us some strength, and then what about a film while we're waiting for it to get dark.' The film was 'Casablanca,' showing for the umpteenth time but they enjoyed it and sat in the back row as lovers do.

They approached the wall carefully because you couldn't say it was really dark, given all the searchlights beaming here and there. But then they arrived and snuggled down with their backs to the wall and waited, and waited. 'It's time' Karl said checking his watch, 'he should be climbing over his wall, just about NOW. I'll look over and see. Yes. YES he's on his way, quick, give me the ladder.' She passed it to him, but as he stooped to collect it, there was a murderous hail of machine gun fire and a muted cry from the other side of the wall.

'I must see!' cried Gudrun, 'I must see.' But Karl stood firm on the bottom of the ladder and would not let her pass. 'Let's go home,' he said, 'Rudi will be waiting for us to kiss him goodnight.'

THE END

'Yes,' thought Rob as he stopped dreaming, 'there are times when a split second can be all important and other times when it could be an hour or even a week'. He reckoned that he had less than a month.

He had asked the Editor and Inspector to come to the Hotel where they might find a quiet corner to discuss the business in hand. It was 10 am sharp as he led them to a small conference room and, after the normal brief introductions he came straight to the point. 'Have either of you heard of Oleg Kuchenko?' he said. His visitors were somewhat taken aback his directness. He seemed like a man in a hurry but they were baffled nonetheless. 'Not me' said Long, 'nor me' said Williams, 'But he sounds kind of Russian. Is he?' Rob waited for a moment before replying then said, 'Well, Kuchenko was planning to attend a Special UN conference convened in London and he didn't turn up, but it may be that your body on the beach is him. I've been told that the body had a number of tattoos and it's possible that these may help to identify him. Can you tell me what they were please and if they make sense, then I'll give you the whole picture.' Alex Williams was as keen as anyone to get to the bottom of the story and the Editor was still hoping to get a story, so they both nodded and Alex passed Rob a sheet from his briefcase. Rob studied it for a moment and then, turning to them both he said, 'Yes it's as I thought. It's him all right and I'll explain why, but, 'he said, turning to the Harold with a rueful smile, 'there will be no story here for some time yet. It'll definitely be under wraps for the time being because, when we're through here I'm going to ask the Inspector to call in MI5. You see we may have an International situation on our hands and it could get nasty.'

Rob then told them that according to his sources, Kuchenko was actually a Ukrainian and, for those in the know the tattoos made perfect sense for one such as he, who had become known as an activist against Russian claims for perpetual hegemony in the region. Rob was what was known as an 'inside-outsider,' able to obtain confidential information, seemingly at the drop of a hat, whilst remaining conspicuously neutral.

The Rose. Not Lancaster but the 'Rose of Georgia'
OK His initials
Liberte An inspiration from France

Pora (not Dora) the pro-Yuschenko group in the Ukraine
UK Ukraine
SJ88 The Lithuanian Baltic movement parallel to Estonia in 1988

'From 2004' he continued, 'I heard that he had been an undercover agent for Viktor Yuschenko the leader of the 'Orange Revolution' in the Ukraine, but in the last few years he had been sent to Russia to support dissidents as they battled to overturn 'illegitimate' elections there (much as in the Ukraine.) With the elections over and riots on the streets, he had been commissioned by the UN to bring any substantiated evidence of vote rigging to an emergency meeting in London. The UN doubted the veracity of the elections, but as claim and counter claim intensified, they sought irrefutable evidence, and this is what Kuchenko was bringing, but not only that, he also claimed that he had clear evidence of Prime Minister Putin's involvement. Some would say that he had to be stopped.'

Rob paused here for a moment to gauge his audience's reaction to all this, but he sensed that they were wondering how it might shed light on the murder of the man on the beach, even if it was Kuchenko. 'I don't know a lot more,' Rob continued, 'my sources weren't sure about his travel plans at all so that's about it.' Now the Inspector made a point, 'It might well be all hush-hush, but the fact is that he ended up on a beach here. He was killed ON the beach here, so it stands to reason that he was meeting someone here but not the person who turned up. Right?' 'That seems perfectly reasonable,' said the Editor, 'but at the moment I'm not sure I can help any more. If you'll excuse me now, I have another meeting to go to but please ring if you need my assistance.' The others thanked him as he left and then Alex asked if Rob might order some coffee. 'It seems to have been a long morning,' he said. 'Done deal,' said Rob and picked up the phone for room service. Then he turned to Alex with a big smile, 'Meeting someone eh? Who might that be then? And why here?' he said.

'I don't know, yet, 'replied Alex, 'but I'll tell you what, there are a couple of leads I've got to follow up. Why don't you tag along.'

Hello again Sue

Later that day the pair arrived at the Edward's house as Alex had arranged and of course Glynis had the kettle on. 'Come in do,' she said, 'Jack's up in his computer room, always up there he is, I'm not allowed in. He pretends it's all a big secret you know, like at Bletchly Park in the war. He was there before we met but I was too young at the time, hardly started school I had. Jack,' she called out, 'Jack, it's your visitors. He'll be down in a minute but, oh, by the way I've got a friend staying here.

She's been sort of looking after me, the shock you know. Here she comes now, 'Come along in Sue,' she said, 'this is Inspector Williams and this is, sorry love I didn't get your name.' 'Robin Watson,' said Sue, 'How are you Rob?' Glynis looked stunned and Alex was surprised as well,

'Seems you two know each other then,' he said. 'Yes, it's a long story,' said Rob, 'Hello again Sue. How are you?' She smiled and just said, 'Fine, perhaps we can meet up later. Here comes Jack.'

Jack strolled into the room looking somewhat blasé about the whole affair, greeting his visitors with a perfunctory nod. 'I've told the young policewoman all I know,' he said, pr-empting the expected questions.

'So what's it all about this time?' Alex greeted him with a warm smile, 'Hello Jack,' he said, 'I'm Inspector Williams, well there's nothing much I suppose but we'd just like to go over a few things. It's the detail you see, just to check that we haven't missed anything. By the way this is Rob Watson from the Press, just helping us out. Is that OK with you?' Jack looked at him suspiciously, 'I told them that I didn't want my name in the Press and Harold agreed. That's the local editor you know.' 'Yes we do know,' said Rob, 'but that's not why I'm here. I'm looking into another case but the Inspector asked me along for company.'

Now Alex resumed his questioning. 'Right, let's make a start then.' he said referring to his notes, 'Let's see, it says here that you found the body at 9am and telephoned the Police. Right?' Jack nodded as if to say, get on with it but just then Glynis spoke up. 'That's not quite right dear,' she said, 'don't you remember that you went out early that day, about eight.'

Alex raised an eyebrow but not much more; he had learnt to stalk a prey quietly and carefully, and he was beginning to wonder if Jack Edwards was on the menu. 'Perhaps you were mistaken Glynis,' he said, 'It was early in the morning.' She looked at him in disbelief, affronted even. What did he know about their retirement regime, she thought, but contained her thoughts by just saying, 'Ask Jack, he'll remember won't you dear.' Alex turned to face Jack again but he just murmured, 'If she says so I suppose it was a bit earlier than usual, storm brewing up and all. Why don't you ask Nelson for a neutral opinion?'

Obviously this was a bit of a slight on Glynis, in other words her opinion was no better than the dog's. Was he hiding something? It was one of those moments when people weren't sure whether to laugh or not, so there was a kind of awkward silence, and Nelson, who was under the table, put his head down between his paws for safety.

Now Alex began to close in, 'Was it usual to vary the time of the dog walk?' he said, consulting his notes once more, as if he had all the times and dates of the dog walks over the last year. Once more Glynis was quick to reply. 'Never,' she said in a very positive manner, 'It's always nine o'clock, but maybe it was New Year that threw him. Right Jack?'

She was trying to make amends of course but Sue couldn't help thinking about the saying, 'Don't dig deeper if you're in a hole already.' Jack didn't reply but was obviously getting irritated, so Alex changed tack.

'Do you know who it was?' he said, and this certainly put the 'cat amongst the pigeons.' The question had the shock element that he knew it would, and he waited for the answer like a cobra ready to strike. It seemed to have the required effect because Jack went into defensive mode, 'No, how could I?' he asked, now more irritated than ever, but Alex wasn't giving up. 'Well, did you see his face?' he asked. 'No, I did not.' came the reply, 'just what are you getting at?' By now Glynis was getting flustered as well so Alex thought it best to ask pass the questioning on to Rob who had signified that he had something to say.

'What he's getting at Jack, is that we think that you know more than you are telling us, and just to help you out I'll tell you what we know about you. Let's see now, worked at Bletchly during the war and then moved to Bath to work in the Civil Service. Right?' Jack nodded, 'All that's no secret,' he said, 'Well, how about this then,' continued Rob, 'Your Civil service was the MOD (Ministry of Defence) and, far from being finished with codes and encryptions, you became one of the foremost authorities in that field. Now is that correct?' Jack remained imperturbable, 'Yes it is but I left all that behind a very long time ago.' he said.

Here Sue had a word to say, 'If you're anything like my Bruce was,' she said, 'you can never leave it alone entirely can you, once you've retired I mean? He was so interested in Police work that he kept a shelf of books on the subject, just as you do with your codes and tales of Spies like John le Carre. In fact I've been reading one since I've been here. It's called 'The Politics of Non violence,' about Gandhi and civil disobedience.'

'Is it by Gene Sharp?' asked Rob. 'Yes, I think it is,' she said, 'Why?'

'Because the dead man Kuchenko and others, were greatly influenced by him as he wrote about power struggles in the Ukraine and elsewhere, so perhaps now Jack will tell us what more he knows.' he replied.

Bruce looked at Alex and they both looked at Jack. His shoulders slumped, 'Well I suppose you'd have found out sooner or later but I've been under the restrictions of the Security Act up to now, and I can only co operate insofar as my information might lead you to the killer. I think that the best thing for me to do is to type up a statement while Sue and Rob get acquainted. Perhaps you might make some tea Glyn.' he said and left the room. He was back in 10 minutes and handed out his report.

'I hope this will do,' he said, 'I'll try to help a bit more if I can but don't forget I'm under strict instructions and the game isn't over yet.'

<u>Statement by Jack Edwards. Field Officer MI5 No.279321</u>
(Also known as Viktor Zharin. Russian Passport No. R9700491.)

I have been a 'sleeper' agent for MI5 since I left the MOD in 2001. Before and after that date I made occasional clandestine visits to Russia and it's satellite states, and also kept a watching brief on low level internet 'chatter' from here in Portsmouth. In early November 2004 I received an activation email from 'George', my Whitehall contact. 'Sorry to say that N is not very well and needs urgent attention.' This was the coded form of contact that now had to be confirmed.

'Tell H to give him a kiss and I'll be there soon,' was my reply.

HQ double confirmation was as follows. Many thanks, let's meet up in the Square on Thursday.'

As I write this now I am somewhat amused by the rather naïve coding guidelines. Admittedly they had to be changed frequently but this set was my idea after we got Nelson, our dog. So the first encryption is Nelson (refers to action required) the second is Hardy and the third Trafalgar. As I said I'm not proud of it and I fear it might have been easily broken. In fact it was a similar oversight that led to the breaking of the Enigma code during the war. German Operators cut corners and that was fatal.

The upshot was that I was to make immediate contact with a man called Oleg Kuchenko through a 'safe' email channel, London to Kiev. He was a right hand man to Viktor Yuschenko the leader of the 'Our Ukraine' political party. In the previous month Yuschenko had been poisoned with dioxin and was only making a slow recovery. In the recent Presidential elections, following the resignation of President Kuchma (in accordance with the constitution), the winner had been declared as Viktor Yanukovych, known to be close to the Russian leadership, but allegations of corruption were rife. Demonstrations had already begun as thousands gathered to protest waving the orange flags that came to symbolise the movement that became known as '<u>The Orange Revolution</u>.' In a somewhat mild retaliation, the opposing camp chose blue, but there was nothing mild about the mobilisation of 10,000 MVS (Internal Ministry) troops to disperse the crowds. The next day, after calls to 'prevent bloodshed' by the GUR (military intelligence) they were recalled by their commander (General Popkov), before serious injuries or deaths occurred. My job was to give as much help as I could, unofficially of course, to ensure that the rerun of the election, which had been called for December 26th would result in a favourable outcome from our (the West's) point of view. The result was close, 'Orange 52%, Blue 44%' so we got our man. As far as I was concerned I went back to my 'part time' job of monitoring the situation in the Black Sea region, but the 'Blues' won the replay in 2010 when Yanukovych won the election, apparently fairly.

Things seemed quiet for a while but then I received another activation message, equally daft I might say now in hindsight, because I do believe that our messages and codes have been broken regularly. My contact, 'George' had dreamt these up, namely, 'G-K-K' standing for Gordon, Kitchener and Khartoum, but anyway the message was the same. I had to get in immediate contact with Kuchenko again, this time to unravel and report on flawed elections in the Russian Federation itself. There had already been widespread demonstrations on the streets, a factor blamed by Prime Minister Putin and others, on the influence of the 'Orange Revolution' next door. (Not without some truth it must be said). Oleg Kuchenko had already been into the region and obtained what he termed 'irrefutable' evidence of vote tampering, and what's more he said there was no doubt that Putin, was involved. He planned to bring this evidence back to London where a special meeting of the UN were looking into such allegations. The point is that Putin is standing for a third term as President in March 2012 and such revelations would undoubtedly weaken his chances. From 'our' point of view, Mevdedev is a far better bet.

Through our 'secure' channels I was told to meet Oleg on Hayling Island Beach at precisely 8am on New Year's Day. The plan was that he would be dropped off by a freighter, met by me and then escorted to London. As you know he was already dead when I got there, and his clothes were dry. I deduce that the boat that brought him to shore landed him safely and handed him over to the 'contact' on the beach. I further reckon that they were on their way back to their 'mother ship' when he was shot. This must have all been well before 8am so I further deduce that 'my' timing schedule had been infiltrated and changed. He didn't stand a chance. It is likely that I will be involved in securing a second set, but of course they must be original documents for them to be taken seriously. It will be up to me to find a way to deliver them safely. I have an idea about this but I'll say no more for now.

In closing I offer my heartfelt apologies to my dear wife Glynis whom I have kept in the dark all these years for her own safety. It must have been difficult for you darling but I have always loved you and always will.

<u>End of Report</u>

Much of this confirmed Rob's previous information on the subject, but Alex was glad to obtain just a few more details about the murder on the beach. He thought that Jack's observations were probably all too true and thanked him warmly. 'I hope you don't think that we gave you a hard time,' he said. 'But now I hope that we can work together if you think of anything else. Obviously we've still got a lot of work to do to find our killer.' Jack agreed and, as they left they could see Glynis holding on to his arm, obviously very moved by the words to her in his statement.

Back at his hotel Rob lost no time in following up on Sue's invitation to 'meet up later.' He organised a hire car and then phoned Sue to ask if she would like a day out. Of course he should have done it the other way round, but he thought that that would smack of indecision, but then again she wouldn't want to be taken for granted would she? 'Damn,' he thought, 'Why am I in such a muddle? It must be love.' With that thought he headed for the whisky bottle and told himself not to be so daft.

Rob Watson was an idealist. To him the adventures of love would have to have a serious purpose with the promise of a happy and enduring outcome. But then again he was a realist, and life had taught him that even the best intentions could come to grief on the altar of Eros. This dualistic approach to love mirrored his perception of the world as a whole. While others were just 'getting on with it' he was often beset by an indecision that prevented the good for fear of the bad. Fortunately he had his mother's moral compass to guide him and that never failed, even if he allowed himself some 'licence' from time to time. She had brought up a family of three as a widow and remained faithful to her husband's memory and the Catholic Church throughout her life. Such strictures were not for Rob but his 'faith' remained a touchstone from which a moral guiding light always seemed to be present. To be truthful he was a bit of a maverick in the eyes of the Church, supporting 'Liberation Theology' and other groups such as Amnesty International, or even the Democratic Party in the USA as they proposed more lenient laws on abortion. He liked to think that 'God' would understand his reasoning. And, inasmuch as the Church prayed for him, he would pray for them.

He did not and could not accept that part of 'realism' that hinted at compromise, and this attitude had prevented some 'progress' in the eyes of some in his chosen profession as a journalist. Nevertheless, and possibly partly because of this intransigence, he had acquired a reputation for absolute integrity. 'You can trust Rob Watson,' his peers would say.

However, within the 'whirly world' of love things were not quite so simple and there his twin pillars of rectitude clashed. He knew that he would always seek a long-term partner but he'd also learnt to accept that this was not always possible. Therefore he had settled for what he termed a number of 'Loving Liaisons,' hopeful for it to work but sanguine if it didn't. So it was with considerable trepidation that he approached the idea of a 'date' with Sue. He could have done without his own 'Mr Negative' at his heels once again, 'You don't want to hurt her and you don't want her to hurt you,' the voice said, 'so why bother?' It certainly needed thinking about, but optimism won out on this occasion and a song was needed to set the tone and provide inspiration, 'You've got to Accentuate the Positive, Ee liminate the Negative, Latch on to the Affirmative, and don't mess with Mr In Between.' he sang, quite out of tune. So he'd made the call and fate would decide. He sat back, fingers crossed.

In her turn Sue was delighted to accept the offer of a day out, but then again she was also extremely apprehensive. She'd been asked out quite a few times since Bruce died and only once or twice had she accepted. On both occasions it had turned out to be a bit of a disaster, 'once on the starting line and once on the back straight,' she had told her friends with a laugh. But it didn't seem funny any more. Could she risk it all again?

The next day the car pulled up outside the Edwards' house at ten am. Sue was waiting and tripped down the steps like a young schoolgirl, then slowed down and checked a rose bush so as not to look too keen. Rob stepped out of the car and opened the passenger door, 'Hello again Sue,' he said, 'your carriage awaits.' She smiled and stepped in, and when he was seated she said, 'Let's go, shall we? I can see Glyn peering through the curtains and she'll ask me so many questions when I get back.' 'Right,' he said, 'I thought we'd take a trip out to 'Bucklers Hard,' it's not too far. Maybe you've been there.' She thought for a moment, 'No. I'm sure I haven't, although Glyn has taken me to the docks and the shipyards down there. Remember I'm a landlubber. Salisbury via Bath you know.' He laughed, 'Yes I know,' he replied, 'but it's not a 'Yard,' in fact it is a 'Hard,' maybe the only one for all I know, but it does have something to do with ship building. There's a leaflet in the glove compartment if you want to know more.' 'You seem to know such a lot,' she said, 'Shipyards and all that stuff back there about politics.' 'Well, I don't know much about you for a start,' he responded. Sue wasn't quite ready for this, boats and politics, politics and boats, that's fine, but now he was getting too close to her comfort zone. However she decided to mask her feelings for now and just responded by saying, 'And I know even less about you.' So there it was. Out there a battle line, or perhaps a less formal skirmish line had been drawn, and now both stepped back in order to reconnoitre the field. An awkward silence hovered over them until Rob broke the ice. 'Shall we have some music?' he said, 'I've got Vaughan Williams' sea shanties here. What do you think?' 'That's a lovely idea,' she said, 'and I'll have a look at the booklet.' Those first hesitant moments were over. It was not so much that a salvo of heavy artillery had been fired or that a fusillade of musket fire had taken place, but something had occurred. A first round perhaps, or maybe just two people casting seeds into the wind to see whether they fell on good soil or on hard rock. Sue opened the leaflet and began to read.

BUCKLERS HARD

On the banks of the Bealieu River, in the heart of the New Forest, you will find this peaceful haven. Originally called Montagu Town it developed as a thriving shipbuilding village in which some of Nelson's fleet were constructed, including HMS Agamemnon. The town was built to service the West Indies sugar plantations, but with the abolition of the slave trade, plans for expansion became unviable. It is likely that it was the solid 'hard' riverbanks that made it suitable for shipbuilding.

Visit the old cottages and the lovely St Mary's Chapel, and then take a walk along the river. Cruises are available from May to October.

Enjoy your stay and visit us again

They did enjoy their stay and they did have lunch and a walk along the river. It was rather blustery so she took his arm but not his hand. That would have been too much on a first date. One could take hold of the arm of a friend or relative in a gale she thought, but a hand was something different, hinting at an intimacy that existed or was to come. The first was hardly the case and she wasn't at all sure about the second, but it felt good all the same. He was just happy to be close to her there on the riverbank, and back at the house she kissed his cheek as he leant across to open the door. 'Don't be a stranger,' she said, and was gone.

The Odessa File

Jack Edwards was given the assignment that he expected. In simple terms it was to go into the 'Lions Den' (Russia) and bring out some of his teeth (The documents) without waking him up. Some chance! However MI5 were not without ingenuity and resourcefulness, judging that Russia might be off guard having already seized and destroyed all the incriminating papers, as far as they knew.

MI5 reasoned that an attempt to secure a second set, and then get them out of the country would have seemed most unlikely. So Jack Edwards became 'Professor' Alan Beasdale, foremost expert on hydro electricity at Cambridge University with an NGO (Non-Government Organisation) brief to bring much needed expertise to a potential flood area on the Dnieper River at Zaporozhye, just south of Kharkov. Legitimate planning meetings had been organised with top Moscow officials so a London to Moscow flight would be the first step. It was there that Jack would meet his contacts and secure the papers. Security checks on internal flights via Kursk and Kharkov down to Dnepropetrovsk would not be a problem, but thereafter, on leaving Russian territory, he could expect to be thoroughly searched. The plan therefore was to leave Zaporozhye for a few days 'fishing break' on the lake and make his way with 'Pora' helpers, to Odessa. From there he would post the parcel back to the UK, marked, 'Children's Books,' to 'Kathy's Kindergarden', Kensington, London. He hoped then to travel back to the UK under his Russian Passport, as 'Viktor Zharin' trade delegate to the European Union.

Within a few days Jack had carried out his assignment without a hitch, and now he sat back in the Black Sea Hotel overlooking the esplanade in Odessa. He had posted the documents and felt very relieved that it was all over. Up to this point the plan had succeeded very well, or had it?

Love from a Cold Climate

While Sue and Rob were out for the day, Inspector Williams hadn't forgotten that he had a murder case to solve. If all the information gleaned so far was correct there was one person he wanted to see, badly. That person was Bernie Hill, but Alex would need his mother's permission first. Putting it as politely as he could in a telephone call to Maureen, home in Salisbury by now, he suggested that Bernie might help the police with their enquiries. What he had in mind was Bernie's unexplained disappearing act on New Years Eve, the fact that he was found in the sauna area and that a witness had seen two people, a man and a woman, she had said, enter the Pool area after midnight. Alex wanted to know if there was any connection, because it was sometime between midnight and 8am that a man had been killed not more than two hundred yards away. Was Bernie that man, was he with the woman and had either of them seen anything suspicious?

Maureen agreed and asked only that Sue might attend the interview as a friend and as a witness. That being agreed the Hills set off from Salisbury and arrived at the Police station at 2pm, which was the agreed time. After the usual niceties the pair sat down with a smile at Sue who was already there. The Inspector began with a few ground rules then began.

The Interview

AW is Williams, BH is Bernie Hill, MH his Mum and A is Anna.

AW Thank you for coming in for a chat Bernie. Now there really isn't anything to worry about, just a few questions about New Year OK? Let me see now, you told us that you got drunk and couldn't remember anything. But perhaps you've remembered something since. Have you?

BH No Sir I haven't.

AW So did you drink alone all night then, or were you with someone?

BH Who do you think?

AW Well, I don't know. A girl maybe, there was an aroma in your room.
(He had in mind the perfumed pillow in Bernie's room)

BH No, I was alone.

MH Come on dear, tell them what you told me about the cleaner.
(Maureen knew what he meant and was quick to nip it in the bud.)

BH Oh yes I remember now. When I got back to my room after lunch that day I found the room cleaner fast asleep on my bed. I told her to clear off but I suppose it was her shampoo or perfume that left a smell.

AW Why didn't you tell us this before then? It's a serious offence to withhold evidence and could be called 'perverting the course of justice.'

BH I didn't think it was relevant

AW Let me be the judge of that, but what would you say if I told you that we've spoken to a girl who says that you made love to her in the sauna?

MH Just a minute Inspector. What's all this? You didn't mention a girl. Who is she and why should any of us believe her?

AW Well I'd been hoping to save us all some embarrassment but seeing as you mention it, let's ask her. Show her in Constable.

(This was an unexpected turn of events and all eyes turned to the door to see who would walk through. There was a sudden gasp. It was Anna.)

AW Hello Anna and thanks for coming in. We won't keep you long. Just trying to get our stories straight you know. Now you say that you were with Bernie from just after midnight until about 6am. Right?

A Yes sir, I tell you before. We meet up earlier, and he show me his room and he kiss me. I like. Then I say come to pool tonight.

AW And did he?

A Yes he did. He very good lover you know.

(Williams looked across at Bernie who was shaking his head in denial. Sue was trying to comfort Maureen who seemed she would faint.)

AW I'm sorry Anna, I know that this is awkward for you but you told WPC Cope that sometimes you kept a memento, or let's say a 'trophy' of your encounters with men and that you did so on this occasion. Now we need to know whether your story is true so will you please show it to us.

(Once more those in the small room held their breath as Anna stooped to open a small bag at her feet. She took out and held up a pair of men's white briefs and then pointed somewhat mischievously to a red smudge.)

A My lipstick very nice, Number 7 Poppy king in Glamour.

(You could have heard a pin drop before the Inspector spoke again.)

AW Well Bernie what have you got to say for yourself now?

BH I'm sorry Mum, yes it's all true. I didn't mean it to go that far but once it started I just couldn't stop. I felt trapped but I still couldn't stop.

AW Take him in the other room for a statement Constable. That's all for now then. Thank you Anna and thank you Maureen.

End of the Interview

With the others gone Alex looked across at Sue who seemed deep in thought. 'What's up Sue?' he said, 'don't you believe her?' Sue continued to look pensive for a while before something seemed to click and she sat bolt upright. 'Oh, I believe her all right but it's all too pat. It's as if she planned the whole thing. It reminded me of the Bill Clinton and Monica Lewinsky case, but briefs instead of a dress. Now why? Because she needed an alibi, that's why. Because she is the killer. Too far fetched for you? Well take this on board then. There's her size for a start, a lot shorter than Oleg and what's more I noticed back at Warners that some of the girls had tattoos and hers was 'Nashi.' Now at the time I thought no more of it assuming it to be a boyfriend such as 'Boris' but then Rob I remembered that Rob has told me about a Pro-Putin youth group with the same name, a bit like the Pan-Slav movement of yesteryear. But to cap it all I have my own test. Anna didn't bat an eyelid throughout the whole process because she had no misgivings about the murder, (in a just cause in her opinion) and of course she is still convinced that she has got away with it. She has the arrogance of a fanatic and, if you want my opinion you should search her room and check out her hard drive now.'

He did want her opinion. He valued her opinion, not only because he knew that she was an ex police officer, but because it all made sense. He set the wheels in motion immediately and within a few hours detectives were taking Anna's room apart. One thing that Sue had got wrong however was that Anna 'was still convinced that she'd got away with it.' There might have been something about Sue's presence in the room that 'spooked' Anna but for whatever reason the bird had flown.

Deja vu Sue

Anna's laptop revealed much of the story as it had developed over some months. It gave details of the Kuchenko mission with the ominous title 'Operation Termination.' It wasn't enough to get the papers back, they had to be destroyed and their courier along with them. The date of Oleg's journey and landing time had to be altered of course and only a very few people were to be told of the plan. As far as the captain of the freighter and the crew were concerned, he was making a bid for freedom to the West and they had been only too happy to oblige, but unknowingly they had led him to his death. They found a Polish passport in her name but hidden away an Estonian one as well. (Sue had been right about that.) Furthermore there was a bonus for Sergeant Andrews and the others when they found one of the actual documents of Russian election corruption, (maybe Anna had been keeping it as a souvenir), but now it was given to Alex and he in turn gave it to MI5 to present to the meeting in London. It was signed with the initials 'VP' which might mean Vice President or even 'Vladimir Putin.' It did not prove his complicity, but it seemed ironic that Jack was even now securing further documents on Russian soil at great risk; but possibly unnecessarily.

The following day Sue was called to the Inspector's office. Waiting there were Rob and two others who Alex introduced as Liz Hamon and T.R. Cody she from MI5 and he of the CIA. She felt a bit out of her depth and wondered why she had been called, but it soon became clear.

Alex spoke first reminding everyone that this was to be a murder investigation and not a political witch hunt. To that end, he said, agents of other departments were welcome especially if they might share information, and he expected Interpol to be involved as well.

Liz Hamon spoke next agreeing that the most important objective was to apprehend Anna Harju, who, she understood was an Estonian citizen wanted on suspicion of the murder of Oleg Kuchenko at Hayling Island on 1st January 2012. It was likely she said, that Anna would have returned to Tallin that was the place of her birth given on her passport and where she might feel safe. If she was in Estonia or another Baltic State there was a fair chance that an application to extradite might be successful, but if she fled over the Russian border it was not likely, so speed and secrecy were of the essence if she were to be apprehended at all.

T.R. now added his voice to the deliberations. 'We think we've got that damned Ruskie, Vladimir Putin dead to rights.' he said, 'but her testimony might be all important to make charges stick, so we want her alive' he paused for a moment and looked around the room, a bit like Gary Cooper in 'High Noon,' 'Or dead.' he added with a smile.

Alex now looked seriously at Rob and said. 'That's where you come in Rob. We've got to find her first and, if she is in Tallin we think that you are the best person to track her down on our behalf. You know the town well and you understand the political groupings there better than most.

Your contacts might help you to get an early lead and that's vital. I've been told that you have an auxiliary MI5 rank of major anyway.'

He now turned to Sue. 'Now this is a difficult one Sue, and please don't take this the wrong way, but I don't know who else to send who might be able to identify her, person to person if you see what I mean. Also you've been there before and you know a bit about local dialects etc, I suppose it might seem a bit like déjà vu for you with Rob there as well, but if you might have uncomfortable memories I'm sure we'll understand. Photos and mug shots are all very well but we need a positive ID and fast. If you agree I have recommended that you take up your old rank of Inspector in the force, temporary of course. If Rob tracks her down we need you to greet her or touch her so that the local police can make an arrest. OK?'

Sue didn't think it was OK at all. Sure she was flattered but International Policing had never been her metier, so she stalled. She also needed to weigh up what the Inspector had said about 'uncomfortable' memories, but no, she thought, they had been wonderful memories. 'I'll need to think it over.' she said, 'but please look out for someone else as well.'

She looked across at Rob and, the cheek of it, he gave her a wink as if he knew darn well that she would not be able to refuse, and was he also thinking, how could I resist an assignment with 'Mr Wonderful' Watson. Well I'll show him and them she thought, but she knew different.

By the following morning she had accepted the plan and had attended a briefing meeting with Rob. By the evening they were on an Easy Jet out of Stansted heading for Tallin once more.

This was to be a 'business' trip of course but it was also so much more.

An understanding, or was it a misunderstanding, had been apparent at Bucklers Hard. Now they had to deal with a situation in which this was being accelerated by their proximity on the plane, and from which there was no immediate escape. A professional 'distance' was called for, so the sparring continued. He asked about her retirement and she about his golf.

'Is it a mixed club?' she ventured to ask, wishing that she hadn't. 'Yes, lots of eligible and attractive women, and men of course.' he said. 'No one special then?' she continued, and kicked herself for asking. 'I'm afraid not,' he replied, 'but I'll know when there is.' To Sue this sounded just like her refrain 'I'll know when my love comes along,' and, as this came into her mind she began to cry. Rob leant over tenderly and handed her a tissue, 'That's enough of that,' he said, but the deed was done.

After touch down at the 'Lennart Meri Tallinn Airport' they took a taxi to the 'Hotel Viru.' Rob knew about the perils and pitfalls of travel in a foreign land so he'd ordered one from the airport desk to be sure.

He'd been told that 'Krooni' were the best, and the driver, whose name was Mak, gave them a card for further service just to prove it. As they approached the booking-in desk, Rob took her arm and said, 'Now this is your first test. You must actually be the person whose name is on your passport, namely Ms Laura Peters, assistant to Mr Rupert Dodd, Art Historian, that's me. Purpose of visit, 'Study of Baltic Art during the Hanseatic period.' There's a book in my luggage if you need to read up.'

Registration went smoothly and for the next few hours they busied themselves with maps of the town. Rob was trying to remember the favourite haunts or districts favoured by rival ethnic an political groups, but after a while he said, 'It's no good, I'm going to go out there after dark. Retrace some old footsteps and see what I come up with. You have an early night, you look as if you deserve it.' Sue agreed at once but then paused. Had he meant that she looked unattractive? She glanced in the mirror and then chastised herself, 'Do I care what he thinks?' she muttered somewhat unconvincingly as she headed for a shower.

At breakfast Rob reported on his night's work. 'I've found out where the Nashi hang out.' he said, 'Strangely enough they meet in the basement of the old KGB HQ Pikk 61 but before the meetings they generally get together in the bars around that area. I suggest we do a 'recce' and then involve the local police if you manage to spot her. Remember there could be informers inside the Police so we might not have long.' Sue agreed, she thought the sooner this is over the better but then she had a rather serious objection. 'Rob,' she said, 'Have we not overlooked the fact that, if I might recognise her, then she might see and recognise me first, and then she'd be off like a shot?' Rob looked stunned. All his planning and expertise had now been challenged, and he was cross with himself for not thinking of the obvious. Somehow though, he was pleased with her because he could see that she was a valuable ally as well as being an attractive companion. 'Yes, of course,' he said, 'Silly of me. You'll have to have a disguise and that means that we'll have to move from this hotel.

I've heard that the 'St Petersburg' has a good reputation, it's up near the Cathedral, but you'll have to get a new 'face' before you register. I think we can keep the old name, but let's hope we don't meet anyone from the Viju Hotel. OK?' Sue thought for a moment and then said, 'Do you prefer Nana Maskouri or Maria Callas? Both dark glasses and rather cover-up clothes.' He laughed, 'Can't say I fancy either of them but that's not the point is it?' Now she pretended to be upset. 'Isn't it?' she said.

That evening Rob went out to reconnoitre once more while Sue obtained her disguise for the next day. It was a balmy evening and she decided to take a short walk up to the splendid Alexander Nevsky Cathedral. She'd seen it on her last visit but that was in the daytime, now it was dusk and the cathedral stood proud and confident under arc lights. There were four 'onion' topped cupulas matched by white buildings with red facings. It was like a fairy tale building, and inside it had a rather discreet grandeur. Icons were everywhere but apart from that it had a rather modest air.

She read from a small leaflet that a major restoration had taken place in 1991 after Estonia became independent. This got her thinking as she sat on one of the side benches there. The Orthodox religion generally favours stand-up worship, so there were none in the centre but she was comfortable and thoughtful. Russia and their neighbours, she thought, so much history, so much love, so much hate and it was still going on.

And what of the 'Russian' Orthodox Church itself? It seemed to be caught up in a seemingly perpetual Schism with the Church of Rome and others. Didn't leaders, past and present make too much of their differences and not enough of their joint heritage, she thought. She was glad that she did not 'belong' in that sense, because she found it hard to justify centuries of antipathy with no end in sight.

'Nana Maskouri' came down to breakfast at the St Petersburg hotel the next morning and greeted her boss. 'Wow!' he exclaimed, 'You really are the business. What do you Greeks have for breakfast?' She laughed and for the next few moments there was a cautious air of companionship about them, somewhat akin to the camaraderie experienced by soldiers going 'over the top' in the First World War. This was it, now they had a job to do. They would be on the street in moments and perhaps everything would change and Rob didn't want to lose the moment.

'Will you come home with me when this is all over?' he said wondering how he found the nerve to ask. She bit her lip before replying, 'Now is that Nana or Sue you are asking?' she said. That did it, 'You Sue, you know that I mean you,' he said, 'these Greek singers are two a penny but there's only one Sue Parker. Daft time to ask I know.' Should she put him out of his misery? No, not yet she thought, 'You'll have to ask her when you back to the hotel then won't you?' she said. He was beaten, maybe somewhat crestfallen but optimistic just the same. 'I will.' he said.

Silver Linings

For the next few days Sue and Rob frequented the area around 'Pikk 61', the old KGB building. An anti-Soviet joke of a few years back said that it was the tallest building in Estonia, because you could 'see Siberia from the basement'. It was now the office of the Interior Ministry so, to some, it was still a rather forbidding building, so dark with small windows and all with bars. However, there were many other kinds of bars all around, and the residents of Tallin mixed happily there with the many visitors who came to town. After a day and a half Sue made a suggestion, 'I'm getting to know my way around a bit,' she said, 'and I have a hunch about what I'd do if I came back from time abroad. First I'd need a job, and secondly I wouldn't want to make myself too obvious.' Rob looked downcast, 'On that basis, we'll never find her,' he said. 'Maybe,' replied Sue, 'but I said that I had a hunch and it's this. Do you remember that Anna and the other girls all had tattoos? Well, that's where we'll find her. Not necessarily working in a tattoo parlour but up there in that arty

(She nearly said farty) district where they make jewellery, sell 'genuine'

'Reval' artefacts (Reval was Tallin's name in medieval times), and offer to do your portrait on the street, a bit like old Montmartre. If she's anywhere here in Tallin, that's where she'll be.' Once more Rob looked at her with admiration. What insight, what a gift. Or could she be wrong?

That evening over drinks he reminded her that they could be in considerable danger. 'It's not just this latest round of stuff in Russia, and the poisoning of Yuschenko in the Ukraine that we're up against. If you were on Nashi's side you'd say they were patriots in the widest Pan-Slav sense, but others would say that their approach borders on fanaticism.

I don't know whether I mentioned it when we were here last time, but the year before that there had been such a fuss when Nashi members held daily protests due to the removal of a statue 'The Bronze Soldier of Tallin' from the centre of town to a military cemetery. In this, and other anti Russian activities they saw, and still see the emergence of a new fascism. I won't say that I have sympathy, but then I wasn't here during the Nazi regime and I can't imagine the horrors of either occupation. Sue looked at him thoughtfully; she liked the way that he carried his heart

'On his sleeve' and allowed the customary peck goodnight to linger.

The next day proved to be another blank as they trudged up and down and drank endless cups of coffee. At lunch Rob admitted to feeling a little tired so Sue left him to read the newspaper in a small dark café while she continued her search, and suddenly there she was seated at a small table in a silversmiths window, over which a sign said, 'Silver Threads'. The girls were placed there of course to demonstrate the very high skills to be employed in their wares, be they bracelets, bangles, necklaces or charms. Each girl wore a grey overall and each had a different coloured headscarf, pinned as one might have seen in an ammunition factory during the war. The scarves partially obscured their faces but then Sue saw the give away 'Nashi' sign on her wrist. Her heart leapt in triumph, but also in fear as Anna's head turned towards her with a smile and 'Nana' smiled back graciously before moving away. 'Phew, no sign of recognition there anyway,' thought Sue, 'but we'd better not waste any time.'

She was back at the hotel in moments and back at the silversmiths within the hour accompanied by Rob, two Estonian policemen and an Interpol Inspector who had been standing by. After a nod from him she went into the small shop, and a lovely silver bell rang out a tune that was then echoed by others all around the premises, a little like a dawn chorus, but the bell was tolling for Anna. A little old lady approached her and smiled, but Sue couldn't think of anything to say except, 'Excusez moi.' Perhaps she thought that French was more in keeping with her Maskouri garb and she never had learnt Greek, but anyway it was quite easy to walk to the window where Anna was working. Sue stood behind her for a moment, admiring the neat and delicate finger work that was transforming an ordinary brooch into a work of art. Then she remembered that it was those fingers that had pulled the trigger only inches from Oleg's chest on that Hayling Island beach, and it was those fingers that had pulled the trigger at least twice more as he lay dying. It seemed so incongruous and such a long time ago. And now Anna seemed so vulnerable as she sat there concentrating on her work and for a moment Sue felt quite sorry for her. How had this sweet girl got involved in something like this, she thought. But then a different kind of feeling wafted over her as she remembered that Anna was the one who had compromised Bernie and killed without scruple in the name of Nashi. She hovered for a moment behind her, maybe a little like an avenging angel before touching her on the shoulder and just saying 'Anna, it's time to go.' She then nodded to the police at the window but could barely suppress a tear as she did so.

The 'Great Game' was over, and Sue returned home gratefully with Rob not only at her side but also in her bed. She remembered how Bruce had said that she should look for the 'Silver Lining' and there he was, yes definitely, with one or two silvery grey hairs. Glynis and Jack celebrated their Silver Wedding Anniversary and Nelson got a new bone.

FIN